WARRIOR OF MERCIA

BOOK 3 THE EAGLE OF MERCIA CHRONICLES

M J PORTER

Boldwood

First published in Great Britain in 2022 by Boldwood Books Ltd.

Copyright © MJ Porter, 2022

Cover Design by Head Design Ltd

Cover Photography: Shutterstock

A CIP catalogue record for this book is available from the British Library.

Paperback ISBN 978-1-80280-773-8

Large Print ISBN 978-1-80280-772-1

Hardback ISBN 978-1-80280-771-4

Ebook ISBN 978-1-80280-774-5

Kindle ISBN 978-1-80280-775-2

Audio CD ISBN 978-1-80280-766-0

MP3 CD ISBN 978-1-80280-767-7

Digital audio download ISBN 978-1-80280-769-1

Boldwood Books Ltd
23 Bowerdean Street
London SW6 3TN
www.boldwoodbooks.com

To my girls. You do an amazing job of putting up with me. Thank you for all your support.

MAP OF EARLY ENGLAND

Designed by Flintlock Covers

CAST OF CHARACTERS

Icel, orphaned youth living in Tamworth, his mother was Ceolburh
Brute, Icel's horse
Edwin, Icel's childhood friend, although they have been separated
Cenfrith, Icel's uncle, brother of Ceolburh and one of the Mercian king's warriors, who dies in *Son of Mercia*
Wine, Cenfrith's horse, now Icel's alongside Brute
Wynflæd, an old herbwoman at the Mercian king's court at Tamworth

The Kings of Mercia
Coelwulf, King of Mercia r.821–825 (deposed)
Beornwulf, King of Mercia r.825–826 (killed)
Lady Cynehild, Beornwulf's wife
Wiglaf, King of Mercia r.827–829 (deposed) r.830–
Queen Cynethryth, Wiglaf's wife
Wigmund, Wiglaf's son
Ecgberht, King of Wessex r.802 onwards, r.829 in Mercia

The Ealdormen/Bishops of Mercia

Ælfstan, one of King Wiglaf's supporters, an ally to Icel

Beornoth, one of King Wiglaf's ealdormen

Muca, one of King Wiglaf's ealdormen

Oswine, an ealdorman who died fighting the East Anglian king

Sigered, a long-standing ealdorman, who's survived the troubled years of the 820s

Sigegar, Sigered's grandson

Tidwulf, an old ally of King Wiglaf

Wynfrith, an ealdorman who died fighting the East Anglian king

Coenwulf, the son of King Coelwulf

Ælflæd, Coenwulf's sister

Æthelweald, Bishop of Lichfield

Ceolbeorht, Bishop of Londonia

Rulers of other kingdoms

Athelstan, King of the East Angles

Ecgberht, King of Wessex

Lord Æthelwulf – Ecgberht's son, designated King of Kent by his father after the battle of Ellendun

The Ealdormen of the East Angles

Herefrith

Godwulf, East Anglian warrior

Mercians

Ælfred, ally of Lord Wigmund

Ælhun, refugee

Æthelflæd, a widowed woman in Tamworth

Æthelgifu, her small daughter

Æthelmod, Mercian warrior

Berhthelm, Mercian warrior

Betrand, refugee

Cenred, Mercian warrior

Cuthred, inhabitant of Tamworth

Eahric, commander of the king's household warriors

Edith, refugee

Egbert, Mercian warrior allied to Ealdorman Sigered

Eomer, the reeve of Budworth, Icel's inherited estate

Frithwine, young Mercian warrior

Garwulf, young Mercian warrior

Gaya, previously a slave woman with a talent for healing, now freed

Goðeman, Mercian warrior

Hild, refugee

Hunberht, an ally of Lord Wigmund

Kyre, Mercian warrior

Landwine, Mercian warrior

Maneca, Mercian warrior

Offa, Mercian warrior

Ordlaf, Mercian warrior

Osmod, Mercian warrior

Oswald, at Kingsholm

Oswy, one of Wiglaf's warriors

Redmudh, moneyer in Lundenwic

Theodore, previously a slave man with a talent for healing, now freed

Uor, Mercian warrior

Waldhere, Mercian warrior

Wicga, ally of Lord Wigmund

Wulfgar, Mercian warrior

Wulfheard, a Mercian warrior, Ealdorman Ælfstan's oath-sworn man

Bada, Wulfheard's horse

Places mentioned

Bardney, a Mercian royal site

Kingsholm, associated with the ruling family of King Coelwulf, close to Gloucester

Lichfield, close to Tamworth and one of the holy sites in Mercia

Londonia, combining the ruins of Roman Londinium and Saxon Lundenwic

Peterborough, the site of a monastery in Mercia

Tamworth, the capital of the Mercian kingdom

Kingdom of the East Angles, part of Mercia at the end of the 700s but reclaimed its

freedom under King Athelstan of the East Angles, the king-slayer

Kingdom of Wessex, the area south of the River Thames, including Kent at this time, but not Dumnonia (Cornwall and Devon)

Repton, a Mercian mausoleum, where her kings are buried

River Welland, running from the Wash, through the kingdom of the East Angles and into Mercia

River Nene, running from the Wash, through the kingdom of the East Angles and into Mercia

River Ouse, running from the Wash, through the kingdom of the East Angles and into Mercia

THE STORY SO FAR

Young Icel is a healer no more but is instead becoming a warrior of Mercia, keeping to the oath he swore to his king at Bardney, even though in doing so, his beloved uncle, Cenfrith, lost his life fighting the Wessex invasion in the borderlands with the Welsh.

Having made a name for himself by saving King Wiglaf's life in the Welsh borderlands, Icel has been tested once more. Forced to live with his enemy behind the high walls of Londinium, living on his wits, he has made some powerful enemies and, more importantly, allies as well.

Instrumental in assisting King Wiglaf to reclaim control over the double settlement of Londonia – consisting of the market settlement of Lundenwic and the ruins of Roman Londinium – Icel has fought and killed, even those he thought were his friends. He has come to realise that enemies aren't always enemies, and allies aren't always allies. With Londonia once more secure, and King Ecgberht of Wessex restricted to the south of the River Thames, Mercia is whole again under her restored king, Wiglaf.

THE MERCIAN REGISTER
AD830

King Wiglaf is once more the rightful king of Mercia. King Ecgberht of Wessex has escaped from Londonia with his life and holds on to the formerly Mercian kingdom of Kent, won in the aftermath of the battle of Ellendun five years previously, his son ruling there in his name. There is no peace accord between the Wessex and the Mercian kingdom, and Mercian warriors remain in Londonia, fearful of a Wessex resurgence.

King Wiglaf of Mercia is acclaimed as the rightful ruler of Mercia, eager to reclaim all that King Ecgberht has stolen in the south and King Athelstan of the East Angles has taken in the east.

1

Wynflæd assesses me with a sweeping gaze.

'It's true then?' she demands to know.

I consider what she sees as she gazes at me. Does she see Icel, the scrawny lad she's been imparting her knowledge to for much of my sixteen years, or does she see a Mercian warrior before her? Does she notice my height, and muscles, the bruising on my face, the bandage tied tightly around my right hand, the annoying scuff of black hair on my chin and cheeks? Does she care for me or is she merely using me as a means to find out what's happened while the king's warriors have been absent from Tamworth?

'What's true?' I retort, but I know to what she refers, and I think it better to admit it than continue my denial. Certainly, I see her as she's always been, back in her rightful place as Tamworth's healer, having been forced to flee when King Ecgberht of Wessex claimed the settlement as his own. 'King Ecgberht escaped. His son as well,' I admit, chin jutting out defiantly. I won't take her criticisms and slights, not after what I've been through. The Wessex king and his ætheling might have escaped, but I played my part well, and it wasn't for lack of trying that the Wessex bastards both still live.

'Then what was the point in sending all those men, and losing all those warriors? Their widows will have at least expected Mercia's enemy to be dead.'

I'm cold and tired, and ache all over. I could do without her harsh words, spoken to me outside her healer's workshop, where I rushed to assure her that I'm well as soon as I could fight my way through the wall of returning men and horses. I've been forced to leave Brute outside Tamworth's walls. There was no possibility of both of us gaining entry in the press. I'm not entirely sure why I bothered now. The welcoming has hardly been warm. I curse my need to seek her out. She isn't my grandmother. She's no relation of mine, and yet, she's all I have. I confess, I expected more from her. Maybe even some joy that I yet live.

'Perhaps,' I mutter under my breath so that she can't hear me, 'they should have come themselves.'

I hear her sharp intake of breath, so she hears me well enough, that sense never having faltered despite the years she wears, but luckily, Theodore and Gaya appear beside me. They've travelled to Tamworth on two abandoned horses, their original owners dead on the slaughter field. I don't think either Theodore or Gaya have enjoyed the journey, but they've managed well enough with the relentless tedium of it.

It's been cold, and the nights bitter. I'd have welcomed a warm hearth each night rather than the firmness of the hard winter ground at my back. I'm sure Theodore and Gaya would have welcomed three hearths to warm them despite the layers of cloaks they wear over their black and brown skin. They might have looked out of place in Tamworth, as opposed to the bustling port of Lundenwic, but, of course, everyone is so used to Ealdorman Tidwulf that they don't earn a second glance.

And they must think it's all better than having Ecgred as their master, and being forced to expend their skills on trying to heal men doomed to die, merely because those were the ones who had the coin that Ecgred demanded in exchange for any assistance.

'Who are you?' Wynflæd snaps.

I'm relieved they're suddenly the focus of her attention, and not me. I examine Wynflæd as she barks her questions. She seems well. Very well. When I last saw her, she was even thinner than usual, her fleeting hair little more than wisps in the wind. In our time apart, she's managed to put some flesh back onto her bones, and lost her sense of shame from having to flee Tamworth when King Ecgberht claimed the settlement. She might have questions for me, but there's still much I don't know about her and the long life she's led. There's still much I don't know about what happened when King Ecgberht was king of Mercia as well as Wessex.

I've heard rumours about him employing magicks that Wynflæd has no belief in, and which a Christian king has no right in using. I'd sooner not believe those reports and Wynflæd's part in them. They belittle her, but then, she might well have been compelled to do as he demanded. After all, Ecgberht was Mercia's king by right of conquest. She can't have expected King Wiglaf to win back all that he lost so quickly, and especially not when Mercia's king had fled rather than fight.

'Wynflæd,' Gaya announces in her lyrical voice. 'Icel has told us a great deal about you. I am Gaya, and this is my fellow healer, Theodore. He does not yet understand everything we say. We are from the far distant southern kingdoms, over the cold sea that surrounds your land and then even further south over lands that slowly warm until the sun burns hotter than a furnace. Icel freed us from our cruel master inside Londinium, and now Ealdorman Tidwulf says we are a freeman and a freewoman to ply our craft

wherever we choose.' Gaya stumbles over the unfamiliar words of
freeman and freewoman. I don't believe they've always been
slaves, and yet here, in Mercia, the distinction must be made
clear. Slaves have a master. Freemen and freewomen might well
swear an oath of commendation to their lords, but they're free.
They are free to choose to whom they pledge themselves, should
they desire to do so.

On this dull day, Theodore and Gaya look resplendent, even
as tired and exhausted as they must be. How their lives have
changed in recent weeks. Or, at least, how I assume they have.
They're no longer enslaved but revered for their skills and accomplishments at healing. Theodore is learning to speak our tongue
well, but before Wynflæd's scrutiny, even I quake to speak.

Wynflæd's eyes flicker from me towards Gaya, thin tongue
licking at her even thinner lips. 'Hmm,' she eventually says.
'You'd better come inside.' And she indicates her wooden workshop in whose doorway she stands.

Theodore bows his head beneath the low door, while Gaya
rushes in before him, pleased to be in the warmth of the small
space.

I think I might get away from Wynflæd then, only for her to
reach out and grip my arm with her too-strong fingers. They look
weak and aged, but aren't. I'm sure that most people with so many
years behind them should have a much less severe grip. Wynflæd
is used to holding tightly to her patients, as they writhe beneath
her ministrations. I should have remembered that.

'Well done, Icel. I'm relieved to see you yet live. I'll hear all
about this later. But don't think this means I've forgotten my
questions.'

I dip my chin, and stay there, waiting for the soft shuffle of her
feet to disappear over the wooden floorboards, and the hum of
conversation to spring up inside her workshop. Only then do I

spy young Cuthred, a boy once better known for climbing trees when he shouldn't have done, who now aids Wynflæd in my place. He can be no older than ten or eleven. He's still slight of build.

Cuthred watches on with an open mouth, a bucket of water held in front of him by both of his hands. With a solid lump in the pit of my stomach as my hand aches from its burn, he fiercely reminds me of the life I once led. I smell myself, realising I stink of blood and death, even now, so many days on from the slaughter of the battle for Londonia.

'That looks heavy,' I offer when he doesn't speak.

'It is, yes,' Cuthred huffs. He's grown a finger's width in my absence, but no more than that. He doesn't yet have the ability to carry a full bucket in each hand.

'Tell me, how's Wine, my uncle's horse?'

At this, Cuthred's face alights. He drops the bucket where it is, sloshing water onto his feet and not seeming to notice as he turns to me. 'Come, I'll show you. She's been well. I've ridden her, once or twice,' he quickly clarifies, turning to meet my gaze. I know it'll have been more than that, but I'm not angry with him. Wine is a pliant animal. She'll have been a good introduction to horse ownership for Cuthred. Perhaps one day he might have his own horse. It depends on what happens with him and Wynflæd and whether or not he's called upon to fight for Mercia.

If Mercia's future is devoid of war, then perhaps he can become a healer, as I once thought I'd become. If Mercia's future is to be embroiled in a war against her enemy to the south, then the role of a healer will not be his. He'll become a warrior, just as I am becoming. The thought saddens me. I hope he can lead the life I wanted. But, then, perhaps he wishes to become a warrior. I remain conflicted. I know what I know about healing, and it has helped me and my fellow warriors more than once, but equally,

I'm learning to kill, the very opposite of what I thought I'd become. Do I miss being with Wynflæd? I do, yes, I can't deny that, and yet, I'm honest enough to admit that becoming a warrior, having such friends as I now have, is also appealing.

All around us, men and women stream to be reunited with their lovers, fathers, brothers and sons, or sob quietly on knowing they'll never see them again. King Wiglaf has been formally reunited with his wife and queen, Cynethryth, and son, Lord Wigmund, in an official ceremony of welcome, during which King Wiglaf was buoyed by his success, whereas his queen looked as stiff as her richly embroidered cloak. I can't say that either the king's wife or his son looked enamoured of Wiglaf's acclaim, even while Mercia's warriors cheered the resurgent king and the success we had against the might of Wessex.

No doubt the queen has enjoyed having the management of Tamworth and Mercia in her husband's absence. I imagine Lord Wigmund would sooner his father hadn't returned as well if I've correctly interpreted his facial expression on seeing King Wiglaf's pride, his eagle banner flying high in the stiff breeze overhead to indicate Mercia's victory.

I blot out the echoes of Edwin's mother greeting her long-lost son, my childhood friend. I'm pleased for her, even if Edwin and I are no longer the allies we once were. We might have held the bridge over the River Fleet between us, but I can't say it's eased the unhappiness we feel towards one another since Edwin was left at Kingsholm by my uncle, while Cenfrith and I resumed our wandering journey to evade the reach of the Wessex warriors. It feels a lifetime ago, and not earlier in the year.

We both blame one another for what happened. I won't hear him criticise my uncle, while Edwin won't admit that my uncle acted to save his life. After all, Edwin's now a member of the lord of Kingsholm's warriors. The same would never have happened if he'd remained in Tamworth. The queen and the king's comman-der, Eahric, would have seen to that.

Edwin and I have ignored one another on the journey north, even while I've been overly aware of him. I've tracked him with my eyes, known where he was and what he was doing. I can't see that he's done the same with me. He seems comfortable with the rest of Lord Coenwulf's warriors. He's been accepted by them far more easily than I've been amongst Ealdorman Ælfstan's men. But then, Edwin has always wanted to be a warrior, and his father was one before him. Edwin knows how to speak to men who are prepared to lay down their lives for their lord. My position has been more uncomfortable. After all, I've not trained to become a warrior, and yet, I've won the notice of the king as someone who saved his life with a blade, and not with a healing poultice.

The stable is busy with young lads and girls running hither and thither, helping the stablehands to contend with a suddenly full stable. As soon as I walk beneath the sagging roof of the building, I catch sight of Wine's intelligent face hanging over her stall, from where she's been brought inside from the summer grazing lands. Has she, I consider, been waiting for me? She's ridden in and out of Tamworth enough times with my uncle to know when a war host is returning. Has she been standing there, anticipating my return?

One of the more experienced stablehands has taken control of Brute outside Tamworth's walls. Brute gave the man a friendly bite on the ear for his troubles. I sympathised but didn't offer to help. I had other matters to attend to.

'Hello, girl.' I hold out my left hand and let Wine smell my sweat. My right hand remains tightly bound. Theodore assures me the angry scar will grow less visible, but I can't see it. I imagine the welts from the copper wiring that decorate the hilt of my seax will permanently mark me as a Mercian more easily than the Viking raiders and their inked markings do them. Administering to Oswy with my seax has emblazoned the burn on my hand. Where before it was faint, now it stands proud. Others might proclaim their allegiance with trinkets and sigils around their necks or along their arms, but I have Mercia burned into my skin. I don't think I can get more loyal than that. Not while I live, anyway.

Wine sniffs my hand, and then licks it, tasting the salt of my sweat, a warm welcome from her. She hangs her head low then, low enough that Cuthred can reach up to run his hand along the long line of her grey jaw. It seems the two have become firm allies in my absence, for all he's only just tall enough to be level with her head. How he's mounted to ride her is something I don't wish to consider. I just hope it hasn't involved a tree and a helpful branch.

'Tell me,' I ask him, moving inside the stables to check Wine more completely. She seems well enough. Certainly, Cuthred has ensured she's not eaten too much while being kept indoors rather than out on the Mercian roadways, as Brute has been. 'What's been happening in my absence?'

Cuthred steps away from Wine's side so that he can see me more easily. He shrugs his narrow shoulders. Wynflæd needs to see to him having a new tunic and cloak for the coming cold weather. I can see his wrists and the flash of his arms below the elbow when he lifts them. His tunic looks uncomfortably tight as well, along his chest and down his arms. With all the buckets of water he must carry for Wynflæd, muscle has finally begun to cord his slim frame. 'The queen managed well. She saw to matters of justice and taxation.'

'And?' I push him. Ealdorman Sigered was so convinced that the kingdom of the East Angles would attack that I need to know more.

'There was a small altercation on the borderland with King Athelstan of the East Angles, to the east of Ermine Street. A few cuts and bruises.'

I smirk. Cuthred speaks with the authority of Wynflæd. I hear the echo of her voice in those words.

'And, of course, Queen Cynethryth has been negotiating with Lord Coenwulf on behalf of the king in regard to his assistance at Londonia.'

In all honesty, this interests me more than another potential war with the kingdom of the East Angles. I've killed so many men in the last few months, that I welcome not having to do so for the foreseeable future. I want only to have the wooden gates of Tamworth slammed shut on my back and to face the winter with nothing more taxing than trying to keep warm.

But Lady Cynehild's future, the former queen of Mercia, does concern me. Whatever passed between her and my uncle, Cenfrith, I know he would expect me to ensure she's treated fairly by King Wiglaf now that he's no longer here to do so. I still don't know the importance of the small object I was ordered to give to her, but I appreciate that it meant something to both my uncle and Lady Cynehild. Once, she made my life torture, when she was married to King Beornwulf. Now she's the one whose life could be in peril.

'What do you know about the negotiations between the queen and Lord Coenwulf?' I ask him, trying to find a smile for my suddenly tight face.

'Not a lot, only that Wynflæd was muttering about it all.' I just imagine she was. Wynflæd told me not to speak to Lady Cynehild of another marriage when she was placed in the nunnery at Winchcombe, even though it's to be expected that a woman of Lady Cynehild's standing should be found a second husband by her new king. The king's wife hasn't done her predecessor the same favours. 'Wynflæd says it's a pity that King Ludica's wife, Lady Eadburga, remarried so quickly. It would have been better for her to be given to Lord Coenwulf in marriage, rather than wasted on a king's thegn.'

I quite agree, but hold my tongue. King Ludica's widow is still very young. She might be more likely to breed, as I know she already has, but I can't imagine she'd bring the dour Lord Coenwulf any joy.

'So, the marriage will happen then?'

Cuthred shrugs once more, and I realise I'm asking the boy questions he can't hope to know the answer to.

'It doesn't matter. Tell me of everyone else. How have they been?'

I've not been gone for longer than two months, and yet anything could have happened in my absence.

'Old Beornwyn died. Wynflæd was saddened by it, but then said the old cow had been holding on for far too long, and her old body needed a rest. Another winter would have killed her, so better to go while the days weren't short and dreary.'

The knowledge saddens me, but it's far from unexpected. Beornwyn had long been old and riddled with twisted fingers. No amount of ointment prepared by Wynflæd could unknot them forever. Just how old Beornwyn was has never been answered. I consider whether it's because Wynflæd is older than her and doesn't want to admit it. Not that it matters now.

'The bishop was a git about burying her. Said she had more than a hint of the Old Gods about her, but Wynflæd ensured it all happened as it should, even if her body lies closer to the river, and not the church. Wynflæd ensured her grave lay east to west, and not north to south, as the bishop directed the gravediggers. He didn't want her to see her Lord on the Day of Judgement.' Cuthred shakes his head as he speaks. Once more, I hear

Wynflæd's words mirrored in his. I consider how much of what I used to say was actually me just repeating Wynflæd's words. I wonder how much of what I say now is not simply more of the same.

'Icel.' I hear Wulfheard's rough cry and turn towards the stable doorway. He's standing there, hands on his hips, looking far from impressed. Ealdorman Ælfstan's commander, and my ally, needs to bathe, shave and lose the sour expression on his face. His face is pinched with cold, and his cloak drags into the churned earth of the ground outside. 'Go and tend to your bloody horse. He's broken two buckets and bitten two people, and you're here, having a nice little chat with the healer's boy.' The disgust in Wulfheard's voice brings a grin to my lips.

I glance at Cuthred, and he returns my smirk.

'I'll see you later,' I console. 'You should get back to Wynflæd. No doubt she needs something doing.'

'Tell me, who were those two people?' Cuthred queries first, taking his chance because Wulfheard has turned away already, his shouted instructions to Oswy covering the extra question.

'Theodore and Gaya? They were enslaved by a Wessex healer inside Londinium, that's the one the giants built high with walls of stone, not the trading settlement.' I speak as though I've always known this, which, of course, I haven't. 'Ealdorman Tidwulf has made them free and they'll be healers now, like Wynflæd. Well, I freed them from Londinium,' I admit, feeling I really should take some acclaim for my part in all this.

'She won't like that,' Cuthred mutters, and I chuckle as I leave the stables and make my way through the seething mass of men and horses towards the open gate. Wynflæd bloody won't like it. Not one little bit. Maybe I shouldn't have been quite so quick to claim responsibility after all. I could have placed the blame at Ealdorman Tidwulf's feet. I wish I had. Cuthred, with the best will in the world, won't be shy about sharing what I've told him, and Wynflæd's fury will be squarely directed my way.

As soon as I've fought my way through the open gateway, where the guards try desperately to keep some sort of control over the flowing thoroughfare, and fail most abysmally at it, I can hear Brute's shrill screams, even above the commotion of King Wiglaf's conquering war band returning home. I shake my head at the sharp cry of the horse.

'The stablehand said he could control him,' I mutter to Wulfheard, coming upon him as he directs carts and horses just to the far side of the ditch and embankment. I can feel the eyes of the inhabitants of Tamworth on me. No one looks impressed. And they all know that Brute is my horse. I've heard the whispers and complaints. Men and women don't like the gift the king gave me, even if I know none of them would be able to control my horse. Jealousy is a strange beast.

'Well, he bloody lied.' Wulfheard is far from placated by my words, as I amble to a run, heading to the low-lying land where warriors and horses are separating after their long journey along Watling Street from Londonia.

I shake my head at the sight of Brute bucking on the end of a tether, while in the distance the twin rivers glint sullenly beneath low-hanging clouds. It's been threatening to rain for much of the day. It'll be bloody typical if it does so now when we're all nearly back beneath the shelter of the king's hall; when the promise of warm hearths is almost a reality.

I feel all the aches and pains of a few days in the saddle as I continue to dart through carts and beasts.

'I'll take him.' I snatch the harness from the stablehand, realising with surprise that it's not the same one as before. No, that man is on the mud-churned ground, hoof marks everywhere, curled around some pain that Brute has inflicted. Bloody horse.

'Brute.' I hold the rein firmly, waiting for my horse to acknowledge me. He rears, and kicks out once more, just missing another stablehand, who shrieks and dashes out of the way.

The other horses have all moved aside with a caution the stablehands have failed to show. Brute comes to a sudden halt, chest heaving with his rage, his breath hot and furious in my face. His eyes are wild and confused.

'What's this all about, then?' My tone is softer than the words I use. 'Making a bloody fuss about nothing.'

As soon as he's down on four hooves, I hold him steady, and then begin to work my way around his body. Have I missed some wound? Has he stepped on something, or gone lame? Has he thrown a shoe? Of course he hasn't. He's just unhappy.

'He's a monster,' the first stablehand interjects into my perusal, the words coming in a single huff as he gasps with pain, still squirming on the ground.

'He is called Brute,' I confirm, absent-mindedly, surprised the connection hasn't been made by them. What sort of fool doesn't realise the name fits the beast? Why else do men and women name their daughters as Godgifu, or gift from God, if not to earn some favour in our Lord's eyes? As a people, we do tend to name our children and animals with some intention behind them. If Brute wasn't always his name, then my horse has certainly earned it since.

'Does he even let you ride him?' I turn then, meet the eyes of King Wiglaf's son, Wigmund, the derision ripe in his voice.

Wigmund hasn't changed in my absence – well, apart from the fact he now has more of a beard and moustache on his slight face. I run my hand along my own chin, grimacing at the stubble there. Wigmund carries his blades in a weapons belt, but they shimmer with the oil of polish and not the gleam of blood, sweat and tears, as mine do. I imagine the last thing he killed was a rat amongst the thatched rooves. Perhaps he even had someone catch the animal for him before skewering it to death. The games of small boys are far from caring for the vermin that infests our homes.

'Yes, my lord.' I bow slightly, my one hand very firm on Brute's rein. It would be typical for Brute to forget himself once more. 'He does allow me to ride him. I've not run beside him all the way back from Londonia.' I keep my voice even. Wigmund means to add oil to the fire, but I'm not inclined to argue with him. Brute is just that, a brute. He'll never be any different. I'm learning that. The stablehand at Bardney thought he shackled me with a terrible horse that would embarrass me and perhaps result in my death if I was thrown from his back. The man actually gave me an excellent one, but one that needs a firm hand. It's a heady combination. I'm learning to be the master. Brute remains an unwilling student, all the same.

'The king, my father, should never have given you such a horse.' It seems Lord Wigmund is disinclined to bring his argument to an end.

I sigh softly. I've just arrived home. Wigmund has done nothing but sit on his skinny arse for the last however many months, kept safely away from the fighting so that Mercia wasn't once more left bereft of men who could be named as king, should Wiglaf die fighting the Wessex king. He was sheltered inside the monastery at Bardney. He's not been in the borderlands with the Welsh kingdoms, or plunged amongst his enemy inside Londinium. Lord Wigmund's not fought to stay alive. He's not had to contend with the enemy as friends. He's not had to bury his uncle and say goodbye to the only family he's ever known. I knew Wigmund was infuriating. Now I appreciate that he really could become my enemy if he means to test me in these smallest of ways.

I consider what he sees before him. Does he smirk at my dishevelled state? Does he look at my hard-worn boots and see me as poor? Does he look at my wrapped hand and see only the wound? Does he even know what I've done? I doubt it, but now really isn't the time to further expound on the actions that made the king beholden to me for his life.

'I'm indebted to the king, your father, for his gift.' I try to defuse the situation, but Wigmund continues to sneer. I meet his gaze evenly, but he's been joined by more people. In our absence, Lord Wigmund has begun to develop his own collection of allies, it seems. I note that not all of them are as young as we are. Even some of the older men surround Wigmund, those who didn't ride to war.

I narrow my eyes. At whose instigation has this been started? The king's? It seems doubtful. At Wigmund's? Again, I can't see it. No, I'm sure it'll be his mother. Queen Cynethryth isn't blind to the fact that, of all Mercia's recent rulers' wives, she's the only one to have a son who could become king should something befall his father. And his father has ridden to war not once but twice since the summer. While King Wiglaf might have been victorious, other powerful enemies remain on Mercia's borders.

I suppose I should be pleased with the development, but it makes me uneasy. I've heard of over-powerful women in the past. They can cause just as many problems as the over-powerful men. If I asked Wynflæd about it, she'd tell me the story of King Penda's son's wife, the Northumbrian princess, who killed him because she detested him so much, slipping her blade through his chest while he slept. She would also tell me of how another of King Penda's son's wives was killed by her Mercian bodyguard. She'd tell me it was because women can be just as much a threat as men. I heed those words.

'Lord Wigmund.' Someone thinks to save me. I recognise the

voice as that of Ealdorman Tidwulf. Has he suddenly become more favourable towards me? It would please me to add another to the small number of men I can count as a friend in the king's court.

Without further words, Lord Wigmund and his entourage turn to face the dark-skinned ealdorman, and I flash him a smile of thanks over the head of the king's son. Ealdorman Tidwulf doesn't seem to notice me, but I'm sure there can be no other reason for him distracting Wigmund in such a way. Perhaps, as I brought him Theodore and Gaya, he means to repay that kindness with one of his own.

Eagerly, I face Brute once more, desperate to make our escape before my horse becomes spooked once more. 'Shall we?' I enquire, and my horse moves forwards, head bowed, suddenly pliant now that I've returned to him, his black and white coat shimmering, even with the overcast sky.

He might have ridden to war, and back again, but he's fit and well, the length of the road disappearing beneath his hooves with ease.

'Apologies,' I call to the men who've fallen foul of Brute's evil temper. 'I would seek out Wynflæd for those bites. And she'll have something for the bruises as well,' I add helpfully, thinking of how I'd treat them if they were going to ask me for assistance. I think I'd opt for yarrow, woodruff, wild carrot and the leaves of a dandelion. That would do the trick. Provided I could find a dandelion. It's not truly the season for them. I'd need to have kept some stored from the bountiful early summer to ensure they contained the right potency.

So spoken, I lead on to the gate inside Tamworth, but not before pausing to examine the defences of the king's capital, tinged with my new-found knowledge from Londonia. There's no stone to be found anywhere along the walls and ditch. There's a deep trench, filled with a damp mess of drying grasses and other, less pleasant, items, discarded from cook pots and also from the latrines. There are also tall wooden walls above the ditch, and along them the guardsmen can keep a good watch when the traffic in and out is much reduced. But I'm reminded of Londinium and its huge grey walls. How did those giants who constructed it – and I'm inclined to believe as Wulfheard does, that they must have been giants – ensure the stones stayed upright?

'Icel.' My name rings through the camp, and I wince to hear the fury in the voice, even as I slip onto Brute's back, and hasten onwards.

'What is it?' I demand on nearing the gateway into Tamworth, only to see Ealdorman Sigered looking smug and pleased with himself, as the queen glowers at me. Just what has Ealdorman Sigered done now? And just what does the queen think I've done?

2

'That horse is a menace,' Ealdorman Sigered informs me through gritted teeth. At his side, Queen Cynethryth is white of face.

'He shouldn't have been anywhere near Lord Wigmund,' the queen commands, her tone imperious, for all it trembles a little.

I feel my forehead furrow, trying to make sense of this. I open my mouth, but notice Wulfheard shake his head from his place on the road into Tamworth. A space has opened up around the queen, and me. Lord Wigmund isn't anywhere to be seen. Who then has been telling of our brief conversation? I'm sure I was polite to the king's son, even if I didn't wish to be

'My queen, my apologies.' I bow from my saddle, ensuring my control of Brute is maintained by gripping him tightly with my thighs.

Ealdorman Sigered stands in front of the queen, or rather, he almost does. In fact, it's the queen's guard who shields her, with the ealdorman hiding just behind them. What a warrior the man is.

'A horse such as that has no place in the king's war band,' Queen Cynethryth persists, her words too strong. She isn't truly fearful, I surmise – at least, not for herself. 'The beast should be shackled to a plough. That's all it's good for.'

'What's this?' Ealdorman Ælfstan appears at the commotion taking place before the gate, and I'm aware that everyone is watching what happens now; no one moves. I run my hand down Brute's left shoulder, hoping he'll remain calm.

'This animal is wild,' the queen announces, chin high, defiance on her lined face. The queen is no longer a young woman, her son a man grown, and she tries to hide her wrinkled face with artfully arranged hair, and a thin veil to cover her silvering locks, but here, in the daylight, all her years are laid bare.

'If not for this animal, I'd be dead,' Ealdorman Ælfstan confirms, his tone bland. 'The king has gifted the horse to young Icel, for his actions in saving his life. The horse was the king's to gift, and he did so.'

I'm unsure why Ealdorman Ælfstan says this. The queen must know. Certainly, everyone else does.

The queen flashes an ungrateful look towards Ealdorman Ælfstan. Perhaps she doesn't wish to be reminded that her husband almost died in the Welsh borderlands. Certainly, she doesn't wish to be reminded that she should show any gratitude towards me.

'He must be kept away from the king's son,' she continues, as though the ealdorman hasn't spoken. 'And, indeed, from any of the king's other horses. He's a menace. He'll cause disruption in the stables.'

'He'll do no such thing.' Now the king is involved, as his voice rises above all other. I don't know who's alerted him to this as well.

I wish I was wearing my helm so that I could hide the astonishment on my face. Brute is but one horse. I'm unsure why he's causing such a commotion. It's not as though Lord Wigmund was ever in danger from Brute. He might have been from me, but not from my horse. And even if Brute nipped him, that's only what any animal would have done.

'Take him inside the settlement,' the king commands from his position at the gateway, where he's been standing, speaking words of encouragement to his exhausted warriors as they trudge inside their home.

'Go,' Wulfheard whispers sharply, stepping to my side. 'Get the animal settled beside Wine, and tell him not to draw any more bloody attention to himself.'

I nod quickly, bow once more to the queen and Ealdorman Sigered, and only then lead Brute over the wooden bridge and beneath the gateway. All the time, I'm aware of eyes on me and sweat trickles down my back, pooling at the top of my trews. I only breathe deeply once I dismount, and my two animals share a nicker of welcome with one another, heads touching over the side of their stables.

With Brute finally settled, and perhaps as bemused as I am about all the fuss his appearance has caused, I turn to make my way to Wynflæd's workshop before remembering that it's no longer my home. No, I sleep with Mercia's warriors now, in a bunkhouse, where all of the unmarried men sleep. Cuthred has my place in the workshop. I'm not sure how I feel about that.

The bunkhouse is not uncomfortable. If anything, it actually smells better than Wynflæd's workshop on some occasions, but it's not truly my home. I've been given my uncle's sleeping space. When I first slept here, in the short space of time in between returning from the borderlands with the Welsh and riding to Londonia with the king's warriors, I found little of Cenfrith's possessions. After all, the Wessex warriors had been making use of it in Wiglaf's absence from Tamworth. Still, there were two tunics which were once Cenfrith's. Even now, they smell of him, and I won't wear them, and neither will I get rid of them. They're my reminder that this was once his place, and his home, no matter that he's gone from my side. I keep them in my wooden chest, alongside my few other possessions.

I lower myself onto my bed, mindful that I stink of the road. If I lie down, I'll sleep, and I need to wash the muck from my matted hair first. But the temptation to sleep is also great.

I look around me. There are other men bending to return tunics and trews to their small wooden chests from their saddle-bags. There are also those arguing or embracing, or weeping at the gaps left in the bunk room by the absence of those who died retrieving Londonia from the Wessex king's grasp.

I don't know if a full accounting of the dead has yet been made. I'm sure that someone, somewhere, will know the names of all those who died. Some clerics will have been given the task. I close my eyes in memory, seeing the sightless faces of all those forever staring men I trampled over on the slaughter field at the end of the battle. Purposefully, I don't consider the dead Wessex warriors, other than Tyrhtil. He was a good man. I'll mourn him even if he was my enemy. I saved his life inside Londinium, and in turn, he helped keep me alive. The younger Brihtwold I won't mourn. He tried to kill me, in the end. I can't deny that I'm pleased I live, while he's dead. But Tyrhtil deserved to live. A man as honourable as him shouldn't have died the way he did.

From nearby, I hear the raised voices of my fellow warriors Garwulf and Frithwine. I'd forgotten they'd be in the bunkhouse as well. I could do with not having to listen to them. They're so filled with confidence after events in Londonia that I think they've forgotten Frithwine was almost crushed to death by his fellow countrymen before they could make a name for them-selves as part of Ealdorman Ælfstan's infiltration of Londinium.

I listen to them now from my place in the bunkhouse, as I

prepare to take myself outside to bathe in the huge wooden tubs the servants are struggling to keep filled with clean and hot water. Frithwine and Garwulf have found some youngster to regale with their battle glories. Damn fools. They'd be better served in keeping their mouths shut and allowing others to mourn now that we're finally somewhere it's possible to do so and can lower our guard as there are others to protect us.

I can hear them even through the walls of the bunkhouse, as I strip, unheeding of those who might see my nakedness, and settle into the warmish water. It's not big enough for me, my knees almost touching my chin, but I crave being clean.

My mind revolves to the memories of my time in Londonia, and if not for the warmth of the water, I'd shudder with cold.

It was a grim day when we buried the dead in one of the many churchyards in Lundenwic. A visibly relieved Bishop Ceolbeorht, free from the Wessex overlord, intoned over the bodies, his pleasure at being free from King Ecgberht's commands easy to see. The grave wasn't a small one, but rather large enough to take the bodies of all the Mercian dead. I counted close enough to fifty men – thirty-three of them from the failed attack on the mint.

I recognised the faces of the dead, and heard familiar names being wailed by their surviving allies and friends, but many of the men were strangers to me. I mourned them as Mercians, and pitied them their deaths, as the jolting of bodies flung callously into the deep ditch exposed wounds and nakedness for all to see. A great deal of pale flesh was displayed that day. Many vomited at the sight of so much destruction, but I stood and watched, just as Ealdorman Ælfstan and the king did. Ealdorman Sigered showed himself to be craven, turning aside, his face as pale as the dead. Theodore and Gaya stoically stood and watched; I could only imagine their thoughts at being free from Ecgred.

The ceremony was sullen, but only for a while, even the

bishop unable to keep the joy from his mournful dirge. Men victorious in battle seemed little concerned with sorrow, giddy only with being alive and living to receive praise and silver from their king as soon as the earth was pushed back into place over their less fortunate comrades.

As for the Wessex warriors, some of the dead were burned close to the River Thames, on a pyre made from the ruins of the ships used in their unsuccessful strike on Lundenwic. I watched the sodden sail of the ships, festooned with the Wessex Wyvern, burn with a ferocity that should have been impossible for something so wet and soaking. I thrilled to know that our ravages would be clearly visible from the Wessex side of the River Thames.

It was both a warning for those sheltering Wessex men who still lived and an easier means of disposing of so many dead from the final attack. Lord Æthelwulf and King Ecgberht would have seen the smoke as it filled the sky, and known only too well its portend.

There were many more dead Wessex warriors than Mercians, even before we'd entered Londinium. I counted over a hundred pairs of lifeless limbs, stripped of all they'd once owned and claimed. I witnessed old wounds, long since healed, and the gaping holes of those fatal losses. The healer in me calmly considered how such wounds could be treated had not men lost all of their lifeblood in the attack.

The smell of the charnel house infected Londinium, as the flames leapt higher from the funeral pyre outside the settlement, the bank of smoke almost blocking out the dim light from the watery sun.

The fort building, which Ealdorman Ælfstan commanded we occupy as our first action inside Londinium, was stripped of its dead; everywhere else still being strewn with the dead. I witnessed men I'd healed in Ecgred's hut lying beyond all means of my assistance as I walked the by now familiar roads inside Londinium.

With Wulfheard to one side, he recounted the story of events inside the fort building itself. While Ealdorman Ælfstan had managed to gain entry, alongside the rest of our small Mercian force of Frithwine, Garwulf, Cenred, Wulfheard and Ælfstan, Oswy and I had been too slow to do so, but it was a bloody battle for them.

'We had to fight through the Wessex warriors trying to stop us. Cenred led the way, with Æthelmod and Goðeman doing the same from inside the fort. It was a bloody mess at the end. The doorway was too small for such a fight. We needed you then, Icel. Cenred took a bad wound, and was no good to any of us. The cut almost severed his left hand.'

Gaya told me that it will take time for Cenred to regain the same function he once had. But, as Cenred told me, smiling around his pain, he can at least hold out hope that he'll be able to wipe his arse with his left hand again one day.

'I must have missed it all,' I commiserated. By the time I arrived at the fort, I'd known that Oswy and I wouldn't be able to gain admittance, thanks to the howling Wessex warriors outside it.

'Aye, lad. Well, you saved Oswy. So, you have my thanks for that. A bloody stupid design,' Wulfheard further grumbled. 'Building the fort to the side of the roadway and gates.'

Bloody stupid, I agreed, but only for those stuck inside it. Not for those thinking to use it as a final means of sanctuary.

Still, we trod the roadway through Londinium, first to Ecgred's workshop, where Theodore and Gaya were carefully removing everything that would help them in their new life. I smiled to see them.

Theodore bent to inspect my hand, shaking his head, while Gaya translated his words for me.

'Is it so hard to keep it dry?' he chastised, using her voice.

'Yes,' I replied. 'When there's a bloody great big battle going on, and I have to cross a river to get to the enemy.'

Swiftly, he and Gaya moved to change my bandage. I wanted to ask them about Tyrhtil. He'd died here, but his body was gone. Theodore offered me a sorrowful glance, and I swallowed heavily. It was better that I didn't know.

I walked away from the workshop, grateful that I would never have to see the place again. I'd not wanted to return to it at all, but the pull of the place couldn't be ignored.

The matter of Ecgred's killing will remain a secret. There's no one left to ask after him, and I've no intention of mentioning it to anyone. As far as I'm concerned, Ecgred's death was a matter of life and death, undertaken during a war, of which Mercia were the victors. The part played by Gaya in his death was irrelevant. She didn't mean to kill him by clouting him over the head with a heavy jug. All the same, his death has ensured me, Gaya and Theodore stay alive.

Once more on the roads that led deeper into Londinium, we'd come across King Wiglaf and the ealdormen. Ealdorman Sigered rode with a cloth held close to his nose, determined to keep the rancid smell away. But, between the smoke still smouldering from the ruins close to the river gate and the ripe smell of the boggy ground close to the River Walbrook running through the settlement, I'd found it difficult to smell anything.

Wessex bodies had been pulled out of the king's way, and Wiglaf was focused firmly on the ancient two-storey building where we had attacked Ealdorman Wassa and his men.

'Icel. Wulfheard. Escort us to the forum,' the king commanded, my name coming easily to his lips.

I swallowed against the unease in my stomach. I knew what we'd find, and if anything, it was even worse than my fears. The ripe scent of blood reached us even there, with the white statues, and their inscrutable expressions, watching us from their places outside the building.

When King Wiglaf demanded Wulfheard and I precede him into the building used as the ealdorman's hall, we had to force aside prostrate bodies, lying cold and marbled. I eyed the man I'd killed there. The one who'd thought to crush me, but who hadn't quite managed to do so, thanks to Oswy. I heard the telltale scamper of rats and other beasts, disturbed from feasting by our footsteps, breaking the silence of the grave.

Immediately, I was forced to turn aside, almost running into King Wiglaf with my speed. He said nothing, and while Ealdorman Sigered refused to enter the building, Ealdorman Ælfstan and Tidwulf accompanied the king. The king wanted to see the face of his enemy.

Wulfheard reappeared first, his face pale, so that the bruises and cuts taken in the fight at the fort were starkly etched on to his face. He came to my side, eyeing me with understanding on his lined face.

'A nasty business,' he confirmed, only then turning away to vomit noisily onto the stone of the forum floor.

I turned my back on the building, distracting myself with examining the ancient statues once more. They were already missing noses, hands, feet and ears, but now many of them were also painted with the shed blood of the Wessex warriors. What had they witnessed in their years? I considered. No doubt events about which I was entirely ignorant. The blood, I decided, would wash from them, eventually, with a few heavy rainstorms, and still, they'll stand. The thought astounded me. If only I could know all that they'd seen. Would it make me wiser? I shook my head at such folly, even as I took the time to examine the smooth faces, hands, arms and legs. I'd truly never seen anything like it before. Even the stone, so glossy beneath my fingers, was a wonder to me. What sort of person had possessed such skill to wrought something so perfectly from sullen stone, I'd thought. And then, my mind swirled around me. These ancient statues resembled men and women such as me, and Wulfheard, Wynflæd, and Lady Cynehild. What had they possessed, that we so lacked, to build such as they had?

'Burn it.' King Wiglaf's voice lacked some of its usual severity as he reappeared from inside the corpse-strewn building of the forum. I was pleased with his decision, even if I knew the stone of the forum wouldn't burn. 'Bring what combustibles we have. That place will never be clear of the taint of the Wessex scum if it's not entirely cleansed by fire,' King Wiglaf further commanded, and every man there pretended not to hear the wobble of the king's voice.

And it wasn't easy to accomplish, for if Londinium could have provided such things as wood and animal dung for burning, then Lundenwic need never have sprouted to the west of the River Fleet. We were forced to pull what we could from buildings that retained turf roofs, and when that didn't produce enough material to burn, we ripped clothes from bodies and used those to fuel the flames.

I was forced back into the building to accomplish the king's commands, a strip of linen over my face. Gazing upon the bodies of the men I'd killed, I bowed my head low over Brihtwold's savaged body. His eyes, thankfully closed, didn't judged me. Yet I shied away from touching his corpse. He lived for hardly no time at all, no older than I. It pained me to see the outcome of our attack, even if the victory was much-needed.

The king demanded that Ealdorman Wassa's body be

removed before the burning. He determined it should be returned to the Wessex king, a task he bid a trader from Lundenwic carry out for him later that day. I didn't watch the small craft bob across the River Thames. I certainly didn't want to see how the Wessex forces received the body.

And then we visited the river gate. Here, so much had burned already, and yet bodies aplenty remained. A few, held in place by the remnants of the wooden quayside, jutted out into the river, bobbing, white and blue, with the rise and fall of the water. Others had been savaged by creatures attracted by the scent of blood. Few kept their eyeballs. Even fewer showed no sign of being gnawed or pecked at.

While Ealdorman Ælfstan stood stoic, even the king was disturbed by what he saw.

'And it's from here that they sent the ships to Lundenwic?' he demanded from me.

'Aye, my lord king, from here,' I confirmed.

'And it's to here that Lord Æthelwulf brought his reinforcements, only to discover that you held the fort?' This he directed to Ealdorman Ælfstan.

'Yes, my lord king.'

'And so, they returned to their ships and made landfall close to the River Fleet and attacked the Mercians from there?'

'So it appears.'

'And it's from there that they escaped?' King Wiglaf's voice thrummed with annoyance. I was surprised to realise it wasn't directed at the ealdorman, or at me. Rather, the king stared across the murky River Thames, towards Wessex. Wessex were the enemy. The fact they had retreated from Londonia just wasn't enough. That King Wiglaf determined to treat the dead ealdorman with the respect he deserved didn't mean he'd forgiven, and he'd certainly not forgotten, but a wise king always showed some respect for his enemy. 'The bastard still lives, and he should be dead,' King Wiglaf continued, confirming my suspicions, and everyone else's.

'We can't risk following him into Wessex.' Of course, it was Ealdorman Sigered who spoke so. There wasn't a man there who wouldn't have risked the River Thames to reach bloody King Ecgberht. Even I opened my mouth, but Wiglaf beat everyone to it.

'Thank you, Ealdorman Sigered.' His tone was icy. 'I think we all know the difference between what must be done, and what we can achieve.'

And so, King Wiglaf swept from the river gate, taking with him many of the ealdormen, but not Sigered. Sigered watched the king with an unfathomable expression, before hurrying to catch him.

Ealdorman Muca has been left to hold Londonia. To him, alongside the king's commander, Eahric, has been given the unenviable task of ensuring the Wessex king understands Mercia's intent to never lose Londonia again.

'Icel.' I look in surprise to meet the gaze of Wulfheard. It's evident he's been standing there for some time, as he taps his foot impatiently, while I reminisce about the aftermath of the battle for Londonia, the water around me filthy and cold. 'Come on. Get dressed. It's time to be feasted by our lord king, and to determine just what we must do next to ensure Mercia's freedom.'

I'm grateful to be pulled away from my memories, from the dreams of blood and shattered bone I see behind my eye whenever I sleep, and sometimes, even when I'm awake. It was one thing to kill my enemy and to know they were my enemy, but now, I realise that my enemy could easily be my friend, such as Tyrhtil was, and that is no longer as easy to reconcile as it once was.

3

For the first time, I enter the king's hall with my eyes level. There's no longer the need to hide behind any who might shield me from the wrath of the king's wife. Not that I much care for Queen Cynethryth, and, of course, I've almost made my peace with Lady Cynehild at Winchcombe nunnery. All the same, it's a strange experience to join the king's warriors on their benches that line the long boards upon which the king's servants have placed platters of food and mugs for drinking. For the first time in my life, I realise how narrow the hall is. There's little room for my shoulders amongst the crush of men seeking their sustenance. I don't believe more than four men, with my shoulders, could stand across the width of the king's hall. The knowledge astounds me.

I'm startled to see Wynflæd seated with the king's wife. Queen Cynethryth seems fully recovered from her earlier altercation with me and drips with jewels and fine fabric, her hems stiff with dazzling embroidery tipped with costly golden threads usually reserved for the bishops and their robes. Wynflæd wears her usual serviceable clothes. I look down at my bandaged hand to hide my amusement. Wynflæd will never change. If anything, her refusal to adopt the ceremonial dress of the king's servant actually marks her as more special. She's her own woman. She serves the king and his family at her discretion.

I look behind me then, and my eyes fasten on Theodore's, with Gaya beside him. The two sit amongst a group of esteemed members of the settlement of Tamworth, Edwin's stepfather amongst them, his mother as well. Also included are the corpulent moneyer, the broomstick-thin silversmith and the short miller, who understands how the mill works with a quickness of wit that startles me. Such skilled individuals are a true asset to the king.

I can see that Edwin's stepfather has been scoured clean by his wife. There's no hint of the blackness of the forge coals upon his face or his clothes. He's no doubt had a busy time of it since our return. There are many horses who need new shoes for their hooves, or even just one replacing after our journey. The roadways are hard on some of the animals' hooves. Not all of the horses require horseshoes, but those that do seem to need them far more often than I was ever gifted with new boots.

Wulfheard eats eagerly beside me, his elbows knocking me time and time again. He's not spoken to me since we left the bunkhouse when I dressed hastily in clothes that didn't hold the stink of the slaughter field.

'Sorry,' Wulfheard huffs, food spraying from his mouth as he does so. 'I'm bloody starving.'

He hands me a platter filled with baked trout, and I hook one of the creatures, no doubt fished from the Tame, and place it on my thick slice of bread. There's also good pottage and thick slabs of pork. It is indeed a feast for this time of year. Surely, this will beggar the settlement and leave nothing for the coming lean time.

'Eat it before the other fat bastards get to it,' Wulfheard urges me in a dark tone.

I shake my head and begin to spoon the fish into my mouth. At the last possible moment, another sits to my right, knocking my spoon so that my teeth clamp down on nothing but air, the fish landing back on the bread, and just avoiding the snapping jaw of one of the king's hounds, squirrelled away beneath the table for just such an opportunity as this. I glower at the animal as its jaw snaps shut on thin air. I curse that I can't grip even my eating knife with my hand as well bandaged as it is. I should have tried my left hand.

'Apologies,' a voice I know too well says and I meet Edwin's eyes. He doesn't offer me a grin. If anything, Edwin appears haunted by what he's seen in the last few weeks. When he thought to become a warrior, it seems he didn't consider that meant killing and leaving bodily remains behind. I've been aware of him, more than once, losing the contents of his stomach, when tasked with clearing away the dead, bloated bodies found festering long after the majority have been removed in and around Londonia.

I open my mouth to speak to him, but King Wiglaf has risen before us, on the raised dais at the front of the king's hall. I make to stand once more, only for Wulfheard to hold me down with a firm grip, as I crane my neck around to see the king.

Edwin has no one to offer him the same, and he stands, alone, facing the king. His face blossoms red, while King Wiglaf fixes him with a perplexed expression, as he realises no one else stands. Quickly, I reach out and grip his arm as tightly as I can, pulling Edwin to my side. I can feel the tautness of his muscles, and also the way he seems to shake. Edwin has been embarrassed, but I believe his trembling is caused by something else entirely.

'My brave warriors.' King Wiglaf is expansive this evening. Mercia's warrior helm has been brought forth for him to wear, complete with bright horsehair adornment covering its crown. He wears his weapons belt, and now I realise that, behind him, a stolen shield of Wessex has been displayed prominently on the wall of the king's hall. Its wyvern's head has been battered, and if I didn't know what creature it represented, I might be unsure. But I know what it is. I doubt I'll ever forget it. The black and white shading would ensure I knew what it was even if the wyvern was entirely obscured.

A cheer greets King Wiglaf's words. At his side, Queen Cynethryth sits woodenly, her son fidgeting beside her. Neither of them looks that impressed with Wiglaf's stance as a warrior king, and certainly not with the acclaim he's receiving from his warriors. They don't approve of his weapons belt worn into battle, the blades easy to see, or the fact that he's won the respect of men who'll kill in his name.

I turn my eyes to the king. I don't want to see their sour faces, not when Wiglaf is resplendent. If my uncle could see him now, I don't believe he'd think him the same man who lost Mercia's kingship to King Ecgberht of Wessex. I believe, and hope, that my uncle would be pleased to name King Wiglaf as his lord, and ally.

'Tonight, we feast our victory, and drink as well.'

Another cheer, and even I add my voice to this, even though I'm not about to drink as much as many of the warriors might do. I've yet to acquire the liking for the bitter brew.

'Tomorrow, under the direction of Bishop Æthelweald of Lichfield, we'll mourn our dead.'

A heaving sob fills the suddenly still air. I wince to hear such raw grief while rich food and ale sits before us. King Wiglaf pauses, to acknowledge that not all is to be celebrated, although his face is far from bland at the unwelcome interruption.

'But tonight, we feast and we drink, knowing that the bastard king of Wessex will never again darken Mercia with his shadow. Londonia is once more Mercian.' As Wiglaf holds his drinking vessel aloft, the light catches the many-faceted edges of the silver goblet, flashing on to his face, and I startle. Wiglaf seems more kingly than I've ever seen him. It's almost as the bishop would have us believe: the holy oil of the coronation marked on Wiglaf's forehead has made the king different to the rest of us. I thought him just a man, and one who can be wounded and killed like the rest of us, but maybe he's truly loved by our God. Certainly, I find myself growing more and more fond of the man, and it's not because he gave me Brute. Far from it.

As the applause and cheering recede, a man and a woman seat themselves before the king's dais. She carries a small drum, and he has some sort of flute to hand, and together they sweep into a rousing tale of Mercia's hero pagan king from nearly two hundred years ago, Penda, and all he accomplished during his long lifetime. He beat back the Northumbrians and their kings and the kings of Wessex who champed at him from across the divide of the River Thames. For over three decades, Penda was king of all on this island, and no man could overthrow him, although I have heard some say that there was a holy man who tried to make it sound as though the Northumbrian kings were the victors. We all know the truth about that.

'I see the king means to become a conqueror, not just a king of his realm.' Wulfheard's eyes show none of the excitement of the other drink-addled warriors. 'But first, he needs must kill that bastard, Athelstan of the East Angles. Before Athelstan kills him.' Wulfheard's tone is filled with foreboding.

* * *

The following day, most wake with aching heads and bleary-eyed. I don't, but the groans of others assure me that many have been foolish enough to drink as much as they can fit inside them, with no thought for the tedium of the religious service we must attend today. We've feasted, and now, we must mourn Mercia's losses. We must honour those who gave their lives for Mercia's independence.

I dress quickly, keen to be away from the stink of day-old ale and the farting of men who've eaten their fill as well. Pork on the way out smells much as pork on the way in. It's making my stomach growl hungrily, and that disgusts me even more.

It's a bright but cold day, the sun finally making an appearance even though it's much later than during the summer months. Winter almost has its hold on Mercia. The puddles in the road have thin sheets of ice covering them. I hear someone forcing the bucket through the surface of the well to ensure the ice there is broken. I'm aware that the weather is different here than in Londonia. It's cooler. I'd not realised such a distance would make such a huge difference. I return to my bed and collect my thick cloak, encircling myself with it and welcoming the heat that quickly builds.

My breath plumes in the air before me, and I'm about to make my way to Wynflæd's workshop when I realise someone is calling my name. I look up, and meet Lady Cynehild's eyes. Behind her, the guards are on duty, stamping their feet and huddling around a brazier as they ensure no enemy enters the king's settlement on what is already a bleak day of mourning.

Lady Cynehild is enveloped in a thick cloak, with warm boots around her feet. I can see where she's just dismounted, and my heart quails. I meant to speak to the king about Lady Cynehild. Clearly, I'm too late to do so if she's already been summoned from the nunnery at Winchcombe to Tamworth.

'My lady.' I bow low, half an eye on her feet, but her boots are well seasoned and a sensible colour. There's no hint of the red shade from when we last met. I almost miss seeing them. Has she already lost the spark that made her so bright even when banished to the nunnery?

'Oh, stand up, Icel. I think we know each other well enough.'

I don't think we do, but I do as she asks. There are a group of mounted men leading their horses away. I also catch sight of someone in a long dark robe beneath a functional cloak of drab colour. I take it to be the abbess of Cynehild's nunnery. Some might take the colour of her clothing to mean she's a woman of little worth, but it's not easy to find the dyes needed for such dark clothes. While she cloaks herself with the night, she proclaims her position as easily as if she wore gold and silver jewels on every cuff. It's understated, and in that, just like Wynflæd beside the jewels of the queen, the abbess speaks volumes about her prestige and position.

'What?' I start to ask, but Lady Cynehild stops me.

'I'm sure you must have heard of my impending union.' Her words are right, but her voice sounds off.

I nod, miserably. It's been barely two months since we last spoke. I can't see that she'll have had a change of heart about marrying. 'I have, My Lady. Yes. I'm sorry.'

'You've nothing to be sorry for, Icel. Our lives are both in the hands of the king,' she murmurs.

'And the queen,' I bite. I feel rebellion stirring in me. Last night, King Wiglaf spoke of Mercia's triumph, but at what price for Lady Cynehild?

Her eyes are sharp at my barb. 'Yes, and Queen Cynethryth,' Cynehild concedes. Her eyes are focused on the king's hall. I can't tell whether she's pleased to be here or not. It was once her hall when she was married to King Beornwulf, and now it isn't. She once laid claim to rule over the unruly men of the king's guard, and the servants. To her fell the task of keeping the hall well maintained. It was she who had the twisting images carved on the wooden posts that hold up the great hall and its roof. That they shimmer with oil now is more to her commands regarding their initial construction than anything Queen Cynethryth has since ordered. That they went against the bishop's command is something else I recall. He decried their heathen nature, as he termed it. Lady Cynehild argued that they honoured Mercia's prestigious line, begun long, long ago, in heathen times, naming King Penda. Lady Cynehild's words had more power than the bishop's. The same can no longer be said.

'I would speak, on your behalf,' I interject. I feel it's my role to do something. She has no husband to speak for her. I don't even know if she has any other family. I assume she doesn't. Although, she once must have done. I can't see that King Beornwulf, with all of his ambitions, would marry a woman when the union would have brought him nothing he hungered for. I consider then which family she belongs to? Which of the dead ealdormen might have been her father or brother? I've never considered this before, and it's evident that I should have done.

Lady Cynehild's face softens, her bright eyes on my face. 'Icel. My thanks, but I'm resolved to my fate. It's not as unexpected as you might believe, even if I would have preferred to take my holy vows. I understand Lord Coenwulf is a good man.'

I grimace at that. I don't have enough experience to know if he's good or not. What I saw of him at Kingsholm revealed a man who wallowed in remorse on the death of his father. He never even tried to claim Mercia as his own to rule, although he must have spent some of his life believing that one day he would be king. He's not a warrior, either. But I don't say any of this.

'Then you're content?'

Lady Cynehild's head jostles from side to side, dislodging her bound hair so that a tendril breaks free from the clips holding it away from her face. Cynehild should probably be wearing a veil, but then, she hasn't actually become a nun. If she had, there would be an outcry about her marriage, no matter the wishes of Queen Cynethryth. A nun may not marry, no matter the commands of kings. Or queens. 'Content is too strong a word. I'm accepting, as you are of the fact you're pledged to King Wiglaf when you wished to spend your time with Wynflæd healing people – not healing them from wounds gained in battle.'

I nod, uneasy that the comparison so easily spills from her tongue. I don't want to think I'm like Lady Cynehild. She's being married against her wishes. Am I still training to become a warrior against my wishes? I can't say I thrill to be in the shield wall, but I've accomplished a great deal for the good of Mercia. I do feel some pride in that, even if it's been through more luck than skill.

'You seem to know a lot about what I've been doing?' I think to query.

She nods, an expression on her face I can't quite interpret. 'As the Lord of Budworth, your actions are spoken about.'

'Hmm,' I sigh, unhappy at the reminder that I inherited my uncle's lands after his death. I've only been to Budworth once, where it lies, to the north and west of Tamworth, to bury my uncle. It didn't feel like my home. I was pleased to leave. I can't see that being Lord of Budworth in name means a great deal, not when all I really am is one of the king's oath-sworn men.

Lady Cynehild chuckles at my less than enthusiastic response. 'I'm sure Ealdorman Ælfstan would assist you if you needed help.'

But I'm already shaking my head. 'Budworth is a small place, with a well-respected and efficient reeve, Eomer. I don't believe

I'll need to visit there often.' I don't say that I don't wish to go there, because that's where Cenfrith's body lies, in the small graveyard surrounding the even smaller wooden church with its square tower. That grief is still raw. Sometimes, even now, I expect to see him striding towards me, some complaint on his lips about the king's decisions, irritation on his face that only softens a little on seeing me.

'Perhaps not, but don't be as much of a stranger to the place as your uncle was. The people there deserve to know that their lord is a good man.'

Again, I feel unsure how to respond. Am I a good man? I killed men who thought I was their ally. And I've also killed many men now. I can remember most of them, but not all of them. There are only so many sets of terrified eyes that I can encounter before they begin to merge into one set. I see some of the men alive, some of them dead, most of them are a blur, apart from Brihtwold, and I didn't make the killing blow.

Lady Cynehild doesn't press me further, but rather walks beside me as we wind our path through the settlement. It's springing to life, people hunkering into cloaks and scurrying against the icy blasts that barrel their way down the neat street pattern. I look around me. This is my home, and yet, compared to Londinium, and even Lundenwic, it's a small place.

'I take it you're going to see Wynflæd?' Lady Cynehild queries.

'I am, yes.'

'Good. I was going to see her as well.'

We walk side by side, but really, it's no more than twenty steps to Wynflæd's workshop, and once there, I indicate that Lady Cynehild should enter first. She bows her head below the sagging roof, at exactly the same moment that Cuthred emerges, carrying an empty bucket, eyes bulging from his face.

'Apologies, my lady.' He bows low, the bucket dropping with the movement so that when he moves off, he kicks it, and winces.

'What are you doing?' Wynflæd's tone is far from reassuring. It's as though she has eyes everywhere.

'It's Lady Cynehild,' Cuthred calls quickly, hopping on one foot.

'Come in, my lady.' Wynflæd's voice shows no greater respect for Lady Cynehild than for one of the other inhabitants of Tamworth, and I grin, dropping my chin to try to stop Cynehild from seeing.

'Come on, Cuthred, I'll help you,' I offer softly so that Wynflæd doesn't hear me.

'I'll speak with you again,' Lady Cynehild assures me with a meaningful look in her eyes, and I mutter and move away. I don't need to hear what the two women are going to talk about. I just hope it isn't about me.

'Tell me more about the feeling inside Tamworth, Cuthred?' I indicate the settlement of Tamworth, and Cuthred sucks his lower lip in thought, and then begins to speak.

'The queen is a difficult person to please, and her son is just as finicky. But if you mean the people in general, then everyone is muddling along. It's a relief that King Ecgberht has gone. He didn't do a lot of damage to the buildings, but with so few people remaining in Tamworth, a lot of the steadings needed repair work done on them. The blacksmith is constructing a second forge, and they had to replace part of the watermill as well. But, over-whelmingly, people are content to know that King Wiglaf is back in control.'

'So, he has more support now?'

'Not more, no. But he does have people's backing. They don't look to Lord Coenwulf as an alternative. No one really knows who he is, although they will after his marriage to Lady Cynehild.'

At the well, I pull on the rope, lowering and then lifting the bucket, surprised that it doesn't make me sweat with exertion. Cuthred watches me with admiration, and I don't appreciate his next question.

'How many men did you kill?' he asks me, his eyes alight with mischief.

'More than enough, thank you.'

'And the king, how many did he kill? And Ealdorman Tidwulf and Ælfstan, and those healers you rescued, cor, they don't half know about healing. Wynflæd can't decide whether to like them or hate them. It's quite funny watching her.' At that, Cuthred stops his constant questions and silence falls between us. 'Sorry, Icel, I didn't mean to—'

'Cuthred, it's fine. Don't worry about it. Theodore and Gaya do have a huge amount of knowledge. As does Ealdorman Tidwulf. I'm sure that Wynflæd might be pleased to have some help, and also a little aggrieved at the same time.'

'Do you think they'll stay in Tamworth?'

'Now, that I don't know. It might be that Ealdorman Tidwulf takes them away with him to his ealdordom. I don't know. Do you think you could treat everyone if they went away, and after Wynflæd was no longer here?'

But he's already shaking his head. 'No, not at all. She says I don't remember anything I'm told and that I'm too fidgety when she tries to teach me things.' Cuthred's tone is martyred, and now I laugh at him and reach over to ruffle his thatch of dark hair.

'She used to say the same to me. Don't worry about it. I tell you this much, you'll be learning much more than you might think. And it might all seem tedious and boring when she sets you to spinning spiders' webs from the corners or cutting the herbs in such a way, but she's making sure you know how to do things properly, even if you're sure there are better ways of doing it. Quicker ways,' I clarify, watching him, careful now that I've swung the bucket away from the well.

Cuthred gazes at me in thought. 'You might be right, Icel. But, well, I think I can still teach her a few things.' His laughter is infectious, and together, we make our way back to Wynflæd's workshop.

4

The ceremony of remembrance for the dead men of Mercia is a tedious affair inside Tamworth's church, dedicated to Saint Chad. Bishop Æthelweald seems to have determined on the slowest possible delivery of his words, and over the sobbing of the widows and children, road brothers as well, I can hear the entire church full of people shuffling uncomfortably despite the number of us standing to attention.

It's cold in here. Despite our cloaks and warmest clothes, it feels more bitter than the middle of winter, when snow might lie shin-deep on the ground. I've mourned for the dead. I wish the bishop would just bloody get on with his Mass and service of remembrance. I would sooner remember the dead in my own way and not with his constant exhortations to God and assertion that these men will thrive in heaven. I saw the ruin of their bodies. I know the pain they suffered. Nothing God can do will take that away from me.

I didn't get to speak to Wynflæd before the ceremony. I was summoned to the church by Wulfheard, gruff and white-faced having drunk too much the night before. Ealdorman Ælfstan's warriors stand together, in a place of prominence, nearly at the front of the church. The ealdorman thinks this an honour, or at least, I assume he does. I haven't actually asked him.

I eye the line of warriors. It's strange to think that I've won acceptance amongst such a collection of seasoned men. Oswy still looks pained by his wounds, but he can get around easily enough now. He continues to limp, but the movement is slight. The seared wound on his chest has finally knit together, as I rub my left hand over my right, which is taking much, much longer to heal. I've taken my bandage off to allow some air to get to the wound. I find it ironic that his life-threatening wound is now almost whole, whereas mine – little more than a burn, as Oswy sometimes taunts me when he catches me itching it, or trying not to use my right hand at all – is taking so much longer.

Uor stands with his belly sucked in tightly. He doesn't like to be reminded of what happened to him outside the walls of Londinium, when he was too fat to enter via our narrow entrance beneath the walls. I believe he's decided to spend less time drinking and eating, but, as of yet, he's all hot air. Landwine carries a collection of new scars on his face and hands, whereas Wulfgar is struggling to grow back his beard from where his chin was sliced by one of the enemy during the battle for the bridge over the River Fleet.

Cenred has his wounded left hand strapped tightly across his body. Æthelmod stands beside him. The welter of bruises that covered his face from where he was struck by a shield boss has finally begun to fade. The attack didn't split his skin, but it's been very painful. For a time, he could only see out of one eye. And it was certainly his weaker eye. His shins have been almost as black-ened as his face from walking into objects he couldn't see well enough. It's a wonder the skin on his hands is still whole. He's fallen many, many times.

Maneca is pale of face, but I think that's more to do with the mead he drank the night before than any wounds he carries. Kyre has a smirk on his face, no doubt because of Maneca's swaying and constant swallowing as though to hold back nausea. More than once, I've seen him sharply elbow his fellow warrior to ensure he stays awake. I can only hope the ealdorman hasn't noticed.

Godeman's nose is red, and he sniffs almost constantly, thanks to a chill he's caught from being outside in the cold too long. Osmod glowers, whereas Waldhere stands as though a statue. I admire him for being so still. He's the only one who doesn't seem to feel the cold or the effects of last night.

The men all look smart, in clean tunics, wearing emblems of their faith and sigils that proclaim their allegiance either to the eagle of Mercia or to Ælfstan, who's adopted the boar as his emblem.

Frithwine and Garwulf, now honoured amongst Ealdorman Ælfstan's warriors, of course, look like they've been dragged through a hedge backwards after their night of feasting and drinking. I'm pleased I look better than they do, and haven't earned myself a swift rebuke from Ealdorman Ælfstan as he passed them to take his place at the front of the church, close to the king and the other ealdormen.

Lord Coenwulf is in attendance as well, summoned to Tamworth by the king so that he'd be waiting when the king's force returned to Tamworth. Not that Lord Coenwulf quite managed it. He arrived more than halfway through last night's feast.

Opposite us, Lord Coenwulf's warriors have similarly been

honoured at the front of the church, although I can't truly say that they did a great deal in the fight for control of Londonia. Edwin and I held the bridge over the River Fleet, and then Wulfgar and Wulfheard, with Ælfstan's men from the fort, assisted us in ensuring we kept control of it. It was Ealdorman Ælfstan's men who chased down King Ecgberht. We might have failed to detain him, but we tried bloody hard, even venturing into the River Thames in an effort to capture him.

Even now, I know that Ealdorman Ælfstan suffers from dizziness when he wakes, having been clobbered around the head by the enemy. He was sick more than once all over my boots before we could drag him away from the battle with the Wessex horsemen. The Wessex warriors all died, but we didn't. It was a victory, even if sometimes that's forgotten about.

Behind us, Ealdorman Beornoth and his warriors stand. It was they who chased down Lord Æthelwulf's waterborne force and sent them scurrying back to the ship – well, those who could. The Mercians under Beornoth made a bloody slaughter of the enemy, and that should truly have been the end of it. But, while I confess, I'm not wise in the ways of politics and war, King Ecgberht has been altogether too quiet since his defeat for my liking.

King Wiglaf has left Londonia reinforced with the might of Ealdorman Muca and Commander Eahric. But, it seems, no one truly expects King Ecgberht to renew his attempt to reclaim Lundenwic's mint or Londinium. That might be wishful thinking on their part, or it might be confidence from a reckoning of the Wessex dead, I'm unsure. The width of the River Thames is an alluring boundary and yet one I fear can be all too easily breached in the future.

And Wulfheard has reassured me, in his far from reassuring

way, that further east the breadth of the River Thames becomes little more than a brook over which horses and men can jump. It's not quite the boundary between two kingdoms that I've long perceived it to be. There, the Wansdyke provides a divide, and Wulfheard assures me it is similar to Offa's Dyke, which demarcates the Welsh kingdoms from Mercia, a slit between the land, with a deep ditch and a higher bank. It's never stopped the bloody Welsh, and that concerns me as well.

The coins from Londonia's mint that were struck to show the image of King Ecgberht of Wessex as king of Mercia have been recalled on the orders of the king, and even now Ealdorman Muca oversees the restriking of the coinage to show Mercia's rightful king, Wiglaf. In the war of blades and kingdoms, I confess, this determination over whose face is on the coinage surprises me.

King Wiglaf has decreed that the coins of King Ecgberht are no longer valid. He's made everyone inside Lundenwic, and a little further afield, powerless to conduct business unless they avail themselves of the services of the moneyer, or use older coins, struck when Wiglaf was king before King Ecgberht took Mercia under his command. He's even allowed that the coinage of his predecessors can be used, provided they were Mercians, and not Ecgberht.

And what a job the moneyer of Lundenwic, Redmudh, had to convince King Wiglaf of his continuing loyalty to Mercia. I pitied the man, but at least the king let him, and all of the inhabitants of Lundenwic who survived the fire, keep their lives. If King Wiglaf had killed all those whose loyalty he doubted, there might have been no one left inside Lundenwic, and Mercia would have been poorer for that, or so Wulfheard has assured me.

Indeed, if King Wiglaf chooses to punish the people of

Lundenwic any more than by nullifying much of their coins for a short amount of time, then no doubt, they'll invite King Ecgberht to reclaim the place. None of us wants that, not after the battles we've fought and the men Mercia has sacrificed.

And still the bishop's words drone onwards. I watch him, eyes narrowed, wishing that my thoughts could make him bring the elongated service to a close. There's no reverence for the dead men in prolonging it, as he does. I can't imagine that any intervention on the part of the bishop will aid the men in heaven, if that is where they've gone. I've seen little to make me believe death is the honour it's portrayed to be. My mother is gone, my uncle as well. I don't think that praying for them will reconcile me to their deaths, or make their God look on them with more favour.

Edwin catches my attention then, pulling me from my thoughts. He's standing rigidly, not offered a seat, although Lord Coenwulf and his sister have been honoured with such. I startle. I'd not realised Lady Ælflæd was to be part of Lord Coenwulf's expedition to Tamworth. I try not to stare, as she sits, head bowed demurely, while Bishop Æthelweald continues his diatribe. No doubt to win the support of the king, the bishop laments the Wessex king and how ungodly his actions in claiming Mercia were in setting aside an anointed and consecrated king of Mercia. I don't miss that Lord Coenwulf nods along with the sermon. His father was an anointed and consecrated king of Mercia. The bishop could just as easily be talking about the folly of his usurpation. But I only listen with half an ear, my attention entirely consumed by Lady Ælflæd.

I consider whether she might remember me. After all, I aided her sick horse at Kingsholm, and it wasn't that long ago. I ponder whether the horse is fully recovered and well. It would please me to know I didn't kill two horses when I was at Kingsholm with my uncle.

Abruptly, Lady Ælflæd turns and meets my gaze. I think to look away, but recognition flashes and she smiles, before bowing her head once more. I feel a glow form on my cheeks, and Wulf-heard leans over.

'Keep your eyes on the bloody bishop,' he whispers, the words overly loud, so that Ealdorman Ælfstan flashes both of us a furious look.

I nod, bow my head, and try my very hardest not to focus on anything the bishop has to say, but rather to reminisce on my time spent at Kingsholm. And, of course, with that memory comes many of my uncle, and once more, I'm reminded how truly alone I am, despite these warriors of Mercia who think of me as their ally, and who drank and ate with me last night.

I'm no longer an outcast, or ridiculed by them. They still tease me, remorselessly, about some of my actions, and when King Wiglaf is close, they're wary of what I might do next to win his regard, but I sit at their fire now when we travel along Mercia's roads. Of them all, it's Oswy who surprises me the most. I find myself strangely grateful to have the huge man as my ally. I can't imagine that Edwin thinks highly of me for that, but then, Edwin and I are hardly friends these days. We have different lords and different experiences. Edwin might have witnessed the horrors of war, but he's not fought the same battles that I have. He's not killed Viking raiders, and Wessex warriors, and saved the life of his king, or of an ealdorman.

Finally, I become aware that the bishop has ceased his drone and lift my head, slumped on my chest, to realise that Wulfheard beside me snores deeply. My eyes startle wide, and I catch sight of Ealdorman Ælfstan, his lips compressed in a tight line, as the king and queen, their son trailing behind them with a bored expression on his face, exit the church building, with its square wooden tower over our head. I nudge Wulfheard, hard, in the ribs, and he snorts awake, drool dripping down his chin.

His movements are even sharper as he digs into Cenred's chest and so on, all along the line of warriors. Neither are we alone. I see others rousing as though from a long sleep, and I even catch a glimmer of amusement on the king's face as he walks past us. Of course, the queen looks furious, her eyes firmly on the door, which stands wide open, allowing the icy bite to penetrate inside the church. The bishop, thankfully, gone from his place before us all, waits to share words with the king and queen; no doubt hoping to receive their praise for his extraordinarily long sermon. I shake my head and catch sight of the delighted face of Lady Ælflæd, only to tear my gaze away to a commotion taking place close to where the king was not long ago sitting.

I narrow my eyes, wishing I was less sleep-addled, and finally make sense of what's happening. The bishop might have left the front of the church, but his monks have remained, and now one of the grieving widows attacks the monk at the centre of their group, fingers reaching for his dark robes, her wails echoing around the wooden structure. I watch, mouth agape, as others attempt to pull her away, and I understand her sorrow and her grief.

Without thinking, I forge a path to her side through those who stand and gawp, and with hands that are stronger than I realise, I release her claws from the monk's robes and crush her to my body. I can feel her shaking, her thin sobs, her distressed breathing. I hold her. I whisper words that mean nothing but are soft and filled with understanding, and when she's once more in control, I unwrap her from my care. Only then do I realise that while the monks have scuttled from the church, as though whipped by their master,

Ealdorman Ælfstan's warriors surround me. They block all who might think to look at this poor bereaved woman, and her small daughter, fingers wrapped into her mother's pale green dress, a bump at the woman's belly showing there is yet to be another child.

I meet Wulfheard's gaze, and he nods solemnly, as do Oswy, Cenred and even Ealdorman Ælfstan.

'Come now, Æthelflæd.' Wynflæd's voice is as calm as mine, filled with understanding and love. 'Come now. We'll get you and young Æthelgifu here something to eat and drink, and then we'll ensure you get some sleep.'

Slowly, the woman allows herself to be led away, Lady Cynehild to her other side, which surprises me.

I swallow against my sorrow. It's all well and good to speak of triumphs and glory, but this is the cruel side to it all and it stabs at me, even as Wynflæd turns and smiles at me, a rare treasure from her.

Grief for my uncle engulfs me.

'Come on, Icel,' Wulfheard beckons, making me jump even though he speaks at a normal volume. 'I know just what you need,' he assures, leading me from the church and to the king's hall, where he places a beaker of ale in my hand, seating me beside the fire, because my entire body is chilled, as though my lifeblood has turned to the ice of deepest winter. 'Drink that, and for a moment, you can forget as well.'

* * *

Later, with a belly pleasantly warmed by ale, I watch Lady Cynehild as she sits beside the king and queen, the feast this evening demure and devoid of the scop to tell tales of Mercia's glorious past. I consider whether Lady Cynehild remembers all those times I tried to avoid her scrutiny, as I now try to catch her eye.

I'm unsure why she sought Wynflæd, but I'm no longer so young that I don't have a good idea. Does she believe, even now, that she might be able to carry a child? I don't know, and fear stalks me. She's not as young as many of the breeding women. I've asked Wynflæd about it, but she's bid me hush my tongue, as though I don't walk with blades around my waist these days.

Neither is Lady Cynehild alone. Lord Coenwulf also attends the feast. This union is to take place sooner rather than later. King Wiglaf is eager to prove himself a man of his word. And he's still buoyant following his victory, even if King Ecgberht yet lives.

I flick a glance to Edwin, sitting amongst the faces of the warriors from Kingsholm. He doesn't meet my gaze, but rather eats quickly, drinking little. I've suddenly become invisible to everyone, and the irony isn't lost on me that I wanted this for many years and now don't bloody like it.

Beside Lady Cynehild sits Lord Coenwulf. He looks better than when I last saw him. It appears his deep grief has left him. I should be pleased for him and Lady Cynehild. Perhaps she won't be forced to marry a man made old by grief. But as much as I want Lady Cynehild to meet my gaze, it's not because I wish to ensure her well-being, but something else entirely.

The queen, dripping with her baubles, sits beside her son, a sullen-looking Lord Wigmund, and beside him perches young Lady Ælflæd. She's fresh-faced, eager to please as she chatters to Lord Wigmund, who seems to only grunt in response to her questions, unless his domineering mother encourages him further, and my heart doesn't know what to feel.

Lady Ælflæd and I hardly spoke when I was at Kingsholm, and yet I can't deny that I've not thought about her in the intervening time, no matter the disgust she threw my way when her brother banished my uncle and me. And then today, she met my look in the church. Yet, it seems, to my eyes at least, she's being considered for an even less envious role than wife to Lord Coenwulf; that of wife to the king's son. While King Wiglaf seems oblivious to this, I can sense from the glances shared between the queen and Ealdorman Sigered that I'm far from foolish to draw such a conclusion.

I find my food tastes of little more than ashes. Why, I think, should Lord Wigmund be allowed to form a union with the brightness and intelligence of Lady Ælflæd? He has nothing to commend himself, other than, one day, he might rule after his father.

And this is why I try to catch Lady Cynehild's attention. I need to know if she's aware of this. If Lord Coenwulf perceives where the queen's thoughts have taken her. King Wiglaf might not have the Mercian pedigree, but he has the military might, as he's shown. If his son is united with such an ancient royal line as that which ruled Mercia for nearly twenty-five years, then it'll be a coup for the queen.

Such a union would legitimise Wigmund's kingship, when it comes, in a way that's not been possible since King Coelwulf was deprived of his title before King Beornwulf claimed Mercia. In the intervening five years, Mercia has had the misfortune to have four kings – well, three, as King Wiglaf has ruled twice. To return the royal line to that which is said to descend from King Penda's brother, then it could be claimed that the unruly years of Beornwulf and Ludica have been brought to an end and Mercia restored to its former self. Other than the fact that Kent is seemingly forever lost to Mercia, now firmly in the hands of the Wessex ætheling.

The kingdom of the East Angles is another matter entirely. I've heard the rumours. I know what's planned. King Athelstan might think he has the upper hand, having murdered two of Mercia's kings, but King Wiglaf, optimistic after his victory over King Ecgberht, means to continue his expansion. Come the warmer weather, Mercia will be at war once more.

But, first, there must be a marriage union, perhaps even two of them, and I'm unhappy about both.

5

A MONTH LATER

Lady Cynehild looks resplendent in the rich clothes that the queen has prepared for her marriage. They're the finest linen, almost rigid with symbolic embroidery depicting the emblem of Mercia's royal family, the eagle. And more, the symbols of fertility, picked out in stunning detail hopping all over the pale blue linen gown, in bright orange and darker hues of russet browns. I note that the gown isn't threaded with gold, such as the queen's, but all the same, it's been an expensive item to produce, and not just in terms of actual coinage, but also in time and effort. I confess I'm surprised by the care that the queen and her women have put into the item. I didn't expect it from her. I thought the queen was made of pure ambition and nothing else.

Lord Coenwulf looks equally fine in his clothes, as the pair sit and feast at the front of the king's hall now that they're officially husband and wife. I'm aware that Wynflæd and Lady Cynehild have spent more time together since my return. While the winter has advanced, bringing with it snow that lies thick on the ground, and a fiercely biting wind that turns ears and noses red as soon as a door is opened, Wynflæd's workshop has been busy,

stuffed to the limits with Wynflæd, Theodore, Gaya, Cuthred and
Lady Cynehild. I won't deny that I feel excluded from the select
group, especially as I'm the reason they've been brought
together.

Now, I allow myself to enjoy the good food, and fine ale. This
time, Lord Coenwulf's warriors have been seated in a place of
honour, much closer to the raised dais, and from where they can
watch their new lady with varying expressions. It would be interesting to know of their thoughts, and whether Edwin, with my
childhood experiences of Lady Cynehild, has tempered their
view of her. I hope my feelings have been ignored; Lady Cynehild
isn't the woman I once thought her to be.

Lady Cynehild glows. She smiles softly when Lord Coenwulf
bends to speak to her, and on the far side her new sister, Lady
Ælflæd, also calls on her attention. Lady Ælflæd is similarly
dressed in fine clothing. Not the silks of the summer, but rather
warmer linen, over which she wears a thick cloak, fastened with
brooches of glorious gold, shimmering in the glow from the
candles and the hearth. For once, the king and his queen have
taken themselves away from the centre of the dais. They may
have arranged this union, but they're playing no further part in it
other than that of beneficent overseers.

'The lady looks well,' Wulfheard offers me. He's done little
but eat and drink since we sat down, savouring everything on
offer before him. The fare isn't quite as fine as the one enjoyed
when Mercia was victorious over Wessex, but considering the
midwinter feast is not far away, the excess is suitably pleasing.

'She does,' I confirm, trying not to reveal my true feelings on
the matter. I find it strange to watch Lady Cynehild radiant on the
king's dais once more. I don't recall her ever being like this while
her first husband was king. Then, she was mean and narrow-
eyed, always able to pick me out in the gatherings, and never easy

with a smile for me. Her time at the nunnery has changed her, but so too, I think, has the death of my uncle.

I consider whether she carries that small emblem still, of my uncle's obvious affection for her. Does she wear it over her heart? Does she even think of him any more? I don't know what they shared, but it was clearly something, and what else could it be, other than love?

I know a moment of mutiny. I still grieve my uncle on waking every day. His loss comes fresh with each slow dawn of winter. I don't see that she does the same, but I can't ask her about it, although I should like to finally understand what our exchange outside Winchcombe nunnery was all about. While I have to physically exert myself daily to control my grief, Lady Cynehild almost seems to have none at all.

Wulfheard and I have taken to training each day. I do it to fight off my lethargy and grief and to grow stronger with my left hand; I fear the right might never fully heal. He does it to show me that no matter what I do, or the numbers of men I've killed, he's still far more skilled than I am. I think we both growl at one another, venting our frustrations that the winter has grounded us when we've become so used to being free from the confines of a smoke-filled hall. Whatever our reasons, I know that, unlike Lady Cynehild, I will never forget my uncle.

'He's a lucky man, that Lord Coenwulf,' Wulfheard continues. 'When she was the queen of Mercia, she did good work on behalf of the king. She endowed churches and ensured the people of Tamworth were always well cared for, even during the freezing winter of twenty-five. Do you remember it?'

I shrug my shoulders. I probably should, but what she did that was special I'm unsure.

'You were perhaps too young to appreciate that men and women risked dying in their sleep from the cold. All over the midwinter feast, it was so perishing that both rivers froze, and it was necessary to crack the ice over the well water each morning, noon and evening. It simply wouldn't stay liquid.'

I nod, a faint memory playing in my mind. I was a child then, after all. My concerns weren't the same as others. I answered to Wynflæd and to my uncle, and to Eadburh, Edwin's mother, and to precious few other people. I certainly attempted to avoid Lady Cynehild as much as possible.

'She ordered that the stored furs and cloth all be distributed to the old and the children. She had extra supplies of grain made available, despite the miller's complaints, and welcomed everyone to the king's hall for warm food. She had bread baked every day because it kept the place hot, as well as fed everyone. The pottage pot was never empty but constantly refilled. The food might not have tasted of much, but it was all about the heat. She said it was only with so many people all together in one place that we could keep warm enough. She even made some of the bread herself. She said it was to stop the cold, but she had the furs to shelter beneath without bestirring herself to such tasks.'

I nod now. I do remember. Suddenly, I consider how I could have forgotten the terrible month I spent trying to keep the cold from my fingers and toes in the hall even while I evaded Lady Cynehild's glowering looks.

'She made Bishop Æthelweald pray for release from the foul weather, and when he complained that his church was cold as well, she told him to light a brazier in the church so he could keep warm, and that it was much more than others had.' As he speaks, Wulfheard shakes his head from side to side, and I almost grin at him, but there's a memory playing at the edges of my mind, and I need to focus on it. It's something important. It's something I would never have remembered without Wulfheard's reminiscences.

I see it now. I'm small, hiding beneath the table closest to the central hearth, with Edwin at my side. He's snoring softly, rolled tightly in a bundle. I know it's late because the entire room seems to rumble with everyone's snoring. I think it's a game to stay awake so late. I know I should be asleep, but here, hidden beneath the table, which is the only safe space for someone as small as me in a hall filled with adults trying to find room for the night, no one knows if I'm asleep or not.

Not that Edwin and I are entirely alone. His mother sleeps on the floor to the side of the table, the blacksmith beside her. It's not even warm in the blacksmith's workshop. I remember that now. He can't make the nails for the horseshoes, or even the horseshoes for the horses, without his breath freezing before him. The fierceness of the furnace isn't enough with the harsh winds blowing outside.

The animals, I recall, are all squashed into the stables. Sheep bedfellows of horses, the cows sharing with the few goats, and the hounds tumbling over one another so that it's not their fur that lies closest to the cold, wooden floorboards.

My uncle is yet awake, as are a few other people, but it's the image of bright red shoes shuffling to a stop beside the table that makes me realise the person he spoke to that night was Lady Cynehild. How, I consider, have I never remembered that before?

'My lady?' My uncle's words are soft, almost sibilant.

'Lord Cenfrith.' Hers aren't as soft. 'You should take him from here. His being here is a reminder for everyone of what happened.'

'This is where he belongs, with what family he has,' Cenfrith answers. There's no heat to his words, and I think this argument has been ongoing for some time, or rather, it's not the first time they've exchanged such words.

'He makes a fool of himself with those gifts of fine clothes.'

'And yet, my lady, you're doing the same, even now, with all the ancients and youngsters in the settlement.'

'I'm doing what must be done, and if it covers up what he shouldn't be doing, then that's also good. I don't deny it.' The words are hot, flavoured with more than just fury.

'Then there's no problem.' I hear a jug being placed on the table. My uncle must drink, or perhaps Lady Cynehild uses it as an excuse for sharing words with him.

'There is a problem, and you know it. You must take him from here. While he remains, he's at risk. People will remember.' These words are even softer but edged with the coldness of the icy wind that even now howls outside the hall, every nook and cranny stuffed with rags and hay to try to keep the wind at bay.

'From who? If he'd not been foolish enough to share the information with you, then you wouldn't know. No one would think anything of it, if only you could temper your fury about the whole thing.'

'I am not furious,' Lady Cynehild speaks, her pitch soft yet filled with malice. I realise the words entirely contradict the tone she employs.

'You do more to bring attention to the matter than any other. If you kept your eyes away, then none would even heed it.'

I hear someone shift in their sleep, and the voices above my head fall silent, while rhythmic breathing I've been only unconsciously aware of stopping resumes once more.

'If you took him away, it wouldn't be for me to ignore.'

I hear my uncle sigh, the sound filled with a thousand hurts, I now realise.

'Will you all shut up and get some sleep?' a querulous voice calls across the room. I don't know who speaks, but there's an authority in the sleep-addled words.

Again, there's silence above me, and I almost think Lady

Cynehild must have left, only her shoes are still there, visible in the dim glow from the hearth. I remember now. The fire was never allowed to gutter at night. It was kept going all night long, the servants taking it in turn to sleep and carefully placing logs on the blaze to keep it ongoing, emitting enough warmth, even while we slept.

When my uncle speaks, I startle awake, eyes wide, peering at the lengths of wood that are nailed together above my head to create the table.

'I have little choice. Here he's cared for, and he's safe. I'm not the right person to raise a child, and yet I do it, all the same. Mostly to spare you, but also to spare him.'

'It isn't right, and you know that. Please, Cenfrith, for all we ever shared with one another.'

There's another thud from above my head, jolting me to full wakefulness. I don't know what's happened between my uncle and Lady Cynehild. The words, this time, are tortured.

'I had no choice, you must see that,' Lady Cynehild pleads.

I don't believe my uncle will reply, and when he eventually does, it's in a voice that's older than the stars.

'I don't see it. No. You had a choice, and you made the wrong one. And you know it. And so does he.'

'Icel, are you listening?' Wulfheard's dig in my ribs jars me from my memories, and I realise I'm looking at Lady Cynehild, although I don't truly see her. She's impervious to my gaze, smiling brightly, caught up in conversation with Lord Coenwulf. They'll journey from Tamworth tomorrow, to Kingsholm, where she'll become the lady of the settlement, the one who holds the keys to the coffers and directs the servants to perform their tasks of ensuring she, and her new husband, are well cared for. It's she who'll kneel to pray in the church there. It's she who'll ensure King Coelwulf's grave is correctly tended. One of

Mercia's kings, but not given the honour of a mausoleum at Repton.

I realise, belatedly, that Lady Cynehild's probably visited Kingsholm before. No doubt, she knew Lord Coenwulf's father before he was usurped by her first husband. Suddenly, I appreciate that for all she made my life hell while King Beornwulf was king, she's a royal woman, of noble birth, and like Wulfheard and others, including Ealdorman Ælfstan, knows far more of events than I can perceive. Do all of them, I consider then, know who my father was? And was that why, in my dream, Lady Cynehild prevailed upon my uncle? Was she speaking of me?

I mull the memories over in my mind, even while I listen with half an ear to the scop with his tales of Mercia's past, and the fruitful marriages that have ensured Mercia's long royal line. I'm considering what Lady Cynehild knows of my father and whether I truly want to know the answer after all this time. Only, slowly, the scop's words permeate even those thoughts, and I realise I'm not alone in listening, barely breathing, as the scop speaks of something other than Mercia's greatness. Why I wonder, would a man share such tales as he does now, and at a marriage feast, of all things?

I look towards the king and his queen, but both of them are as caught up as the rest of the hall. Even the servants and hounds have stopped their tasks. All is silent, all apart from the scop, with his straggling silver hair and elaborate robes, decorated with swirling symbols, so reminiscent of the pagan symbols etched outside on the doorposts. He beats a small drum in time to his words, and I realise I've been caught by the increasing tendency of those small booming noises, punctuating his words as his voice lifts and drops and then rises and falls. I'm as swayed by his words as everyone else within that room, for all I've missed much of the tale.

'Helmsman of the chariot of the sea, the steerer of the sea-horse. You made ready your armoured ships and you mustered the red shield at sea. The wind filled the canvas and you turned all your prows westward out to sea. You carried the shield of war and so dealt death mightily, giving swollen flesh to the raven and marking men with the print of the sword's edge. There was food for the ravens from the spears as you fought. Red spears soared as you fought on. Eagles flew over the rows of corpses left in your wake, and beaks of the ravens dripped red while the wolves tore at wounds. You offered Mercian corpses to the wolf by the sea. Dwellings and houses of men burned, many times you caused the people to give warning of deadly attack while your men reddened the land of the Saxons. You broke the raven's sleep as the waker of battle, blunting swords upon weapons. They could not defend their strongholds when you attacked. The she-wolf received wolf's food, and the raven did not go hungry as the stud-horses waded in blood.'

The drumming ends abruptly, the scop breathing heavily, and I swear he glowers at me, his gaze intense, even as I realise my chest heaves. What has this scop done? And why now would he speak of the triumph of the Viking raiders against Mercia and the Saxon kingdoms?

Silence fills the hall. Only broken when King Wiglaf eventually stands from his position to the side of the dais, his expression perplexed as he looks from the scop to Lord Coenwulf and Lady Cynehild.

'This is a marriage feast,' the king calls to the scop, flicking his hands angrily, his voice growing stronger. 'It's a time for joy and fruitfulness, not for tales of our enemy.'

'My lord king.' The man stands and bows, making it clear he'll relinquish his place, but the hall is silent. There is no acclamation for his songs. I can hear the breathing of others, and realise my heart hammers in my chest. His words have reminded me too fiercely of the attack on my uncle and me. Of the violence of the Viking raiders, and of their preoccupation with slaughter and savagery.

As the scop rises unhurriedly from his place, I feel his eyes on me even as he gathers his drum and finds a seat for his bony arse. As music springs up from drum and flute played by more jovial entertainers, I move aside, with the rest of the warriors and inhabitants of Tamworth. The tables and benches are cleared away, and cheering erupts as Lady Cynehild and Lord Coenwulf are prevailed upon to dance. But the joy in the moment is gone. I can't wipe away the memories. Watching Lady Cynehild dance with her new husband, I consider whether it should have been my uncle with her. Were they lovers, or just friends? What was it that they shared?

Whatever the scop's intentions, I see only those men my uncle fought on the Welsh borderlands, with their swirling inked arms, and their fearlessness and desperation. I hope to never see their like again.

6

I lead Brute outside onto the frozen ground. It's bitingly cold, and yet both of us crave leaving the warmth of stable and hall. I can tell in the way Brute kicks his stall, and even Wine is restless at his side.

Cuthred is beside me. The youth grins, revealing a jagged tooth. I hope it's one of his childhood ones.

I shake my head at this fresh sign of his impetuous nature. 'You can't ride Brute.'

His smile falters, but only a little. He has a new cloak, and it's lined with fur, although from what animal, I'm unsure. He also has warm boots, presented to him by Edwin's mother. It seems that Cuthred's needs have been noticed by more than just me. They're not new boots, but neither are they scuffed and at least they fit his feet.

'Wine is better, anyway,' Cuthred muses.

I grin as Brute whinnies in disagreement. I swear Wine looks pleased with herself as she lifts her head higher, eyes clear. Both animals understand far too much.

'She can almost gallop as fast,' I confirm. We've checked both animals, and content that neither has any injuries, we've saddled them, Cuthred helping me when my bandaged hand was a hindrance, and now we walk into the gloom of a winter's day. We won't be going far, but I know that's not the point. We just need to be going somewhere. As much as I craved a quiet winter behind Tamworth's walls, the events of yesterday have unsettled me. I don't want to think of the Viking raiders, or of my half-remembered conversation between my uncle and the newly married Lady Cynehild.

'Icel.' The startled word of Lady Ælflæd fills the air, and I just stop myself from colliding with her and her horse as they return to the stables as I'm trying to leave it.

The feast of last night and the words of the scop about the Viking raiders still sit uneasily with me. But all the same, I find a smile on my face at seeing her, and the fact that she does, in fact, remember my name.

'Lady Ælflæd.' I bow quickly, dropping my eyes to the ground, only to notice she wears thick boots, padded with soft grey fur, and the leather of the boots has been dyed a bright red. I would comment on how alike she is to her new sister, Lady Cynehild, but the words die on my lips as I catch sight of who escorts her. Ealdorman Sigered, and of course, Lord Wigmund, both still astride their horses, although Lady Ælflæd has dismounted. Her cheeks are pink with exertion. They must have been awake much earlier than I was. My dreams have been unsettling, filled with images of wolves with blood-red muzzles, the screech of raven and eagle, and ships crashing against Mercian shores.

'How do you know Icel?' Ealdorman Sigered demands imperiously, just about beating Wigmund to it. I notice a wariness in Lady Ælflæd's eyes, unseen by the two men, and she's quick-witted with her reply.

'He healed my horse at Kingsholm, nothing more,' she confirms, her words suddenly bland.

'Did he now?' Lord Wigmund gloats. 'He's the healer's apprentice.'

Now it's Lady Ælflæd's turn to look unsure, as her gaze sweeps my appearance, Wine and Brute just behind me. 'But he's dressed in the garb of a warrior?' She turns to Lord Wigmund, an incline of her head to show her confusion. 'And he has the horse of a warrior – in fact, two of them.' For once, Brute is still at my side. He doesn't tug on his reins or even stamp his hoof with displeasure at this interruption. Wine is placid as well.

'Well, yes... well, um, yes, he is one of my father's oath-sworn men. Now. He was to be a healer, before.' Lord Wigmund trips over his words.

'And his horse?' Lady Ælflæd moves forwards, reaching out her hand to approach Brute, and I know a moment of trepidation. I hope my horse doesn't bite her hand, as he did with the stable-hand on our return from Londonia.

'Was a gift,' I offer when no one fills the silence. I don't add that Brute was a gift from the king. That would be overly boastful and would cause Lord Wigmund's confused face to twist angrily.

'Ah, then that makes sense to me.'

Brute sniffs Lady Ælflæd's hand as she speaks, and then allows her to stroke his long nose. I release a breath I didn't realise I was holding, and Ælflæd winks at me, as though she's heard of Brute's reputation and knew her attentions weren't guaranteed to be welcomed.

She's dropped the reins of her horse, and I nod towards her.

'How is Sewenna?'

Lady Ælflæd smiles with delight that I've remembered the animal's name who trails behind her, eyes bright and alert. 'She's all recovered, thank you. I'm surprised you remember such a small thing, with all that's befallen you, since.' Her words are tinged with understanding. She has no father, and I've lost my uncle. We both know what it's like to grieve.

I don't know how to respond. I do remember Sewenna. I also remember the look Lady Ælflæd gave me when her father's horse died, and I was thrown out of Kingsholm, with my uncle. But it seems she has forgotten some of the events of our earlier meeting, or refuses to remember them. I'll happily do the same.

'Well, Lady Ælflæd, shall we hand the horses over?' Ealdorman Sigered queries, his voice loud and ringing in the chill air. I don't look at him, but he sounds cold. I sense, more than see, that those who are about have ceased their activities to watch what's happening.

'You go ahead,' Lady Ælflæd offers. 'I'd like to speak with Icel about some small matters.' Lady Ælflæd doesn't even turn to ensure her idea is acceptable to the ealdorman, but instead looks to Wine. 'I remember you,' she coos. 'Such a beautiful colour. So unusual.'

'She's a fine horse,' I agree.

'And yet you have another?'

I nod, my throat suddenly full. There are too many memories at play today.

'Wine was my uncle's horse.' I can't say more.

'Of course,' she murmurs, and now Cuthred pipes up.

'I look after her, for Icel. He lets me ride her.'

'Then I won't stop you. In fact. I'll join you.' Lady Ælflæd turns aside, takes the reins of Sewenna from a waiting stable-hand, eyes darting between Lord Wigmund and me. She looks around for a means to mount.

'My lady,' the ealdorman announces sharply. 'You were to accompany Lord Wigmund to the church.'

'Yes, but there is time yet.' She dismisses the ealdorman's concerns, her tone imperious.

'You'll escort us, Edwin and Oswald,' she calls to the two members of her brother's war band, who must have done just that already as they're waiting patiently with their horses. 'I don't believe Sewenna has exercised enough today.'

'My lady, this is most unusual,' Ealdorman Sigered announces. 'Icel is merely one of the king's oath-sworn men, who has some luck with a seax.'

'And I'm in need of protection, and so I have what I need,' she calls brightly, already mounted, having made use of a handy collection of empty wooden barrels to do just that. She looks expectantly at me. I dare not risk looking at Edwin, or Lord Wigmund. Or Ealdorman Sigered.

'My lady.' The next to speak is none other than Lady Cyne-hild, appearing from the king's hall, and I eye her, hoping for some assistance out of this awkward situation. She provides it readily. 'I'll ride as well. Perhaps, we should all make the journey.' Her new husband is at her side, dressed in a thick cloak and calling for his horse, without seeming to understand what's taking place before him.

'Of course.' Ealdorman Sigered bows, his objections evaporating in the wake of so much support. It's unsettling to see his oily ways at work.

'But I'm cold,' Lord Wigmund complains. 'I need to warm up. I'll not escort you.' As he speaks, Lord Wigmund dismounts, his expression mutinous. 'You must be cold as well,' he calls in Lady Ælflæd's direction. 'It would be better to have warm wine and relax before the fire.'

I really don't know what to do. I thought this would be nothing more than a ride with Cuthred to exercise the horses, but it has become fraught with unease.

'Then you rest before the hearth, and I'll join you shortly, and then we can visit the church. Now, come on, sister dearest,' she calls to Lady Cynehild, 'and brother dearest. We have quite the honour guard.' And without pausing, Lady Ælflæd turns Sewenna back towards the open gateway, and Brute follows in her wake, now that I've mounted, Cuthred perched astride Wine, while Lady Cynehild and her new husband hasten to join, their horses prepared and waiting for their riders.

I say nothing and look only on the roadway in front of me. I hope that the awkwardness of what's just happened will soon evaporate. Cuthred, for once, holds his tongue beside me. Edwin and Oswald lead the way, joined now by three other members of Lord Coenwulf's household warriors. Lady Cynehild rides beside Lady Ælflæd, and I try to turn Brute to the rear of the group, but Lady Ælflæd will have none of it.

'Icel, ride with me, please,' she calls, her tone brokering no arguments.

'You better do as she says,' Cuthred murmurs to me, his sudden wisdom assuring me that whether he knows it or not, he's learning the ways of politic from Wynflæd.

I move forward, Lady Cynehild moving aside to allow me room, so that I ride between the two of them. She has a faint smile on her face, a blush to her cheeks, and I consider that she might just be happy with her new husband. Brute makes no complaint, even as I fear he'll buck or shy in such close proximity to the two horses.

'Hatel and Pega still speak of all you did for my father's horse, Ansfith. Don't they brother?' Lady Ælflæd seems determined to cause me as much discomfort as possible.

I can barely breathe for fear Lord Coenwulf will react angrily.

'What?' he calls to his sister, from his place beside Lady Cynehild. He seems distracted as we make our way over the bridge that spans the river and out towards the area of trees in which I once hid on escaping from Tamworth with my uncle.

'Hatel and Pega, they still speak of all Icel did to aid Ansfith.' Her words are slow, as though they mean more than they say.

'Ah, yes, young Icel.' I feel the heat of his scrutiny, but as I meet his eyes, I catch sight of a small smile on Lady Cynehild's face. That reassures me. 'Hasty words and actions. I would apologise for my behaviour. Your uncle was a fine man, loyal, always, if not always to the right man, but loyal all the same. I'm only grateful that I have young Edwin as a consequence of what happened, and I've mourned your uncle as well. A good man. All things considered.'

'My... my lord.' I'm astounded and unsure what to say. I could be angry and blame him for my uncle's death, but while our banishment set off the events that led to my uncle's death, in the end, it was a Wessex blade that killed him. Not a Mercian one.

'Icel, I believe, would thank you for your words, my lord,' Lady Ælflæd interjects, and I nod, switching my head from the sister to the brother, unsure what I should say, and how I should say it. I can't help but think that there'd be no apology without the intervention of Lady Ælflæd. Perhaps, she wasn't angry with me on that day, after all. Perhaps, her rage was all for her hot-headed brother. Not that I could ever ask her.

'Now, Icel, show us all Brute's great speed,' Lady Cynehild calls, and as though he's been waiting for the command, Brute takes off, leaving the others in his wake, with his hooves thundering on the hard ground. I grip Brute's side with my thighs and hold tightly to the reins with my left hand, hoping that, in this, my horse won't embarrass me and leave me tumbling to the hard, frost-covered earth, beneath his hooves.

Despite Lord Coenwulf's words of apology, which I never thought to hear, and also never thought to need to hear, the spectre of the Viking raiders my uncle and I fought lingers in the words of the scop. If I weren't so busy trying to stay mounted on my horse who tears up the ground so quickly I think we might just return to Londonia in little to no time, I might just muse on the images the scop conjured.

7

TAMWORTH, AD831

'You must learn to watch your foeman all the time.' Wulfheard and I are once more on the training ground outside the settlement of Tamworth, on the fallow ground that stretches all the way to the twin rivers. The weather is cold, but not too cold. There's no snow on the ground, and that means we can fight one another without fear that one of us will slip and be declared the loser. My breath plumes before me, but the cold doesn't infiltrate my clothing and leave me feeling exposed.

'I am watching you,' I retort. I know my face is red with exertion, and my tunic sticks to my sweat-slick back.

'Then it must be with one eye shut,' Wulfheard counters, his seax flashing before my eyes, while he holds back his shield. I know very well what he's about to do, but still, the shield hits my right arm and I growl angrily.

'It's not that I don't watch you. I'm merely too slow to react.'

'Then react more quickly,' Wulfheard orders me. I only wish it were so simple.

It's long past the midwinter. The days are slowly starting to elongate, and all Wulfheard wishes to do with the extra daylight is spend more time berating me for not being able to overcome his advances, even though I'm learning to battle with my left hand, as opposed to my right.

I'm aware of Oswy and his recovered strength. Wulfheard doesn't make him train fully just yet. I'm almost jealous that he gets to sit in the king's hall all day and be fed and assisted by the servants, even while Wynflæd, Theodore and Gaya tend to him. But then, he doesn't need to learn to fight all over again. He merely needs to allow his body the time to fully knit together.

Even Cenred is doing better than I am. His wound is little more than a flash of puckered skin.

A clash of Wulfheard's seax against my shield, and I lower it, glowering at him. He does me the courtesy of looking slightly abashed.

'Apologies,' he offers before I can voice my complaint. 'I forgot.'

'Don't you always,' I murmur, my eyes caught by something taking place closer to Tamworth. I haven't been aware of the thunder of horses' hooves, but I should have been, as now, a collection of about thirty mounts await entry inside Tamworth. 'Who's that?' I query. I'm assuming it must be one of the ealdormen. While Ælfstan and Tidwulf have remained at Tamworth, and Ealdorman Muca continues to hold Londonia, Eadwulf, Athelhard, Mucel and Beornoth have returned to their estates to eat of their own land while winter ravages the kingdom. Ealdorman Sigered is absent from Tamworth as well. His alliance with the queen has not run quite as smoothly as he might have hoped, or so I understand it from Cuthred. Wynflæd really does manage to gather more news than anyone else within the settlement.

But Wulfheard shakes his head as he focuses on the banner being displayed by one of the riders. He tenses, and I almost think he'll run after the final swishing tail of one of the horses. I'm aware that he growls and turn to face him.

'Who is it?'

'That, my boy, is the emblem of the king of the East Angles.'

I feel my forehead furrow. 'King Athelstan?' I'm not sure I believe him.

'Yes, bloody King Athelstan. Now, what is he doing here?' Wulfheard is already marching back towards Tamworth itself, when Eahric, the commander of the king's troops, steps into his path. He's finally been allowed to leave Londonia. It seems, with the icy weather, that Ealdorman Muca believes King Ecgberht of Wessex will not bestir himself to attack Mercia. I think he's right, but King Wiglaf didn't take the arrival of his commander with quite such good grace, and even now, Eahric's temper is evil. I've even heard him say he'll return to Londonia – I wish he would.

'It's not for you to concern yourself with,' Eahric murmurs, caution in his voice.

'What?' Wulfheard stumbles as he hears those words.

'The king of Mercia has welcomed a delegation from the king of the East Angles.'

'Why would he do that?' Wulfheard and I aren't the only two Mercian warriors to have stopped their labours. More and more circle Eahric, and I watch as the king's commander stands a little taller. It seems he has, at last, gained the ear of Mercia's king.

'I'm not privy to the king's decisions,' Eahric informs everyone, trying to counter the murmur of unease. I have no particular hatred for the king of the East Angles, but I'm aware that many Mercians died in the two battles against him. There are still widows behind Tamworth's walls, and throughout Mercia. To me, it seems that King Wiglaf is playing with fire by even allowing this delegation. King Athelstan threatened Mercia while she was at war with Wessex. The fact nothing came of that is irrelevant. The kingdom of the East Angles is an enemy.

'As I say. I'm not told more than you are, by your oath-sworn lords. All I know is that Ealdorman Sigered arranged to escort the party, and that his men are in command of the visit. I'm not to involve any of the men of Tamworth.'

This news, again, encourages growls of fury from the warriors. I turn to look at some of the men I know. Waldhere wears a face of fury, while Osmod is breathing heavily, his eyes flickering from Eahric to the gates, his lips tightly compressed. I can well imagine the thoughts running through his head.

'Now, get back to your training. If you're not so inclined, I can assure you I have some less than pleasant tasks I could lay at your feet. And assisting the stablehands is the most pleasant of them.'

Slowly, Wulfheard walks away from Eahric, back to where we stood not so long ago. Where we fought, the ground has begun to thaw from the movements of our feet. Others of the men take longer to move aside, and Wulfheard has yet to lift his shield or seax and resume his warring.

'I would have expected Ealdorman Ælfstan to inform you of this?' I eventually say what's on my mind.

Beside us, Frithwine and Garwulf are clumsily clashing with one another. I would laugh at them, but there's some reasoning behind their actions. While the one pretends to be either unskilled or wounded, the other is determining how best to defend themselves from sloppy strokes, and then, how to land the killing blows.

'I would as well, which makes me think, he doesn't know about it.' Wulfheard's tone is hard, the edge of his anger easy to detect.

'And what would he think of it?'

'How would I know?' Wulfheard rounds on me. 'But I can't

see that it would please him. He was an ally of Ealdormen Wynfrith and Oswine, good men who died beneath the blades of the men of the East Angles when they fought beside King Beornwulf and Ludica.'

Wulfheard still doesn't reclaim his weapons. Now I'm starting to shiver because the sweat has dried on my skin, cooling me. I think longingly of donning my cloak even as I swing my arms around, trying to bring some warmth back to my body.

A thud from beside me, and Frithwine lands on his arse, the breath knocked from him.

'Be careful, you bloody fools.' Wulfheard isn't distracted enough not to realise what they're doing. 'That'll bruise,' he follows on conversationally.

Garwulf's smirk slips from his face at Wulfheard's complaints.

'Wulfheard.' Ealdorman Ælfstan's single word snaps with command from atop his horse, the animal gently steaming in the air. It looks to me as though horse and rider have ridden far and quickly.

I notice a few others of the ealdorman's men behind him. There's a deer flung over the back of one of the spare mounts. The ealdorman has been hunting. How we've not heard his return, I'm unsure, but then, the ealdorman has ridden from the south, not the east.

'My lord.' Wulfheard is quick to run to the ealdorman from where he waits, to the side of the training field, on the roadway that links the bridge to the settlement. I follow on, because I'm getting even colder, and my cloak is flung over a piece of fencing that delineates the training ground from the road, and from the better grazing land to the east.

'Who's that?' the ealdorman queries, pointing towards Tamworth. Great plumes of smoke rise into the air, driving back the cold from the king's hall and the workshops and homes of the inhabitants of Tamworth. I shiver, gathering my cloak over my shoulders, ensuring the clasp stops it from slipping from my shoulder.

'Eahric informs me it's an embassy from King Athelstan of the East Angles.' Ealdorman Ælfstan's face is flushed from his riding, and the thrill of the hunt. His blond hair and beard are astray and yet I watch his face drain of all colour at the news.

'Is he sure? The king mentioned none of this to me.'

'Aye, my lord. Eahric said he's been instructed to hold his men away from the settlement. Ealdorman Sigered has arranged the whole thing, and is in command of security during the meeting.'

'Bloody Ealdorman Sigered. He's always too keen for peace,' Ælfstan growls, and I consider I probably shouldn't be listening to this. 'I take it the men are uneasy?' Ælfstan scans the training field as he speaks.

I turn to look as well. Other than Garwulf and Frithwine, arguing rather than fighting, no one has yet to resume their previous endeavours, aside from Eahric and the man he battles against. The sound of the two shields and their muffled weapons rings loudly through the day, as though summoning the people to church, but everyone ignores the call. The majority of Mercia's warriors stand around in small groups, talking to one another, their faces trained on Tamworth's south-facing gate, which is wide open, although there's a full contingent of warriors standing across the roadway.

'Do they mean to deny us entry?' Wulfheard asks.

'I don't know. But I'm going to find out,' Ealdorman Ælfstan confirms. 'Come with me. I would have you at my side in the king's hall. You too, Icel,' the ealdorman continues, and I wince to have my presence so openly acknowledged. I really shouldn't be privy to this. And yet. 'Let's see if you share your uncle's knack for understanding what's happening before even the king is aware of what result his actions will bring about.'

Together, Wulfheard and I jog alongside the horses, the ripe smell of blood from the dead deer pervading the air because everything else merely smells of the cold, but the dead animal promises a hint of warmth, even if it's slowly fading.

Ealdorman Ælfstan does his best to keep his horse in step with us, but the animal is just too fast. He arrives moments before we do, but I can hear the conversation easily through the still air.

'My lord, respectfully, we've been ordered not to allow you entry at this time.' The man who speaks is puffed up and flushed. He gleams with the freshness of a new day, his shield and spear both in hand before him.

A further ten men block the entranceway across the ditch that surrounds Tamworth. Due to the rampart, it's not possible to see what happens inside Tamworth. I can only catch a glimpse of people scurrying to and fro, huddled inside their cloaks through the open but barred gateway.

'And who gives this command?' Ealdorman Ælfstan asks, filling his voice with confusion.

'King Wiglaf, the first of his name,' the guard retorts.

I eye him. I think I know who he is.

'Egbert,' Wulfheard announces, stepping forward. 'Do you truly expect me to believe that the king himself has forbidden Ealdorman Ælfstan from entering?'

Egbert's eyes flicker dangerously from Ealdorman Ælfstan to Wulfheard. 'I don't expect you to believe anything. I expect you to take this as the word of the king, your oath-sworn lord, and obey his injunctions.'

I watch the other guards. They're all uneasy, and I'm far from surprised. I'm perturbed and I'm not truly a part of this. While I'd welcome some clean clothes, and warm food, I could, if need be, wait a little longer to gain admittance to my home. But that isn't really the point.

'The king has given no instructions and I spoke to him only last night. We discussed today's hunt. He bid me ensure the kill was good and plentiful enough to provide a bountiful feast. I don't believe he would have asked me to do such, and then prevent me from entrusting the sport to the cook.'

'If you leave the beast with me, we'll ensure the cook receives it,' Egbert retorts. To me, he's almost enjoying this. But then, if Egbert's an oath-sworn man of Ealdorman Sigered's, he'll be used to causing upset and being at the centre of problems. That's about all the ealdorman is good for. Certainly, he doesn't encourage a battle, and neither does he embolden his men to take part in them.

'I'll do no such thing, Egbert. I've carried out my king's instructions and now demand to be admitted with my burden.'

'You'll have to wait, my lord.' Egbert's voice no longer reflects any respect for the ealdorman. I wince to hear the man's tone. Even I'm considering wiping the smirk from his face.

'What's going on?' The voice is a bark, and I look up, unsurprised to meet the face of Ealdorman Sigered himself. He's surrounded by five more of his warriors, all of them looking fierce, although I notice the lack of battle scars on their faces, and more importantly, how straight their noses are. I can't see that they're seasoned warriors as Wulfheard is, or even Eahric, the king's commander, for all I don't much like him after what happened with Edwin and the king's son. Still, at least I know he has the stones to stand in a shield wall and fight Mercia's enemies.

'I'm being denied entry by one of your men, who informs me it's on the king's orders.'

'Well, yes,' Ealdorman Sigered confirms. 'It's true. There are orders to ensure you don't disturb the meeting between King Wiglaf and the ealdorman of the East Angles, sent here on their king's order to discuss a peace accord between the two kingdoms.'

'And who gave that order?' Ealdorman Ælfstan presses. I realise, replaying the words in my mind, that indeed, Ealdorman Sigered hasn't confirmed the order is that of the king's.

'The order was given. That's all that should concern you.'

'But it isn't all that concerns me. I believe, Ealdorman Sigered, that should I press the king, he'd inform me that the instructions didn't come from him. Now, order your man aside. I'm coming into Tamworth, whether he moves or not.'

'Now, my Lord Ælfstan.' Sigered's words are all honey and mead, but I already know that Ælfstan will refuse to heed them, and equally, Wulfheard has been joined by others of Ælfstan's war band, Uor and Wulfgar most prominent amongst them. It's quite possible if Ealdorman Sigered doesn't order Egbert to stand aside that there might well be a battle here, amongst the Mercians, even as a peace accord is allegedly being discussed between King Wiglaf and King Athelstan's representative.

 Wulfheard menaces the guard directly in front of him, a thin whip of a man, who looks as though he might be blown over if the wind changes direction. I bite my lip, unsure what to do. Ealdorman Ælfstan is furious, as are his warriors, while Ealdorman Sigered seems determined to incite a fight. The air is filled with blades, and one wrong move could set it afire.

'What's the meaning of this?' For the first time in my life, I'm grateful to see Lord Wigmund, and his collection of adherents streaming behind him. I notice the men, and the older sons of some of the other ealdormen, and I consider whether they're truly so desperate that they're already prepared to form an alliance with the snivelling Wigmund.

I'm surprised to see one of Sigered's grandsons with the

king's son. Sigered's son has long been dead. He had more honour than his father ever had, or so Wynflæd has told me. Sigered's son died at the battle of Ellendun, prepared to fight for Mercia, unlike his father. Sigegar is a few years older than me, I imagine. He has his grandfather's gaunt appearance and snake-like eyes.

'My lord.' Ealdorman Ælfstan is the first to show his respect. 'I'm returning with meat for the king's feast, but there are some problems gaining entry.'

Wigmund looks between the two men, the faint lines of humour on his young face. Perhaps he's not stupid, even if he's no warrior. 'Let the ealdorman through, good man. On my orders, as it were. I'm sure my mother and father would welcome the deer caught by the ealdorman. And, the rest of his men, well, I was making my way to the training ground. I should like to see how the warriors are progressing. Come now, Wulfheard, isn't it? Lead on, good man.'

I sigh softly. Ealdorman Ælfstan has what he wants and also what he doesn't want.

The warriors barring our path move aside, and Ealdorman Ælfstan directs his horse through, having first inclined his head towards Lord Wigmund in thanks. And yet, the guards quickly block the way as soon as Ælfstan and the horse carrying the dead animal have journeyed through. I daren't turn to Wulfheard for further instructions. Ealdorman Sigered has a smirk playing about his lips now, no doubt curious to see what Ealdorman Ælfstan will do.

'Come on then, Wulfheard. Show me what you've been teaching young Icel here. My father is filled with praise for Icel's battle prowess, as we all know. I should like to see it.'

With no time for further conversation, Ealdorman Ælfstan turns to face Wulfheard just before he moves out of sight, and gives a small shake of his head, either a warning or an instruction, and continues on his way.

'Come, Ealdorman Sigered. When I'm free of my horse, I'll escort you into the king's presence to seek clarity on your orders,' Ælfstan says, loud enough for all to hear.

I look down at my feet, not wanting Wigmund or Egbert to see my smirk. Ealdorman Sigered might think he's won, but I'm far from as sure about that. Mind, I must now do battle for the king's son's pleasure.

* * *

'Bloody bollocks,' Wulfheard mutters under his breath as we return to our previous position. I'm at least warm once more, even if I'd sooner not have to fight with Wulfheard again. My right hand is yet to regain all of its strength. Each night, I'm constrained to bind it with salve, while every morning, I run through a series of exercises that Theodore and Gaya say will rebuild the strength in my hand. I know that Wynflæd is yet to be convinced, but she doesn't caution me against following their instructions. She's as curious as I am to see if what they say will work.

'Eahric.' Lord Wigmund's voice is overly loud as he summons the king's commander to his side. 'I would watch these men fight. I should like to know that the fine food provided by my father throughout the winter hasn't made them too fat to be quick and lithe in the battle line.'

'Aye, my lord. I assure you that while they've been enjoying the king's bounty, they've been careful to remember the need to stay fit and healthy.' Eahric's voice is filled with respect, but not approval.

'I'll inform my father of this. Now, I'd see Icel fight, against someone he doesn't usually train with. Suggest someone else who'll test him.'

'My lord,' Eahric begins, but Wulfheard speaks over him.

'My lord, Icel and I often train together. I, too, would like to see him fight another, perhaps Wulfgar would be a good opponent for him.'

'My thanks.' I glower at Wulfheard, but I'm aware that in speaking up he's done me a huge service. Wulfgar is a mean warrior, and yet we share respect for one another. He might suffer from a larger belly than mine, but I hope he won't go too hard against me.

'No, no, Wulfgar is one of Ealdorman Ælfstan's men. It must be someone else. What about...' Wigmund pauses, and I half close my eyes. I can predict who he'll suggest, even before the name leaves his mouth. 'Horsa.'

Horsa is one of Wigmund's allies. I know that. He doesn't stand with the king's son now, because he's a warrior, and he prefers to power his way through his enemies than stand and strut beside the king's son. Horsa even overtops me, and I'm a tall man now. He's also at least three times wider than I am, and I've seen him rubbing a special salve into his arms to ensure they stay strong. I've asked Wynflæd about it. Her response made me chuckle.

'The bloody fool. He buys it from the shepherd's wife, and he doesn't know that it contains little more than sheep shit, a slab of butter, and slices of sweet herbs to make it smell nice. It'll do him no good, although, well, in the right light, it does make his arms shine nicely.' I laughed then, but now I'm not so sure. Despite the cold weather, Horsa is wearing a tunic cut short to his shoulders. His arms glisten, and not with the cold. If this was to be a hand-to-hand battle, I'd stand no chance. I'd slip from his arms, and be unable to get any sort of grip on my opponent. But now, when it'll be shield to seax to shield, I think the possibility of me evading some nasty bruises, and possibly some cuts as well, is very slight.

Wulfheard turns his back on the growing crowd of men and beckons me closer. Wulfgar comes as well, and that surprises me.

'He's not very quick,' is the first comment Wulfgar makes, below his breath. 'He looks the part, but that's about as far as it goes. Get beyond his guard, and you might never fell him, but he won't be able to attack you either.'

Simultaneously, Wulfheard speaks. 'Stay out of reach of his shield. If he punches you with that, you might not regain your senses for months.'

'Wonderful.' I glower at both of them, working my right hand loose, and trying to decide whether I should place my seax or shield in it. My decision will make my attack, or my defence, the weakest part of the coming bout. 'What did I do to deserve this?' I mutter.

'You saved the king, and then you saved the ealdorman, and our young prince can lay claim to neither of those things. And, if the rumours are to be believed, you also won the attention of Lady Ælflæd,' Wulfheard mutters with no sympathy.

'And will he ever do any of those things?' I murmur to myself, but Wulfheard must hear because ice flashes in his eyes, although he holds his tongue.

'Icel, Horsa.' Eahric has taken command of the coming spectacle.

I can't help wishing I'd stayed abed that morning, or perhaps joined Oswy, taking my ease before the king's hearth, but there's nothing for it.

I turn around and see that the king's son and his allies crowd together, Wigmund to the fore. His eyes are glittering with malice beneath the fur-lined hood he wears to keep the chill from his ears. His face is the pinkest I've seen for months. Most of us are

haunted by the cold and it rests on our features. Not so the clos-
eted king's son.

I move my head from side to side, trying to loosen my neck
from where it's become constricted because I've not been
sweating for so long. My right hand feels too tight as well. What
little I've done with it this morning has been more than enough
for one day. I grip my shield in that hand, and pull my seax into
my left hand. It's not such a natural movement for me, and yet I'm
certainly improving.

Wulfheard has finally trained me with spear, and I'm better
with it in my left hand than my right, but the seax is a weapon
that takes more skill. I already know I'm going to lose the bout,
but I don't truly think that matters. I just have to show that I can
battle with the tallest, widest, dumbest of men. That should prove
something to the king's son, even if he won't like the lesson.

'Now, let me check your seaxes are blunt enough,' Eahric
commands, ripping the sack covering from the blade and
revealing it to the crowd.

Wulfheard stands beside Wulfgar, and I feel some pleasure in
seeing the others of the men I went inside Londinium with there
as well. Kyre grins at me, whereas Cenred's face shows his anger
at what's about to happen. None of them, I confess, look confident in my skills. I'll thank them for that later. Maybe, if Oswy
were here, he'd remind me of how I kept him alive inside
Londinium, with little more than my seax as a weapon. But he's
not here, and he was wounded, despite my best efforts. Perhaps
he wouldn't be a comfort after all.

'Now, Horsa, your blade is too sharp,' Eahric confirms,
looking slightly pained where his finger bleeds a little. 'You'll
need to exchange it for this one,' and he hands the other man a
slightly longer blade, but one with a thicker edge. 'Icel, yours is
fine,' the commander assures me, his back turned to Horsa, a

strained expression on his face. I think he wants to tell me something, but he bites his lower lip and moves away from the space that's been left for Horsa and me to fight in. Eahric and I are far from allies; all the same, he knows that this match is far from equal. 'Ready. Then fight,' Eahric announces.

Horsa makes no move towards me, but rather stands there, testing the handle on his new blade, a faintly perplexed expression on his face.

I find my gaze sliding from Horsa to Wigmund, even while the men around me jeer and shout their advice to me. No doubt, some of the buggers will have placed a hasty wager on who'll win. I'm surprised anyone will bet against Horsa. I wouldn't.

And still, the other man does nothing.

'Hurry up, Icel, it's damn cold,' Waldhere calls, and I'd curse him, but he's right. I'm only getting colder now I've removed my cloak.

I make the first move, aiming a blow towards Horsa with my shield. He's right-handed, and I'm currently left-handed, so our shields face one another, and our seaxes do as well. The shields clash together, and the power behind his defence shudders up my right hand. I gasp in pain, wanting nothing more than to remove my hand from the shield and shake it to try to get some feeling back into it.

Distracted, I don't realise that Horsa attacks me with his seax until I feel the thud of it against my byrnie. With a dull blade or not, I huff in pain. There's going to be a bruise across my chest, probably by tonight. Spurred to action, I counter with a slash of my seax, and somehow, despite his size, manage to miss him.

'Hurry up, Icel,' Waldhere calls once more, only for Wigmund to lift his face from watching the attack, no doubt to glower at my fellow Mercian. Others shout him down and I grin. I can just imagine the expression on Waldhere's face.

Horsa returns my attack with a swing of his shield. He uses the protection as though it's nothing more than a seax. The edge of the shield crashes into the side of my body when I'm too slow to counter it, too twisted by having my seax and shield in the wrong hands to counter a right-handed opponent. I didn't really think it through. I should have stayed with my seax in my right hand, even though it would have made my attack weaker.

I just about keep my feet. I eye the giant before me. I imagine he barely realises that we're in a fight. I'm no doubt little more than an annoying fly to him, and that gives me an idea. Flies move quickly, and before man or beast can truly sight them, they're gone again.

I hurry my movements, stabbing out with my seax, and punching with my shield, darting around on my feet, first one way and then another, and at one point, I even make my way to the rear of him. Horsa follows my movements, but too slowly. Not that I land a blow immediately. Not until I'm almost level with him again do I finally impact him, and even then, my blade glances off the thickness of the padded byrnie, and I'm once more where I started, although Horsa isn't quite there yet.

The men continue to encourage, and so I persist, with fast stabs, with seax, and then shield, trying to ensure there's no discernible rhythm to what I'm doing. Seax, shield, shield, shield, seax, seax, shield. Still, I don't manage to secure many blows, but they do slowly become more frequent, and I think I might just stand a chance against him. The men are shouting my name, over and over, they must sense it as well, and I almost find a smile on my face. And then Horsa hits me full face with his shield, my nose crunching with the impact, and I fall to my hands and knees, spitting blood, shaking my head to try to clear my flashing vision.

The shouting of the men fades away. I'm aware it's not

because they've stopped, it's just that, like inside Londinium after the disaster of the attack on the bridge over the River Fleet, my hearing has been compromised.

I taste blood on my lips and wince around the sharp pain in my nose. But I push myself upwards, for all I sway. Horsa, however, is no longer standing where he was. He's moved aside, and Eahric stands before me, a look of sympathy on his face. Wulfheard is there as well, a faint smirk playing around his lips.

'Bastard,' I exclaim, my hands both throbbing, my nose pulsing. Only then do I realise that Lord Wigmund is laughing, his eyes wide with delight, as he praises Horsa, trying to lift his arm high to show he's the victor, only Wigmund's too short. Horsa's hand is barely taller than where it normally rests.

And then I hear the words.

'It seems to me that my father rewards a man who has no claim to even being a fledgling warrior of Mercia. None at all. Look at him, spitting blood and crying like a baby.'

Wulfheard's hand is on my arm before I can so much as take one step forward. I'd fight him off, but I feel weak, and my eyes can't truly focus on anything.

And it seems I don't need to be the one to stand my ground anyway.

'My lord,' Oswy calls, his words coming to me from far away. I don't know when he arrived. Perhaps he tired of warming his arse before the king's hearth. 'I'm proud to fight with Icel. Proud to stand beside him in the shield wall, and your father is the same. Mercia's king owes his very life to Icel, as does Ealdorman Ælfstan. Horsa might have the brute strength of an ox, and welcome to it, but he would have arrived far too late to save either your father or the ealdorman. I'd think on that, my lord. I really would.'

I'd gasp at those words, but I'm aware that Oswy is much

thought of by the queen. When he was a member of her personal guard, they forged a link. I see that Wigmund realises that as well. The malicious smile slides from his face, and I hope that'll be the end of it, as the world tips on its side, and I land amongst the legs of Eahric and Wulfheard.

8

'What's he done to himself now?' Wynflæd's words are like a salve for my soul.

'A fight. His nose,' Wulfheard confirms, his words coming to me through the fog of my hearing.

'Do you think I lack the ability to see?' is the snapped response, and I blink, opening my eyes on the roof of Wynflæd's hut. It's been repaired. I can tell because it's not possible to see the sky through the gaps in the old sagging roof.

'No. My apologies.' Wulfheard sounds suitably chastised, and I feel a grin on my face, only for Wynflæd to move into my field of vision.

'And you can stop smirking.' Wynflæd's words are sharper than Horsa's blade.

'Dorry,' I try, but my words sound funny, and a smirk appears on Wynflæd's lips.

'You sound funny.' Cuthred's youthful voice is the next to be heard, his head popping into my field of vision after I hear his words.

'Dit's my dose,' I try again, but then give up. I do sound funny.

'Bloody fool,' Wynflæd snaps again, but the words are less sharp. It seems I've been forced to fight, and now they're all to enjoy laughing at me. 'I'll clean you up, but you'll have to sleep sitting up until your nose is better, or it'll hurt too much and your head will pound. Did he lose his senses?' Wynflæd continues to harangue Wulfheard.

I imagine Wulfheard wishes he'd not been the one to bring me here. I'm surprised he was allowed entry into the settlement. Perhaps Ealdorman Sigered's men took pity on my slumped body.

'Yes, but not straight away.'

'Then he must stay here for the night, at least. I'll watch him and ensure his sleep isn't too long, and too eternal.'

I shudder at the news, but appreciate Wynflæd's care for me. I know full well she wouldn't usually allow one of the king's warriors to stay in her workshop for such a wound. She'd send them away, to be cared for by Eahric, or rather, whomever of Eahric's men he determines to task with such an onerous all-night duty.

The comforting smells and sounds of Wynflæd's workshop fill my senses, and my eyes close once more. It's warm in here, a fierce blaze driving back the cold, and I have furs to cover me. But Wynflæd's wizened hands on my nose jolt me awake, as she must set the bone with a sharp snap.

'Dow,' I howl.

'That's the worst of it,' she mutters.

Wulfheard seems to have gone. I can no longer detect his hulking menace in the room. Cuthred remains, and he moves to place a rolled-up fur beneath my head, a look of sympathy on his young face. I finally get a better look at the room, but it's spinning once more. I feel my stomach roll, and turn to retch, only for lights to flash before my eyes.

'Don't sit up,' Wynflæd snaps, but I don't believe she truly means for me to vomit all over myself, as I sink back down on the bed. 'When you can, drink this,' and she offers me a beaker filled with a murky-looking substance.

'Whad dis it?' I query.

'A potion to ease your belly, and your head. Once you can list the ingredients of it for me, I'll know you're on the mend, until then, you can just drink it and sleep. I'll be here, and so will Cuthred.'

I hear Cuthred moan and consider what feast he might be missing, and then I remember.

'Whad dappened with the king and de representative from the East Angles?' I enunciate my words as clearly as possible, trying not to add in unnecessary d's.

'I don't know, not yet,' Wynflæd murmurs. 'They're discussing everything.'

If I could, I'd smirk, pleased to see that Wynflæd has lost none of her knack for knowing what's happening in the king's hall.

'I'll tell you that Ealdorman Ælfstan now sits beside the king. And that's all you need to be told, for now. Sleep, and then, when you're better, I'm sure you can tell me what all this fuss is about.'

I want to ignore her words. I want to send Cuthred to the feast, but instead, my eyes close, and I'm just grateful that I don't feel sick any more.

* * *

When I wake, it's light in the workshop, and Wynflæd and Cuthred are murmuring softly to one another. For a moment, I keep my eyes closed, luxuriating in the familiarity of my one-time home. Looking back on my time here, which I confess, I resented on occasion, it's impossible not to wish I'd enjoyed it more. This was the only home I ever knew, with Wynflæd and my uncle caring for me, along with Edwin's mother, Eadburh.

I hear footsteps outside, and then Wynflæd speaks.

'I know you're awake, so come on, let's see if you can sit without decorating my floor with your innards.'

I groan. My nose aches and my throat is sore, a sure sign I've been breathing through my mouth all night. But I do make it upright, even if my hands grip the side of the bed to stop me from lying down. There's an ache of pain across my chest, and I remember the smack I took from Horsa's shield.

'Let me look at you.' Wynflæd's words show some sympathy for my plight.

I raise my head to meet her fierce eyes. She nods, as though pleased with my small accomplishment, reaching out to run her finger over the side of my nose, which hurts like a bastard, but she seems pleased with what she finds.

'Now, drink this and tell me what's in it.' I'd wrinkle my nose at the strong smell, but appreciate that's just going to hurt even more.

I take the beaker and don't even peer into its confines, preferring to just swallow it back as quickly as possible.

'Well?' she demands as I hand her back the beaker with a shaking hand.

'Dutter,' I say first, wishing my words weren't so muffled by my nose.

'And?'

I feel on firmer ground now that I have one element correct.

'Mild from a dow?' I continue. I'm sure I catch a smirk on her face, and Cuthred is chuckling in the corner, his eyes bright with mirth.

'Are you asking me that, or telling me that?'

'Delling you,' I murmur. 'And darrow and beddony,' I speak before she can say anything else.

'Obviously,' she manages to say, the hint of amusement on her face.

'Dorndoddle and dennyroot.'

'Very good. And I think you meant butter, milk from a cow, yarrow, betony, corncockle and pennyroot. But you know that recipe as well as I do. What else was in it?'

I'd shake my head at her, and glower, but I know it's going to hurt too much.

'Doo also added some deddles. And, I believe dey're early-summer deddles, before they truly addain their dodency.'

Wynflæd truly grins at me then, showing me the gaps in her front teeth, while her white-haired chin catches the light from the fire that's behind her. 'Good,' she confirms, offering no further praise, even though I'm feeling quite proud with myself. 'Now, come and sit before the fire. You can leave, but only when you've eaten, and I've told you all I know. And don't jump from the bed,' she further cautions, as I'm just about to do so.

I move more slowly then, lowering one foot and then the other, allowing the room to spin a little, before I can focus on her. As soon as I'm standing, I wish I wasn't, for my nose aches, and I can already feel a terrible dull, pulsing pain throughout my head, even as my chest tightens and I find it an effort to get a good breath in.

'It'll pass,' she assures me.

I see then that a stool is waiting for me, and I perch on it, more relieved than I should be not to have to stand. I reach up with my hand, and she slaps it aside.

'Leave your nose alone, or it'll hurt twice as much. And don't be picking it. If it starts to bleed again, come back to me, but it'll just be a matter of waiting for it to heal. Don't get into any more fights. I can only straighten a nose so many times before it's just always going to be bent, and the men in the barracks won't thank me for your loud snoring then. Here, eat this.' She passes me a bowl of good pottage, that stinks of garlic, even through my clogged nose.

I eat it eagerly.

'Now, I know what happened yesterday. Ealdorman Sigered is once more not beloved of the king, while Ealdorman Ælfstan remains furious at what happened. However, both men managed not to have an outright argument while the ambassador was here with the king. The East Anglians left at first light.'

It seems I've slept for a long time.

Wynflæd continues. 'There's much talk about whether the king has formed an alliance or not. For now, no one knows for sure. I doubt King Wiglaf, still filled with confidence after his victory over King Ecgberht, will agree to a peace accord, but what do I know? I expect the ealdorman will inform you soon enough, and then you must tell me. There's a great deal of unease within Tamworth. Good men died fighting the king of the East Angles. Such a sacrifice isn't easily forgotten, especially not by wives, sons and daughters.'

'Do you think he's made a deace accord?' I query, pleased to be able to speak more easily now that I'm a bit more alert. I'm also able to try to form my words with more care.

'I've no idea what goes on in that man's head,' Wynflæd counters. 'As long as he doesn't make peace with King Ecgberht of Wessex, I'll be content. But others won't be.' This sounds like a caution, but what chance do Wynflæd or I have to sway a king from his course? Ealdorman Ælfstan might have some small opportunity if he can get the support of other men of the witan, I suppose. 'But it's not of the king that I wish to speak to you about, but the king's son.'

I still then. I can well imagine what Wynflæd means to say to me. While I might think of her as very much the grandmother I never had, I'm unsure if I wish to listen to her advice as though I were one of her kin.

'Lord Wigmund's mother, the queen, exerts a fiery domination over him. It's she who decides on his friends and allies. It's she who makes him believe he can strut around the place as though he were the king.' I'm unsurprised that Wynflæd's voice has fallen to little more than a whisper.

I consider moving forward to better catch her words but know I won't be able to hear her over the thudding of my head and nose.

'I'm aware of the historic incident between Wigmund and Edwin, and equally, I'm aware that you and Edwin aren't as friendly as you once were. That makes it much easier for me to caution you. You must not do anything else to bring yourself to Wigmund's attention. You might resent the king rewarding you in the way that he has, and you might well wish people would stop discussing how you thrust yourself between him and the enemy, but it's more than Wigmund will ever be able to do. His mother won't allow him to ride to war, whether Wigmund can kill is another matter entirely. He simply won't have the opportunity to win the acclaim of his fellow warriors and future allies. As such, he'll stoop to do all he can to undermine those he fears, and I believe that he fears you and all you have done.'

'Wynflæd,' I murmur softly, echoing her own cautions. 'I'm a nobody. I have no claim as an ætheling. I'm not throne-worthy. No one would ever think I could rule Mercia. Wigmund has nothing to fear from me.'

I can't decide whether it's a trick of the light, or whether a bemused expression crosses Wynflæd's face, or even if I just imagined it, but she shakes her head, eyes holding mine, for all it makes my stomach queasy once more.

'If you're to become a warrior as your uncle was before you, none of those small details will matter. Mercia's rightful ruling line, through Lord Coenwulf, has put aside all claims, and now merely means to pay homage to whoever is king. With King Beornwulf and Ludica dead, and with Wiglaf king, a man with only just more right to rule than you, or anyone else for that matter, there are some who'll think nothing of proposing any man of war who can show himself capable of defending Mercia from her enemies. You've shown yourself capable of that not once, but twice. Should you do so a third time, you'll be even more surely marked as someone who could cause problems, with the right amount of support, especially against a man who'll never make a name for himself as a warrior. Lord Wigmund won't be able to use his father's growing reputation to ensure his own. A man must forge his destiny. The people of Mercia hold King Wiglaf in much higher regard than during his first reign, but that doesn't include his son. Wigmund might be foolish, but his mother is far from that. And so, she means to bind him to Mercia's ancient royal line with Lady Ælflæd.' Once more, Wynflæd cautions me. How she knows so much about my inner thoughts, I don't know. But her words thrum through me as painfully as my healing nose. She knows that there are bones to my fears that Wigmund will be wed to Lady Ælflæd.

'Wigmund's marriage is of no concern for me,' I counter, a little hotly, I'm aware.

'Perhaps it's not, but I think you know of who I speak. And so, you're doubly compromised; you're becoming the warrior that Wigmund will never be, and you and his future betrothed already know each other, and Wigmund is aware of this. And, I'm led to believe, you performed no small assistance for her when you were at Kingsholm.'

I bite my lip then, breaking my gaze with Wynflæd. Why she speaks to me as she does, I'm unsure, but I can't deny she does perceive my thoughts about Lady Ælflæd too easily.

'The union will take place as soon as she's old enough to wed,' Wynflæd continues confidently. 'I know the queen well enough to perceive her ambitions and her plots. While the king busies himself with safeguarding the borders, her eye is only on the future. And I believe she and Ealdorman Sigered share a regard in that respect.'

Wynflæd's words astound me. 'De queen and Ealdorman Sigered?'

'Yes, they're often to be found in one another's company. His disdain for battle means he's often left behind in Tamworth. It's little surprise that he's bending his will to accommodate the queen's. He means to have greater influence, somehow.'

'And dhat's why his grandson is allied with Lord Wigmund.'

'Exactly,' Wynflæd confirms, a gleam in her eye showing me she's pleased with my reasoning. 'Had the old ealdorman a granddaughter to spare, I assure you the union between the two families would have already been secured, no matter the king's distaste for such an accord.'

'So, Ealdorman Sigered wishes do have peace with the East Angles, and he works with de queen. And yet, de king is still determined to have war with the East Angles.'

'For now, yes. But as King Athelstan refrained from attacking last year, despite all the harrying on the borders, there's now room for a different narrative.'

'Doo seem do know a lot for da herb woman,' I announce.

She winks at me, damn her, a smile on her thin lips, her chest rising and falling as she chuckles at my outraged words. 'My boy. I've lived through far too many kings and their wives to find any of this new. Even the matter of the kingdom of the East Angles isn't new. It wasn't so long ago that the East Angles were their own kingdom. It's little wonder that they want to be so again.' She pauses then, stroking her chin, suddenly serious. 'I would hope that one day Mercia will have a king to make her great again, as under Penda, over two hundred years ago, or Offa, who ruled in my lifetime. Those two men made Mercia what it is today. It's a great pity that in the intervening years, ambition and unexpected deaths have allowed her to fall as low as she has. But I know' – suddenly Wynflæd's words thrum with intensity – 'that one day, Mercia will lay claim to a mighty warrior king once more. I just hope I live to see it.'

And there's something in her look that makes me believe she'll do whatever it takes in order to do so.

9

'Welcome back.' Frithwine grins at me when I appear in the bunkhouse. I look to him, my eyes still playing tricks on me as I move from the brightness of day to the darkness beneath the roof.

'Danks,' I murmur, wishing I could speak better, but it's an effort to walk and breathe, let alone walk, talk and breathe at the same time. I settle gingerly on my bed, wondering whether to risk lying down.

'Have you heard?' Garwulf joins his brother. Both of them stand before me. There's no one else in the room. They must be on the training ground, or perhaps hunting.

'What?' I query, pleased to get that one word out without mangling it.

'The king has decided to meet King Athelstan of the East Angles. The plan is to discuss a peace accord then, in person, rather than like this, using intermediaries.'

'When?' I don't much fancy moving any time soon. I hope to be allowed some rest before having to escort the king on such a journey.

'Around Easter, I believe,' Wulfheard offers. I've not seen him enter the door. He looks at me, a wince on his face for my wound.

I wonder why Wynflæd didn't tell me this? I can't believe she didn't know. But then, she seemed more concerned with the problem of Lord Wigmund than what the king was actually doing.

'Well, two black eyes are always better than just getting the one.'

I try to smile at Wulfheard, but my face doesn't want to obey me. I want to ask more, and Wulfheard is no doubt aware of that.

'Can you walk with me?' the older man queries, making it clear what he wants to speak to me about is of no concern for Frithwine or Garwulf.

'I think so,' and I stand from my bed, swaying only a little.

Wulfheard shakes his head at me. 'You'll need your cloak. It's cold.'

I pause, thinking of my cloak, aware I'll have to bend to retrieve it from the bed.

Muttering under his breath, Wulfheard collects my cloak, and even does me a service in twirling it around my shoulders and fastening it at my throat. I sway once more, and Wulfheard offers me his arm for support.

I can smell very little with my nose as it is, but I can still detect the sharpness of the cold day.

'Where are we going?' I query.

'Just shut up, and I'll talk and you can listen,' Wulfheard suggests, leading me slowly towards the gated entranceway of Tamworth as soon as we leave the long wooden hall in which we sleep.

I keep my eyes on where we're going, not on my feet and, slowly, the world stops swaying quite so alarmingly. That is until we stride over the ditch and I feel the ground lurching towards me.

'Didn't Wynflæd give you some mint to chew?' Wulfheard asks.

I'd forgotten that. I fumble in my pouch and pull forth a few leaves. I can't smell it, not at all, but I place it in my mouth, and chew it, wincing slightly as all of my face moves with the action. Still, it does clear my head.

'Mint is good for sickness, even I know that,' Wulfheard confirms, a touch of pride in his voice for knowing something about healing. I'd smirk if I could do so without it hurting. I'd also call him a fool, because, yes, everyone knows mint is good for clearing the head. I'd just forgotten because my head wasn't clear.

Ahead of us, I catch a glimpse of the king's warriors on the training ground, but Wulfheard doesn't walk that way, but rather follows the course of the roadway that leads towards Lichfield and the home of the bishop. Wynflæd told me that, once, King Offa thought to make Lichfield an archbishopric, akin to Canterbury and York. It met with no success, although she didn't know all the details as to why. Although I do believe she muttered something about the bloody pope in bloody Rome, and I didn't really know who she spoke about, not then. Now I know. The pope is some distant figure, far, far away, over the sea, and over more distant lands, and he thinks to determine what men and women think and pray about. I'm astounded the king lets this unknown person have any say in his kingdom, but Wynflæd assured me that all Saxon kings do the same. I find that more than strange.

Wulfheard remains silent after his comment about the mint leaves, and I don't prompt him because I'm too busy concentrating on putting one foot in front of the other and not falling over. Even with Wulfheard supporting me, it's an effort.

'Ealdorman Ælfstan has bid me speak to you, about the king's son.'

I feel my heart sink at the news, when Wulfheard finally breaks the silence. I don't want to be lectured to by Wulfheard or Ealdorman Ælfstan. Not about bloody Lord Wigmund. I've heard more than enough from Wynflæd already.

'The ealdorman is aware that the king's son is a difficult individual. Ælfstan also understands that Wigmund is entirely manipulated by his mother, and in turn, his mother manipulates the king, in some regards. And for one reason or another, you've come to the queen's attention. Unfortunately for you. In turn, that means that Lord Wigmund is fast developing a hatred for you, on top of the unease he already feels towards you for being the recipient of the king's largesse. For now, it's an itch that Lord Wigmund can scratch with such instances as occurred yesterday. But there'll come a time when he's able to do much more than that, and you need to learn to ignore it, as much as possible.'

I open my mouth to argue, but Wulfheard releases my arm and turns to face me. His eyes are narrowed, as he watches me. I realise that I actually have to look down. That surprises me. I think Wulfheard must note the same because he smirks, no doubt struck by the same thought.

'Your uncle was a fine man. He was truly a great man, in all honesty. And he had the advantage of having a king's ear, and with that, he was able to continue after King Beornwulf's death as though little had changed. You don't yet have that same relationship with King Wiglaf. He sees you as too young, and too untried in battle. You might well have ensured he lived and got into Londinium alive, but King Wiglaf just sees your age. He sees you as akin to his son. And his son is allowed no closer to the battlefield than to be taught how to use blunted seax and shield. Wigmund wasn't raised with the belief that he'd one day be king.

He wasn't even an ætheling, throne-worthy until his father over-topped all the other ealdormen to rule Mercia. No. Wigmund's education has been about politics and making a name for himself as one of the king's counsellors, and perhaps, if he was lucky, one of the king's ealdormen. His life has changed, just as surely as yours has since King Ludica was killed and his father became king.'

I hold my tongue. I want to argue my side of this, but it's too difficult with my head pounding with every step I take. I resolve to listen, as though Wulfheard is Wynflæd, and somewhere, amongst all the words used, will be something useful to me, and not an admonition.

'Ealdorman Ælfstan suggests you do your best to avoid the king's son, and the queen, but without making it overly obvious that's your intention. He appreciates it'll be difficult at such close quarters. But there are rumours that the king and queen will shortly travel away from Tamworth, perhaps to Lichfield, or Worcester, they may even journey to Kingsholm to call upon Lord Coenwulf and his new wife, Lady Cynehild. The ealdorman intends to encourage them to do so. You can remain at Tamworth and have some respite from them.'

I nod, just enough that Wulfheard knows I heed his words, and so that I don't cause nausea to bloom once more.

'And now, for matters of politics. Ealdorman Sigered is a slip-pery fish, but the king is wise to his ways. The king means to conduct negotiations, in person, with King Athelstan. As such, nothing will happen, not until Easter, when we'll all travel to the east.'

Wulfheard holds my gaze, and then looks aside, gazing towards Lichfield. The road begins to climb a slight rise, and along both sides of it, thick trees gather. Beneath those trees, I used to collect herbs and mushrooms for Wynflæd. It feels like a lifetime ago, and I know a moment of remorse for all I've lost. It was bad enough when I had to avoid the gaze of Lady Cynehild before I became oath-sworn to King Wiglaf at Bardney, desperate to save my uncle's life by fulfilling the task he swore me to as quickly as possible. I can't say it's any better now.

'There's something about you, young Icel, that either makes men your firm allies or turns them entirely against you. I can't quite determine what it is, but it's a powerful weapon at your disposal. I urge you to use it with caution,' Wulfheard finishes, not meeting my eyes as he speaks.

I feel my mouth open in shock. Does he mean himself when he says that? Or Ealdorman Ælfstan, or perhaps Oswy, Frithwine and Garwulf? I would shake my head, deny his words, but they won't come. I think of Wynflæd, and Lady Cynehild, now my ally and not my enemy, of Brute, and Wine, and even King Wiglaf. Perhaps I'm more like my uncle than I ever thought possible, because, certainly, Cenfrith was a beguiling man. He was able to bend others to his will, or rather, he was able to bend them so that he could follow his own will. I can't decide whether that pleases me or not. Wulfheard is correct to caution me.

That night, Wulfheard doesn't sit beside me at the king's board, but instead Oswy and Waldhere are my allies. Somehow, they refrain from making any sort of comment about my nose, and neither do they expect me to speak. They also see to it that, sitting one to either side of me, with Goðeman opposite me, no one can get close to me. I'm impressed by their forethought, until Waldhere nudges me and leans closer.

'The king's son can't take his eyes from you. Keep your head down and don't react.'

I do as he says, giving no indication that I've heard what's been said.

King Wiglaf is absent from the meal. Rumour has it he's travelled to Repton, to pray at the tombs of Mercia's kings, no doubt for guidance on how to continue with the king of the East Angles. That means the queen and her son are in nominal command of Tamworth, with Ealdorman Sigered at their side. If I lifted my head, I'd see the group of three all toadying up to one another, laughing and discussing politics; ruling over Tamworth with haughty arrogance.

Ealdorman Ælfstan is also absent, as are about ten of his warriors, alongside Wulfheard. They, it seems, have accompanied the king. I almost wish I'd been allowed to go, no matter that each and every jolt of Brute's steps would have sent pangs of pain through my head.

Godeman and Waldhere keep up a long conversation, of which I half-listen, concerning a bout they witnessed on the training field that day. I appreciate them ensuring there's no silence for me to hear the malicious comments of those men who are now Lord Wigmund's allies, where they sit, backs to mine at the table closest to the dais. Even so, I hear the odd word, and chuckle, and even Cenfrith's name, which makes me tense.

'Ignore them, lad,' Oswy urges me. 'One day, you'll stand beside them on the slaughter field, and you'll watch them piss themselves with fear, and it won't matter what they've said about you, because you'll live and they'll be fodder for the crows.'

I find those words strangely reassuring.

* * *

The king doesn't travel to Kingsholm, or even to Worcester, as Wulfheard thought he would, content to have food brought to

Tamworth from his vast estates rather than risk the winter roads himself. That dismays me. I'm tired of constantly watching those around me, and trying to avoid being anywhere that Lord Wigmund thinks to stand. He and his allies, and I've noticed that the number is continuing to grow on an almost daily basis, seem to be everywhere.

With my nose finally healed, and my eyes no longer stained with the black of night, I can at least return to the training ground. Not that Wigmund stays away from there. But with Wulfheard returned from a week-long trip to Repton with King Wiglaf, I at least can be ordered around by him, instead of by the king's son.

Returning from a sprint along the river, which Wulfheard has initiated to ensure his warriors lose their winter-fat bellies before the Easter festivities, I see Wigmund and a collection of his allies watching a fight taking place between Frithwine and Garwulf. Both lads have been late to arrive for the run. Wulfheard might have had words with them, but I think he might allow them some peace because of Wigmund's attention.

I eye the collection of men and boys with Wigmund. There's Ealdorman Sigered's grandson and also others. I look to them with sour eyes. Hunberht is the oldest of them all. He thinks to become an ealdorman, but, as of yet, he stands in the king's council and nothing more. He has lands close to Kingsholm. I imagine, before the union of Lord Coenwulf and Lady Cynehild, that he thought to convince the king to make him the ealdorman there. Wicga is actually younger than Wigmund, I'm led to believe. He has no living father, being the son of Wilfwald, killed fighting King Athelstan of the East Angles, but his mother is as ambitious as the queen. In fact, both of them are as cats to one another. How Wicga has managed to insinuate himself into the small gathering, I'm unsure.

I consider the rest of the men and boys. I know some of them by name, and a few by sight. Ælfred, I believe, is somehow connected to Ealdorman Ælfstan, but I'm unsure of the exact relationship. I spare a thought for him, imagining Ælfstan's rage, and then appreciate that the ealdorman might not be so angry after all, if he's playing politics, which I know he's capable of, even if he doesn't enjoy it.

But it's the other men watching on that surprise me. I recognise them and quickly scan the rest of the group, only for my eyes to settle on Oswald and then on Edwin. He meets my gaze evenly, and I realise that Lord Coenwulf has come to Tamworth and not vice versa. My thoughts immediately turn to Lady Ælflæd, and I'm as nauseous as when I first broke my nose, even as I stop my running, and pant, my breath coming hot and my heart hammering in my chest, only not from the exercise.

Frithwine and Garwulf grabble with one another, until they're both sweating and filthy, the earth beneath their feet churned as we make our way to the training ground. But, when the fight is over, Garwulf hauls Frithwine to his feet and they both laugh. So too does the group of attendant watchers, even Lord Wigmund seems to find some humour in it all, and I slip behind Wulfheard so as not to be seen, keeping my head lowered because I overtop Ælfstan's commander. I've been doing a lot of this of late.

'Well met.' Wulfheard's greeted by Oswald, as the group starts to disperse. My eyes remain on Wulfheard's back, while Oswy, Waldhere and Godeman have gathered there as well. It's all about making it look less obvious, so I've been informed.

'Lord Coenwulf wishes to speak to the king,' Oswald tells him quickly, making it unnecessary to ask the question.

'About the East Angles?' Wulfheard queries.

'You can come out now,' Oswy murmurs to me.

I lift my head and see only the backs of Wigmund and his

coterie of allies. I move aside, and then reach for my practice weapons. There's little point in going for the run and not using my warm body to practise with the rest of the men.

Oswy and Goðeman eagerly face up against one another. Waldhere shakes his head.

'This could get nasty,' he offers me in an aside, indicating the two warriors. 'The two have some disagreement about who truly won the game of chance last night.'

I look to Waldhere. He once had a broken nose and two swollen eyes. I can remember thinking he'd never be pretty again. Unconsciously, I lift my hand to my nose, feeling the strange bump in it now, and thinking I'm perhaps the same, only for my eyes to alight on my scar. With my hands warm from running, it's not as obvious as it could be. Still, I'm only a youth, and already, I'm festooned with the marks of my warrior's life. It's a far cry from when my biggest concern was trying not to slice open my finger with one of Wynflæd's small herb knives.

'I heard the arguing,' I confirm, content to watch them for a moment.

Wulfheard continues to speak with Oswald from Kingsholm, and I'm curious to know about what they speak, but I know better than to seem too keen. I consider how Lady Cynehild fares, and if Lord Coenwulf has come to talk of King Athelstan of the East Angles, or if it's actually about the less than secret discussions regarding the union of Lord Wigmund and Lady Ælflæd.

Oswy is once more able to fight as he used to, while Goðeman is a beast. He bristles, even without weapons, and I'm unsurprised the rest of the men have gathered. Landwine and Kyre murmur one to another, Maneca looks fiery and ready for whatever is about to happen. I just hope it doesn't end with some new injury that will earn us all the ire of Wulfheard and Ealdorman Ælfstan when they realise what's happened.

'Icel.' I turn to meet Edwin's interested gaze.

'Well met,' I return. When he left for Kingsholm after the marriage of Coenwulf and Cynehild, there were no words of parting. Now, it feels strange to have him seek me out. Perhaps he wishes to speak to me of Lord Coenwulf's apology to me, to acknowledge that neither of us was to blame for our separation.

Silence falls between us. In front, Godeman is the first to land a blow against Oswy's shield. The sound is loud in the stillness of the day now that Wigmund and his chattering ravens have gone away.

'My mother speaks well of you,' Edwin offers, the words awkward.

'And Lord Coenwulf?' I feel I need to say something, but I can't accept the compliment, no matter how half-hearted.

'Seems content with his new wife. Lady Cynehild,' – Edwin fumbles for words – 'is much changed as well. She's almost jolly,' he confirms, shaking his head as though amazed to have said the words.

'That pleases me to hear.' I didn't wish for her to be unhappy when forced to wed again.

'Lord Coenwulf was dismayed the king couldn't travel to Kingsholm. He'd determined to play a greater part in the future of Mercia.'

Oswy has managed to land a blow through Godeman's guard, on his shoulder, and now the other man is furious, striking out at Oswy with a mixture of happenstance and cunning. I watch him, the edges of a smile on my lips. It's an intriguing way to battle. It's impossible for Oswy to actually know what Godeman will do next. Oswy is trying to overpower the slightly smaller man, but I can't see that it'll work. It reminds me of the time Frithwine and Garwulf both tried to play the useless warrior, while the other tried to learn how to battle through the unpredictable attack.

'And did Lady Cynehild travel with him?' I ask,

'No, she remained at Kingsholm, alongside Lady Ælflæd.'

'A shame, I would have liked to speak with her.' I'm unaware of Edwin's response to my words, but his next question confirms his confusion.

'She used to hate you?'

'She did, yes. We've reconciled since the death of my uncle.'

'And why was that?' Edwin presses me.

I furrow my forehead and turn to meet his eyes. The fight between Goðeman and Oswy is completely forgotten about, although the sound of iron on wood continues to ring through the air.

'My uncle asked me to give her a message. It was his dying wish. I believe that whatever it meant, she's content now, as she never was before. I was unsure about her union to your lord. I knew she had no plans to remarry. But that changed,' I offer lightly.

There are so many emotions covering Edwin's face, that I don't know what to think. Is he perplexed by what I've said? Does he truly care? Perhaps I shouldn't have offered so much information. I've forgotten that Edwin and I no longer share the friendship we once did. His eyes are uneasy, his jaw tight.

'All those years of avoiding her, and now you merely ask after her well-being?'

'Yes,' is my only response.

A roar of outrage from the fight has me turning to see that Goðeman, as I expected, is victorious. A sliver of blood slides down Oswy's face beneath his helm, and I wince. I hope he's merely caught it on the edge of his helm, and it's nothing more serious.

When I once more turn to face Edwin, I'm astounded to be met, not with his uneasy eyes, but with his fist, and for the second time in as many weeks, I tumble to the ground, wondering what I've done to deserve such an attack when only moments ago we shared our most meaningful conversation since we spoke at Londonia. Whatever I've said has angered him. I only wish I knew what it was.

10

Brute is easy beneath me. We're firm allies now. At last. And together with Ealdorman Ælfstan and his warriors, we ride to the borderlands with the kingdom of the East Angles, taking the Foss Way northwards from Tamworth.

I returned to Tamworth from Londonia along Watling Street as winter bit at our heels and now I ride from it once more, with frost crisp underfoot. King Wiglaf is impatient, and so, it seems, is Ealdorman Ælfstan. Even I'm not dismayed by our new orders. I'm just grateful to be away from Tamworth, the queen and her snivelling son. If they won't leave Tamworth, then I most happily will.

If I thought I could get away with it, I'd punch Lord Wigmund and break his nose. I'd wipe the smirk from his face and ensure he was never a handsome man. And yet I don't. And it's not just because my own nose is now tilted to one side thanks to both Horsa and Edwin.

How I despise Wigmund, and all of his followers. I note, not for the first time, that it's Ealdormen Ælfstan and Tidwulf who lead the Mercians eastwards, the king and his men there as well, but not the king's precious son nor any of his growing circle of adherents. No. They'll be staying at Tamworth, or travelling to some other of the king's properties. They'll be kept safe in the very heartland of Mercia, while others potentially don battle gear in the king's name, knowing that, one day, all that we accomplish might well be held in Wigmund's name.

King Athelstan of the East Angles appears genuine in his attempts to draw together a peace accord between the two kingdoms, for all that I distrust Ealdorman Sigered's part in the whole scheme. And the queen's. King Wiglaf meant to ignore it, despite firm rumours that we'd travel east for Easter so that the two kings could meet face to face. No, King Wiglaf wanted to expand Mercia, and even reclaim Kent as well. But King Ecgberht hasn't been quiet, sitting in Winchester nursing his wounds, and berating himself for his failure in holding Mercia. King Ecgberht of Wessex has made overtures towards King Athelstan of the East Angles and that has changed everything.

The roar of outrage when King Wiglaf was informed of this yesterday is why, now, with barely enough daylight to make travel possible during the dark time of the year, we're riding towards the borderlands with the kingdom of the East Angles, and it is far from Easter time.

Neither has Lord Coenwulf and his Kingsholm warriors joined the king on this expedition, even though they were at Tamworth when news of King Ecgberht's latest outrage was received. They may have come to discuss the problem of King Athelstan, and to arrange the marriage of Lord Coenwulf's sister to the king's son, but Lord Coenwulf was very eager to leave Tamworth at the first sign of trouble, with bloody Edwin at his side. Lord Coenwulf's men might have assisted at the battle for Londonia, but they won't be there for the peace with the kingdom of the East Angles. Or the war if the peace should fail and war be declared.

'What ails you?' Wulfheard's voice carries all the sympathy of a sharpened seax.

'Nothing,' I growl, and he shakes his head. I'm ill-tempered, and no matter what I do, I can't shake it away from myself, even with the smooth gait of Brute beneath me, and the distance between Tamworth and me growing with every breath I take.

I grip the reins tightly, and then loosely, with both of my hands. I'm sure I can almost battle as well with my left hand as I can my once dominant right. Wynflæd assures me that I carry too much bile and that's why it's taken so long to heal.

Theodore and Gaya have been slightly more sympathetic. Theodore, now able to speak my tongue in more than just halting words, has assured me that in overusing it immediately after I gained my injury, I've slowed the healing process. He also says that the dank weather of the winter months, which has seen him huddled up close to the fire, and almost encased in two cloaks, hasn't aided the wound. He says, when the sun is once more ascendent, it'll finish its healing and all will be well. I hope so. Although, I can now stab and slash with both hands, and at least I don't carry the slightly lopsided stance of some of the Mercian warriors who battle predominantly with either their left or right hand.

'Aye, nothing. And it's been nothing for months now. A man can only mourn for so long.'

Wulfheard's words, unbidden as they are, bring an unwelcome tightness to my throat. I've missed my uncle's presence during the winter months. Not that he was ever at Tamworth a great deal, but his arrival always occasioned some lifting of the tedium of another winter.

'A man can mourn as long as he must,' I retort, annoyed to

have my temper questioned, and to have Wulfheard assume it's caused by my uncle, when I think it has more to do with Lord Wigmund and Edwin. Or, perhaps, I'm honest enough to admit it's both of those things.

'You just need to face an enemy. That'll do more good for your ill humour than anything else. It's always the same. Men trained to fight must always have someone to fight against.'

I shake my head at his words, turning aside to catch the gloating expression of Frithwine. I really do think that Ealdorman Ælfstan would have done well to relieve himself of the two youths of Frithwine and Garwulf. But, of course, he's done no such thing. Ælfstan's keeping them close, because despite all their faults, they've learned to fight much better over the winter, and they've proved themselves fiercely loyal to the ealdorman, and to Mercia. I think perhaps their slim build is one of the reasons as well. Ealdorman Ælfstan doesn't ever intend to have his plans scuppered by fat warriors.

'Where are we actually going?' I ask, eager to change the subject.

'Towards the kingdom of the East Angles.'

'But where exactly?'

'Wherever the king takes us?' Wulfheard responds, very unhelpfully. And then he relents. 'The king means to take us to Bardney, to give thanks for their assistance in sheltering him when King Ecgberht claimed Mercia. From there, it'll be wherever King Athelstan of the East Angles determines the peace meeting should be.'

We ride in silence then. I try to force myself from my grumpiness and allow my thoughts to turn to the kingdom of the East Angles and Athelstan. When I was a child, I didn't understand the lure of that kingdom. I didn't truly understand why two of

Mercia's kings died fighting for it. I think I know a little more now.

Like the lost kingdom of Kent, the kingdom of the East Angles is important to Mercia. If King Wiglaf gained a hold over the kingdom of the East Angles, Mercia could lay claim to a coastline, complete with a network of trading settlements. Without it, Mercia has rivers along which trading sites can grow, just as at Lundenwic, but not the easy access to the sea. And, of course, Mercia relies on its trading networks. Salt, lead, copper and Mercian oak are much in demand, whereas Mercia itself needs exotic objects from faraway shores to reward the elite when the king is disinclined to part with more of his landed possessions or even to reward them with titles.

But, of course, it's not towards a war that we ride. No, this plan of a peace accord is once more what drives King Wiglaf on. He'd sooner have peace with King Athelstan than allow King Ecgberht to forge a treaty with that kingdom. Bad enough to have Wessex to the south, without also having the eastern kingdom beholden to Wessex also on Mercia's border.

And, just like Lundenwic, there's a mint in the kingdom of the East Angles, and Mercian kings once had their image on those coins, but now it's King Athelstan's face that shows on them. I consider then whether King Wiglaf truly yearns to triumph over King Athelstan in the same way he did over King Ecgberht, or whether this is something else entirely. After all, if not for King Athelstan's murdering ways, King Wiglaf would never have become king. King Wiglaf essentially owes King Athelstan a debt, whereas King Ecgberht's usurpation of Mercia had to burn for an entirely different reason.

'Icel.' I turn and meet the eyes of Oswy. He's lost some of his girth, but now he's working hard to reclaim all that bled away from his body when he was unwell.

'Oswy,' I retort.

He smirks, and in doing so, draws even more attention to his huge nose. 'Wulfgar and I were hoping you'd help us out with something.'

I shake my head at his words. Oswy, while according me more respect than in the past, is still likely to torment me. Of late, he and Wulfgar have taken to asking me about the more personal conditions I might know how to treat a man or woman for. It's becoming tedious very quickly. 'What is it you wish to know now? Is it why it hurts to piss, or something else?' I opt for the least salacious of the recent questions.

'Well, we all know why it hurts Oswy to piss. He should really leave off with the sheep.' Kyre laughs from behind us all, earning himself a menacing glower from Oswy. Not all of the men like one another, that much has become clear with the number of wounds inflicted, even with wooden or bound weapons, upon one another.

I shake my head, trying not to smirk.

'No, no, it's not that,' Oswy counters, but he's not embarrassed enough to leave off altogether. 'It's that Edwin. He used to be your friend, didn't he?'

I think I'd rather he asked me about his piss or his stones. I don't want to talk about Edwin.

'I mean, you're sporting a nice black eye there, and we all saw Edwin give it to you.'

Instinctively, I reach up and run my hand over the inflammation around my eye. I would welcome a salve of yarrow, wild carrot and woodruff to take the heat from it, but, of course, I can't ride with the stuff sliding down my face. Hopefully, when we stop for the night, I'll be able to tend to it better.

'I don't deny it,' I confirm, hoping that'll be enough, but Oswy has recovered his memory of the time that I stood by Edwin's side when he was beaten by Lord Wigmund, and also recalls that Edwin left Tamworth when I did.

'Why does he hate you so much? Why is he a member of Lord Coenwulf's war band and not the king's? He was raised at Tamworth, wasn't he? His mother and stepfather live in Tamworth, don't they?'

'It's a long story.' I try to deflect, but Oswy isn't to be put off.

'We're not going anywhere. Well, we are,' he clarifies. 'But as we're heading in the same direction, you may as well tell us what happened.'

'Leave the lad alone,' Wulfheard interjects, but I either tell the story now or they'll keep asking me about it.

'Edwin and I were parted at Kingsholm. He remained behind, and my uncle and I travelled onwards.'

'When you killed the old king's horse?' Kyre queries.

'Icel didn't kill the old king's horse,' Wulfheard counters. I'm surprised he's prepared to argue on my behalf, but I appreciate it all the same. 'The horse was old and full of shit. Icel eased the poor beast's suffering and then he died. That's the story. Icel isn't a horse killer, as you all well know, and as Lord Coenwulf has ensured people know.'

The men do know this. While no longer supposed to tend to Wynflæd's constant requirements, I have been learning what I can about horses from the stablehands. Horses, while so much larger than man, woman or child, suffer from remarkably similar ailments on occasion. And they're all stubborn bastards, the lot of them. Order them not to eat fresh grass, and they'll break their necks trying to reach their neighbours'.

'So why does Edwin hate you then? Enough to punch you in the face the day before you ride out with the king's war band?'

'He just hates me. That's what happens. Sometimes you stay friends with people, sometimes you don't, and sometimes your enemy becomes your friend.' I raise my chin to meet Oswy's eyes, hoping he'll grasp what I'm trying to say and shut up.

'I heard it was something to do with Lady Cynehild, wife to Lord Coenwulf,' Kyre continues to taunt.

'Why would it be anything to do with a lady?' Wulfheard demands.

I'm staggered that these men spend their time talking about me. What a waste of their thoughts and breath.

'Yes, Kyre, why would it be anything to do with Lady Cynehild? She never much liked Icel. I remember now. The poor git used to have to avoid her at all costs.' Oswy is watching me as he speaks, and I can see he's thinking, his mouth hanging slightly open so that he resembles a carp. I don't appreciate his scrutiny. I certainly don't want him to realise that Lady Cynehild and I were once enemies. I don't want him to think that there's anything between us. Even I don't understand her interest in me, other than she was once something to my uncle. What that 'something' was, I don't know. I don't want these men to tell me if they know, either. If my uncle loved his king's wife, I would sooner not soil his memory with the knowledge.

'So why did he hit you?' Kyre persists.

I breathe in deeply and consider how long this conversation could go on if I don't tell them something. Admittedly, it won't be the truth because I don't know why he hit me. He didn't say. And I was in no fit state to find him once I was sensible once more.

'He's been angry with me ever since we held the bridge over the River Fleet. He thinks what I made him do was reckless and I should have asked another.'

'They say he cries himself to sleep at night.' Kyre leans over his mount's head so that he can see me, Wulfheard, Oswy and Wulfgar, who are also involved in this conversation. 'They say he whimpers in his sleep, and fights imaginary foes. I heard his mother wanted Wynflæd to make him a charm to keep away evil spirits.' Kyre spits over his horse's head as he finishes speaking. I notice he reaches up to run his hand over a small emblem that sits at his throat. No doubt it's a cross or some such. Kyre, surprisingly, is particularly fervent in his beliefs. He's often to be found on his knees listening to the bishop drone, or rather, one of the bishop's priests. Bishop Æthelweald likes to show his devotion by having other men attend the church and speak the words that he should.

'Edwin is a warrior of Mercia,' Wulfheard growls. I'm grateful for his intervention. I would sooner not defend Edwin to these men I've fought in battle beside. 'There's enough of us who don't sleep at night not to make fun of the youth who struggles having made his first kills. You should be lauding his accomplishments, not belittling them.'

I hope that puts an end to it, but Oswy is a persistent bugger. That's one of the reasons he's so lethal in battle.

'Well, I also heard that Edwin fancies himself a mate for Lord Coenwulf's daughter. I imagine that good old Icel here was merely defending our Lord Wigmund's prior claim to her.' Kyre chuckles darkly, as does Wulfgar, but Wulfheard casts a sideways look my way and I'm pleased to ignore it.

'What's all this?' Ealdorman Ælfstan has worked his way back to our line of warriors. We've lost the tight formation from when we first left Tamworth. Ælfstan looks far from pleased. I realise then that the rest of the men, either under King Wiglaf's command, Ealdorman Tidwulf's or Ealdorman Beornoth's, are keeping to their formation.

'Nothing important, my lord.' Wulfheard bows his head in apology and Oswy and Wulfgar pull their horses back behind Brute and Bada.

'Yes?' Ælfstan queries Kyre, only for Kyre to grin and turn his mount's head.

Over his shoulder, he calls, 'I'm just trying to find out why our young protégé has an eye that's currently every shade of purple and green.'

Ealdorman Ælfstan pauses and looks at me then, as though noting my wound for the first time. 'You can still wear your helm?' he questions, without a drop of sympathy. I wince at the reminder of trying to force it on over my eye earlier that morning, when we received the unexpected commands to prepare for our journey north.

'Aye, my lord. I can, if I must.'

'It would be better if you kept your personal grievances amongst yourselves. The king doesn't wish to see that.'

I nod, feeling ashamed, and wishing for the hundredth time that I'd actually countered Edwin, rather than allowing him to hit me. But I'd have needed to know that was his intention.

'Go and ride with Landwine. I need to speak with Wulfheard.'

'My lord,' and I encourage Brute onwards, more pleased than I should be when the animal takes my commands easily.

Landwine rides a beautiful bay stallion with a coronet on his face. The animal is a little shorter than Brute and so I tower over the squat man when I'm level with him.

'Icel,' he murmurs on an exhalation. He has a deep voice entirely at odds with his appearance. I can't say whether he likes me or not. I don't know if I like him either. He's one of Ealdorman Ælfstan's men and is fiercely loyal to him, and only then secondly to King Wiglaf. If it came to it, I know he'd rush to aid the ealdorman before the king.

'Landwine,' I reply, and then we fall into an easy silence, punctuated only by the sound of hooves over the road. It's been a cold winter, and very wet. I can see the ravages of it in the dislodged stone of the road, and the way the drainage ditches lining the road are choked with water and other detritus. The smell is ripe as well, reminding me of my journey under the wall at Londinium far too vividly.

'What they talking about?' Landwine asks me.

'I've no idea. I was asked to leave.'

'Well, it'll be something the king's demanded, as usual, that the ealdorman doesn't agree with. It's often the way. Or the king might have a special task for the ealdorman. Ealdorman Ælfstan trusts no one more keenly than Wulfheard.'

I nod. Landwine's not telling me anything I haven't already come to realise. When Ealdorman Ælfstan ordered Wulfheard to train me, he actually assigned a good teacher. I'm grateful to him for that. The process is far from done, but already, I feel better able to protect myself, and my fellow allies, than when I fought outside Londonia.

'What happened to your eye?' Landwine asks, with a smirk, and I realise he's heard much of our earlier conversation anyway.

'I walked into a wall,' I mutter, while he laughs softly. Bloody Edwin. He's done me no favours, with his impromptu attack, and I've not had the time to discover what drove it. Luckily for him, we've been called away from Tamworth before I can seek out some answers. Even more luckily for Edwin, he's not a part of the king's contingent of warriors.

11

It takes us two days to reach Bardney. We arrive as the clouds grow thick, and fat raindrops begin to fall. The small space behind the walls and ditch is crammed with horses and warriors, all of us trying to get out of the freezing deluge. The monks, I notice, do all they can to stay away from us, sheltering in the meagre comfort of their wooden church, and scurry to their prayers as soon as possible. We don't all fit inside the church, for the king's service of thanksgiving, but we can hear well enough from inside the comfort of the hall. When the morning comes, the king orders us on our way again, south towards Londonia. Whether he means to have war or peace with the kingdom of the East Angles or not isn't even mentioned. Instead, King Wiglaf demands we stay alert for an early assault from the Wessex bastard.

Ealdorman Ælfstan is given the most onerous task. As we ride, far more alert than when we left Tamworth, I'm not the only one to muse on it, as I hunker beneath my cloak, wishing the wind would drive the rain onto my back rather than into my face.

'Would it not have been bloody easier to ride from Tamworth

to Londonia and then north along Ermine Street?' It's Oswy who bemoans our current task, but he's not the only one to be thinking it. Certainly, if I had my way, I'd be sharing a few choice words with the king for our current predicament.

'That's not for you to question,' is Wulfheard's immediate response, but I know Wulfheard thinks the same. He told me while we readied our horses for today's journey.

Having taken our time to reach Bardney, we must now push our horses at a quick gallop to reach the far end of Ermine Street, almost to where Londonia lies, but not quite. While Ealdorman Tidwulf and his warriors ride a more sedate patrol along the upper part of Ermine Street that borders the kingdom of the East Angles, we must push our horses hard, and even the horses don't appreciate being exposed to the elements in such a way. Ealdorman Beornoth is to stay with the king. His men were still abed when we were roused to wakefulness. I was far from alone in purposefully making a racket as I dressed and left the settlement of Bardney.

Not that Brute seems to mind. He's keen beneath me, but some of the other horses are far from as young, or fit, as Brute. Bada is easy enough beneath Wulfheard, but Oswy's poor horse is already sweating even with the bite of the trailing winter keen in the air. No doubt that's why Oswy bitches as much as he does.

'We do as the ealdorman commands, and he receives his instructions from the king,' Wulfheard informs the man, but even I can see the problem. Wulfheard's not blind to it either. And we've only been travelling for half a day. 'We'll slow our pace,' Wulfheard raises his voice above the clattering of hooves and I quickly pull Brute to one side. Brute takes the instruction unwillingly, and I'm forced to fight him. 'Go and stop the rest of 'em,' Wulfheard orders me when those far in front don't heed the order.

Brute resumes his onward gallop, and by the time I reach the ealdorman and can let him know what's happened, I've lost sight of Wulfheard and Oswy because the clouds lie so low to the ground, moisture covering everything, even though the rain has finally stopped falling. I can't envisage it being long before the drizzle once more turns to fat raindrops.

'The horses?' Ealdorman Ælfstan asks me without heat as he finally reins in his mount. His face is well hidden beneath his fur-edged cloak.

'Yes, my lord. Too old and slow for such a turn of speed.' I think both of us realise how similar this situation is to the one beneath Londinium's walls. Neither of us comments. Fat men and old horses. It's a wonder that they've survived these bloody times as well as they have.

Ealdorman Ælfstan nods, unsurprised by my words, as he dismounts and guides his horse to a gently tinkling stream. Ælfstan leads about half of the force of fifty warriors, well, fifty-one if I include him in the reckoning. Frithwine and Garwulf are amongst those numbers. They ride young horses, but I can see that they've pressed them too much in an effort to keep up with the ealdorman. Both animals are blowing hard, sweat along their muzzles and forelegs.

'The old men too slow,' Garwulf calls jauntily to me. It seems the dankness can't dim his enthusiasm.

'No, just their horses. They know not to push them.'

The ealdorman hasn't missed what's happening, and Garwulf's smirk drops from his face. 'Get some grasses and wipe the sweat from your mount or she'll be no good for anything. We don't want a horse going lame on us.'

I hide my amusement for the berating of my fellow warrior, but really, Garwulf should know better. A winded horse will be no good if he needs to escape from a trap laid by the men and women of the East Angles. And not far from where we pass is the kingdom of the East Angles, and whether they're enemies or allies has yet to be fully determined.

I've been eyeing the border as I travel onwards. There's nothing to demarcate the two kingdoms. There's no ditch, no dyke, nothing. I can't even see any differences in the way the land is cultivated, in the animals or the people about their tasks. It's just another reminder that, as so often, the clashes between kings and their warriors mean little or nothing to the people they fight over. We're all Saxon. We all, just about, pray to the same God. We all sicken, and thrive in the same circumstances. And yet, unease has made my back slick with sweat, and every strange noise has me reaching for my seax.

'There's nothing to fear,' the ealdorman murmurs to me. 'This is a show of strength on King Wiglaf's behalf, but I don't believe King Athelstan of the East Angles will attack us. He's intelligent enough to realise that King Wiglaf is an entirely different man from both of his predecessors. That's why he decided to propose peace. King Wiglaf has lost his kingdom and regained it. The men of Mercia, even with our numbers suffering from those battles, will fight for their king. They'll protect him. And, at the moment, neither of them intends to force a confrontation. If they did, we'd already be at war.'

I nod, reassured by the words, but I can't dismiss the feeling that we're being watched. 'Then why do this at all?' I query, just to say something rather than allow my worries to run rampant.

'Mercia must prove herself once more. The king means to do similar along the Welsh borders, when he's content that the king of the East Angles and bloody King Ecgberht have begun to realise that what went before will not be possible again. He'll ensure King Ecgberht realises he can't turn all Mercia's enemies on her at the same time.'

I nod. I've heard these arguments from Wulfheard, sitting around the campfire at night, and still, I'm far from convinced. King Ecgberht and his son have already taken too much of Mercia. It's not the kingdom it once was. Wynflæd is right when she cautions me that King Beornwulf did Mercia no favours when he usurped the kingship. Sometimes, I believe her caution encompasses something else as well, but what that might be defeats me still. I know better than to ask her to speak plainly. Whatever passed between King Beornwulf and Wynflæd, it seems I'm to remain ignorant of it.

'I believe the king will be successful in his endeavours,' Ealdorman Ælfstan further shares. 'He knows how lucky he is to still be king of Mercia. He intends to remain in that position.'

'My thanks, my lord,' I reply, turning Brute away as he's drunk his fill and there are others waiting to take our place. In the distance, I see no sign that Wulfheard and the rest of the spent horses are walking to join the rest of us. That worries me. I open my mouth to alert the ealdorman to the delay, but before I can, a cry rips through the air.

''Ware,' Frithwine chokes.

I move around Brute, to where he's pointing along Ermine Street, towards the south. I'm not alone in reaching for my seax and pulling it free from my weapons belt.

'Be careful,' Ealdorman Ælfstan warns us all, turning to glower at his warriors. 'It might merely be merchants and not our enemy.'

I peer at the specks on the horizon, wishing Wulfheard was here with the rest of the warriors. I also hope that the people coming towards us are merely merchants, keen to trade, and not our enemy.

Expectantly, we all wait, and when they come close enough to us, I feel my forehead wrinkle. I don't know what I expected, in all honesty, but it isn't this.

'Hail.' Ealdorman Ælfstan stands in the middle of the road, arresting the advance of the ramshackle collection of men and women. They have an ox pulling a cart laden with everything from dented pots to an elderly man lying snoring beneath a thick cloak. Some of the men carry bandages around upper arms and legs and yet others seem hale. They're all cold, faces bleached of colour. They look as miserable as I feel in the dampness of the day. 'I'm Ealdorman Ælfstan. Where are you from? What's befallen you?'

They look no more pleased to encounter us than we are to see them.

'We was attacked.' It's one of the women who speaks. She carries a babe clasped to her breast beneath her threadbare cloak and her lips are thin and near enough blue. She offers Ealdorman Ælfstan no great respect for his rank. I'm unsurprised. Her shoes are caked in mud, and the cloak can do nothing to keep the biting wind and drizzle from her skin.

'Who attacked you?' the ealdorman probes, with far more respect than that offered to him.

I move in front of him, wary that near enough everyone is limping or carries some other wound. The woman watches me, eyes flashing angrily, but doesn't attempt to stop me, as I reach up and gaze at the older woman trying to direct the ox from the back of the lopsided cart. One of the wheels seems to be a good few inches smaller than the other. The animal has eagerly moved over to crop the line of grass valiantly showing to the side of the road. He has a deep gash across his wide back, but that's not what concerns me. I can see where the woman's one arm hangs loose to her side.

'Let me see,' I urge her. 'I have some healing skills.' I haul myself up and kneel beside her on the cart.

The woman glowers at me. She stinks of pain and fear, her face lined with her years and her fury. 'They tried to take the ox, and I wouldn't let them take the old boy. He's been with me for years.' As she speaks, I detect a roll to her words, as though she comes from the south. Painstakingly, she drops the reins and shows me her left arm.

I touch it gently, feeling all the way along it. It's not bleeding and there's no corruption, but she's clearly wounded, all the same.

'Did you hold on when they tried to take the animal from you?'

'I did, yes. It was a nasty fight, and then my husband, God rest his soul, stuck the fork through the foul attacker, and he finally let go of my animal. A pity my husband didn't realise there was another just waiting to kill him, right behind. But I have my beast and my husband is to thank for that.'

I nod, running my hands along her arm, all the way to her shoulder. She winces as I do so.

'You need to strap your arm tight to your body and leave it that way for at least two weeks. Use it for nothing, and then the feeling should return to it, and the pain go away.' I reach for a strip of linen cloth from beside her, poking through a leather bag, indicating it with my eyes. When she makes no complaint, I loop it around her neck and adjust the tie on it, until I'm sure it'll hang just right.

'You think to tell me something I don't already know,' she growls, but there's only pain in her words as I secure her arm.

Content I've done all I can, I turn to look at the old man, sleeping in the cart.

'He took a blow to his head, but he's getting better every day.

You should help Edith. She has a nasty cut to her face. She keeps it covered with her hair, but it's not healing properly.'

I jump to the ground, and go where the woman points.

Ealdorman Ælfstan continues to speak to the woman and the babe, and I half-listen to the words. News of an attack is unwelcome, but as of yet, I don't think the ealdorman has determined where the attack came from, or from where these people hail. It's easy enough to cross borders between the Saxon kingdoms for those who don't ride as part of a war band. They might be from Wessex, or Kent, or even from the kingdom of the East Angles. I certainly think that's where these people must come from. I don't think they'd have travelled much further than that in the state they're in.

'Edith.' I approach a woman who clasps the hand of a youngster tightly within hers. She startles at me naming her, and I offer what I hope is a smile. Her eyes are dull with pain and I wince in sympathy. 'She says you have a wound. Can I see it?'

Edith's eyes fill with refusal, and the woman behind me calls to her: 'Let him see, or you'll not live for that boy of yours.'

Only then does Edith release her grip on the youngster, no more than five or six winters to his name, and pull back her tangled dark hair. I gasp at the mess on her cheek, close to her eye.

'May I?' I ask, and she doesn't say no, so I get even closer, peering at the wound. It requires stitching, of that I'm sure, but first, I need to clear the filth from it before it infects the rest of her skin, as the sides of the wound are already pink and inflamed. 'I need to get my supplies,' I caution. 'I'll return.'

Ealdorman Ælfstan's voice rumbles over my actions, but I don't catch his words. As of yet, I'm the only one to assist these people, and that frustrates me.

'They won't harm you,' I mutter to Garwulf as I return to

Brute's side, but he stays firmly mounted and behind the ealdorman.

I reach for my saddlebags and pull my collection of healing supplies from it. I really need boiling water.

'Can we light a fire?' I call to Ealdorman Ælfstan.

He nods but says nothing further to me.

As he doesn't scold me, I take it as permission to continue with my task. He's examining the men and women, and I notice that he's finally ordered others to keep watch, and that one of the horses, tail high in the air, is galloping back towards where the remainder of the men are resting the horses. I think it might be Uor, but I could be wrong. It's difficult to tell in the gloom.

'Frithwine, can you gather some wood and start a fire?' I call to him.

I think he'll argue with me, but a quick glance to the ealdorman and Frithwine, an unhappy look on his face, lands in a deep puddle and moves away from his horse into a small patch of low trees, where he stoops to pick up sticks and the driest pieces of grass. I dismiss him from my thoughts. I need the hot water, but first, I can perform other tasks.

'Come, sit here for me.' I indicate a patch of worn grass to the side of the road over which I've flung a blanket from my saddle-bags to stop the water from seeping through.

Edith does as I ask. I look for the boy, but he's taken himself to the cart and now sits beside the older woman. She's smiling at him, offering him the reins, while she moves to drink from a water bottle. She's sharing her cloak with him, and so she must realise how cold he is.

'How did this happen?' I ask, gathering the woman's long, straggling hair so that I can secure it away from her wound using a leather tie.

She doesn't answer me. Her eyes are fierce, as though braced for whatever I might say.

'I'm going to clean it,' I inform her, tipping some of my water onto a piece of clean linen. It would be better if it was hot water, but this will do for now.

The blood is congealed and difficult to move and every time I press on her cheek, I fear the wound, which has barely begun to knit together, will pull apart once more. I notice that her hands are tightly clasped, one inside the other.

'Sorry,' I murmur when she emits a single gasp of pain, and a solitary tear falls from her eye. I breathe in deeply, smelling the scent of the fire. 'Can you put me some water to boil over the fire?' I call to Frithwine.

He does as I ask without complaint. I realise that Ealdorman Ælfstan is standing behind, watching me, and that all of the mounted men have converged on this one place. Wulfheard is speaking to the older woman, their conversation easy to hear above the murmurs of everyone else.

'My husband died in the fighting,' Edith says, when I sit back from her to examine what I've accomplished so far.

'I'm sorry,' I murmur, and her eyes harden.

'Are you a warrior?'

'I'm training to become one, yes, and a healer.'

'Then you'll kill the men who decimated my village? And killed my husband?'

I meet her gaze. 'If we can, then yes. Are they still there?' I query.

She goes to shake her head, but then stops. 'No, they took all our coins, weapons and metal pots and left, in a ship.'

My heart stills at this, and I feel Ealdorman Ælfstan's hand on my shoulder. He must already have determined that these people were attacked by the Viking raiders. Damn the bastards. It seems to me that they sneak along all of this island's waterways, causing havoc as they do so.

'Then we'll do our best to find them,' the ealdorman confirms, his voice filled with reassurance. I wish I felt the same.

'The water's ready,' Frithwine calls.

'My thanks.' I stand to retrieve it, but Frithwine appears with the bowl, holding it wrapped in his cloak because it's so hot. I smile at him, but he stumbles on seeing the ruin of the woman's face and almost spills the boiled water over himself. 'Just put it there for me.' I indicate the spot on the ground and reach for my supplies to find pigs' gut to knit the wound together. 'Can you put some more on the fire?' I ask him. I've not yet looked at wounds others might have.

Eager to get away from the disfigured woman, Frithwine moves aside, and now I dip a clean edge of the cloth into the water and finally manage to pull aside the more persistent pieces of filth in the wound. Fresh blood pours from it. The woman looks horrified.

'Better it bleeds afresh now,' I assure her.

With careful hands, I thread the needle and begin the delicate task, ensuring I pull the needle away from her line of sight so that she won't flinch.

The ealdorman still watches me, but Wulfheard stands beside him. The pair of them speak quietly, and I can't quite catch their words over my laboured breathing as I concentrate carefully on what I'm doing.

'There you go,' I offer, peering at the five neat stitches to ensure they'll hold. 'Leave them for at least a week, and then have them removed. Keep it clean and dry. And hold your hair away from it so that it doesn't tangle with the stitches.'

'My thanks,' she murmurs, her hand hovering over the

wound, only for her to move it away. 'May I keep the thong for my hair?'

'Of course. Use it well. Now, is anyone else wounded?'

'I believe there are some cuts and bruises,' she offers, standing again, to check where her son is, a strained expression on her face when she sees him still with the older woman. 'Most of the injured died from their wounds. We're the lucky few who survived.'

'Where are you headed?' I ask her.

'North, where there are no rivers.'

I nod, and look to the ealdorman.

'I'll have four of my men escort you to Peterborough Monastery. They'll ensure you arrive safely. There'll be somewhere for you to start again, in the heart of Mercia, if you so wish it. I can guarantee that.'

'Then you have my thanks,' the older woman calls from her place on the cart. 'Come, Edith. Sit with me and your son, and we'll continue on our way.'

While I'm listening to the words, I'm also moving through the other survivors, checking to ensure Edith spoke the truth. But while the women are bruised and have some small cuts, it's only the old man in the cart and another youth, no older than I am, who seem to be badly wounded. And the youngster's long sweeping gash on his arm is showing signs of good healing when I pull his bandage aside.

'I'm Icel,' I say to him. He's sitting on the ground, leaning against a sack he must have been carrying. He raises weary eyes to look at me, and my worry returns. 'Do you have more injuries than just your arm?' I ask him.

He looks at me, sullen-eyed, and I see a conflict there. But his lips are thin and cracked, and the smell of him is slightly off.

'I have another injury. To the inside of my thigh,' he confirms.

'It hurts, from all the walking, but I can't go in the cart. Old Bertrand's in there. My name's Ælhun.'

'Show me.'

He bites his lip and then undoes his trews, wincing as he does so, and the smell of corruption is suddenly ripe in the air. The wound is in a strange place, almost as though he's sat on a seax, or even a spear. The higher up his pale leg the wound goes, the deeper the cut.

'That looks nasty,' I confirm, grateful then that Frithwine has been heating more water for me. 'Wait here, and I'll be back in a moment.'

I thread my way through the mass of people, pleased that the horses have been moved to encircle us and so can't further cramp the small space.

'I need the water, please,' I say to Frithwine. His small fire is already starting to gutter and go out.

'It did boil,' he informs me, wiping an ash-covered hand through his hair.

'My thanks,' and I reach for the bowl, using a wad of linen to hold it, and walk back to Ælhun. He's not moved, and from a distance, he looks even paler than I thought he did. I consider then why these people have no healer amongst them, and quickly realise it could well be that their healer was killed in the attack.

With gentle hands, wincing when my burn mark touches the water which is still not far off boiling, I tend to the wound and clean it. I don't believe it needs stitching, but I do find a wad of moss and soak it in some vinegar.

'This will hurt, but you need to keep it bound around the top part of your leg. I'd also suggest that you ask for a seat behind the woman on the cart.'

Ælhun shakes his head defiantly. 'I'm not sitting with old Hild. She's got a tongue as sharp as whip.'

'Would you sooner rub this and delay the healing longer?' While we speak, I'm also ensuring his arm injury is free from infection. It looks red and angry, but no worse than I'd expect for such a wound. 'When you get to Peterborough, ensure the monks check both of your injuries.'

Ælhun looks defiant once more, but he offers nothing further. Perhaps he has no love for monks. I don't know.

I ease him back to his feet, when the moss is secured around his leg and his trews once more covering the injury. He hobbles a little, but then strides with more confidence, wincing every so often.

'It feels better,' he confirms for me.

'Well, it'll feel even better if you rest it.'

I'm busy tidying away what's left of my supplies and pouring the water away into the clogged drainage ditch of the road. I stand and stretch my back, cramped from all the close work, and realise that the party of refugees is ready to move on. Ælhun has made no effort to seek a seat on the cart, and I determine not to interfere. I don't know these people. Perhaps he and the older woman detest one another for some long-standing feud. I just don't know.

'Uor, Kyre, Frithwine and Cenred, you'll escort these people to Peterborough, and ensure the monks there know they come at my command. It shouldn't take more than a day to reach, perhaps two at the most, at the pace of the ox. Come and find us after that,' the ealdorman instructs them. I notice that the ealdorman is splitting the two brothers, and I think they might argue, but Wulfheard shakes his head to caution Garwulf.

'My lord, perhaps Oswy could also accompany them, or go in place of Uor. His mount is struggling with the pace.'

Oswy glowers at Wulfheard when he speaks, but it's true enough. Even I can see the animal is threatening to turn lame.

'Aye, Oswy, you go in place of Cenred, then.'

Slowly, the cart and the refugees begin to traipse onwards, the ox bellowing at being forced from its rest, and Ealdorman Ælfstan turns to face us all, his expression lined with worry.

'I believed we were securing the border and stopping King Ecgberht, but it seems that we might have Viking raiders to contend with as well. We'll continue as agreed, but we'll also travel to their village and see what we find.'

None of us speaks to argue.

'Well done, Icel. It seems your skills will be well used, even though you're almost a warrior of Mercia.'

I bow my head to acknowledge the praise, but the words remind me that even here, having done what I've been training for throughout my youth, I must still pick up a seax and shield and fight for Mercia. If it came to it, Ealdorman Ælfstan would expect me to fight, not heal. Even now, I battle against that knowledge.

12

We rest that night on the side of the road. The ealdorman allows us to have two fires, and we huddle around them, cooking food and filling our ravenous stomachs, trying to warm cold bodies.

Wulfheard sits beside me. Goðeman and Æthelmod are on watch duty, Goðemon to the east of us. We're stopped on a very slight rise along the generally flat road. From here, it's possible to see a good distance, while the light lasts, which, of course, it doesn't for long at this time of the year.

Ealdorman Ælfstan is not his usual talkative self, and in fact, most of the men are quieter than usual. I can understand why. We thought to have won a great victory over Wessex and her king, but the kingdom is still far from secure. We might have convinced ourselves throughout the winter months that our victory was decisive, but now, in the cold reality of the coming summer, it's evident that's not the case.

'I imagine that bastard, Athelstan, king of the East Angles, has more to worry about than what King Wiglaf might be up to and what alliance King Ecgberht might dangle before him,' Wulfheard mutters as he finishes his food. He's stretched out on the ground before the fire. The night is clear, but cold, the paltry heat from the sun fleeing as quickly as darkness fell.

'You might be right, there,' Ealdorman Ælfstan confirms. 'It'll be up to the king to decide whether to take advantage of the distraction offered by the Viking raiders, or not.'

Ælfstan and Wulfheard, using what local knowledge of the area they have, have determined that the village the refugees lived in must have been somewhere along the River Welland. The river, I now know, runs from inland to the Wash, through something called the Fens, according to Wulfheard, who, as so often is the case, seems to know far more than everyone else about Mercia's extent. He assures me the Fens are a dank place, rife with a strange fever that sends men and women delirious. I don't much want to visit there, if that's so, even if he tells me it happens during the warm weather, and one thing is for sure, it's not warm.

'So, King Athelstan would have been alerted to the Viking raiders?'

'Perhaps. It'll depend on how many people survived,' the ealdorman muses.

I shake my head at this new problem. 'I encountered the Viking raiders, a small party of them, on the borderlands with the Welsh.'

'Aye, lad, you did. But the pestilent scourge get everywhere,' Ealdorman Ælfstan confirms. 'It might only be one ship, or at the most two, but the places they raid are small and unused to such fighting. You might not think we've had much peace during your lifetime, Icel, but when Mercia was superior, no one dared attack her. Not like in Northumbria, and not like over the sea, in the Irish kingdoms. The Viking raiders have been making sporadic attacks ever since they invaded and destroyed Lindisfarne over three decades ago.'

The mood of the encampment is a little dour. I'm not

surprised. The Viking raiders my uncle and I encountered in the woodlands were lethal and confident – a more dangerous combination it would be difficult to find. The fact Cenfrith overpowered them, with virtually no help from me, reminds me of just how skilled he was with seax and war axe. The words of the scop, never far from my mind, return to remind me of just how deadly the Viking raiders can be.

'Icel, you and Garwulf will take the second watch,' Ealdorman Ælfstan informs us, as we're all about to settle into sleep.

I nod, stifling a yawn, while Garwulf growls. It's the worst watch to take, a night interrupted by sleep, and Maneca mumbles something under his breath. I don't doubt it's derogatory.

'They must learn,' Wulfheard growls at Maneca before reaching over and gripping my arm tightly. 'Whatever you do, don't fall asleep when you're on watch.'

I meet his gaze evenly. I want to tell him that, of course, I won't fall asleep, but I'm exhausted, and before I can think of anything clever to say, his snores fill the air, and I join him not long after, words of denial still on my lips.

When Godeman wakes me, I blink grit from my eyes, and suppress a yawn. I feel as though I've only just fallen asleep, but overhead it's black as night gets, the clouds lowering once more. I fear it'll be raining again before too long.

'It's all quiet,' Godeman informs me, before turning aside, to roll in his cloak and sleep.

I stagger to my feet and walk through the darkness, offset only a little by the glowing embers of the fire, to where I believe he was keeping watch. I follow the outline of the slope, and just before it starts its descent, I reach to finger my seax and stand, alert and ready. I yawn immediately. I'm so tired.

From inside the camp, I hear a scuffle and turn, seax drawn, only to hear the murmur of Garwulf and Æthelmod trading places.

I peer into the gloom, returning the seax to my weapons belt, and grit my teeth against the cold that's already making me lose feeling in my feet. There's a slight breeze, clouds scudding overhead against the slice of the moon.

I focus on the moon, and the stars, anything to keep me awake. I hunt for the shapes amongst the stars that I've heard others speak about, but they're just spots of brightness to me. I consider what they are, and where they are, and why they're so small, and my breathing calms. I hear nothing above the odd hoot of an owl and the flap of wings overhead. No small creatures are tempted close to me, and eventually, my legs and feet begin to ache from standing for so long. Even upright, I feel my eyes start to close and pinch my forearm to keep myself awake. Being so cold isn't helping me stay alert. If anything, it's making me even sleepier. I would like nothing more than to wrap myself in a thick fur before a raging fire and sleep until daybreak, if not longer.

I startle to full wakefulness, some noise reaching me that's different to anything else I've heard. What was it?

I strain to hear, hoping I've not truly been asleep, but just resting my eyes.

My hand snakes once more to my seax, and I remove it from my weapons belt. I don't want to be caught off guard and unable to defend myself.

With my heart beating more quickly, I peer into the gloom. It's darker now, even the thin piece of the moon obscured by heavier-looking clouds. I think the rain will start to fall soon and then I'll be soaked as well as cold. The thought is far from cheering. But what have I heard?

I'm not able to tell how much of the night has passed. I don't know if perhaps the noise I perceived was Garwulf exchanging his watch with Ordlaf, or if mere moments have passed, and I still have a long stretch to go.

I try to still my heart, and calm my breathing, even as I strain to hear whatever it was that startled me.

And there it goes again. Now I know I'm not hearing things. There's someone, or something, out there, in front of me, towards the east, where King Athelstan and his East Angles men might be. Or where Viking raiders might have come ashore along one of the three huge rivers that cut the land, such knowledge I have thanks to Wulfheard. There is more than just the River Welland that dissects the kingdom of the East Angles, and runs into Mercia itself. There's also the River Ouse, and the Nene.

I turn my head, first one way and then another, as though I might be able to see something even in the murkiness. For a moment, I consider running back to the camp, waking Wulfheard to tell him that we're not alone, but I've not seen anyone yet. I need to know. I hold out the hope that it might just be a stray sheep or a cow, or perhaps even a wolf or a fox, but then I hear the unmistakable sound of metal and I know I'm not making it up.

I turn to head towards the camp, my eyes seeking out the thin slice of embers I saw before, but all is darkness. The moon has gone, the stars are obscured by the gathering clouds, and my worst fears are realised, as rain starts to thud onto the ground. I slip, my leg sliding out beneath me. I recover my balance, hoping the rain might wake the men better than my alarm, and head in the direction from which the noise of the horses can be heard, alongside the odd fart and very loud snores.

Whatever is out there, they mean us harm. But should I shout and wake everyone, or reach Wulfheard's side and then wake the men silently, so that our enemy don't know we know they're there? I argue with myself, and it takes so long to reach a decision that I'm falling over one of the sleeping warriors before I can even shout.

'What the...' a sleep-fuddled voice demands.

'We're not alone,' I counter, rushing back to my feet, wincing at the pain in my hands and knees from my fall.

With the heavier rain, all of the men are disturbed and, as I rush through them, towards my target of Ealdorman Ælfstan where he sleeps closest to the fire, I urgently whisper the same warning.

The ealdorman doesn't need waking when I reach him. He's already standing, peering at me, hand on his seax. Wulfheard is beside him, eyes white in the gloom, his bright teeth visible where he grimaces.

'I don't know how many or where from, but we're not alone.'

'Garwulf,' Wulfheard mutters.

I'd forgotten about him in my dash back to the camp.

'They come from the east,' I reiterate.

I hope Garwulf isn't dead. I hope his cries of alarm haven't been cut off.

'Bring the horses inside our circle,' Ælfstan informs Wulfheard, who turns to issue the command to those close enough to where we left the horses.

I hear the jangle of harness, but I'm staring out across the expanse I just ran across, and with my eyes narrow, I just detect the flash of something metallic.

'There,' I urge the ealdorman and he focuses on where I'm looking and nods.

'Stand ready,' he urges the rest of the warriors in a low voice that shows no fear. 'Show yourselves,' the ealdorman calls in a voice so loud I jump and almost drop my seax from where I hold it in my right hand. I can feel the ealdorman arching his eyebrows at my actions and feel like a bloody fool.

There's no reply, but I do hear the scampering of feet coming from behind, just one set of feet, and determine that Garwulf has heard the shout and is making his way back to the camp.

'Show yourselves, or there'll be trouble,' the ealdorman tries once more, his voice loud and easy to understand, but there's still no reply. Then I hear the feet of more and more people moving over the area where I kept guard only moments ago. 'Hold yourselves steady, men,' Ælfstan encourages us. 'It'll be short and over quickly, and then our enemy will be dead.'

At that, a howl of derision echoes from the east and the first of our enemy runs at Osmod and Goðeman, where they stand just in front of Ealdorman Ælfstan.

I grip my shield tightly in my left hand, ready for the attack, seax loose in my right hand. It's the first time I've battled with my scarred hand since Londonia. After my encounter with Horsa, I believe it's best to use my more natural hand, no matter the problems of the tightness caused by my scar.

And then, more and more of our enemy surge over the slight hill. I see them more in the flicker of weapons than their actual bodies. It's as though they're coated in the night, with only their blades to give away their presence.

Osmod and Goðeman are already engaged with the enemy. I see a little more, because our foemen are close to us. They carry war axes and seaxes, but have no helms.

'Steady,' the ealdorman roars.

I plant my feet, waiting for the first blows, and Goðeman stumbles before me and falls to his knees. Without thought, I leap into the space left by his departure, shoving my retrieved shield into what I hope is the face of our enemy.

A crunch of bone greets the action, but then I can hear nothing else because our enemy attack and all is chaos and screaming, cries and howls of rage and the thud of weapons against shield.

I feel a weight on my shield, and realise that my foeman is trying to rip it from my hand. I growl low in my throat. With his weight on it, it's difficult to move, and so I stab around it blindly, and my seax meets resistance, although I wince around the pain from my hand. The weight on my shield abruptly disappears, as I feel fluid over my gloved hand. My shield flies upwards with the loss of weight. I quickly hold it level once more, and an elbow emerging from out of the darkness just misses my nose and eyes, which have only just started to lose their greenish shade from Edwin's punch. I watch where the elbow goes and stab out immediately, hoping to catch my enemy beneath his arm.

I'm aware of Osmod battling beside me. He has a shield on his right arm and lashes out with his left. All who come against him, and it's as though they're creatures born from the fenlands and not truly like me at all, judder and die on his blade. They don't even have the chance to skip aside from his violent attack.

And then Wulfheard is next to me, and I'm conscious that the ealdorman has ordered everyone to meet the assault, moving aside from where we camped so that our legs don't become entangled in discarded items left beside the fires. For all we helped the refugees yesterday, and set a guard, I know none of us truly expected an enemy to attack during the night.

I duck a blow that comes from far away, the glimmer of the point of the blade just catching my eyes before it impaled me. I'm grateful I kept watch with my helm in place, even though it was bloody uncomfortable.

I jab and stab, thrusting my shield at any who thinks to get past my guard. Wulfheard and Osmod are doing the same, but in the darkness, it's impossible to see anyone else, until the flames from the two campfires crackle upwards, the warming glow making it easier to make sense of the shadows to either side of me.

My seax is running with blood, but I don't know if I've managed to kill our enemy, or merely arrest their advance. My mouth tastes of blood and sweat and still the enemy comes against us.

'How many are there?' I huff. I feel half-blind, unable to see how many we face, or when the battle might come to an end. Bad enough to fight in daylight, with a shield wall restricting your view, but this is so much worse. I want to keep my eyes forward, but dancing shadows keep dragging my eyes away every time I sense movement.

'Enough,' Wulfheard growls as he replies, the ring of his seax against a shield assuring me that the attack is far from over.

I'm unsure how these foemen managed to travel without detection. Have they been following us, or is this purely bad luck? I wish I knew. They make almost no sound, other than grunts of effort, and so I have no idea if they're Saxons from the kingdom of the East Angles, or Viking raiders, or even the bloody Wessex warriors.

I thrust my shield upwards, even as I stab downwards with my weapon. I can't see my enemy, but I can smell him. He brings with him the scent of stagnant water, and it makes it difficult to breathe, the fog almost choking me. The rain is doing little to clear the smell, even though it falls heavier and heavier, thudding from the sky in a torrent. The ground beneath my feet is slick, either with water or battle dew, and still, I stab and jab with my seax and shield, even though I can see no one. Not even white-rimmed eyes.

But men are dying on blades. I hear howls of pain, some abruptly cut off, others malingering as they attempt to crawl away. I hope Godeman is well and not dying behind me. Something terrible must have happened to him as he's not returned to the fight.

I jab and cut, and a blade looms out of the darkness, scoring a thin line along my scraggly bearded chin, and I shriek with the unexpectedness of it all. I can't see how we can win this.

A shrill whinny from one of the beasts alerts me to the fact that the horses are in just as much danger as my fellow warriors. I turn to rush to them, but Wulfheard senses my movement.

'Stay where you are,' he growls. 'The damn horses will run if they can't evade them. They won't want one of the bastards on their backs.'

Another blade startles me, and I don't have the time to knock it aside with my shield. The point comes so close as to almost take my eye, only for the blade to immediately retract. I follow it, thinking it'll disappear into the darkness, and it does, but downwards. The man who wielded the weapon is dead already.

I suck in a much-needed breath, aware my feet are tangling with lifeless limbs, and then, as abruptly as it started, the battle is at an end. I jab with my seax, but there's no one there, and neither do Wulfheard or Osmod face an enemy.

'What's happening?' Wulfheard huffs, his voice too loud in the silence.

'They've gone,' Ealdorman Ælfstan responds immediately, so I don't know if he was going to say those words anyway. His voice is just as laboured as Wulfheard's and it's then that I remember the horses.

In the still dancing flames of the rekindled fires, I turn to look for Brute, or any of the horses. The view that greets me is horrifying. The reason the flames lick higher and higher is because a man lies, burning in the fire. His hair is a spark of brightness, and then the flames look for fresh fuel along his arms and upper body.

'Who's that?' I call. Should he be one of the Mercians, I think I could attempt to treat him, but the pain will be unimaginable from such burns. Half of the hair sparks abruptly, sending super-heated blues curling over him, and while I squint against the glare, I can't see the body move, not even a finger, or a foot, any sign that he might live, in fact. The man must be dead, whomever he is.

'An enemy,' Wulfheard assures me. 'Garwulf, are the horses well?' he further calls, and I realise then why he was so assured they would be well. 'Garwulf,' he calls again when there's no answer, and I'm not alone in making to move towards where I left Brute.

'Hold your positions,' the ealdorman's tone is sharp with command, echoing despite the driving rain. 'This might be a trick,' he calls. 'The horses haven't been harmed, I believe. Now, stay in position. No one is to move, not even to help a fallen ally. Stay in place. It'll be light enough soon, and then, when we can see once more, we can assess what's happened here. Stay on your feet. All of you,' the ealdorman admonishes, and I consider who's ignored his orders and slumped to the floor. But more than anything, I want to know where Garwulf is and who the dead man is, who even now lights the space behind us as his body burns and crisps, turning the air ripe with the smell and sizzle of fat. I grimace at the sound of the burning flesh, the hiss of the rain doing little to quench the flames. I hope the man is dead. I hope the man is one of our enemies – whomever our enemy might be.

'Goðeman,' I call, remembering the man who fell before me.

A grunt is the response. I'd turn, but I still wouldn't be able to see him.

'I'll live,' he grumbles, voice edged with pain. 'I think,' is his less than reassuring follow-up comment. I can hear him doing something.

'If it's a cut, then bind above it,' I call to him. 'If you've been impaled, don't move, and don't move the weapon.'

'I can't bloody see,' Godeman replies. 'I'll do what I can.'

None of us can see outwards, despite the fire. The rain makes it impossible, even if the darkness could be beaten back.

The night drags. I gasp much-needed air, and try not to focus on the myriad hurts that are making themselves known, most notably on my right hand. My grip has been tight on my blade, tighter than I've had it for many months. My hand aches, and my scar throbs. I could do with a drink, and a piss, but I hold my place, peering into the gloom, trying to see when it's impossible to do so. If the dark wasn't bad enough, the streaming rain is making it even more difficult to perceive anything beyond the edge of my nose. And the noise of it drowns out all but my breathing. For a moment, I feel as though I've lost the use of my ears, and my breath comes suddenly faster until I swallow and realise that it's merely the drumming of the rain on the grass that makes it difficult to hear.

I turn to Wulfheard, and he nods at me in the murkiness. I can see his face but little else.

'You did well,' he assures me, leaning heavily on one leg.

'Are you wounded?'

'No, just winded. I took a heavy blow to my chest with a shield.'

That doesn't mean he's not wounded, but I allow it, and turn to Osmod. The other man stands easily, his shield tight in one hand. Osmod is clearly far from convinced that our enemy is gone. I grip my shield as well. I don't want to be caught unawares once more.

I'm too easily reminded of the battle my uncle was forced to undertake in the borderlands with the Welsh against the Viking raiders. I consider they must be our enemy. Would King Athelstan of the kingdom of the East Angles attack in such a way? In the past, he's been honourable, meeting Mercia's kings on the battlefield, not sneaking around in the dead of night. He might have triumphed in the battles, but that's more because Mercia's kings weren't warriors, as Athelstan clearly must be.

I turn to gaze at the smouldering body once more, trying to determine against the dampening flames if he wears the inkings of those raiders, or if he's a Saxon, but an enemy Saxon. But it's impossible. I feel my legs begin to shake and wish I could sit, or drink, but I stay upright, obeying the ealdorman's words.

I don't know where Ealdorman Ælfstan is. Of those that I can see in the dome of light from the fire, none of them is the ealdorman, and neither is one of them Garwulf. I spare a thought for the young man. I hope he's well. I hope he wasn't caught nearly sleeping on guard duty and that it was the last act he did.

Finally, and slowly, the rain not lifting at all, a thin tendril of light begins to emerge on the horizon. It hovers, grey and uninviting for too long, and it really doesn't lessen the dreariness. The clouds, I realise, are low and forbidding. They promise no let-up in the rain, and I brace myself for a long and dismal day.

I must close my eyes, although I don't intend to, and then, next thing I know, Wulfheard is speaking to me, and it's light enough to see the aftermath of the fight. I turn to Goðeman, and wince to see him looking so pale and almost lifeless on the ground, but he grins at me, and points.

'I've not been impaled,' he confirms, the words more joyful

than I expect from a wounded man. 'But the bastard sliced me, look,' and he points to his leg.

I bend then, examining the length of the injury. It starts just above his right knee, and extends all the way to where his stones rest, cutting his trews in half. I whistle through my teeth, moving closer to get a better look. It's bad, but not terrible.

I look up and see that Ealdorman Ælfstan already moves amongst those who died, Wulfheard at his side. I yawn widely, and scratch my face, swallowing nothing but the salt of my exertions when I lick my lips. As much as I want to know who our enemy were, I need to drink more, and help Godeman.

I make my way to where I briefly slept the night before and retrieve my water bottle. My sack of possessions is sopping wet as I turn to scamper back to Godeman. I lift his possessions, thinking he might appreciate a dry cloak. Only then do I drink, casting a glance at the remains of the body in the fire.

The fire was bright but short-lived, only embers there now. It was certainly not hot enough to fully consume the body, and much of it remains, the bones and any metal the man wore, holding the body together in a parody of the living.

As I greedily drink, I turn to eye Garwulf. He's not with the other men, and neither is he close to the horses. I can see Brute watching me from amongst the other mounts. I make a quick count and realise that all of the horses are there. None of them have been wounded. But where, then, is Garwulf?

'I'm going to bind it for you,' I inform Godeman as I return to his side. There's no warm water, and I can't see that we'll be staying here long enough to get the other fire going again, not when it's so damp. Neither do I wish to go any closer to the dead man.

I open my sack and quickly find all the items I need. I realise that if this continues, I'm going to need to keep much more than just the collection of jars and herbs that I have. I need a lot more linen for bandages as well. Hastily, I find the vinegar, cushioned between my collection of spare rags, and wince as the sharp smell reaches my nose as I fumble the top open with my left hand, not my right. My right hand is cramping. I need to spend some time opening and closing it, and slowly getting the full movement back, just as Theodore informed me.

Godeman watches my actions. 'This is going to hurt?' he asks me wryly.

'Like a bitch,' I concur, and then pour some of the fluid directly onto the wound. The smell is sharp and sour, but he doesn't cry out. I look from what I've done to his face and only then realise that his fists are clenched tightly in an effort to alleviate the pain.

Swiftly, I clear away a few pieces of cloth that have stuck to the wound and then, taking a wad of moss, bind it tightly. When I'm done, the bandage runs from just above his knee to the top of his thigh. It's not going to be easy to ride with such a wound.

'Icel.' The ealdorman summons me.

I stand and dash through the meandering men, busy about the task of trying to find something to eat and drink, to stand beside him and Wulfheard. They look down, sorrowful eyes, and I swallow to see a man wearing Mercia's colours, prone on the floor. I don't recognise him from behind.

'It's Offa. Can you help him?' the ealdorman asks me.

I try to remember who Offa is, but can't place him. Carefully, I run my hands over his back, wanting to turn him to check if he yet lives, but knowing to do so might be foolish. Beneath his byrnie, I can feel no wounds, but that doesn't surprise me. I also check his legs, and that's when my hand encounters the blood. So dark, I can't see it on his clothing thanks to the rain-drenched sky.

I touch his back then and don't feel his chest moving up and down.

'Help me,' I ask Wulfheard, and with a creak of his damp byrnie, he does so.

A cold, white face greets us, the red of Offa's beard making his face seem even paler.

I bow my head. I don't need to look any more.

'He took a wound, to his inner thigh. It was fatal,' I inform the ealdorman.

Ælfstan's face, already bruised and drenched from the rain, looks severe.

'Goðeman took the same, but he'll live,' I tell him.

'My thanks,' Ælfstan offers, but his words are choked.

I look around me then, noting the other bodies. There are perhaps twelve dead warriors. It's not possible to see if they're Mercians or not, but I take comfort in knowing that the ealdorman only asked me to try to aid Offa. He dismisses the others, and so I take them to be our enemy.

'Viking raiders, or East Anglian Saxons?' I ask then, standing, having rubbed my hands through some damp grasses to clear away Offa's dark blood from my gloves.

'Viking raiders, I believe.' It's Wulfheard who answers. Ealdorman Ælfstan looks pensive as he gazes into the distance, or what little of it can be seen. 'They must be the men who attacked the refugees.'

'Then there's a river close by?' I ask, turning, as though I might see one, although I don't.

'Maybe, yes. This isn't good,' the ealdorman confirms. He stands, seax in one hand.

'Did they come from this direction, or surround the camp?' I'm still thinking of Garwulf. I've not seen him yet.

'They surrounded the camp. You raised the alarm, Icel. You did well.'

'And Garwulf?' I take a chance and ask the question, noting as I do so that the ealdorman's lip compress in a tight line.

'He was struck by a heavy object. He's not yet regained his senses,' the ealdorman comments.

Now I understand. Garwulf was overpowered. I consider whether he fought first, or merely succumbed to the attack. I doubt the ealdorman will tell me.

'Shall I ensure he's well?' I ask.

'He's fine. I've checked him this morning. He'll come round soon enough.' There's menace in those words, and I look down, examining my boots so as not to give away how I feel knowing that Garwulf has lost favour with Wulfheard and the ealdorman.

'Gather the dead together,' the ealdorman orders. 'We'll add them to the fire, and leave it as a warning. Now, I need someone to return to the king, and inform him that our threat is now twofold.'

'I'll go, my lord,' I offer.

But the ealdorman shakes his head. 'No, you'll stay here. If we come under attack once more, you're more use to me as a healer as well as a member of the war band. I'll send another. Who has the fastest horse?'

I'm unsure if it's a question I should answer, and I see a flicker of amusement on Wulfheard's tired face. We all know Brute is the fastest of the horses.

'Landwine's mount is quick,' Wulfheard eventually concedes. The man is a good rider, even I can see that.

'Then send him to the king, with all haste.' The ealdorman has turned aside once more, peering towards the east. I consider what he's seeking. Does he believe our enemy is watching us even now? Or is he pondering just how many of them there were and whether their intent is to attack Mercia?

I knew Mercia had more than one enemy, but now, no sooner have we chastised King Ecgberht of the kingdom of Wessex, than another foe has reared its head, and it's not whom I suspected. I look at the dead men, and at poor Offa, and my fingers tighten around my seax despite my intention to rest my right hand. The coming summer is going to be just as bloody as the last. I must still fight for Mercia, and for all I hold dear.

13

Ealdorman Ælfstan is efficient as soon as the bodies have been placed close to the fire, beside the ruins of the half-burned man, and new wood added to the smouldering remains of the previous night's blaze. It'll be an effort, but the flames should begin to consume the flesh of our enemy.

Offa is buried away from the fire, in a shallow grave, making use of a deep field ditch to cover his white, cold flesh. His face, when he's laid into the dark mud, is surprisingly peaceful. I consider whether he knew his death was coming, or if it surprised him. Such wounds lead to a very quick end.

Offa's valuables are taken from him and placed with the rest of his possessions, and tied to the saddle of his horse. The animal looks confused at what's happening, and when we mount to ride out, and Offa has still not returned to her, I hear a faint nicker of complaint.

Garwulf's sent back to the king alongside Landwine, tied in his saddle. The ealdorman will not allow him time to regain his senses. Sooner Garwulf's gone than slowing down the rest of the warriors. Goðeman should be sent away, but he glowers at me, and at Wulfheard, and even at the ealdorman, and he's allowed to remain. The damn fool. The pain he's in is evident in the laboured way he limps to his horse, and the extended time it takes him to mount. Does he not realise how close he came to dying? Does he not see what happened to Offa? I shake my head at his contrariness and catch sight of Oswy as I do so. I'm reminded, once more, that these men are made of greater than their flesh and blood. They have resolve, stubbornness and a refusal to ever admit defeat.

With six men gone from the ealdorman's troop of warriors, I can't help feeling as though we're outnumbered by our enemy. And yet, we killed many of them, eleven all told, and so I hope we might still be equal to the task should we encounter them.

Ealdorman Ælfstan is grim-faced as he announces his orders. 'We continue as the king commanded, but eyes wide, and at a slower pace. This weather is a bitch anyway. Ensure your horses step carefully. We can't afford to lose one of them. Ride in your byrnies, helms and with your weapons to hand.'

We've been doing so anyway, but the truth of what could face us has become a reality. I peer into the eastern lands with more caution now, opening my eyes wide to try to see everything, but the greyness of the day, the rain falling in such huge swathes, makes it impossible. It's not as though there are even any gaps in the rain. It's one vast storm. When I spent a winter in the hut on the side of the hill with my uncle and Edwin, I could stand and watch the rain and snow, see it in the darker patches that flanked the sky. Here, on Ermine Street, it's impossible to obtain such a view. Even the smouldering remains of the fire are impossible to see. Not even the smell of roasting flesh reaches my nose.

'Bloody weather,' Wulfheard grumbles to me. He's hunched inside his cloak, rain pinging from his helm.

'It's always like this here,' another voice grouses, and I spy

Æthelmod, looking fiery with his fury. The ealdorman rides in the centre of the group of remaining warriors. I can't say that anyone looks happy, or settled. It's a far cry from when we left Tamworth and rode with good cheer to Bardney, when they teased me for my black eye. Well, they were in high spirits, I was angry and bad-tempered, my eye thudding with each hoof step. I confess, my grumpiness has left me now, but only to be replaced by fear. 'Be careful underfoot,' the ealdorman cautions once more, as his mount slips and quickly regathers his hooves without mishap.

I feel wet and miserable and, worse, sleep-deprived. I've had no more than a third of my usual rest. Fatigue is threatening to close my eyes, and with it, my grip on Brute's reins. Yet my mount is curiously sedate today. Perhaps he senses the unease, or maybe, and I consider this seriously, he hates the rain as much as the rest of us. Certainly, when I look down, his black coat shimmers with heavy raindrops, and while I wear my helm, I also have my cloak to at least try to drive the rain away from falling down my face and obscuring my vision. Brute doesn't have the same. He rides, head upright, eyes focused forwards. The rain must be stinging his eyes.

More than once, Brute shakes his head to dislodge the water, and I find myself burying my gloved hand in his coat to encourage the water away. It's going to take a long time for him to dry. And the rain is cold as well. The sun is barely visible behind the bank of almost black clouds. I can see that we're going to be forced to stop very early, or risk riding in the dark. I'm unsure of the ealdorman's intentions, but I do have a good idea of his plans.

All too soon, I realise that I'm correct in my thinking, as we veer away from Ermine Street, and begin to trek along a smaller, much less-travelled route, and one which runs alongside a river that gurgles and surges with the vast deluge falling from the sky, the wind picking up small waves along its course. The ealdorman means to visit the village of the refugees, and no doubt, he hopes to find some evidence that the raiders who attacked us were one and the same.

'Aren't we in land that King Athelstan claims?' I offer softly, hoping Wulfheard will hear me without having to raise my voice further. I don't want to announce my ignorance.

'Perhaps not just yet,' is his less than reassuring response. 'I doubt the East Angles king's men will be out in this,' Wulfheard offers sourly. 'No mad bastard should be out in weather like this.'

The path is so narrow that we're forced to ride one behind the other. Ahead, Maneca leads the way. His mount is short and stocky, almost entirely covered by her rider's cloak. I can barely see her, but I know that Maneca has excellent vision. That's been proved on this journey already, when he spied an eagle, far overhead, that none of us could see, although we could all hear the creature screeching her fury.

My unease returns. There are too few of us, and there's no one who knows where we're going or what we're doing. More than once, I'm jostled awake by Brute's missteps, and I almost bite my tongue to stop myself from crying out. My eyes are itchy and painful, and I'm unhappy to be placed in such a predicament. Is this, I think to myself, how my uncle felt when he was sent out on his solitary journeys for the king? Did he fear he was riding into danger, or did he believe his position as the king's man, as a warrior of Mercia, protected him? I wish I'd thought to ask.

We smell the smoke before we see the ruins of the settlement.

''Ware,' Maneca calls, as the day draws ever darker.

I shiver, my fingers cold inside my gloves, my thighs long since beyond all feeling – and my feet and toes? Well, when I finally dismount, I'll be forced to hold on to Brute before taking any steps.

The ealdorman passes the command down the line, and I wince as I try to grip my seax, where it rests in my weapons belt. The cold has made my right hand ache all over again. I can feel the burn as though it only just happened and fear I'll be no good to anyone should we encounter the enemy.

My eyes turn to the river, turgid and grey, running faster and faster with the incessant rain, and I gasp.

'Wulfheard,' I call to him, my voice sharp.

'Aye, lad, I know,' he reassures me.

In the river, there's a glistening white body, turning endlessly side over side, snagged between branches of a low-hanging tree. It might not be from the raider attack, but I imagine it's related.

I lick my dry lips and cough away my thirst, even as Maneca leads us into the remnants of a village. It's a dead place now. I can tell just from looking at the ruins. The homes and what remains of the grain store are smoking shells, the odd puff of smoke erupting from them, revealing just how hot the fires became that reduced the place to little more than a smudge of ash and charcoal on the ground.

There's a small quayside, jutting into the river, and I can see another body wedged in the wooden struts, but there's no sign of a ship.

'Spread out, secure the settlement,' the ealdorman commands. He doesn't dismount, and I take it to mean none of us should, only for Wulfheard to slide from Bada and hand me the reins.

'Stay here and stay out of trouble,' he urges me, slipping his seax from his weapons belt, and taking his shield as well.

He's not alone. Five other men do the same. It's difficult to tell whom everyone is beneath their cloaks and with the rain still falling, but I believe Waldhere, Osmod, Maneca, Cenred and Æthelmod escort Wulfheard. Their actions seem well tested as they separate, weaving a path around the ruins and ensuring the perimeter isn't missed.

I hold steady, barely breathing, turning more than once to check that no one can attack us from the rear, but Wulfgar and Ordlaf are behind me, and they've both turned their horses to peer back the way we've come.

All is silent, apart from the wet slap of something on wood, which I take to be the dead body in the river. Brute is restless beneath me, moving forwards and backwards, and even sidestepping away from the river. I can hardly recall him to order with my hands and legs so cold. Bada nudges him, and the two settle, but I can sense how alert Brute is. He might be tired from the trudge through the rainstorm, but if he must, he'll gallop from this place to ensure he reaches safety.

'It's abandoned,' Wulfheard eventually announces, his voice echoing eerily.

The village isn't huge, but I can tell that it was once wealthy from the thickness of the walls on the dwellings, and the quantity of scorched wooden poles that still stand, eerily marking where the wattle-and-daub walls used to stretch between them. Now, it's as though they're the carcass of a dead animal, alluding to the life that once lived between those blackened bones.

Ealdorman Ælfstan nudges his horse forwards. I follow on behind, curious to see more, and trying not to hear the dead flesh thud from the quayside, which rises even above the dripping rain and the sound of horses on the move.

Along the main street we go, and I get a sense for the size of the place and the number of people who must have died here. There are the remains of a large hall, no doubt used by whoever claimed this place as theirs to rule, whether they lived there all the time or not. To the side of it is another building, which I take to have been a stable or a barn as there's disturbed hay leading from it and the ripe smell of slaughtered animals.

Further down the street are a number of homes and work-shops, a few jars all that remain, their contents disturbed, cracks and missing lids showing they weren't carefully emptied. And there's also what I take to have been a blacksmith by the black-ened earth of a huge hearth at the centre of the building, and another hut that stinks of old water. These people fished the river, that much is sure.

'The dead have all been buried,' Maneca points to another building, away from the others, and I sense that this must have been the church, from the disturbed plots of land that show where the dead now lie, the ground slightly raised, or slightly concave. To walk through the churchyard, I'll really need to keep my eyes open or risk tripping.

The ealdorman has said nothing, but now Ælfstan dismounts and walks among the remnants of the village. He bends to retrieve something, but I can't see what it is. Others have dismounted now as well, and I think I must do the same, or I might never reclaim the feeling in my feet.

'We'll stay here tonight,' the ealdorman confirms, his voice just as echoey. 'There's half a roof on that building there.' He points to one I've not yet seen, set back from the main throughway a little. It'll be a cramped night, that's a certainty. 'Set fires at the perimeter. I want them to know that the place isn't abandoned if they're still close by. Perhaps they'll come and see what happens here.'

I can't quite determine Ealdorman Ælfstan's intent. It's almost as though he wants the raiders to attack.

'Aye, my lord,' Wulfheard confirms.

I don't listen to the rest of his words, more focused on trying to dismount without falling on my arse. I direct Brute to a piece of very green grass, sodden with rain, hoping that if I do fall, it'll be a softer landing. His hooves splash muddy water everywhere, and I realise that if I do fall, I'm not going to get any wetter than I already am, although I don't welcome a sheen of mud to add to the dampness.

'Here we go,' I murmur to myself, forcing my right leg over the back of the saddle with a barely suppressed cry of pain.

I land on the ground, mud reaching over my boots to splash my knees, and turn to see Osmod laughing at me.

'Are you a youth or an old man?' he calls.

I growl, but that only makes him laugh more. I'm not alone in being uncomfortable. I jump up and down on my toes, hoping to encourage some feeling in my feet. Only then do I lead Brute to where the other horses are being encouraged beneath the thin remains of one of the roofs. I begin the process of removing Brute's saddle and bend even lower to place it beneath the slanting edge of the rest of the roof. Everyone else is doing the same. I offer Bada similar, as Wulfheard hasn't returned to his horse, and then I grab handfuls of dubious-looking hay from the floor of the stable and use it to slick the water from both animals' long bodies. By the time I've finished, I can feel my feet and all of my toes again, and even feel warm for the first time all day.

The smell of poorly catching fires reaches my nostrils, and I pity those asked to set them. With the torrent we've endured, I can't imagine there's anything dry for a huge distance around us.

I offer Brute and then Bada some oats, and only then emerge back into the darkening dusk. There's a hive of activity taking place. Ealdorman Ælfstan continues his examination of the ruined buildings, moving amongst them all, and Ordlaf has been given the unfortunate task of removing the body from the quayside. He and Æthelmod are shouting one to another, their distaste for the task easy to hear. And there's no lessening in the rain.

'Wulfheard.' I find him beside the ealdorman. 'I tended to Bada,' I confirm.

'My thanks,' he murmurs, but his eyes are on the ealdorman. I fear I've interrupted an important conversation and go to move away, but then the ealdorman speaks.

'Icel, tell me, what do you make of this?' The ealdorman places an object in my hand. It's cold and hard and yet also very familiar, and I feel my eyes narrow as I hold it up to what little light there is to get a really good look at it.

'It's one of King Ecgberht's coins, proclaiming him as Mercia's king,' I say in surprise.

'It is, isn't it?' the ealdorman mutters, and I look from him to Wulfheard, and Wulfheard looks very far from happy at this unexpected development.

14

'So, this is Mercia then?' I ask into the silence, hoping for them to confirm this for me. Wulfheard doesn't look at me, and neither does Ealdorman Ælfstan. I still don't know the name of the river we've been following for much of the day.

I turn the coin between my fingers. It's a dull silver colour, despite the fact the surface of the coin is sharp and angled beneath my finger. I grip it in my left hand, and it disappears beneath my fingers when I curl them over it. The coin is new. That can't be denied. It might never have been used for any reason other than to pay for a single item. But what was that item? I don't truly want to consider it.

'It could have come from anywhere, my lord,' Wulfheard murmurs, but I know we're all thinking the same thing. It could have come from anywhere, but it must have been minted at Londonia and it must have come straight from there. Has the Wessex king determined to send his enemy to attack Mercia? Or are we all imagining something because of where we are, the dank day and the even more insidious threat of an attack that surrounds us?

'Is this what you found in the debris?' I ask the ealdorman.

He nods, just once, and turns aside, his cheeks lifting in an unhappy scowl.

'What does this mean?' I demand from Wulfheard, and he refuses to meet my eyes as well.

'I can't say, not for sure. But I don't believe it's good. Not this far from Londonia. Yes, King Ecgberht ruled for over a year, but even so, the people of this settlement should trade in the coins of the East Angles, not of the Mercians.'

I swallow down my fear, wincing at the sharp slap of the dead body finally being pulled from the river and no doubt being laid onto the quayside.

'Come with me,' Wulfheard commands, and I follow, uneasy at what I'm going to find, because we're now heading towards the quayside.

The smell of pottage makes my stomach rumble, and I spare a glance towards the half-roofed building under whose thatch others of the men are resting themselves and drying before the large hearth fire. I'd sooner be there, than here.

Wulfheard carries a brand before him, and it sizzles as rain slides over it but manages to stay alight, somehow. No doubt, the rushes must be infused with oil to do so.

At the quayside, the two men are bickering.

'You take his bloody hands, and I'll take his feet,' Ordlaf orders, but Æthelmod already has the feet.

'Bugger that,' he exclaims. 'You get his hands, and I'll carry this part of his body.'

The flesh is shockingly white, a wreath of blond hair almost blinding beneath the light of the brand. I don't know if this man is a Viking raider, but I suspect he is, from the dark band of inkings around the top of his left arm, so similar to the ones I saw on the Viking raiders my uncle killed on the Welsh borderlands.

'I'm not touching his sodding hands,' Ordlaf judders.

I can see that both men are even wetter than I am. They've removed their cloaks and one of them must have been in the churning river water to haul the body upwards, using a rope tied very tightly around his midriff. I think they're lucky the body didn't break into two, what with the flesh that's sloughing from it thanks to being immersed in the water for so long.

'Stop titting about,' Wulfheard urges the two of them. 'You can both take one hand and one foot, and have done with it.' There's no empathy in Wulfheard's voice as I bend to see what killed the man.

I reach out, not truly wanting to touch the corpse but, all the same, yearning to confirm my suspicions. I touch a flap of the severed flesh at his neck, only to jump back as a small wave of water bursts from the cut.

'Urgh.' Ordlaf turns to vomit into the river, and I too have to swallow down my bile at the sight.

'A slit throat then?' Wulfheard confirms.

I nod. I don't believe he needed me to tell him that.

'Any other wounds?' he presses me.

'Well, that depends on whether he had only one eye before the battle, and I don't believe that's the case.' The eye socket is vacant and filled with yet more river water. It's truly a horrifying sight.

'So, he had his throat slit and lost an eye. I hope the bastard who did this lives to fight another day,' Wulfheard muses.

Ordlaf is wiping vomit from his beard, using the rain to clean it. He looks deeply unhappy. 'Can we not just toss him back in the river?' he queries. 'It's easier than carrying him away.'

'No, his body will pollute the water. He needs burying or burning,' I'm quick to counter, earning for myself an evil glance from Ordlaf.

'Then you can bloody carry him,' Ordlaf announces, rubbing his hands together for warmth. I notice that his fingers are almost as pale as the dead man's.

'No thank you,' I reply, hoping Wulfheard won't order me to do so.

'We'll get something to carry him on,' Æthelmod interjects. 'Then we don't have to do more than roll him onto it. I saw a piece of wattle-and-daub fencing over there. It might hold him.' And he walks away, only to curse. 'Bloody bollocks,' he exclaims, hopping on one foot, the rattle of the kicked stone sounding too loud. It's almost too dark to see by now.

'Icel, help him,' Wulfheard says, handing me the brand, so that I can light the way for Æthelmod. The blast of heat close to my head is welcome, although I quickly start to cough, turning into the wind so that the smoke doesn't choke me.

'This way,' Æthelmod directs.

The smell of pottage occasions a further growl from my belly, and Æthelmod laughs.

'You see a body like that, and you still want to eat? Oh, the joys of being a youth.'

I make no response to his comment. I'm not hungry because I saw a body, but rather because I'm just plain hungry.

I follow him, paying careful attention to where I step. Quickly, we reach the remains of another of the buildings, where, for some unknown reason, an entire piece of the wall hasn't burned. Here, I can see that thin strands of branches have been carefully worked through one another to create a kind of lattice. There are chunks of other matter there as well, no doubt to block the many holes.

'Help me,' the older man demands.

I bend to do as he asks, placing the brand in my left hand to make use of my right. The wood is surprisingly smooth, and light, as we turn and retrace our steps. Now, the brand is next to no use, doing more to blind me than to show me the way. But the sound of the churning water directs our steps, and soon we return to the quayside and the dead man.

Wulfheard has remained. He bends and helps the other two place the flaccid body onto the temporary stretcher, and then I illuminate the path towards the remains of the church. Here, Wulfheard takes command. Ordering the man placed on the ground, wiping his hands on his drenched trews.

'We'll tend him in the morning, when we can see further than the end of our noses,' he commands. 'I'm bloody starving.'

Without a backwards glance, we all return to the dubious shelter of the half-collapsed roof. As I thought, there's little room for us all, but the rest of the men make way for us so that we can all sit beneath the slanting roof, staring out at the ruined settlement while we eat our fill and eventually wrap ourselves, still drenched, in our cloaks and sleep. I'm grateful to be spared watch duty that night, my eyes closing before I'm even lying down.

* * *

The following morning, every part of my body aches, and when I open my eyes, I have another man's stinking arse in my face and someone else pressed tightly to my side. I can hardly breathe, as I focus on my surroundings.

Æthelmod grins down at me, already standing and awake. 'Here, I'll help you up. We need to burn the dead man,' he informs me.

I shudder at the thought, but grip his hand and emerge from the mass of bodies with a soft plop. Many of the men still sleep, but not the ealdorman and not Wulfheard. And two others have already resurrected the fire and, again, the smell of pottage wafts through the air.

Outside, it's a whole new world. The sun isn't shining, but there's a soft white glow to everything. Stretching and groaning at the same time, I realise that it must be far warmer than the day before, now that the incessant rain has stopped, for fog curls from the river, shrouding all.

'You can't see in front of your nose.' I glower, following Æthelmod to where the men have been using the remains of a mud-cut ditch as a latrine. I empty my stream and then turn. It's difficult to get my bearings. I can't even see the shelter of the night before, although the sound of the river does give some inkling of where we are.

'Ealdorman Ælfstan called in the guards for the third watch. Said there was no damn point as no one could see anything.' Even sound moves strangely on days such as this.

'Which way?' I ask.

'This way, but we need to collect wood first.'

'Can't we just use the remains of one of the buildings?' I grumble. It would be much easier than finding enough dry combustibles.

'They're all wet,' Æthelmod announces. 'They won't catch fire, and the ealdorman says we can't leave until the man is burned.'

I shake my head. The ealdorman has given us a thankless task.

Staying close to Æthelmod, I follow him as he meanders between the old buildings. I hope he knows where he's going. The wrecks of this place seem to appear with regularity, but all of them startle me, black hulks taking shape through the layer of thick cloud. Anyone could be out there and we wouldn't know.

More than once, my aching hand strays to my seax, and I turn my head, hearing the slightest sounds and assuming the enemy have returned.

If Æthelmod notices my unease, he doesn't comment, as he leads me unerringly towards a small plot of trees, their branches sagging with the dampness of yesterday.

'Through here,' he continues.

As we forge a path, the fog seems to ease and we can finally see more. I turn to Æthelmod and grin. 'How did you know this was here?' There's a pile of logs neatly stacked on the ground, just waiting to be used in someone's hearth.

'I was on guard duty last night,' he smirks. 'I fell over them. Come on, the sooner this is done, the better.'

Eagerly now, I bend and lift as many logs as I can in my arms.

I ignore the small earwigs as I can't dislodge them, and when I can carry no more, retrace my steps and emerge once more in the gloomy day. As we stack the wood around the body of the dead man, I take a final look at him. Nothing's changed now he's dry, although his skin has lost the soggy look of a body kept in the water too long.

'I wonder who he was?' I ask Æthelmod.

'Who cares? He's dead now, and I'm pleased about that. One less for us to kill.'

I shrug. Æthelmod's correct.

We collect more logs and then set a brand to the drier wood and watch the flames begin their work. Only when we can be reassured that the blaze will do its job do we return to the rest of the men, and it's only just in time.

'Shield wall,' the ealdorman calls, his voice emerging from the fog.

I open my mouth to argue because we've not eaten, although

it seems everyone else has, but the thunder of horses' hooves from somewhere close by makes me snap my mouth shut and instead reach for my seax once more. What's happening now?

15

Hands on seaxes, Ealdorman Ælfstan urges us to form a defensive line in the middle of the fog-shrouded ruins of the settlement. I taste bile and wish I'd had a chance to eat something or drink something before setting the body ablaze.

Wulfheard glowers at me from beside the ealdorman, and I return the look. It's hardly my fault if we have an enemy coming towards us now. But, I consider, that's probably not what the look is for. I'm just behind the ealdorman and Wulfheard. He no doubt wishes I'd consigned myself to the back of the group, where the men with less experience should stand. I know the men say I don't know my place.

'My Lord Ælfstan.' As the pounding of the hooves ceases, the voice rings out through the fog, and I immediately relax. It would be difficult not to recognise Oswy's tone.

'Oswy.' The ealdorman returns the call. 'Why have you returned?'

With that, the four warriors that the ealdorman sent away with the refugees emerge from the bank of thick clouds. Oswy,

Kyre, Frithwine and Uor. I consider if they've met Landwine and Garwulf on their journey.

'My lord.' Oswy is riding a different horse to his usual mount. The animal looks strong and well, breathing heavily, but easily able to take Oswy's weight. They must have been riding all night to reach us, or have risen very early. 'The king has summoned you to Peterborough.'

'Why?' the ealdorman queries, but he's already directing us to mount up and follow Oswy and the others back along the track we took only yesterday, to discover the remnants of this place.

'He's heard of the raiders, and, also, there's something else.' Oswy looks around fervently, and Ælfstan beckons him closer. I'm trying to watch and listen, but the line of men has once more spread out, and so whatever happens between the two is lost to me because I'm now close to Frithwine, and think he might tell me, but his lips are set in a thin line.

I cast a look back the way we've come, relying on Brute to keep our path straight, and see a burst of orange, no doubt from the funeral pyre. The fog is beginning to lift, but ahead, the way is still blank to me. The sound of hooves over the sodden ground is all I can hear from the front of the line of horses and warriors.

I consider why King Wiglaf has countermanded his own orders so quickly. It must be something to do with the Viking raiders, as Oswy announced, but there's evidently something else happening as well. I wonder what that might be, as I follow the horse in front of me, a dappled animal, a little shorter than Brute, ridden by Cenred. Cenred makes no attempt to speak with me, and in fact, the line of men is remarkably quiet, until, at some indeterminate time much later, we finally emerge from the fog to be greeted with a brighter landscape. I wrinkle my forehead and turn to face back the way we've come. The fog still lingers there.

'The water,' Cenred informs me, now we can ride more than

one abreast. 'The water clings to the fog. It's often sunny here, but not there.'

'Ah, my thanks,' I mutter, looking for the ealdorman and Wulfheard. Both of them ride ahead. Now that we can see, they've spurred their animals onwards, and we all ride at a much faster pace. Oswy remains close to the ealdorman, whereas Kyre and Uor lead the way. I'm not to get any answers, not yet.

I peer into the heartland of Mercia, seeking out the telltale sign of smoke, as though that might answer my questions. But there's nothing to see. The day is clear, not particularly warm, but I feel warmer anyway, just from seeing the sun and finally being free from the cloying fog and the rain of the day before. The smell of ripe, damp ground is redolent in the air, and I almost enjoy the ride, despite my worries about what this summons might mean. I'll get my answers eventually, I know that.

As the day descends once more into the night, the fug of smoke over a settlement assures me that we've either reached our destination or that we won't be sleeping under the stars that night. The sound of a solitary voice speaking in a garbled tongue is the next thing I hear, and I know we've reached the monastery then. I've never been to Peterborough before, although I've heard of it on many occasions.

I seek out the complex of buildings. Peterborough is a Mercian monastery. It's been tempting King Athelstan of the East Angles ever since he was proclaimed as lord of his kingdom, but, as of yet, he's not taken command of the place. I can understand why it's appealing. If I'm right, it's just inside Mercia's border. The buildings are large and of good construction, with a wooden palisade and ditch encircling it, built mostly of Mercian oak, Mercian branches and Mercian shit, while worn stone comprises the church, with its small tower above it. It's rare to find a church built entirely of stone.

It's a hive of activity, with men and women rushing in and out of the gateway that looks out on to the river gurgling beside it. The land is remarkably flat, aside from the complex of buildings, and the river seems almost too close. I wouldn't be surprised if the river level has risen thanks to the prolonged rain of the last few days.

I can hear chanting coming from the church. It must be time for one of the holy offices.

'My lord.' A strong formation of ten watchmen allows Ealdorman Ælfstan entry to the complex after we've crested a sturdy-looking wooden bridge. They watch us with hard eyes as we follow him inside the walls. There are horses everywhere. It's chaos, just as when we went to Bardney. And then King Wiglaf emerges from inside a long, wooden hall, his eyes on the ealdorman before I can even dismount.

Given the vantage of Brute's height, I remain where I am, curious as to what's happening.

'You encountered the Viking raiders?' the king demands, his voice tight with fury.

'Yes, my lord king. We killed as many as we could.'

'You did well, but there's a bigger problem, as Oswy told you. Now, come with me. I'd heed your counsel.'

Jumping from the back of his horse, the ealdorman turns to Wulfheard, and some words are exchanged between them, and then the ealdorman is gone.

'Get down here, Icel, and I'll tell you all you need to know,' Wulfheard calls, as soon as the ealdorman is just out of sight. I startle, unaware that I'd been seen, but, of course, a solitary youth sitting on his horse when all others have dismounted was perhaps going to bring me to Wulfheard's attention.

He waits for me, while the rest of the men move their horses to where there's water and feed for them, and I eye him, a little reproachfully.

'Curiosity might well be the death of you,' Wulfheard muses, censorship and humour in his words.

'I just...' I start, but he shakes his head.

'Or it might aid you, who knows?' And he shrugs his broad shoulders. 'The king has summoned Ealdorman Ælfstan to discuss an emerging situation with King Athelstan of the East Angles.' Immediately, my hand reaches for my seax, but Wulfheard shakes his head once more. 'It's not of war against one another, but rather the talk of a united war against a common enemy that drives this sudden change.'

I feel my forehead furrow in consternation at the words.

'King Athelstan wishes to make a temporary alliance with the king. It seems, the Viking raiders we encountered are the least of the problems for the kingdom of the East Angles. There are at least two other ships wreaking havoc on the waterways. King Athelstan thinks to involve Mercia because some of these waterways reach into Mercian land and affect Mercians.'

'So, there are more of them?' I ask, just to be sure I've understood what Wulfheard is telling me.

'Yes, there are more of them, and King Athelstan believes that if Mercia and his kingdom work together, they can better deal with the menace. He was prepared for a truce anyway. Now it seems, he has even more need of one.'

I feel my mouth open in shock. 'And the king means to do this?'

Wulfheard shakes his head and bites his lip in thought. 'The king doesn't know what to make of it all. He fears a trap, and yet, the presence of the Vikings raiders, and what we saw in that village, can't be denied. The refugees we found are also a testament to what happened.'

'And what if the two sides do join together?' I ask. I can't see it happening. The Mercians have no love for the men of the East Angles, not since they killed not one, but two kings, and sought their independence. It comes back to what Ealdorman Sigered attempted to bring about, with the connivance of the queen. No one was happy then. No one will be happy now, even if both kingdoms face a common enemy. And, of course, there is the matter of King Ecgberht's name on the coin in the destroyed village.

'What if, indeed,' Wulfheard muses. 'Now, tend to your mount. I can't see our stop here will be anything but brief. Take Bada with you. I'll follow the ealdorman,' Wulfheard confirms, and I sigh softly. Once more, I have two horses to tend to before I can think of filling my aching belly.

The chanting of the monks in the monastery buildings is a strange counterpart to the mundane task of cleaning and feeding the two horses. Brute might be badly behaved for me, but just as when Wulfheard is around me, he's strangely pliant with Bada watching on. I eventually leave the two animals, saddle-free and contentedly eating hay, and make my way to where the rest of Ealdorman Ælfstan's warriors have long since disappeared, having only one horse to contend with.

Thinking myself all alone, I'm surprised when Oswy matches my steps. I eye him and he explains.

'My horse just needs rest, but no one here has had the time to feed her, or clear out her stall.' It seems, then, that I'm not the only one to have two horses to care for.

'What happened when you arrived here?' I ask.

'The king was already here. Our encounter with the refugees had occurred long after King Athelstan had already considered some sort of peace accord and had sent a messenger to King Wiglaf. I heard he's already lost two of his ealdormen in surprise attacks along the River Nene and the River Ouse. These Viking raiders have chosen their paths wisely, evading the larger settlements, and preying on the weaker ones. King Athelstan is said to be incensed. He sent one of his three remaining ealdormen to speak with King Wiglaf because he didn't wish to leave his kingdom at a time like this. The two met at Peterborough only yesterday.'

'And what will those men who survived the last attack on King Ludica make of this alliance?'

'I can tell you I think it a bad idea,' Oswy confirms, shaking his head unhappily. 'Should the Viking raiders decimate the kingdom, and kill all the ealdormen, then Mercia can reclaim it, just as King Ludica wanted to do.'

I breathe deeply at those words. Oswy won't be alone in thinking them. I believe that perhaps King Wiglaf would be foolish to even ruminate on the possibility. He'd made it clear before that he didn't want to consider this alliance, but it's evident he's changed his mind, and that makes me believe he'll agree to it.

Inside the wooden hall, a large fire warms the tight space, and it's cramped with so many warriors inside it. I seek out the king and find him deep in conversation with Ealdormen Ælfstan, Beornoth and Tidwulf. I look for the refugees as well and find them on another one of the benches, close to the fire. They all have rosy faces and have lost the terror that infused their features when we first met. I also see those I healed, pleased to note they all still live.

'Shift your arses,' Oswy instructs Landwine. Along the row of men, a strange dance takes place where they all have to stand and move further up the bench, one after another. I watch them, knowing there'll be no room for me, and wanting nothing more than to grab a piece of bread from the board before them. And then I hear a clatter. Looking up, a smile splits my lips. There was only so far they could all go, and now poor Frithwine has been upended onto the floor, running out of bench to sit upon.

He glowers at the others as he attempts to reclaim his seat, while Kyre, taking pity on me, reaches over to the centre of the table and hands me a piece of bread. I eat it eagerly. It has the vestiges of heat. I didn't expect to eat fresh bread with so many warriors in attendance.

I stay standing as a bowl of watery pottage is placed into my hand by Wulfgar and I eat eagerly. If there are this many Mercians here, some of us will need to sleep outside, I'm sure of it. I'm already eyeing up where I can place my head when the king calls everyone to attention from his place at the front of the hall.

'My fellow warriors.' The king's voice is infused with authority.

I once thought King Wiglaf a man who grasped a position he had no right to hold. My uncle believed the same. But, in recent months, circumstances have made Wiglaf Mercia's strongest hope and he's growing into his role with every day. A pity, I think, he's saddled with his wife and unpromising son.

'We hear reports of Viking raider attacks along the waterways, even close to the monastery. We have people here, amongst us, who have survived such attacks.' The king indicates those we sent to Peterborough, and they all look uneasy at suddenly being the centre of attention. 'I've received a plea for mutual assistance from King Athelstan of the East Angles, from this man, Ealdorman Herefrith, sent by King Athelstan.'

I'd not noticed this man on the dais earlier. Now I eye him with surprise. He's not a tall man, but rather wiry, and really rather old. He must have known King Beornwulf, and even King Coelwulf when he was Mercia's king. I consider what stories he might be able to tell me of that time. I contemplate whether he was at the battles that killed both kings Beornwulf and Ludica.

'King Athelstan has called on us all, as the united Saxons, who share illustrious ancestors and trace our descent from the god Woden, to defeat this terrible enemy. King Athelstan tells of men and women tortured, raped, beaten and killed just trying to protect their children and livestock. Ealdorman Herefrith here has witnessed babes ripped unborn from their mothers' bellies.'

Now there's fury in the hall. I see men reaching for their weapons belts as though the enemy were here, now. It's one thing to face the Wessex bastards, and even the East Anglian ones, in battle, but to have people attacked just for going about their day-to-day business is something else entirely. Men and women who tend sheep and fish for their livelihoods are never likely to triumph over men sworn to kill all they encounter.

'The agreement is simple. We'll scout the rivers – the East Anglians from inside East Anglia, the Mercians from inside Mercia's borders – and we'll ensure the Viking raiders are forced from the two kingdoms if they don't die on our bloody blades.'

This announcement receives exclamations from the warriors.

The agreement sounds reasonable enough to me. No one is being asked to fight on another's territory, no matter that we are all Saxons, as King Wiglaf has reminded us.

'The East Anglians will simply force the Viking raiders over the borders into Mercia,' a disgruntled cry rings out.

I nod my head. Whoever speaks makes a good argument.

'Aye, and we can do the same to them,' another calls.

King Wiglaf, the hint of a smile on his lips, holds up one hand. I cast my eye over Lord Herefrith. His expression is surprisingly bland.

'I'm aware the solution is not without its problems,' Wiglaf confirms. 'But I'm minded to agree to it. After all, these Viking raiders seek Mercia along the lengths of the rivers that begin at the East Anglian coastline. The East Anglian warriors are taking more of a risk than my Mercians. We're merely here to ensure that none manage to slip beyond their guard and into Mercia as Ealdorman Ælfstan encountered a few nights ago when one of his men was slain. We'll send men along the Rivers Nene, Welland and Ouse, as far as we can reach into the kingdom of the East Angles.'

'And what of the southern border?' Again, a voice demands more details.

I nod along. Thanks to Wulfheard, I'm aware that the River Ouse breaches Mercia high on the eastern border, and the other two rivers, even higher.

'King Athelstan has avowed there'll be no attacks into Mercia from further south. His focus is only on the Viking raiders, and not on attacking Mercia.'

An uneasy acclamation ripples through the crowd. I eye the men I've been riding with. Frithwine, standing at the far end of the board, shows little to no interest at all, but others are clearly unhappy. Kyre and Wulfgar both have mutinous expressions on their faces. I imagine that they both lost friends in the battles against King Athelstan. I pity them having to now think of the man as an ally of Mercia, even if the alternative is equally disquieting. Garwulf looks perplexed by what's happening, but then, Landwine said he'd not long since woken from his stupor.

'Tomorrow, I'll have Ealdorman Tidwulf begin to journey north once more, to the River Welland. Ealdorman Beornoth will take the River Ouse, and, Ælfstan, you'll have the shorter journey, to follow the River Nene back to the borderlands, and you'll have Ealdorman Herefrith as your guide.'

Each of the three ealdormen inclines their head in agreement, but my eyes focus on Ealdorman Herefrith. I've realised there's a small collection of warriors with him. They sit close to the front of the hall, within easy sight of Herefrith, and he has two of his warriors standing to either side of the dais as well. Herefrith looks like he'd slip away easily enough, if there was trouble. I can't say the same for his two warriors. Both of them are hulking giants. I imagine they're there to intimidate rather than because they actually possess great skill.

'I would drink to the success of this joint venture,' King Wiglaf finishes. 'And when King Athelstan realises the worth of Mercia's intervention, I'm sure the agreed price will be readily paid,' he further informs his warriors.

The ealdorman of the East Angles shows a flicker of mutiny at such words, and I consider what Wiglaf is trying to extract from the kingdom that was once part of Mercia. Maybe, after all this time, he means to have some sort of geld paid to Mercia to counter the loss of the taxes and easy trading routes since the kingdom declared its independence. Or perhaps he demands the wergild for two dead kings. Such a cost could devastate a kingdom. The wergild for a thegn is twelve thousand shillings. For a king, it must be many times more.

'Wonderful,' Wulfgar murmurs below the desultory drinking to this new venture.

King Wiglaf is unperturbed by his warriors' less than fully appreciative response. I catch sight of Ealdorman Ælfstan, and he too looks less than enamoured of what we must now do. At least, I think to myself, we're not now riding to war but, rather, to stop the Viking raiders before they can actually get more than a toehold inside the Mercian kingdom. Perhaps it is war, after all.

16

The East Anglian ealdorman and his ten warriors ride before us as we set off along the western side of the River Nene, having crested the wooden bridge once more. It's not raining, and there's no fog. For once, it's almost warm beneath the glow of the sun. It's a stark contrast to the last few days.

Ealdorman Ælfstan has taken his warriors to one side and spoken to us all. We've been warned not to start a fight with the warriors of the East Anglian ealdorman. I think those words were specifically meant for the uneasy warriors, those who'd rather kill one of their allies than accept they are an ally.

I've yet to decide what I think of these men. I accept their bravery, in coming on to enemy land. I also appreciate that the king of the East Angles is either a desperate man or a cunning one. I've ensured my seax is sharp, and my byrnie free from any rust after the rain and damp conditions we endured. I've also ensured I've stretched my body from the tight confines of last night's sleeping place. When the Viking raiders attack, I'll be ready and prepared for them. I think. I've also spent some time exercising my right hand. The skin remains tight though. It's well covered with a coating of the salve Wynflæd made for me before I left Tamworth.

'It won't be far, and we'll reach the border,' Wulfheard assures me. His opinion on what we're doing isn't hard to determine. He's not uneasy, but neither is he happy about it. 'And then we can bring this farce to an end.'

The river here is wide, the far bank a very cold and wet swim away, and one that the horses will probably enjoy far more than the riders.

'Will the Viking raiders not simply use their ships and go to the far side?' I ask, curious as to why everyone has crossed the river and now rides on this side.

'No,' is his only response. I think, perhaps, this might have been overlooked when settling the arrangements. I think of the words of the scop. Of how he spoke of the blood and slaughter that the Viking raiders bring with them. And I consider all that I've seen of these men. Are they, as my uncle told me, all desperate for food? Or is it something else that drives them onwards? I know of the attack on the holy island of Lindisfarne, for all it happened decades before my birth. I know the Viking raiders stole and killed. I know that ever since there have been periodic attacks on other areas of this island, but why there are three ships now, I just don't know. This has the feeling of something else about it. Do these men merely mean to attack and return to their homes, far to the north and over the whale road, or are they after something more tangible? Do they seek battle glory?

The Viking raiders who attacked us on the side of Ermine Street were lethal, for all we killed many of them, in the end. They had no problem striking at night. They thought to take us unawares and showed no fear when their attack was discovered.

While the East Anglians ride at the front, to the rear, Oswy and Wulfgar are on watch duty. It's to be hoped that the Viking raiders won't come from behind us, but the ealdorman is taking no chances. And while the three ealdormen of Mercia perform their tasks, King Wiglaf has determined to remain at Peterborough. He, and his household warriors, will ride out in assistance, should this prove to be more than just a simple exercise in ensuring the rivers are clear of our joint enemy.

I'm unaware of whether Ealdorman Ælfstan spoke to Wiglaf of his suspicions regarding the coin we found at the abandoned settlement. I must assume he has. Perhaps that's why Wiglaf has determined to assist King Athelstan. Perhaps there's a worry that rather than just trying to ally with the East Anglians, King Ecgberht has also attempted to make allies of the Viking raiders. But what do I know?

Garwulf has finally recovered from being knocked insensible. He sports a rather evil lump beneath his hairline, but one only visible when he reveals it to me, as he has. I've winced and consoled him. He laughed it off. Garwulf, it seems, isn't about to be left behind.

Behind me, Frithwine and Garwulf are engaged in a wearying conversation. I wish I could not listen to their words, but it's impossible.

'You're wearing my cloak, and I'd have it returned to me,' Frithwine orders his brother.

'It's my cloak, brother, and you well know it,' Garwulf counters. 'See, there's a mark on it here, and that makes it mine.'

'No, that's the mark I made with my seax to stop these tedious arguments,' is the hot reply.

'No, it's the mark I made to ensure you'd always know which cloak was mine,' Garwulf retorts angrily. 'If you'd not mixed our cloaks, we wouldn't be having this argument.'

'I didn't mix the cloaks, you did, and I know you did it

purposefully because the cloak you wear has been better treated against the weather. I know it because it kept me dry when you were wet.'

I shake my head at the querulous tone of the two brothers. But both cloaks do look identical, and I can imagine it must be easy to confuse them. Perhaps it would have been better if any distinguishing marks had been made with more thought, and remembered, by both of them.

I allow their words to tumble all around me, trying to think of anything else. The matter of the coin has plagued my sleep, and I've tossed and turned, only perhaps truly sleeping when the grey edges of the new day started to lighten the room. For all that, I feel well-rested, even if my thoughts are consumed by the motivations of the Viking raiders in the kingdom of the East Angles. Would the Wessex king truly invite an enemy into his Saxon neighbours' kingdoms? I can't easily dismiss the notion. I think it is likely. King Ecgberht is certainly ambitious, and he believes he should rule Mercia, so why not the East Anglian peoples as well, as the Mercian kings once did? King Ecgberht has shown he's a man with massive ambitions. He took Mercia, he also tried to quell the Northumbrians and the kingdoms of the Welsh people. Perhaps his dismissal from Londonia is only a temporary setback for him.

Brute is steady beneath me. Perhaps an evening spent close to Bada has settled him. Or maybe he's just determined to enjoy the warmer weather. After all, what is there to complain about? We ride at a steady trot, the pace set so that the horses can tolerate it for a long time. Admittedly, the smell from the river is occasionally a little too rich from all the rain that's fallen recently. There's little space between the water and the riverbank, but the river hasn't overflowed itself and, hopefully, won't do so.

'And you have my seax.' The words of the two brothers once

more disrupt my thoughts. 'See, mine has the better blade, the one that I've spent a great deal of time sharpening. This one is far from as sharp. I doubt it'll be much good for cutting through the finest silk,' Frithwine complains. I roll my eyes at the two of them.

'No, it's my seax, and you know it. Look, it fits my hand better.'

I turn then, curious to see if the two are riding with their blades drawn just so they can argue over who has whose weapon. And, of course, they are. If the horses should spook or if we should have to rein in sharply, they'll cut themselves, or their mounts, and it'll hurt, whether the blade is blunt or not.

'Put them away,' a voice barks before I can suggest the same. Æthelmod, riding behind them, sounds furious. 'We have no need for them at this time, and so they should be on your weapons belt. You could slice through your horse's neck with that.'

'It's not a problem,' Garwulf announces haughtily. 'We're not small children. We know how to handle our weapons.'

'Do you now?' Æthelmod offers. 'And were you taught to ride with blades unsheathed? I don't believe you were.'

I think Frithwine will argue, but at that inopportune moment, Brute gives a shiver of fright. I redouble my grip on his rein, as his rear legs kick out, and suddenly we're rushing along the line of warriors, while outraged shrieks greet Brute's antics as horses react to the thunder of his hooves.

I haul on his reins, unsure what's spooked him, although a flicker of brightness close to his head makes me think it's just an insect or a fly. My damn horse is a monster but frightened by the smallest of things.

This time, rather than fearing Brute will run and run and never stop, I have a little more respect for my skills. If I can just stay mounted, then he'll stop eventually. When hauling on his reins has no impact at all, I bend low, over his shoulders and allow the passage of wind to dislodge the front of my hair, where it escapes beyond the confines of my helm. With half an eye to where we're going, and the other half on where we're passing, I try my best to guide him with my hands and knees, even as I speak to him, hoping he'll hear my words over the rushing of his gallop.

We overtake the East Anglian ealdorman and his warriors, shocked cries reaching me on the wind, but Brute is still far from reassured. He dashes onwards. If we're not careful, we'll be in the kingdom of the East Angles, and for a moment, I fear we might encounter the Viking raiders alone. And then Brute stops. The movement is so abrupt, that I only just keep my saddle, breath heaving through my tight chest, as I bend and rub his shoulder, before getting a good look around me.

We're still by the river, and as I turn, I can just about see the rest of the warriors, provided I squint against the glare of the sun.

'What was that about?' I ask Brute.

His lack of reply, as he bends to nibble on grasses bowed by the weight of the rain, reassures me that whatever it was, it's over with. For now.

I consider returning back the way we've come but can see little to recommend such an action. I decide to stay where we are. There's no sign of any enemy close by, and the surface of the River Nene is smooth here. There are no bodies in the water, borne along by the current, and no sign of any enemy ships either. The land and river are remarkably flat. I can see a good distance all around me.

I don't believe we've ridden past any settlements, but there's a smudge of smoke on the horizon to assure me that the men and women of the kingdom of the East Angles do make the riverbank their home. The air is scented with the vestiges of a good downpour, but it's not raining. I consider whether the smell is always

so fruity. There are marshes close by, beckoning to the unsus-
pecting traveller.

'What are you doing?' an angry voice calls to me from some
distance away. I turn back and see one of the East Anglian
warriors. He rides a chestnut animal, snorting loudly as it trots
towards me. I can see where the beast has been run at a faster
speed, but has been slowed.

'He startled. A butterfly, I believe. Damn thing. Being terrified
of something as small as that.'

The warrior, an older man, with grey hair and a beard turning
all too white, narrows his eyes as he comes closer. His eyes take in
Brute's size and obvious power, and then he nods. 'They can be
stupid, sometimes,' he confirms, and settles to wait beside me.
'It's happened before?' He speaks into the silence. I imagine he's
considering the lack of response by any of the Mercians to what's
just happened.

'The first time I rode him, he took off quite fast. I had some
help on that occasion,' I confirm. I'd not expected to spend the
morning talking of my horse with a man who should truly be my
enemy but isn't. For the time being.

'He's a horse worthy of a king. Who are you?' he queries, his
words filled with respect and also confusion.

'I'm no one, not really. The horse was a gift from the king,
though,' I confirm.

'So, you're beloved of your king?' the man presses.

I wouldn't really call it that, and neither would Wulfheard,
but I nod my head. After all, the man is an enemy. I should
present myself as being one of the king's warriors, even if Wiglaf
wouldn't claim me as such.

'I performed a small service for the king, and received the
horse in exchange.' I smile, trying not to think of the result of that
small service.

'Kings must reward their warriors well.' The man almost smiles, although his lips are set in a tight line. I can't determine what he means with his words. 'I'm Godwulf, oath-sworn man to Ealdorman Herefrith. I was once a man of Mercia, but then the kingdom fell to King Athelstan, and he's now my lord.'

'I'm Icel. Oath-sworn man to King Wiglaf.' I realise as I say those words that I've never given an oath to Ealdorman Ælfstan, and neither has he ever asked for one. I imagine that the majority of the men I ride beside have spoken the words of commendation to their ealdorman. I consider then why I haven't. I might chaff about my oath to the king, but I would happily offer myself to the ealdorman.

'Icel. An unusual name,' Godwulf replies, slowly.

'I don't know,' I shrug my shoulders. 'I've never truly considered it.'

'Ah, well, then you should know it's most unusual. I once knew a man who had a young nephew called Icel. We were allies, for some time, until the split with Mercia.' I feel my chest tighten at his words. 'It was a strange relationship. I never knew who the boy's father was, and he was a tight-lipped individual. Would that happen to be you, the nephew? Are you Cenfrith Lord of Budworth's nephew?'

'I am, yes,' I confirm. 'Unfortunately, my uncle died last year, fighting against the Wessex bastards.'

A flicker of sorrow crosses Godwulf's face, but I hardly notice it. For a moment, I considered that he might have news of who my father was, but he's made it clear he doesn't.

'And have you, young man, determined the identity of your father?' Godwulf questions.

'I have not, no. And you don't know who it is either?' I ask him, just to be certain.

'No, I don't. But your mother was a beautiful woman. She

could have married the king for all I know. Your uncle was very protective of her. Whoever she married, it would have been a good match. A pity she died birthing you.'

I open my mouth to say more, but of course, the rest of the mounted warriors have joined us by now. Ealdorman Herefrith wears a scowl on his lined face. His cheeks are flushed with the speed of their passage.

'Control your bloody horse,' he orders me, and I bow my head, moving aside to allow the East Anglians to resume the lead of our line of men. I only look up when Ealdorman Ælfstan calls to me.

'What was it this time?' he asks, no rancour in his voice.

'I believe it was a butterfly, my lord.' I dip my chin as I speak.

A deep chuckle greets the admission.

'You've heard him, men. Ensure you protect your horses from the hazard that is a butterfly.'

I find a smile, although I don't feel any mirth at what just happened, and rejoin the line, my thoughts consumed with the knowledge that Godwulf knew my uncle. Surely, I consider, there must be someone who knew whom my mother married? Was the service not conducted by the bishop or one of the priests? Why I think, not for the first time, was it shrouded in such mystery?

'A butterfly?' Oswy taunts me, dragging me from my thoughts.

'Aye, a butterfly,' I confirm, hopefully for the last time. 'And if you're not careful, you'll be in the same position as me.' Here, beside this stretch of the river, with the first signs of growth along the hedgerows, there's suddenly a multitude of brown and orange-tipped butterflies. It's a sure sign that the better weather is on the way, but it concerns me. I don't want a repeat of what just happened.

'I can assure you,' Oswy announces, 'my horse won't be spooked by something as small as that.' Oswy still rides his new mount. He's left his older beast at Peterborough. His new horse is the colour of clay, but, as of yet, I don't know his name. He's almost as tall as Brute, though. The two keep pace together well.

I lapse into silence, allowing the amusement to ripple through the men. My mind is on what Godwulf has told me. Does he, perhaps, know more than he suggested? I don't believe he does, but still, I didn't expect to find someone who knew my uncle amongst our enemy. It makes me appreciate, once more, just how close our kingdoms once were. Perhaps, they could be again? My eyes narrow as I look to where the East Anglians lead us onwards. Is there something else at play here? Is King Athelstan's request for assistance genuine, or does he hope to overrun Mercia by leading her protectors into danger? Has the king even considered this? I wish then that Wulfheard was closer so I could seek out some reassurance from him. Maybe even from the ealdorman. But I'm almost at the back of the line of riders, and I really can't draw even more attention to myself than Brute already has. I'll have to keep my suspicions to myself, for now.

17

We camp that night on the outskirts of a settlement that stinks of fish and sheep combined. A heady combination. The East Anglians are welcomed into the hall of the man who governs the place, but Ealdorman Ælfstan isn't. I don't think it unduly upsets him.

We set a fire, and men are posted all around the impromptu camp, set just to the edge of a small coppice of trees, which have spindly limbs and seem to be struggling in the damp conditions.

We're brought food from the settlement, even though there's also a good pottage on the go.

'My thanks.' The ealdorman bows low and accepts the offerings from a collection of six men and women, who present the food. There's a baked fish on a wooden platter, clearly taken from the river, and also some birds. What there isn't is enough for everyone to take their fill. I'm grateful for the hot pottage when I only manage to snag a mouthful of the oily-tasting fish.

'Are they Mercians or East Anglians?' I muse to Wulfheard.

'Here, it'll depend on who they think they are. They've honoured the East Anglian ealdorman, but that's no doubt because he rode through here on his way to Peterborough. If we'd arrived first, it would be us enjoying their hospitality, and not the East Anglians.'

Wulfheard sounds uneasy, and I turn to face him.

'Could this all be a trick?' I murmur softly so that no one else can overhear my concerns.

'Perhaps, my lad. The ealdorman and the king have considered it.' That reassures me, for now. And then my mind turns to Godwulf.

'One of the East Anglians said he knew my uncle.' I don't add that he almost hinted at my paternity. I don't want Wulfheard believing that's what drives my questioning.

'Well, I knew the ealdorman of old, as well. It's to be expected. Less than ten years ago, and these two kingdoms were as one. And then one of their ealdormen, Athelstan, determined that the kingdom should be free from Mercian interference.'

'Didn't he like the Mercian kings?'

'I don't believe he much liked anyone, but he certainly rallied the other ealdormen to his cause, and now he comes begging for assistance.'

I bite back my reply that he's hardly begging. Wulfheard speaks with disdain. I've noticed it from some of the other warriors as well. Perhaps many of these men, those that are old enough, were once allies with one another.

'How's your horse?' Wulfheard breaks the silence that's fallen between us.

'Happy, provided there's nothing to spook him,' I confirm mournfully, and Wulfheard barks with laughter.

'Get some sleep. You'll need to be well rested for whatever he has planned for tomorrow.'

I know that he doesn't mean the ealdorman, but rather my

horse, as I wrap myself in my cloak. At least, I muse, as I allow sleep to claim me, I don't need to keep watch tonight.

The smell of pottage rouses me. The sky is watery overhead and I groan. It's going to rain, I'm sure of it. Many of the warriors are already up and about, leading their horses to a small brook to drink, or tightly packing their supplies to prevent them from getting wet when the rain does come.

'It always bloody rains in the kingdom of the East Angles,' Oswy muses unhappily, his words just too loud.

'They say the same about the northern kingdoms,' Kyre offers mournfully.

'And the bastard Welsh ones,' Landwine confirms.

'Is it only in Mercia that the sun always shines?' I query, my voice sleep-fogged, but amused, all the same.

'Of course, it's only in Mercia that the sun always bloody shines,' Oswy glowers. 'Everywhere else there are hills or coast-lines, and everybody knows such brings more rain.'

I'm not entirely sure that's correct, and I know from my time on the borderlands with the Welsh kingdoms that it doesn't always rain there, but I'm not about to argue with them. I'd borne the brunt of their jokes for long enough the previous evening thanks to Brute and his terror of a butterfly.

'It rained when we were in Mercia the other day,' Garwulf pipes up, and I smirk as all of the men turn to glare at him. He still lacks the skills to know when to speak and when not to do so.

'It's going to bloody rain, again.' Wulfheard mingles with the rest of us now. His face is darker than the storm clouds brewing to the west. 'I hate riding in the wet.'

'Well, our enemy don't have the same qualms,' the ealdorman announces, his words lacking humour.

I turn to look at him in surprise. He no longer seems as at ease with this task as when it was first assigned to him. I consider what's changed during the night. As far as I know, the Viking raiders haven't been seen. Certainly, nothing disturbed my full night of sleep.

'Be quick about it. The East Anglian ealdorman and his men are already mounted and ready to go.'

Hastily, I tend to Brute. He eyes me with contrition.

'Today, there'll be no butterflies,' I inform him, holding his long nose so that he must see me. 'And nothing else either, no bees, no flies, no nothing,' I further confirm. 'We'll travel with the rest of the men and there'll be no arsing about.'

Laughter reaches my ears, and I turn, furious, to see Frithwine mocking me, his cloak covering only one shoulder, while he fiddles with his horse's saddle.

'He talks to his damn horse. He's surely touched.' But before I can retort, he moves aside, to join the line of already prepared horses and warriors, and I hasten to mount.

Soon enough, we're once more making our way ever eastwards. I can still see no defined difference between Mercia and East Anglia. Even the rain, when it falls in a heavy torrent, is exactly the same. It drenches Brute's neck, but at least it's not bitterly cold, as before.

Peering through the gloom, I begin to take more notice of the river. In places, it's wide, with trees seeming to sprout from beneath the forbidding water, while in others, it narrows so much, I feel it might be possible to run and cross its width with a giant leap.

'Can boats truly make it so far inland?' I ask of no one, but Uor replies.

'The Viking raiders don't always need their ships. Sometimes, they carry them over places where the river is too shallow to take it.'

I startle at this. He nods, as though imparting great wisdom to me.

'Have you seen them do that?' I feel the need to query.

'No, but I've heard it said by men who have seen them lift the ship from the water.'

'They must be strong then?' I ponder. I've seen Mercian ships. They're big and heavy, made with oak, and I'm always surprised they have any buoyancy at all. And when they're loaded with supplies, as at Lundenwic, I think they should surely sink.

'They make their ships in a different way to us,' Uor continues. I consider when he became such an expert on such things. He chuckles, despite the rain landing on his long nose. 'I come from Londonia. Since I was a small boy, I've watched the ships on the River Thames. I've seen huge vessels and tiny things that can fit only two people inside them. I've made quite a study of the techniques of building ships, and how they're kept both river- and seaworthy.'

'And yet, you're a bloody warrior?' Wulfgar interjects.

'Aye, well. I'm a clumsy bastard with adze and axe. They decided it was best to keep me away from them.' As he speaks, he removes the glove from his left hand, and I see he's missing half of one of his fingers.

'That must have hurt,' I console.

'It was too long ago for me to rightly remember. I just know shipbuilding, and being in a ship, wasn't for me.'

'No, you'd have fallen into the whale road long ago,' Wulfgar taunts.

I smirk, but I have questions for Uor. I'd like to know more about Londonia. Even being there has left me wondering about certain things, but at that moment, a cry ripples from ahead, and all conversation ceases.

'What is it?' I demand to know, but my eyes are drawn to the river, something bright catching my eye. I assume it must be a swan, or some other river creature, but then I get a second glance and realise it's none of those things. Instead, there are at least three lifeless corpses caught in the current of the river. I swallow down my unease, reaching for my seax, only to wince at the stab of pain from my tight hand.

Ahead, the line slows. I can hear Ealdorman Ælfstan and the East Anglian men conversing. Despite the dampness of the day, I also smell smoke, the sort of damp stuff that serves only to make people cough.

'I think we might have found another example of the bastard Viking raiders' work,' Uor confirms uneasily.

I nod, my eyes caught by the dead bodies, and not what might lie ahead. I can't help wishing that the selfish gits would at least bury the dead, should they find it necessary to kill Mercians and East Anglians alike. The thought of more bodies abandoned in the water makes me uneasy. I just hope we've not drunk anything that they might have corrupted.

* * *

Ealdorman Ælfstan has us dismount a good distance away from the settlement, and we leave the horses with a guard of four men. Frithwine is one of them, and his complaints are vocal. Cenred, Kyre and Oswy take their instructions more easily.

Ealdorman Herefrith has led his men onwards, remaining mounted, but Ælfstan declines to do the same. When I reach the ealdorman and Wulfheard, I get my first glimpse at the settlement that's been attacked. It's ruined, as the settlement on the

Welland was, but far fewer of the buildings have been torched. There are abandoned bodies littering the single roadway leading through the village.

I shudder, and hold my shield tighter.

'Spread out but stay together. I don't like this,' Ealdorman Ælfstan orders us.

Wulfheard moves amongst the warriors, directing us to places where he wants us to stand. Garwulf is unceremoniously removed from the front row, between Æthelmod and Waldhere. I know enough not to tempt it this time, but Wulfheard shakes his head at me and forces me into the space left by Garwulf.

'At least you know what you're doing,' he mutters.

Only when Wulfheard is happy with the arrangements does Ealdorman Ælfstan join the shield wall. Ahead, I can hear the voices of the East Anglians and their ealdorman. They're certainly not taking the same precautions. I understand why Ælfstan does so. There's something here that doesn't feel quite right. It's too quiet, no bird call in the air, and there's only the sound of the rain, nothing else. It's as though everyone is holding their breath, not wanting to be discovered.

'I don't like this,' Æthelmod grumbles. It brings me no comfort to know I'm not alone with my worries. And then, there's a loud shriek, and the unmistakable sound of iron on iron.

'Bugger,' Waldhere complains.

I lower my shield just a little and catch sight of something happening up ahead. The East Anglians are certainly up to something. For a moment, I worry that this has all been a ruse by King Athelstan of the East Angles, only to catch sight of a fierce battle taking place, the backs of the East Anglian men facing us. The Viking raiders are still here. Their ship must be hidden from view, perhaps drawn away from the river, as Uor had been explaining to me.

'Advance,' Ealdorman Ælfstan orders, his voice tight. I consider whether he's angry at the East Anglians' refusal to take the threat seriously, and their bumbling into our enemy, or whether he's pleased to have found the Viking raiders without having to travel further.

I move with the rest of the warriors. We block the road as we advance. Behind me, Garwulf huffs angrily into my ear, as though it's my fault he was removed from the front row, but I focus only on what we might be about to encounter. We've set no forward scouts, because the East Anglians were controlling the pace and had been trusted to alert us to any danger. We don't know how many enemy there are, or if the East Anglians will be victorious against them or not. I hold out half a hope it's merely that there's a single remaining Viking raider left behind by the rest and the East Anglians are taking their time in killing him.

But that's not the case.

'Hurry.' Ealdorman Ælfstan encourages us onwards, despite the pools of water and the slickness of the grass-lined path we travel along.

With my shield before me, I can't see what's immediately beneath my feet, but I can see just ahead. More than once, I leap over an object, hoping I've timed my steps correctly. Waldhere stumbles, kicking something aside, but although his balance wavers, he keeps upright, and the integrity of the shield wall remains.

Something veers towards me out of the gloom, and I swallow against my rising unease, lifting my shield to keep it away from my face.

A Viking raider has emerged from behind one of the seemingly abandoned buildings. And he's not alone. There are at least fifteen men, and perhaps some women. They all glower fiercely at us, weapons in hand, a collection of war axes and seaxes. The stone, for that's what's been thrown, hits my shield, and bounces aside, falling into the path of Waldhere once more. He growls but keeps his footing this time.

'Attack,' the ealdorman calls as the Viking raiders begin to advance against us. I'm unsure what's happened to the East Anglians. Maybe they've been captured, or perhaps they're all already dead. For now, we need to quell our opponents.

Our enemy has shields, daubed with a bird in flight, and when the two sides crash together, it's nowhere near as noisy as when we first fought the Wessex warriors outside Londonia. But the action jars my shield hand, and I wince against the pain of being brought up short when I was in mid-running stride.

A seax immediately probes its way above my shield. I lift the shield, hoping to dislodge the weapon. I'm unsuccessful, though, because another object threatens me. I have to lower the shield immediately. I eye the edge of the blade, rippled as though with the flood of water, and reach up with my seax. This time, I have more success forcing the blade aside, but the fighting is already fierce. Waldhere huffs between tight lips as he jabs with his shield, no doubt eager to bring the bout to a quick conclusion. I thought there were only fifteen raiders, but if there are only that many, they're a good match for Ealdorman Ælfstan's larger force.

Sweat beads down my back, mingling with the rain, as I try to force my seax through the shields of the enemy, to draw blood. Behind me, Garwulf is screaming with battle lust, but as of yet, has done little but deafen me so that I can't hear the commands from the ealdorman or from Wulfheard.

I hit something soft and fleshy, stabbing with all my might, only for a blade to slice my arm, above my glove, and below my tunic. I gasp with pain and immediately withdraw my hand. I glimpse a thin line of maroon but realise it's more the shock of the cut, than the pain of it, that makes me react in such a way.

I thrust my shield forward, along with Waldhere and Uor, and it clatters noisily against another shield, which tumbles to the ground. I quickly lash out with my seax, and this time it buries itself deeply inside our enemy. A scream of pain must ring out, but it only registers faintly, thanks to Garwulf's ear-splitting cries.

Beside me, Waldhere fights with skill and precision, sliding his seax in and out from behind the shield wall. I follow his lead, not pausing to enjoy the fact I've drawn first blood. The shield wall holds steady. The ealdorman doesn't command that we advance, but rather, hold our place. The Viking raiders seem eager to die on our blades. I'm just as determined to ensure that happens.

I can't hear their shouts or cries, but I'm sure that someone must direct their attack, just as the ealdorman and Wulfheard do for the Mercians.

My actions become almost mechanical: jab with my shield, stab with my seax, retract my arm, and do the same all over again. Time and time again, my seax returns to me reddened and I can feel the slick substance coating my gloves. The enemy doesn't appear to have spears or any arrows, and that means that Garwulf behind me doesn't need to cower beneath the shield, but can instead assist me. His arm snakes forward over and over, but not once do I see it return with blood on it.

'Are you purposefully missing them?' I huff with annoyance, as once more, my blade retracts, bloody and dripping with gore. My words echo strangely in my ears, and I have no idea how loudly I speak.

'My arm isn't bloody long enough,' Garwulf complains, loud enough that I can hear him.

'Then get closer to me,' I urge.

I don't know for how long we've been fighting, but if we only faced fifteen of our enemies, I would hope we'd have triumphed by now. Fatigue is starting to slow my strikes. The next time I stab forwards, I encounter something hard, and only by chance do I retain my hold on my seax. My hand aches from the impact.

'Get closer, and reach through,' I instruct Garwulf. The rain drums on my helm, intensifying so that it's the only sound I can hear. Garwulf does redouble his efforts, and he crows with delight when his blade finally shows that he's drawn blood, if not made a kill. The shield that faces me abruptly sags to the ground, and Garwulf shrieks as he crushes me tighter to my shield.

'What the...?' I ask, but it's obvious that Garwulf's hand has been caught by one of the raiders.

I lower my shield, there's no other way to help Garwulf, and face a long-haired foe who menaces with sweat and grime, black inkings surrounding his eyes so that the whites of his eyes are stark. His teeth are black with blood. I wince away from his half-slit nose. He has hold of Garwulf's arm, and I stab upwards, trying to make him release Garwulf by wounding him elsewhere. But the foeman doesn't even seem to notice that I cut him, or that blood falls, almost as steady as the rain, from beneath his armpit.

'Mad git,' I mutter. I feel exposed with my shield lowered, but I can't lift it, or Garwulf might lose his arm, and perhaps his life.

I reverse the grip on my seax again, using it to slice along the line of the man's neck, but although blood springs up, the man again doesn't seem to notice.

'Bloody hell,' I murmur, shoving my shield into the man's nose, hoping that he will, at last, feel this.

Garwulf's arm surges upright, almost slapping me in the face, and the foeman finally staggers backwards. A wave of emotion covers his helmless face. I consider whether all of my enemy's cuts and wounds have suddenly made themselves known to him. He lurches, and I think he'll go backwards, taking his shield with him, but at the last possible moment, he veers upright, coming towards me. I just manage to lift my shield to stop him and his blade from cutting me, or Garwulf. I can feel our enemy attacking my shield, but I hold it steady, recovering my breath. Eventually, his strokes lose their fierceness, and I sense a movement of air at my feet as his body hits the ground.

I finally resume my attack, only to realise there's no shield there any more. I lower my weapon, and appreciate that Waldhere is doing the same. I look forwards, and then I look down, and then up again, and meet the eyes of the East Anglian I spoke to yesterday. Godwulf holds a bloodied seax in one hand, and an axe in the other.

'You took your time,' he comments, lips curled in a smile of triumph beneath his helm.

All of the Viking raiders are dead, or dying. Godwulf isn't alone in bending to check the enemy are dead, and offering slit throats for those who still linger. I tilt my head, unsure what's happened here. Have the East Anglians attacked from the rear of the Viking raiders? Why didn't the Viking raiders attack them first? It doesn't make sense to me.

'We came as soon as we could,' Waldhere huffs, bending so that his hands rest on his thighs, as he recovers his breath.

'How many of them were there?' I think to ask.

'Twenty-three. They're all dead.'

Twenty-three doesn't seem like a huge number to have held us at bay for so long.

'They were sheltering in the village. They killed everyone and thought to feast before moving on, I imagine. Daft bastards. They should have left when they had the chance.' Godwulf's voice drips with derision. He doesn't respect the Viking raiders, not at all. Perhaps, I consider, he's right not to.

I bend and examine the man I killed, eventually. He has no helm, but he has the build of a fierce warrior. Even in death, I can see the outline of the muscles in his arms, and where his tunic is ripped, I see the tightness of his stomach muscles as well. The man was clearly a well-seasoned warrior.

'It's from all the rowing,' Uor assures me conversationally, as though we've not just fought and killed twenty-three of our enemy. 'Men who spend their lives on the whale road are always in good physical condition. Nothing like rowing to build muscles on top of muscles.'

'So, they're shipmen, not warriors?'

Uor shrugs his wide shoulders. 'They all come with a blade and the intention to steal and kill. I don't care what they are. Dead is what they should be.'

I look away from the men, towards where Ealdorman Ælfstan and Herefrith are deep in conversation. Herefrith seems buoyed by the triumph, but Ælfstan is far less effusive, his stance tight as they continue to speak. I wish I could hear what was being said.

'Where's the Viking raider ship?' I query then. I should like to see it. I saw all sorts of boats and ships at Lundenwic, but not a Viking raider ship. I've heard stories of them, and the scop spoke of them on Mercian shores.

Godwulf fixes me with an unreadable expression, and I consider what I've said wrong. 'Further away from here, I should think, for it's not here.'

I narrow my eyes at that admission. If the ship isn't here, does that mean there are more Viking raiders close by? And if there are, are we still expected to travel with these East Anglian warriors?

While others bend and ensure the lifeless bodies are truly that, I consider what this all means. I absent-mindedly watch the others, noting how treasures are palmed into the hands of the Mercian warriors. I think that only the enemy are dead, only for Wulfheard's voice to rouse me.

'Icel, get your arse over here,' he calls to me.

I stagger to where he crouches low to the ground, bending over someone prone on the churned mud, feet vibrating against the floor.

'Can you aid him?' Wulfheard demands of me. His face is tight with fury as I eye the wounds that Berhthelm has taken. I wince to see the deep slash that runs down one side of his face, where his helm has clearly come askew during the fighting. The chin guard must have been severed. But it's the blood pulsing from around a wedged seax blade that worries me. It's on his chest, but lower down, almost where his trews end.

'Aye, I should be able to,' I confirm, joining Wulfheard and taking my time to examine the wound. The blood that flows is thick and stinks of rust, but it's a mere trickle compared to what it'll do once the blade is removed.

'Don't touch the blade,' I inform Wulfheard and Berhthelm. 'Not until we have everything we need. If you do, you might bleed so much I can't save you, better to leave it where it is.'

'But it hurts.' Berhthelm is sheeted in sweat, his eyes reddening with the pain, his hands clenching and unclenching at his side, his feet pounding against the ground.

I open my mouth to offer some sympathy, but Wulfheard beats me to it.

'Then you should learn to keep your shield in place, and not get bloody hit.'

I startle at the lack of compassion in Wulfheard's voice. But it seems to do the trick. Despite it all, Berhthelm lies his hands flat to the ground on either side of him, his intention to show that the blade will remain where it is, easy to see.

'Stay here,' I caution Wulfheard. 'I need to get my supplies.'

As I skip back towards where the horses have been gathered just outside the small ditch that marks the extent of the village, I consider what I need from my saddlebags. I decide to bring everything with me.

'Berhthelm is wounded,' I inform Cenred when I reach where we left the horses. He hasn't moved forwards with Kyre and Oswy but has kept the horses together, ready should we need to escape quickly, as Wulfheard commanded them to do.

'Well, he should never have been in the bloody shield wall,' Oswy argues. I can see he would sooner have taken Berhthelm's place. I doubt he'd have rather taken the wound.

I eye Brute, ensuring he's well, but leave him with the rest of the mounts. I don't need him to aid me, just the supplies on his saddles.

Hurrying back along the path I've just taken, my eyes focus on my feet, ensuring I don't trip on the wet path and straggling green shoots that mean to fell me, only for a man to block my progress. He's of a similar height to me, blood dripping from a wound on his left arm, where a deep gauge nearly reveals the bones, almost, but not quite, masking the inkings that run the length of his arm.

I meet his eyes. How has the Viking raider made it beyond the guard of Ælfstan's men? Perhaps, I consider, he was never in the shield wall. Although, his wound tells me the opposite. This man has fought, someone, and now he's the only survivor and desperate with it.

He menaces me with a war axe in his left hand. I eye it uneasily. I can see where hair and skin have become stuck to the blade, glued there by the sticky blood of my allies. Who has this man wounded? Did he, perhaps, injure Berhthelm?

The dark-haired man glowers at me, the menace in his stance clear to see.

'What do you want?' I demand querulously, raising my voice in the hope that Oswy or Cenred might hear. I need to return to Berhthelm as soon as possible. But I can't see that this man would show himself unless there was something he wanted from me. Why would he risk himself when he's so vastly outnumbered by his enemy?

He makes no reply, other than to growl low in his throat.

'What do you want?' I try again. I don't have time to fight, and the pathway is wide enough for me to just evade him. It's extensive enough for a cart, and so it should be plenty big enough for a man and a youth. But my enemy jumps into my path, wincing with pain as he does so.

I grip my seax, frustrated by this delay. I can hear the Mercians in the settlement and know that the horses are just out of sight, but, of course, I've stamped here alone and no one will come to my assistance if this should become a fight.

'I need to get by,' I urge him, again, my words too loud. I don't want to kill him to do so, but if he doesn't move, then I'll have no choice. It's more important to save Berhthelm at this moment.

The man frowns at me, showing me his front tooth is missing, perhaps from a brawl, if not from battle in a shield wall.

Briefly, I glance over my shoulder, but there's still no one coming, and the ealdorman hasn't yet summoned the horses. And, no one is looking for me, just yet. I shouldn't have run quite so fast.

'Bloody hell,' I growl, determined to rush the man and stab him if need be.

But he must sense my intentions, and moves aside, only to round on me, hooking his arm around my neck, so that it's an effort to breathe. I buck and twist, stabbing backwards with my seax, but the man has a firm grip on me, and with his other hand he batters my seax to the ground. Panic takes me. I curse my stupidity. But the man does nothing further, just holds me there, ensuring I still beneath him, his stinking breath in my ear, my back to the ground. I consider what his intentions are.

Does he mean to kill me? Surely, he would have done so by now?

'What do you want?' I try once more.

There's still no answer, and I fall silent. The man isn't fighting me. He wants something from me, and if I can just lull him, perhaps he'll drop his guard. And then, I can escape and get to Berhthelm.

18

The man gabbles something in my ear that I don't understand, his Viking raider tongue feeling as though it should make sense to me, only it doesn't. His grip on my neck lessens, as he allows me to gain my feet, and I can breathe more freely. I stay as still as I can. I hope one of my allies will appear, or a shout will come from the settlement itself, but instead, the man pulls me with him, my feet scrabbling over the ground. He moves backwards, away from the path, firstly into the damp undergrowth, and then beneath a tree. The day turns ever darker as we move away from the riverbank.

I allow myself to be guided by him because he has the weapon close at hand, not me. And also, because, at the moment, as soon as he frees me, I'm in much better condition than he is. I can still hear the blood dripping from his wound to the ground. If he's not careful, he'll lose too much blood, and die standing upright.

I watch as the branches of trees close around me. I've been scuffing my boots in the rich loam, hoping that when Wulfheard eventually realises I'm not coming back to help Berhthelm, he might see my missing seax and follow the trail I'm trying to forge. I might move quietly, and as though the man has command of me, but I'm plotting my escape, as soon as I get the chance and the blade is even further from my throat than it is right now.

He stops, then, and turns me around. I gasp at the sight before me. I thought him alone, but there's another man here as well, propped up against a tree trunk, and one with a cavernous wound in his left side. I hear laboured breathing and know he's not long for this world. But the man who caught me thrusts me towards the dying man, his blade held as though he'll strike me at any time.

The two men speak. My captor's words are short and heated, the other man's are arduous and slow. The injured man knows he's dying. I look once more to the wound, considering how the man knew I was a healer, but maybe he didn't. Maybe this is all just the act of a man desperate for a friend not to die.

I sigh and shuffle forward to see if there's anything I can do. The lacerated man, his head shorn tightly so that only thin bristles of dark hair show, feebly batters my hands aside. My knees encounter a slick substance, and his blood touches my skin. It's too cold. A man's lifeblood needs to remain in his body, not pool to the ground in this way.

He holds hands on the wound but they don't cover it, and blood sluggishly oozes from it. He really doesn't have long left. I can't save him. Wynflæd wouldn't be able to heal him, and neither would Theodore or Gaya. I consider whether they'd even try. I hope they would, with a blade just waiting to slice them should they fail.

I move the man's hands, despite his feeble attempts to stop me and gasp at the depth of the cut. I wouldn't be surprised to discover he's pierced all the way through. The flaps of the skin are marbling, his body cooling, and he begins to shake. I turn to the other man, shaking my head, but he steps towards me, menacing with his axe, and I appreciate that now isn't the time to admit defeat.

I scrabble in my bag and seek out what I might need. There are clean linens to mop the blood with, and my bottle of vinegar. Should I dab this man with it, he'll certainly have some clarity in the moments before his death. What I need is boiling water, but I don't know how to convey this, and I don't truly think there's enough time for sticks to be found, a fire lit and the water boiled to make it more wholesome.

Instead, I busy myself with the linens I do have, attempting to clear away the blood even as I try to stop the bleeding. The man doesn't even buck and twist beneath my ministrations, which are far from gentle. I shake my head, pursing my lips. He's going to die. I can do nothing to stop that. His left hand scrabbles on the ground, seeking out the hilt of a blade I hadn't even realised was there. I scurry backwards, thinking the man means to kill me, only to come up against the legs of the Viking raider who's brought me here.

I look at him, seeing both malice and sadness on his face. His friend is dying, and the realisation has finally taken hold. I lick my lips, tasting the salt of my fear. When the man takes his last breath, I must make my escape. If not, I fear that my foeman will kill me as his wound isn't severe enough for him to die from it. Not yet.

The dying man convulses once more and then falls silent. I notice that his hand grips the hilt of his blade. At least, I think, he managed to do that as he died. I know it's important for these Viking raiders to die with their blade in hand. They must do so or they'll never be welcomed to their idea of heaven, to sit beside their god, Odin, while they're feasted each and every day until Ragnarök. That is, if they're chosen by the Valkyries and aren't cast into their underworld, where Hel presides. Once more, I'm indebted to Wulfheard for sharing his knowledge with me.

A howl of sorrow erupts from the man behind me, and that's my chance. I scramble to my knees, and then my feet, remembering to grab for my precious healing supplies. I can't leave them behind.

I'm almost out of reach of the keening man when he startles. I can sense him coming for me, although I don't look back. I dash from the place, bending my head low to avoid the branches, as my sack bounces against my back, something, probably the precious bottle of vinegar, hitting me uncomfortably with every stride I take.

I erupt from beneath the trees and can see the river ahead. I open my mouth to shriek for help, only for another voice to wash over me.

'Get down,' Wulfheard roars.

I crash to the ground, tasting the mud and muck I've traipsed through as I do so, while above my head I hear the sound of something flying through the air. A thunk of it hitting its target and Wulfheard is at my side, helping me to my feet, while I spit mud from my mouth. I've not released my grip on my sack.

'Bastard.' Wulfheard glowers.

I stand, my knees unsteady beneath me, and turn to face the man who tried to kill me. Wulfheard has impaled him with an axe, perhaps taken from one of the dead Viking raiders.

'Why didn't you scream for help?' He rounds on me, fury making his face pink.

'He had a blade at my throat and I couldn't so much as take a deep breath.'

'But you escaped?' he queries, stepping back, and then walking around me, as though to ensure I'm unhurt. I realise then that Wulfheard isn't alone. Oswy is beside him. Both men have faces like thunder.

'His friend died, and I ran for it while he mourned.' It hardly makes me sound like a hero, but it's the truth.

'Good, and there's no others in there?' Oswy glowers.

'No, just the two of them. The other man is dead.'

Now that Wulfheard's rage is starting to abate, and my fear to subside, I'm reminded of Berhthelm.

'I need to get back,' I urge, checking the contents of my sack from the outside, feeling them through the hemp. I didn't take much out of it, but I'm still worried I might have lost something.

'Go on, then. Hurry. He's squealing like a pig. But here, take this,' and he thrusts my dropped seax back into my hand. I grip it tightly, reassured by its presence.

'Aren't you coming?' I ask the two men.

Oswy shakes his head. 'No, we're going to make sure there's no one else around. It seems that the twenty-three men we killed weren't all of the bastards, and we need them all dead.'

I look towards the river and realise I can hear hooves over the pathway.

'We're moving the horses. Hurry and catch the others, before another of our enemies tries to get hold of you.'

Hastily, I rush to do as requested, grateful to see Brute once more. I walk quickly then, to reach Berhthelm, and find him where I left him. Ealdorman Ælfstan fixes me with a firm look as I arrive, out of breath.

'There was a Viking raider. He took me captive,' I confirm quickly. 'Wulfheard and Oswy are ensuring there are no others.'

Ælfstan nods, beckoning me towards Berhthelm, but I can tell he's far from happy at this new development.

'Sorry,' I huff to the wounded man. Maneca is beside him, keeping him company.

'I'm just glad you came back at all.' Berhthelm winces as I bend to resume my ministrations. I eye the seax that's impaled him, pleased to see it hasn't been moved. I can feel Berhthelm's breath on my neck as he tries to look as well. It's better if he doesn't.

'I'm going to need to remove this, and it'll hurt, but I should be able to stop the bleeding and stitch it tightly.' Someone has started a fire in my absence. It seems my constant requests for boiled water are becoming so commonplace that they're providing it without me having to ask.

'Bring us the water,' Maneca calls to Garwulf.

The youngster bends to do as he's asked, and I appreciate that I've probably missed an argument between all these men as to whose task it was to perform each function.

Not that I much care. I have what I need. Berhthelm's shield lies on the ground, and I reverse it and place everything I require onto its curve. Then I curse, for I've left my supply of linens on the floor beside the dead Viking raider.

'Does anyone have a spare tunic I can have?'

'Here, use this.' Uor thrusts something towards me, and I take it. I think it'll probably stink, but it doesn't. That surprises me. He's done a good job of keeping his clothing both clean and dry since we left Tamworth.

I then consider what must be done. The seax is quite firmly stuck, despite my worries that Berhthelm would dislodge it.

'Help me,' I urge Uor as Maneca keeps Berhthelm still using his large hands on either shoulder.

'If I must.' Uor grudgingly takes hold of the seax blade.

'When I say,' I order him. I look Berhthelm in the eye, seeing his fear and trepidation. I wink at him. 'Now.'

Berhthelm screams with pain as the seax comes loose with a plop and blood flows once more, but not as much as I feared.

Hastily, I clean the wound, force the two pieces of flesh back together and, having soaked the pigs' gut, begin the task of binding the wound tightly. Uor watches me from over my shoulder, his breathing loud in my ear. Berhthelm has fallen silent, the pain too much for him to stay conscious, while Maneca winces with every movement of the needle.

Once I'm happy that I've done all I can, I find moss and honey and use a strip of Uor's tunic to bind them all in place.

'He'll need to be careful not to rip them open,' I advise Maneca.

I become aware that Wulfheard and Oswy have returned. They speak to the ealdorman quietly. The East Anglians surround their ealdorman and a tremor of unease runs through my body. This isn't going well. Something has happened while I've been busy with Berhthelm.

'Can you tend this?' Frithwine asks me. He has a deep cut on his forearm.

'Yes, come here.' And so I bind his wound as well, and take the time to check my cut. But, provided I keep it clean, it'll knit together quickly.

Waldhere also approaches me with a deep but small cut that needs sealing, and then I notice that Oswy has returned. He looks pained.

'Is it your old wound?' I demand. It's healed, but the skin remains puckered and angry.

'No, I have a slash to the back of my calf. It hurts.' He lifts his trews to show me, and I wince at the purple bruises already forming there.

'I'll not stitch it. It shouldn't need it. But I'll clean and pack the wound. But, tell me, what's happening over there?' I point towards Ealdorman Ælfstan.

'The East Anglian ealdorman wants us to continue. Ælfstan says we've done what we were asked to do.'

I nod. We have. Although, clearly, there might be more Viking raiders hiding close by.

'Did you find any others?' I ask, making him stand in front of me, holding his trews away from the wound as I work. Berhthelm remains insensible, and Maneca has taken the opportunity to find something to eat. I'm thirsty too, but I decide to drink when I'm finished.

'No. Just those two. That makes it twenty-five.'

'But there's still no ship?'

'No, not yet. It'll be further along the river, I should think.'

'And so there might be more Viking raiders as well?'

'Maybe, maybe not. Perhaps they're all dead.'

I consider the conundrum. King Wiglaf determined that we should help the East Anglians against a common enemy.

'How many ships does Ealdorman Herefrith believe there were?'

'Just the one, at the most two along the River Nene.'

I lapse into silence. I don't relish the thought of riding ever deeper into the kingdom of the East Angles. We're surrounded by people who might think to kill us, even as we hunt down another enemy. If these two Viking raiders managed to escape from our previous altercation, then there are potentially more of them, making their way towards Mercia. Just like the men we encountered on Ermine Street.

'Maybe it would be better to await them at the Mercian border,' I muse, packing away my supplies and wincing at some painful bruising starting to make itself felt around my neck and along my arm.

'Talking politics again,' Wulfheard interjects, but his voice contains no malice.

I stand and stretch my back, while Oswy limps a few times and then straightens his leg.

'My thanks,' Oswy offers me, moving away to leave Wulfheard and me alone, apart from the sleeping man.

'You did well,' Wulfheard offers, his tone filled with warmth. 'I followed your scuff marks and found you. Good thinking.'

'I should have been more alert,' I berate myself. 'I was foolish for believing I was safe.'

'Perhaps, but desperate men are precisely that. The Viking raider thought you could aid him. It seems likely you might have been able to, given all you know.'

I nod, but my hand lifts to my neck, wincing. It feels a little swollen, but it's the ache that's going to cause the biggest problem. Already, I can feel my head starting to pound. After Garwulf screamed in my ear, and the Viking raider tried to strangle me, I feel quite bashed around.

'You need to eat,' Wulfheard advises me, pointing towards the fire. Osmod has been placed in charge of the pot hanging over the blazing fire. The aroma is far from appetising. 'Stir it, you damn fool,' Wulfheard bellows. 'I can smell it burning from here.' He shakes his head, and strides away towards the fire. Berhthelm farts in his sleep, and I smirk. I hope that's all the fighting we need to do today.

19

The men are unhappy the following morning, and so is Ealdorman Ælfstan, as we ride through the abandoned settlement and further along the River Nene. After much arguing, all of it terse and conducted with the utmost respect between Ælfstan and Herefrith, it's decided that we're to follow the River Nene further, until we either find the missing ship or two days have elapsed. Only then will we turn back to Peterborough, and the kingdom of Mercia.

Berhthelm's left behind at the ramshackle settlement. He can't continue on a horse. Maneca remains with him. I don't believe either of them is happy at being marooned in East Anglia. But the surrounding area has been scoured and there are no more living Viking raiders to be found. More bodies were discovered, however, taking the total of the dead to be burnt to thirty-one, but Ealdorman Herefrith believes there will be more. The smoke from the fire follows us on our journey. There was an argument about that as well, but Ealdorman Ælfstan prevailed. We couldn't leave the dead to fester.

'How big are these ships?' I query, frustrated to be riding eastwards and not towards Mercia.

'It depends how long they make 'em,' Oswy chuckles beside me.

I fix him with a scowl and gaze at the river. Oswy's in too good a mood. While my neck aches from being attacked, my ministrations for his leg mean he's not even limping.

The river's suddenly narrowed, and I can see the bottom of the riverbed clearly in the bright light. 'But how would they get it through here?' I muse to myself. I can't see them carrying it, but the water level is low.

'They'd wait for it to fill,' Oswy answers, giving the matter some serious thought. 'Then they'd get through all right.'

'But why? We've not seen anything truly worth stealing?' I want to know what drives these men.

'They just come to kill and take slaves,' Oswy counters. I'm not used to him riding beside me. Usually, he journeys with Maneca, but, of course, he's not here. Brute is particularly well-tempered beneath me. I think he's pleased to be away from the smell of blood and smoke from the small settlement.

'Would you truly risk such a perilous journey across the sea just to kill people and make a bit of coin? There must be more to it than that.'

Oswy falls silent. I assume he doesn't wish to continue the conversation, but then he speaks.

'Perhaps they've nothing at home to keep them there,' and he spurs his horse onwards. I watch him, mouth falling open in shock. I shake myself. I should have thought of that. Equally, maybe, I should have questioned why Oswy is a warrior and not, for instance, a farmer or a craftsperson. I realise I don't know these men well, after all. Where are their families, if they have them?

Ahead, Ealdorman Ælfstan rides with Wulfheard at his side. The two men are rigid, eyes flashing all around them. Behind me, Uor, Wulfgar, Garwulf and Cenred keep a sharp eye, just in case an enemy erupts from beneath the undergrowth or surges up from the river. Wulfheard has no intention of being caught out again. As before, the East Anglian warriors ride to the front. They could lead us into another ambush, and that concerns me.

I run my hands around my neck. It's tender, and while I slept during the night, I must have chosen a strange position. Now my upper back aches while my bruises pulse in time to Brute's steps. I would sooner have taken another day of rest, but Wulfheard roused me early and told me that the ealdorman was keen to resume the journey as the sooner it was done, the sooner we could return to Mercia. I echo those sentiments but regret jumping to my feet so quickly.

I wallow in my misery. Perhaps I should have offered to stay with Berhthelm.

At some point, I must fall asleep, because I blink my eyes open, squinting into the bright light when the cry comes from ahead. I try to peer around the backs of my fellow warriors, but I can see nothing.

'What is it?' I demand of Goðeman. He's riding beside me now. I checked his wound this morning. It's healing well, but the constant riding isn't good for it. Not that Goðeman will listen to my cautions.

'If you'd stayed awake, then you might know,' Goðeman murmurs but then takes pity on me. 'They've found the ship,' he announces. 'The East Anglians rode straight past it, but look.' He points, and it takes me a moment to realise because my eyes are fixed on the expanse of the gurgling river and not inland.

My mouth opens in shock, but he's right. To the side of the river, no doubt taking advantage of the slanting dock that gives access to the flowing water, a long ship has been pulled clear. Or, it had been. There's little more but the burned remains now.

Wulfheard's dismounted and pokes around the ruins of the ship, pulled up and half covered by broken branches, the leaves clearly placed there to cover the wreck of the vessel.

'Why would someone do that?' I query. I'd like to dismount and look as well, but no such order has been given. Instead, everyone stays mounted, alert in case of further danger.

'I'd say it was once a good sixty feet long,' Wulfheard announces, having taken long strides beside the ship. That must mean something.

Others of the men nod, knowingly.

I look to Uor and he chuckles. 'A ship that long would easily take a crew of at least forty, maybe even fifty, or else it would be impossible to use the oars to guide it. They'd rely only on the sail, and that's not as much use along rivers such as this as when it's out at sea.'

'So, we're still missing some of the Viking raiders, then?' My forehead furrows as I realise this.

'Yes, a good number, really.'

'It's possible that some of the East Anglians burned the ship, but that the Viking raiders have covered all signs of that, hoping others will think they're still able to navigate the rivers.' Oswy grunts in agreement, a flicker of something in his eyes. If I didn't know better, I'd think he might have been impressed with my quick summation.

'Where are these missing men?' I continue, peering all around me as though they might just suddenly appear.

'I don't believe we need to find out,' Oswy offers in a lower voice. Of course, he's correct. The ealdorman agreed to assist in finding the ship, and now we've done that. I hope that means we'll be leaving soon. I've not enjoyed the day's ride. The river has become eerily quiet, as though hiding some secret. Alongside my aching neck, it's made me uneasy and likely to jump at every quack from a duck, or bark-like screech from a disturbed pheasant.

The East Anglians have returned by now, summoned back to see what Wulfheard has discovered. Oswy and Uor move aside, many of the Mercians doing the same at a flick of Ealdorman Ælfstan's hand. They scout the surrounding landscape, but I stay where I am, alongside Garwulf and Frithwine. We've not been taught these more secretive workings of the group.

It means I get to hear the heated conversation between the two ealdormen.

'You must still come with us, to the mouth of the river.'

'There's no need. Here's your ship, and it can be no use to anyone, not now it's little more than ashes. Your Viking raiders are dead or fled. The task is complete.'

Ealdorman Herefrith lours at Ælfstan, his hands clenched, and if I didn't know better, I might suspect him of thinking to grab his seax and threaten the Mercian.

'You know, you always were an arsehole. You know full well your king means for you to carry on.'

'I know full well King Wiglaf meant his words to be obeyed. I've done more than he asked for and will risk my warriors no further. Two men were badly wounded, one more than the other. And what did you and your men do? You rode into the fray at the settlement, and here, you ride right past your enemy. If you all bothered to look better, you'd have found them long ago, and we wouldn't have needed to help you.'

'We didn't need your help,' Herefrith menaces. 'Our king asked for it, as a sign of mutual respect between two kingdoms who share boundaries and rivers. He could have easily let the Viking raiders slip into Mercia and thought nothing of it.'

'He could have done, yes. But he chose not to do so. These raiders must menace your kingdom before they get to ours. It's only because you failed to act that they entered Mercia.'

'And it's only with your help that they'll face the ultimate reckoning.'

'We've given you their reckoning. The Viking raiders are dead. Whoever fired this ship will no doubt have ensured the rest of them are dead as well. They didn't come along and randomly burn a great big bloody boat. Had they wanted to, they could have sailed from here, to distant lands, or even sold the craft. Ships such as these take a great deal of coin to build.'

'But there are still more,' Ealdorman Herefrith urges Ælfstan, his voice rippling with unease.

'I see no evidence to support that. And it's possible that the Viking raiders are causing more problems along the two other rivers. Is it not better for us to return to Peterborough and see where else needs reinforcements?'

'No, it's bloody not. My king ordered me to maintain clear passage along the River Nene, both for the sake of his kingdom and for Mercia. He doesn't expect you to turn back now, not when there are still enemy shipmen at large.'

I wince to hear the fury in Ealdorman Herefrith's words. I'm aghast at his insistence. Surely, if the kingdom of the East Angles had been so desperate for help from Mercia, then they'd have been wise to stay a part of Mercia? Or if not stay a part, then perhaps ask for a pact of mutual assistance. This attempt, asking only for the warriors to ally together for a short period of time, won't protect the kingdom of the East Angles. What if we kill these Viking raiders, but more come when it's truly the summer months and when we're back in Mercia? I'm sure they mentioned three ships of Viking raiders along the rivers. So far, we've only found one. And it's still before Easter. The fighting season is during the summer months. I'm sure it must be the same for the Viking raiders and their attacks.

'Then you can continue onwards, but my men and I won't be doing so. We've killed more of your enemy than even you have.'

'Without our help, you and your men would all be dead,' Herefrith counters.

'If you'd had your eyes open, you'd have seen the enemy before we did.' Ealdorman Ælfstan is far from giving up.

'My lord.' The cry is from Oswy, as he comes crashing through the undergrowth. 'I've found them,' he urges everyone. 'There are still at least fifteen of them, and they've taken command of a settlement a little further inland.'

The words shock me. I was as convinced as Ealdorman Ælfstan that the Viking raiders must be dead.

A look of gloating triumph on Ealdorman Herefrith's face has Ealdorman Ælfstan turning aside.

'Lead us onwards,' Ælfstan instructs Oswy. 'Send your men to assist my warriors,' Ælfstan commands his equal. 'It's about time some of your men made a killing blow.'

A growl from Ealdorman Herefrith, and he summons his men to his side.

Oswy looks from Ælfstan to Herefrith, perplexed. Ælfstan turns to me, a gleam in his eye. No doubt he knows I've heard a conversation to which I shouldn't have been privy.

'Go with Oswy,' Ælfstan instructs me, eyebrows raised to communicate something else as well. It seems I'm to inform Oswy of what's happened in his absence. 'I'll remain here, with Garwulf, Frithwine and Godeman. We'll watch the horses.' So spoken, Ælfstan busies himself in instructing my fellow youths on what he wants them to do, while Godeman gives me a quizzical look.

'Come on,' I huff to Oswy.

Many of the men have returned by now from their attempts to locate the enemy, and they follow us, as we walk beyond the ruined ship and follow the path Oswy must have taken to find the Viking raiders.

Wulfheard is behind us, and it would be far too obvious if I tried to inform him of the argument between the two ealdormen, and anyway, it's Oswy and I who need to hold back, to allow the East Anglians, led by Godwulf, to show us the extent of their skills.

'The ealdorman wishes the East Anglians to advance,' I inform the older man under my breath. He grimaces but nods in understanding.

Emerging from a thick line of hawthorn bushes, I can see the settlement ahead. There's the smell of smoke and pork cooking, but other than that, all seems as it should do. There's a man in a field watching a small flock of dirty-looking sheep, a mangy dog at his side. There's a woman walking with a bucket to what I take to be a well, and an old man sitting in his doorway, glaring at all around him.

I turn to Oswy and he nods at me, aware I'm doubting his words.

'They're in the great hall. I heard them talking to one another, and the man with his sheep will not meet my eyes. He didn't even call a greeting to me, but rather looked towards the hall. I knew what he meant and went looking for the Viking raiders.'

Having managed to work our way backwards, so that the East Anglians are ahead, we advance together. Not as an orderly fighting force, but not as a rabble either.

'Hail,' Godwulf calls to the shepherd. 'A fair day?' he offers.

The dog growls at Godwulf, low on his front legs, teeth showing. The sheep abruptly scatter and run far from the buildings that comprise the settlement. There's a small ditch around the extent of the collection of houses, and a reciprocal rampart, although it's really just mud and filth. It's evident that Godwulf's trying to establish what's happening. Behind us, I hear a solitary horse's hooves over the hard-packed ground. Ealdorman Herefrith has determined on riding to the battle. That hardly seems sensible to me.

'Good day, my lord.' The man ducks his head. He doesn't raise his eyes to indicate what's happening here, but he does lift his arm to point towards the hall.

Godwulf doubles his speed, his fellow warriors keeping pace with him.

'We're hardly going to take them by surprise,' I complain.

'They know we're here,' Oswy counters. 'They've known of our presence for a lot longer than we've known of theirs.'

His words prove to be correct, as, abruptly, our enemy surges from beside the largest steading in the village, clearly the lord's hall. They threaten us all. They're attired in byrnies, with helms, weapons belts and shields, which I notice carry the emblem of the East Anglian snake. These then aren't their usual weapons. They've taken them from men they've killed. Whatever happened here, and I consider that we might never know what really took place, the East Anglians fought the enemy, managing to burn their ship, but the Viking raiders still outnumbered them. Where, I wonder, are the bodies of the dead?

A growl of fury rumbles from the East Anglian warriors on seeing they face their own weapons turned against them. I swallow against a sudden spike of fear. And then the East Anglians rush at the Viking raiders, a hail of spears from their hands landing just shy of the enemy, or impacting shields and helms. Not one of the enemy warriors falters. They don't have spears, I notice, but they have war axes aplenty.

Wulfheard catches up to me and Oswy, scrutinising me, as he realises the ealdorman isn't there.

'The ealdorman wants the East Anglians to take the brunt of the attack?' he queries with quick understanding.

I nod. I don't feel right hanging back like this, allowing the other warriors to take first blood and receive the first wounds, but it's what I've been instructed to do.

'Assist me, men,' Ealdorman Herefrith orders imperiously, as though he's our lord, and not just a stranger to me, if not to all of Ælfstan's oath-sworn men.

'Come on.' Wulfheard slowly moves forward, his shield and seax ready. Oswy does the same, a smirk on his lips.

I ensure my helm is firmly in place, despite my pounding head, and hasten to join them. My breath comes a little raggedly, the tightness of my crushed throat uncomfortable.

The Viking raiders are clearly outnumbered, and the East Anglians are scything through them, as though wheat come the harvest. They don't need our help, despite Herefrith's words. Far from it. Wulfheard stands behind Godwulf, Oswy next to him, the rest of the Mercians following suit. But I don't even have to bloody my blade before the Viking raiders all lie dead on the ground. Godwulf turns to face us, a look of triumph on his face. I incline my head towards him, but it's Wulfheard who speaks.

'You fought well. Your men did too,' he further calls to the ealdorman. But if he's expecting some thanks from either Godwulf or Ealdorman Herefrith, he doesn't receive it. Instead, there's an uneasy calm and into it I think anyone could speak and this battle might continue, but East Anglian against Mercian, rather than Saxon against Viking raider. 'We need to return to Mercia,' Wulfheard calls when no one else speaks, not even Ealdorman Herefrith to offer his thanks. I don't miss the look of fury on Ealdorman Herefrith's face.

20

When we return, only three days after leaving Peterborough, King Wiglaf comes himself to question Ealdorman Ælfstan before we've even made it across the bridge, let alone can dismount inside the ditch and rampart that protect the monastery.

Wulfheard bids us all stop on the southern side of the River Nene, while the king questions his ealdorman, and so the words are clearly audible to everyone.

'We found the Viking raiders harrying the people along the River Nene. They're all dead. We killed the majority of them, but I allowed the East Anglians to finish them off.'

'You lost men?' Wiglaf demands roughly.

'Wounded. They travel more slowly,' Ælfstan confirms, and I'm reminded of Berhthelm and Maneca, who keeps him company.

I can't tell if King Wiglaf is pleased by this or not.

'Where's the East Anglian ealdorman?'

'He stayed behind. He said there was no need to return to Mercia, not when he needs to protect the people of the East

Angles.' Ealdorman Ælfstan keeps his tone neutral as he speaks.

Fully appraised, the king finally allows us passage over the bridge, and we follow him inside Peterborough. Once inside, Ælfstan jumps to the ground and walks close to the king so I can't hear the rest of the conversation. I hasten to follow Ælfstan, but for a time, I'm concerned only with my horse, and with avoiding other men's horses.

'What happened to you?' I'm surprised when the king notices me as I walk into the hall to take my place beside the hearth, his voice rising from the dais.

I turn, look around, but quickly appreciate the king is speaking to me and no other.

'I was near enough strangled, my lord king. I'm recovering now.' I half-bow. I don't hear King Wiglaf's thoughts on my response, but, beside me, Wulfheard bids me rise.

'Stop that. He doesn't need you to bob and bow unless we're at Tamworth or it's a warrior-helm-wearing day. Here, we're all warriors together.'

I doubt that but rise eagerly enough, keen to get some warmth into my body from the hearth fire. The weather hasn't been our ally. We've had rain, fog, pervading dampness, and only today, when we're near enough returned to Peterborough, has the sun even considered showing itself. Even then, it's been little more than a watery haze.

'Is there word from the other ealdormen?' I ask Wulfheard when we're sitting together, eagerly eating the warm and well-cooked meal provided by the combined efforts of the servants of the monastery and the king's own people.

'No, not yet. They had further to travel, remember,' Wulfheard informs me.

'What will the king say about Ealdorman Ælfstan's actions?'

I'm aware of an undercurrent of unease. Did the ealdorman flout the king's orders or will Wiglaf be pleased with what we've accomplished?

'Ealdorman Ælfstan did nothing wrong. We killed the enemy. We made only grudging allies with the East Anglians.'

I nod, eating quickly. My neck is no longer swollen, although it's a delightful shade of green and purple. My throat has been sore, but the hot food is finally easing it. I consider that I might need to drink a warm healing potion for some days to come, just to take away the harshness from my throat. Here, it'll be easier to do than travelling along the side of the River Nene.

I watch Ealdorman Ælfstan and the king as they sit beside one another. I can't help thinking they're not as at ease as they might have been in the past. Has this decision by King Wiglaf to aid the East Anglians created a distance between them? I receive my answer just before finding a space to sleep that night.

'The king requests that we return along the River Nene, no further than Mercia's extremities,' Wulfheard informs me. He's making a fuss of finding a large enough gap to sleep in on the floor of the hall, and I'm annoyed with him because I found the space first.

'Stop it,' I order him, forgetting for once that he's my commander and I should show him more respect.

'Then get your arse out of the way,' Wulfheard growls. He settles, and just as I'm falling asleep, he speaks. 'The bloody king is discontent with us. He believes we should have done more, so now we need to chase shadows and shades. There are no more Viking raiders, but King Wiglaf fears that the East Anglians will purposefully allow them access, because Ealdorman Ælfstan has parted from Herefrith on ill terms.'

I sigh heavily. I'd welcome not being in the saddle for a few days, but I'm not to get my wish.

'We leave at first light,' Wulfheard confirms, and more of the men than just me must hear, as there's a loud muttering of unhappiness. I share it. Mercia has many enemies. I'm not sure that allying with one of them is for the best. Not until we know if the Viking raiders have been paid to come here by the Wessex king. I've yet to be convinced that King Ecgberht either has done so or hasn't. He's a devious man. It's just possible he might wait for Mercia's warriors to be in the kingdom of the East Angles before launching an attack into Londonia once more. I hope Ealdorman Muca and his warriors are alert in Londonia. They must be wary of any ship that crosses from the shores of Wessex.

But, I consider, what do I know? I'm merely one youth, almost a man, but not quite, despite the many men I've killed, and equally the lives I've saved.

I sleep, but it's neither peaceful nor restful, and for the first time in my life, I understand the reasoning I've heard from others that, sometimes, it's just a relief for it to be time to wake and get on with the unenviable task that the following day will bring.

The day, I admit, is at least bright and filled with the promise that the warmer weather is finally on the way. The water in the river seems clearer than on our earlier journey, and substantially lower, but the mood of every single one of Ealdorman Ælfstan's warriors is certainly much murkier. We meet Maneca and Berhthelm not long after creating the bridge, and content that Berhthelm is hale, Maneca eagerly rejoins our group, Berhthelm continuing on his way to the monastery. He looks well enough, for a man who was so badly wounded. I'm sure the monks will be able to aid him with a healing pottage.

Ealdorman Ælfstan pushes his horse onwards, and Brute is

almost the only one to be able to keep up with the fleet-footed animal. Bada isn't far behind either, but the rest of the men, even Oswy with his newer mount, flounder behind us, as though the ealdorman leaves a wake that disturbs everyone else.

'My lord,' I eventually call to him over the pounding of the hooves of Brute, when even Wulfheard has been forced to turn aside or risk injuring Bada.

'What?' Ealdorman Ælfstan growls angrily, high in his saddle to allow his horse the freedom to gallop. I'm reminded that Ælfstan is a younger man than Wiglaf, perhaps more prone to burning rages than the king.

'I think we've finally outrun everyone,' I urge him, loud enough that he'll hear, hoping he'll stop. I can't see that it'll be long until we come upon the first village. It'll have taken us less than half the time to reach it than the last time we ventured this way.

'What?' But the ealdorman risks a look over his shoulder and brings his horse to a more gentle speed, before slowing him to a walk. 'Where is everyone?' he calls to me, perplexed.

Brute, despite the distance we've covered, is unhappy when I rein him in.

'Not everyone has a horse such as ours,' I inform him, my words coming out in one long huff, as I pull in much-needed air. We've gone so fast, it's been an effort to keep Brute under my command. It's been even more perilous to keep myself in his saddle. I'm not above prompting the ealdorman that I have a horse bequeathed to me by a king, and not just my oath-sworn lord, as Ælfstan's commended men do. It reminds me, all over again, that I'm not actually one of Ælfstan's men. My oath is to the king. Perhaps, I consider, I should query that.

'Of course,' Ælfstan admits sheepishly. His face is red with exertion.

Silence falls between us, broken only by the huffing off our horses breathing and the sound of the water running beside us. I hardly dare ask him more or say more, even though I'd very much like to know what passed between him and the king to have occasioned such a rare outburst.

'Tell me, Icel. What did your uncle say to you of kings and their wishes?'

I wrinkle my forehead, trying to remember when Cenfrith might have spoken about such things. I shake my head. 'My uncle knew kings were just fickle men,' I offer, the words bringing with them a revelation I hadn't realised I'd concluded.

'Aye, well, he had the right of that. And yet he still served these men?'

I nod. This knowledge has bedevilled me even without the realisation that kings are merely men. 'My uncle lived only for Mercia. The men who ruled her were perhaps an irrelevance to him. He could do only what he could do. But he did it to the best of his abilities,' I conclude.

'He was a wise man.'

'He was, perhaps, but I don't think he always was. I don't believe all men are wise about the same things.'

Now the ealdorman fixes me with a firm glower. 'You criticise me?' Ælfstan demands, his words a snarl.

'No, my lord. I don't.' I sit more upright in Brute's saddle. 'I meant to say that sometimes men can be wise about one thing, but not about another. We're all blinkered on occasion.'

The ealdorman slowly relaxes at that, and in the distance, we both hear the sound of another horse moving quickly.

'I imagine it'll be Wulfheard,' I inform him.

'No doubt. And he'll harangue me, and probably you,' the ealdorman consoles.

'I did nothing wrong, my lord. I followed my lord, to the best of my abilities.' I find a tight smile, even as I rise my eyebrows.

'So it'll be me he chastises?' Ælfstan queries.

'Absolutely, my lord.'

Ælfstan almost smiles at that, and then we turn to face Wulfheard's ire.

'Bloody bollocks, my lord.' Bada is puffing and immediately drops to little more than a walk on realising the gallop has come to an end. 'Your horse is too swift for the men. Either ride slower or get them all better mounts.'

I look down at my gloved hands on the reins and smirk.

'And you.' It seems I'm not to be left out of his tirade. 'My thanks for keeping up with your wayward ealdorman. At least one of us has some sense.' Wulfheard's voice reflects his shock and worry.

I meet his eyes. He promises me more words later, and I doubt they'll be quite as complimentary.

'I needed to think,' Ælfstan counters.

'Well, you could have had all the time in the world to think, had you fallen from your horse, or been waylaid by our enemy. Think on that, my lord.'

I gasp at the sharpness of Wulfheard's tone. I expect Ælfstan to demand an apology, but he does no such thing. He moves, instead, to the side of the path, content to allow his horse to nibble on the drying grasses.

'What did he say to you?' Wulfheard demands from me in an undertone.

'He and the king have clearly had a disagreement,' I confirm. I don't think it's my place to reveal too much.

'No shit.' Wulfheard menaces me, but I stay tight-lipped, and in the distance the sound of more hooves approaching saves me from a further complaint. 'You did well,' Wulfheard murmurs once more, and then the rest of the men arrive in a cacophony of jangling iron, pounding horses' hooves, and the huffing of men caught unawares.

Brute's barely breathing hard, but the same can't be said for the other animals. Ælfstan doesn't turn back to his warriors but instead allows time for the animals to regather their composure.

'We ride on, at a more sedate pace,' Ælfstan eventually assures them. 'Icel, ride with me,' he commands.

That request surprises me, but I do as I'm bid, even as Wulf-heard ensures that Osmod and Kyre ride at the front of the group.

Ælfstan wisely holds his tongue, and I appreciate then that all men, be they ealdormen or merely warriors, must sometimes allow others to know what's best for them. I chuckle, earning a glowering look from the ealdorman, but I don't explain, as we encourage the horses once more and move at a sedate pace where the landscape doesn't blur with our speed, and it might just be possible to see an enemy before they attack us.

Even at this slower speed, it doesn't take long to arrive at the settlement where we first encountered the Viking raiders.

'Check it,' Wulfheard orders Osmod and Kyre.

The pair of them slip through the settlement, but I can tell there's no one there. A place with someone living in it wouldn't be so still, so silent, so entirely devoid of even the smallest breath being taken.

'We'll stop here for the night,' the ealdorman confirms, even though the sun remains high in the sky.

The smell of burnt flesh lingers in the air, and Brute shies away from it. I jump down.

'Come on. It'll be all right,' I inform him, leading him to drink, and then brush down his coat. Some of the other animals continue to look tired from their headlong dash. I'm not surprised. These animals are bred for stamina, not for speed. A

Mercian warrior might need to make their way from the east to the west in no more than a day or two. These horses can do that, but they can't do it any more quickly.

'Icel, you have the first watch,' Wulfheard announces. 'Along-side Wulfgar.'

I grumble at that, and realise this is part of my punishment for being able to keep up with the ealdorman. I don't much appreciate it, but I knew something would happen to ensure I didn't think myself somehow special. All things considered, taking the first watch is a light punishment.

The night is long and dark, although there are a whole host of stars up above to keep me company, and the moon offers some light. At least, I reason, it's not raining.

When Goðeman replaces me, I go to my place beside the fire quickly and sleep like the dead until morning.

Another fine day beckons, although the wind has risen. We set out at an even pace once we and the horses have eaten, and I think it'll be a day as devoid of activity as that before. Yet, no sooner have we left the settlement than Osmod and Kyre, once more scouting ahead, rush back towards us.

Wulfheard watches them approach, his face wreathed in unease.

'What is it?' he calls when they're finally close enough. The horses have slowed, as we all wait to discover what new threat there is.

'Another ship, my lord,' Osmod gasps.

'Full of Viking raiders,' Kyre continues.

I'm not the only one to reach for my seax.

21

'What are they doing?' Wulfheard asks the question from where we're both hiding behind a handy copse of trees, close to the river, but dense enough that the branches, with their thick coating of pine cones, are able to keep us hidden. We're just able to see the burnished longship, gleaming in the water, and the Viking raiders who shelter in the sleek-looking craft. The ship doesn't move, oars extended to either side, one dipping every so often into the water, to stop the current from taking it back towards the far-distant sea. The river here has widened, and they've chosen their location well. It would be impossible to attack them from either side of the glittering expanse of clear running water.

'Waiting for something?' I query. I'd sooner not be here but with the rest of the men, further west, hidden around not one but three bends of the river. But Wulfheard is still punishing me for yesterday and so me, him, Osmod and Kyre are hidden away behind the trees, while the rest of the warriors, alongside the ealdorman, shelter further away.

I've marvelled at the ship. It looks flimsy, and yet Wulfheard

assures me that it's ridden the whale road and that the sea steed,
as I recall the scop called it, is indeed entirely seaworthy. The sail
isn't extended above the ship, but it doesn't need to be. The ship
itself is forbidding enough as it is, with its prow head pointing
westwards as well. The carving is indistinct at such a distance, but
Wulfheard has told me what it means, and my legs grew leaden at
their beliefs. They think to frighten us and take what's ours, be it
silver, slaves or just our lives.

Wulfheard fixes me with a firm glare for my obvious summation. 'What are they waiting for?'

I have an idea, but I don't really want to give voice to it.

I've counted those I can see. There are about forty-three
Viking raiders visible, similar to the number that was killed on
our previous excursion, give or take a handful. Their heads keep
bobbing around so that it's quite difficult to get an accurate
reckoning.

'Another ship?' I try. I'm hoping that's not the case. It'll be
difficult for us to overpower the forty-three, let alone double that
number if another ship should appear.

'Why would Ealdorman Herefrith have allowed not one but
two ships beyond his guard?' Wulfheard murmurs, but I don't
answer that question. It seems obvious to me, that if the
ealdorman has done so, then it can only be for one of two
reasons: he's dead or he's allowed it to happen. Ealdorman Herefrith might well mean to punish the Mercians for not assisting
him as he wanted.

'Where do they intend to go?' Osmod asks. It's a good question, but then, we know this river by now. We know how few
settlements dot its banks. The Viking raiders might not know, or
perhaps they do.

'Peterborough?' I suggest. The monastery there is wealthy,
although how the Viking raiders would know of this, I'm unsure.

Unless they'd been told of it. Perhaps by bloody King Ecgberht, if he's involved in this stealth attack on Mercia. Not for the first time, I consider what might be happening in Londonia in our absence. I hope Ealdorman Muca is alert to Wessex's games. I hope there are no similar ships harrying the people there. Would they, I consider, abandon all that they have to seek sanctuary behind Londinium's steep walls?

'But the king is there?' Wulfheard stammers. He's clearly not had the same thought before and now it shocks him.

'Aye, he is,' I agree. 'Maybe they're just enjoying the weather?' I attempt to jest. 'Perhaps they're fishing?' I know both explanations are terrible, but I don't know what else to make of it, and my stomach is leaden with fear.

'Go back and tell the ealdorman.' Wulfheard turns to Osmod. 'Return afterwards. I want him to know the size of the ship and how many men crew it.' Ealdorman Ælfstan hasn't seen the ship up close. It was spotted by Osmod and Kyre and we were all ordered to stay back. Well, the majority of us were.

Osmod slips away, leaving just the three of us.

I can't take my eyes from the ship. It's impossible not to be impressed by the craft. It looks smooth and sleek, as though it could travel overland as well as over the waves if the wind was just strong enough, or the oars had something to plough through. It sits in the water, but only to a shallow depth. It certainly isn't as round-bottomed as some of the craft I saw at Lundenwic. Is this, I consider, another reason for their success? Do the Viking raiders make their ships in a different way to most other peoples and gain speed and prowess in such a way?

I can just make out some of their guttural language every so often as it drifts on the breeze. They're hiding in plain sight. That worries me all over again.

It's impossible to know for sure, as I don't understand the

meaning of their words, but they sound angry to me, and that contrasts entirely with what they're doing. If they're angry, why would they be waiting, in the middle of the River Nene? Maybe, I consider, they're not angry, and I'm just imagining it, interpreting the cadence of the words as opposed to their meaning. Despite myself, I'm awed by the ship, and the men on board it. When I've caught glimpses of their faces as they move about the ship, I've seen stern-faced men, devoid of helms, but wearing byrnies to protect themselves with. They're a truly mobile force, and their actions can only point to one thing. They must mean to attack.

'I don't like it.' Wulfheard glowers.

'I don't either,' I confirm, once more reaching for my seax, where it hangs on my weapons belt. I need to stop doing that because it only serves to remind me of the tightness of my scar. Equally, the blade isn't about to disappear while I peer at the enemy. It marks me as someone unsure of themselves, and that annoys me, even as I take comfort in the weight of the blade in my hand.

Overhead, the day is drawing on, the heat warming between my shoulder blades. I stand and stretch my body, tight from holding the same position for too lengthy a time. It won't be long and there'll be newborn lambs in the barns. The days might finally become longer and less filled with rain and storms.

'We should send word to the king?' Kyre complains. He's not enjoying being still. I think Wulfheard should really send him back to the ealdorman. If he fidgets much more, one of the men might just catch sight of him as a movement amongst the trees, and then they'll come for us. I don't want to face them alone. I don't want to be killed by them, or worse, captured by them and sold as a slave in some far-distant land, as happened to Gaya and Theodore.

'I'm sure Ealdorman Ælfstan is already doing so,' Wulfheard

counters, showing a great deal of faith in a man he was very angry with yesterday.

'The ealdorman orders us to stay here.' Osmod slips back between us, shoving me so that I have to grip a branch to prevent myself falling to my knees amongst the low-hanging branches. I bite my tongue to stay my complaints. 'Sorry,' he murmurs. Osmod, I confess, is as intrigued by what's happening as I am. 'He's sent Waldhere, Æthelmod and Garwulf to circle round, and see what they can see from further along the river, and to try to catch sight of Ealdorman Herefrith, should he still live.' Osmod's words are bland when he speaks of our erstwhile ally.

I don't much like the thought of that. Neither does Wulfheard.

'They better keep themselves hidden, or there'll be a blood-bath and none of us will be able to help them,' he snarls.

'Aye, well, I'm sure they know what they're doing,' Osmod consoles.

I wish I could be as confident of that. Waldhere and Æthelmod are men I would trust to keep themselves hidden, but Garwulf? I'm not so sure about that.

The afternoon drags. Watching and waiting tries even my patience. More than once, Kyre has to scamper away, desperate to do something with his jiggering limbs. To begin with, I have no sympathy for him, but as time presses on, I do. It's hard. It's not like keeping a watch at night when there's nothing but darkness and the sounds of men sleeping and furtive animals moving around in the night. No, here we must do nothing to draw attention to ourselves, and still, the ship holds its position, oars occasionally dipping in and out of the water, but other than that, keeping its place in the centre of the river.

'It'll be dark soon,' I mutter to Wulfheard, unhappily.

'Well, let's hope they find a brand or something so we can keep our eye on them.' But it's a problem that the ealdorman has considered. The next time Kyre returns to us, he brings a message from Ælfstan.

'We're to retreat, once it's dark. There's no point watching them during the night when they're asleep. The ealdorman says it's better if we're all together and can then counter an attack, if it comes.'

'And how will he keep an eye on the ship?' Wulfheard is prepared to argue.

Kyre shrugs. 'I'm just passing on the message,' he counters moodily. It's been a long day for all of us, better to have spent it fighting or healing than standing and doing nothing, the scent of piss ripe in the air as we've all needed to empty our stream more than once.

But then, just as darkness is creeping over the land and the river, something happens. It's not that we see it in the gloom, rather we hear it. A chorus of voices raised in greeting, and my heart sinks. Just visible, before the darkness of night descends, is another ship. And the shipmen on board are calling merrily to the others. This has been prearranged.

'Where's the bloody East Anglian ealdorman?' Wulfheard glowers.

I'm thinking the same. Where is the other ealdorman? He was so keen to ensure the Viking raiders didn't slip through his guard, and yet now, there are two ships full of our enemy. Does that mean he's dead, as I already suspect? And Godwulf with him? I'd hoped to speak with him again about my uncle. It seems I'm to be denied that chance.

Wulfheard urges Osmod and Kyre to return to Ealdorman Ælfstan and inform him of what's occurring. They do so eagerly.

I stifle a yawn and try not to think about how hungry I am, or the fear that's making my stomach roll just as much.

'We can't do anything, alone,' I urge Wulfheard.

'Maybe we can't,' he confirms, frustration rippling through his voice. 'How many of the bastards are there?'

'It's too dark to see,' I counter.

'I meant in general, not right now. How many of them think to invade the kingdom of the East Angles and Mercia? How many of them have bloody King Ecgberht of Wessex set against us?'

I hold my tongue. I'm unaware it wasn't a question he wanted to be answered, but now that I realise he was merely musing on it, I don't want to rile him further. If it's King Ecgberht's fault that the Viking raiders have come, then how has he contacted them? Not that I ask the question. Maybe they visited Londonia when he was there and set them the task. That must be the solution. I can think of no other for why there would be such a concerted attack, right now. Unless, of course, it is all just happenstance. Perhaps something has occurred elsewhere and driven these ships to the rivers that run through the land of the East Angles? I wish I knew.

The soft shushing of water reaches my ears, and I strain to hear more. The Viking raiders have fallen silent now, and in place of their conversation, there's another noise, one far more unwelcome. It's constant and repetitive, and I turn to Wulfheard, just about able to see the whites of his eyes in the darkness.

'They're rowing,' I mouth, as quietly as I can, aware that if we can hear them, they must be able to hear us.

'Bastards,' he murmurs. 'We need to get back to the ealdorman.'

Not for a moment do either of us think that the Viking raiders are rowing away from Mercia.

22

Frithwine's sent back to Peterborough, mounted on the ealdorman's horse, the order given quickly and in hushed voices. The animal takes the change of rider more easily than Frithwine takes the command. Eyes wide, terror in every line of his body, he resembles a toy on top of the huge horse.

'Tell the king that Mercia is under attack,' Ealdorman Ælfstan commands him. 'Inform him that we're shadowing the two ships, but that he must have men ready to counter the offensive, when it comes.'

'My lord.' Frithwine's voice trembles, and I consider if he's scared of the dark, or just scared. I shouldn't like to be sent away, alone, knowing the enemy was just out of sight, chasing me along a river they have more command of than I do over the path I must forge with a strange horse.

I think the ealdorman will send me, but he doesn't. Maybe, I hope, he believes me a better warrior than Frithwine. I allow a moment of pride before I appreciate that I'm in harm's way, whereas Frithwine might well be safe behind the large earthworks of Peterborough's monastery.

We work quickly to muffle any sound from the remaining horses. Our instructions are simple, we'll follow the ships, as the ealdorman said, because we can't get ahead of them, not in the dark. Hopefully, they won't know we're there. If there's an opportunity to counter them, then we'll take it. I'm not sure what sort of chance we seek, and how there'll be one in the night, but I hold my tongue. If I could, I'd attack them now. I'd wade into that river, and I'd fight, but Ealdorman Ælfstan says the river is too deep, and he won't take the risk. He wants the Viking raiders on dry land before any fighting begins.

I taste the sourness of too little food and water throughout the day and hasten to drink and eat a slab of cheese from my saddlebags as I mount up. Brute has been tended for me, and so we're all set for what looks to be a fraught night, after an equally worrying day.

'Stay away from the riverbank,' the ealdorman urges us all in a harsh whisper. 'We follow a little further inland. No noise must reach the enemy to tell them that we know of their arrival.' Ealdorman Ælfstan looks strange on Frithwine's horse. The animal is a good beast, pliant and with a gentle nature, but it's at least two hands smaller than his horse. I can't stop thinking that his booted feet will scrape along the floor, although, of course, they don't.

In groups of two, we're sent on our way towards Peterborough Monastery. Maneca and Wulfgar go first, allowing the darkness to shroud them before the next pair of warriors rides out, Godeman and Cenred. Ordlaf and Oswy follow on, Oswy fixing me with a firm look before he leaves.

'Fight well my young friend,' he urges me, a glint of his teeth just visible, his voice throbbing with the intensity of what might befall us all before we see one another again.

'I will,' I mumble, wishing my voice sounded as sure as his. 'And you as well.'

Oswy grins and turns aside, as though this is going to be enjoyable.

I'm paired with Uor. In the darkness, I can't tell whether he's pleased or not. I suppose, at least this time, he doesn't have to worry about his overhanging belly and getting stuck beneath large walls. And he does know more about the ships than anyone else. Whether that extends to how to evade the reach of the ship-men, only time will tell. I would sooner have been with Wulf-heard or Oswy, but the ealdorman makes the decisions.

The night quickly envelops us, and yet the sound of the oars moving through the water is overly loud. I can't not hear it, and it makes me tighten my hands on Brute's reins, although I prevent myself from touching my seax, until the urge is too great, and I have to reach out and slide my hand over the reassuring hilt. I appreciate, in the darkness, and with only touch, that my hand fits perfectly to the hilt now. We've been forged together, in fire, and now we must battle together, as though the seax is merely an extension of my hand.

I lick my dry lips, wishing I'd had both more and less to drink, as I need to piss again.

I can't hear any of the horses, or the rest of Ealdorman Ælfs-tan's men. I can only hear the ships, and the men on them are being as quiet as we're being on our horses. This is a deadly game, and the knowledge sets my heart pounding. This could end very badly, for everyone involved.

If Frithwine doesn't return to the king in time, should he get lost or the ealdorman's horse turn lame, then the monastery at Peterborough might well be overwhelmed and we won't be able to do a great deal about it. I doubt the other two ealdormen will have returned from their expeditions yet, the one to the north and the other to the south. The king could be entirely exposed, for all we thought him safe at Peterborough, inside Mercia's borders. Could this perhaps have been the intention all along? Have we been forced to this action, and done only what was anticipated by whoever moves the pieces on the *tafl* board?

I shake my head. I'm seeing conspiracies everywhere. I need to concentrate on what I do know, and not on what can't be determined.

Brute plods along beneath me, even he's moving quietly. Not that it's easy. Away from the path we've followed four times now, the going is more difficult. There are tangled masses of hedgerows and trees, and even some dugout trenches, no doubt put there by those keen to ensure the river, should it burst its banks, can't flood the cultivated fields. They veer out at me unexpectedly. I'm pleased I wear my byrnie and helm, as, without them, I'd be covered in a collection of scratches and bleeding cuts. I'd probably also have bitten my tongue on dropping into one of the trenches.

I keep my mouth shut, not wanting to cut my lips on the sharp branches. It's far from pleasant, and all the time, I can hear the unending shushing noise of oars through the water. The Viking raiders aren't moving any more quickly than we are, but their destination seems impossible to dispute. They want the monastery. Do they, perhaps, foresee there being riches there, as when the holy island of Lindisfarne was first attacked, all those decades ago, or do they come for the king, on the orders of King Ecgberht, or even King Athelstan of the East Angles? Has he allowed them access to rid himself of an uneasy ally? I can't imagine I'm the only one to worry at the problem.

And then we have a new issue. Somehow, most of the night has passed, and the thin edges of a new dawn can be seen from behind. While we might have been hidden by the darkness, the hedgerows and trees won't provide enough protection once the sun's risen.

I look around. I don't want to leave the side of the River Nene, but, equally, we can't be seen by our enemy. We'd be quickly overwhelmed, and I don't intend to die on the edge of a Viking raider blade trying to slip beyond our guard.

'Go this way,' I urge Uor.

He seems to wake from a trance, and blinks, perplexed that he can see me.

'This way,' I reiterate, as I take Brute a few horse lengths further inland to where there's a collection of trees that will make the going more difficult, but that might provide more cover. I hope the others have realised the danger, but it's still too dark to see them up ahead. I've not heard them all night, and the ealdorman was determined that we ensure the staged gaps between us were maintained. I risk a look behind me, but I can see nothing, although my eyes focus on the growing streak of pink on the horizon.

'Bugger,' I huff, as I hook myself on a straggling piece of branch and am forced to hack it with my seax, because it won't release me.

'It's difficult going,' Uor confirms, his voice even. He gives no indication of whether he thinks the idea is good or bad. I'm already regretting it.

'Do you think they'll stop for the day, again?' I whisper to Uor. 'Do they only travel at night?'

Uor tilts his head from side to side, considering.

'We're still some distance from Peterborough. They've not pushed themselves onwards during the night. Perhaps they hope to attack during the following night?'

I hope he's right, but I'm unsure. They've come this far. Why would they stop now? Where would they stop now?

Ahead, I hear the crack of breaking branches and peer into the darkness. I can just see the swaying tail of Oswy's mount in front of us. I'm pleased they've thought to hide away, as we have. But it does mean we've lost sight of the river and the two ships. Not, I consider, that there are many options for the crews. They either continue or stop for the day.

I turn, meet the eyes of Wulfheard, coming up behind me. It's evident he's had the same thought as me.

'We need to hurry,' he urges me in a harsh whisper. 'They plan on attacking Peterborough today. They can't delay, not now.'

'You're right,' Ealdorman Ælfstan has come along the line of trees as well. I startle to see him riding so brazenly now that it's fully daylight, and his words chill me. 'They've increased their pace. They're moving quickly now. All the oars are being used. We need to hurry.'

Erupting from our hiding place, we return to the path, while Wulfheard hurries to race on and join the rest of the warriors up ahead, who're also in the woodlands. We ride as one group, the horses fleet beneath us, because one thing is certain, the Viking raiders have indeed increased their speed, and although we have too, I still fear to see them sliding past me before I can reach the monastery.

The king of Mercia is threatened, and whether it's through devious means or pure coincidence is irrelevant. We need to rescue him, or Mercia will once more face the threat of a new king when her many enemies mean only to overtop her.

Brute is the fastest of the horses. Despite the ealdorman urging me to stay within sight, I encourage him onwards. I need to know. I need to see. Perhaps I might be in time to assist the king, and if not, I'll at least be able to inform the ealdorman of the mess to which we're riding.

I bend low over Brute's shoulder, feeling the passage of the wind over my face. I keep my eyes firmly on where we're going, not wanting to allow him to trip on the uneven surface of the path.

I pass the men in front of me, Wulfheard shouting at me to slow down, clearly deciding the time for silence is past, but I don't. Every so often, I spare a look for the river, but I still can't see the ships. Neither can I hear the men, and they must be making some noise by now, if they're rowing as quickly as I think is required.

Ahead, I see where the river abruptly changes direction from its straight course, angling towards the north. There, finally, I catch sight of the two ships. I also realise that our efforts to inform the king of what's happening aren't needed. Men and women scurry towards the safety of Peterborough from both sides of the River Nene, mothers crying for their children, while fathers look fearful. The people from the village we sheltered in with the East Anglian ealdorman are there as well. Those rushing to safety take only what they can carry, and I'm forced to direct Brute around slower-moving cattle and oxen, abandoned because they simply can't move fast enough. The lowing of cows and outraged bellows from the oxen are a strange counterpart to the thunder of Brute's hooves.

The Viking raiders row and row, someone banging a drum or some such to ensure they keep pace with one another, the oars protruding from the ship like the ribcage of a deer picked clean of meat. I hear the cries and grunts of the shipmen, and I also spot the glint of metal. They're armed. I can see the sheen of sweat on arms when the sun settles on them. The two ships look menacing, cutting through the river, one behind the other, the sun gleaming on the burnished wood of their hulls, the two ship heads standing proud to the prow of the vessels. In the sunlight, I can see that they're painted in vivid red shades, and that teeth painted white and marron menace, jaws wide open. They bring death and I shudder against the fear that threatens to hold me stationary. Ducks quack as they gain their wings to flee the advance of the enemy.

I pull Brute in, allowing him to recover his breath. I scout the way ahead, but I can see no warriors preparing to counter the attack before the ships can reach the monastery. The king hasn't called his warriors to protect the area outside the monastery – not, I think, that there is anywhere that looks defensible other than the walls. I hope that Frithwine has reached the monastery. I spare a thought for his brother as well. I hope he follows on behind us all and hasn't fallen foul of the late-arriving second ship filled with our enemy.

'Icel, wait.' I hear a far-distant command from Wulfheard, but pretend I haven't. I don't know what one man can do against two ships, but I'm aware that if we're not careful, the Viking raiders might take command of the bridge, preventing us from reaching the king on the northerly shore. After Londonia, I appreciate just how powerful a bridge is. I need to try to reach it, and I need to make sure the people fleeing towards it don't get in my way.

'Move aside,' I urge them. 'The ealdorman is coming,' I call to the confused-looking people. They don't know the target is the monastery. They think they run towards the safety of walls and their god, but that's not right. 'The Viking raiders seek the monastery.'

This causes consternation amongst those fleeing, but some of them scamper aside from the path.

'Come on,' I encourage Brute, and together we race towards the bridge, the strangled cry of Wulfheard being cut off with the passage of the wind.

I don't follow the sharp angle of the river, but instead push Brute through a field, lying fallow and waiting for the next crop.

Angry, squawking crows surge in a wave of blackness at Brute's passage. The ground rises slightly, and I again see the two ships just behind me. The oars are being brought in, or so it appears, as the monastery comes into view, the cluster of buildings half-hidden by the defences which suddenly seem meagre and feeble.

A cry of my dismay ripples through the air, but there's no one to hear it. And then, I'm close to the bridge, and from the far side I catch a fleeting glimpse of three monks running towards the still open gates of the monastery. I shout, and one of them turns, only to tangle his legs in his dark flapping robe and tumble heavily to the ground. I wish I'd kept my mouth shut. Why hasn't the king heeded Frithwine's cautions? Why are the gates still open?

Brute launches himself onto the bridge, with a loud clatter of hooves on wood, and I look down as at least twenty pairs of eyes settle on mine, from where the first ship is being run on to the bank, with a crunching sound as the wooden prow plunges up the muddy riverbank. The men are already armed, metalled helms cover their faces, and they're shrugging into byrnies. Their arrogance astounds me. They come, here, into Mercian lands, and they don't even think they need to wear byrnies as they sneak along the river to their target.

I encourage Brute onwards. The Viking raiders haven't thought to split their combined force, but rather to attack the monastery from the northern bank of the river. I need to keep the bridge clear so that Ealdorman Ælfstan, Wulfheard and the rest of the Mercians can race to the aid of their king.

I jump from Brute's back, taking my shield from his saddle. It bangs against my leg in my rush, and I can already feel a bruise forming. I encourage him to return to the southern side of the riverbank and stride towards the entrance of the bridge, aware that my heart beats as loudly as Brute's hooves do over the wooden planks as he retreats. The bridge is wide enough for two horses, or a horse and a cart, and I'm only one man. Yet, I know what needs to be done.

But it seems, the Viking raiders do as well. Three men erupt before me, from beneath the bridge, shields and war axes in hand. Two of them wear dented helms, and the third doesn't have one at all, long dark hair streaming behind him, although the wind isn't that strong. Fierce eyes glower at me. I notice the inkings on their arms, even as my attention is stolen away, where the Viking raiders are tumbling from their ships and surging up the slight rise towards the monastery. I swallow and taste bile. At least the gates have finally been closed with a loud shriek. No one else will be getting beyond the monastery's ditch and rampart, and I hope that includes the Viking raiders.

Burbling laughter recalls me to the task at hand. The long-haired man chuckles at me, eyeing me in mockery. I tighten the grip on my shield, and prepare with my seax, carefully placing my gloved hand so that it fits into the shape of the copper wiring that scarred me. The long-haired man advances, calling something over his shoulder to his allies. One of the men looks quizzical, and then shrugs and moves away. That leaves me facing just the two of them.

The long-haired man menaces with his war hammer, tossing it from one hand to another, as though it'll impress me. I watch him carefully. He's too confident, far too confident.

I take another step, and still, the laughter comes. I consider why. I might be young, but I'm a tall man, with tight cords of muscle along my arms and my stomach. Does he laugh because I don't look like a warrior, or because he thinks I stand alone?

I can hear the shrieks of terror from inside the monastery below the laughter, and I grimace and growl. Our enemy have come to terrify all. I can't allow it.

'Bugger,' I say to myself, and run forward, using my powerful legs to drive me against the chuckling warrior. I catch him, war hammer in mid-air and therefore useless, with the full force of my shield on his upper body and back.

He tumbles backwards beneath me. I stab down and his laughter cuts off with a wet gurgle. I turn to the other man. He fixes me with a disbelieving look and advances. I welcome his attack. Where before I struck without warning, this time, I allow him to encroach, his eyes straying betrayingly to the dead man just behind me.

'Ready?' I ask him, feeling strong, my fear banished.

My foeman hits out at me with a sweeping swing of his war hammer, but my shield easily intercepts it, knocking him aside. He stumbles but regains his feet before I can finish him off. We face one another again. He pulls another weapon from his weapons belt, this one somewhere between a seax and a sword. It glints sharply in the bright sunlight, blinding me until I blink the slash of light from my eyes. I threaten with my shield, and while I'm doing that, skip forward two more steps. I'm only five steps away from him now, almost at the entrance of the bridge, and that's my target, not him.

My opponent thinks I'll use my shield once more, I can tell in the way he braces his feet on the wooden bridge, ensuring a wide stance, so I slash across his chest with my seax. A slither of blood pools through the material, but he's still standing.

He howls with fury, coming at me now, both blades busy before me. I watch the half-sword, thinking it the most likely weapon, only for the war hammer to flee through the air. I jab it aside with my shield, and then close him down, running at my enemy, so that he attacks with his half-sword, or he'll be left without the space to strike me down.

I hold my seax out, aimed for his throat. He thinks to duck away from my attack, but I'm too quick for him. He dies with my seax protruding through his neck, great gouts of blood streaming to the wooden bridge, and then down, into the water below.

I have my bridge, but for how long I can hold it, I just don't know.

Breathing heavily, I look towards the ships and the settlement of Peterborough. The enemy are entirely focused on the monastery. No one even looks my way. They must trust their men to secure the bridge. Or they don't realise that they've been trailed this far along the River Nene by Ealdorman Ælfstan's men.

I steady myself, steal a glance towards Brute, and to where the rest of the Mercians should be about to appear. With them at my back, we'll hold the bridge easily, but holding the bridge won't be at all important if the king and his men are unable to drive back the Viking raiders from the meagre defences of Peterborough.

The ditch and rampart aren't the firmness of Londinium, with its mighty walls. And the Viking raiders are racing towards the weaker part of the defences: the gate that leads into the interior. I just can't see that the ditch and rampart will be a big enough deterrent for them to admit defeat. The walls are no more than the height of two men. Should they have a means of climbing, they'll be up and over the top easily.

Both ships have been abandoned by the Viking raiders far up the muddy riverbank. I imagine horses or oxen could be assigned to them and they might be able to pull them as though carts and not ships. The crafts wallow, almost tipping to the side, without water to either side to keep them buoyant. Only the far end of the crafts remains in the water. I consider how the Viking raiders plan on refloating their craft. It'll take a great deal of effort. All of them will need to lift the ship. I look at them again, I can't take my eyes from them, and then Ealdorman Ælfstan arrives, abandoning his borrowed horse to the far side of the bridge, alongside Brute and the rest of the horses.

'Bollocks,' he exclaims, only then noticing the dead men at my feet. 'Well done, Icel,' he immediately continues. 'You're becoming a mighty warrior.' There's respect in his voice, and that pulls my thoughts away from the two ships.

I become aware of the shrieking and screaming, the bloody sounds of battle from outside the walls of the monastery, as well as the increasingly loud chanting coming from inside. The monks mean to pray their way out of this. I wish them luck with that. If only prayers and the language of their god were as sharp as blades.

'How do we help them?' I query. There's so few of us, compared to the near enough eighty men trying to crack open Peterborough's gates. I don't believe there's enough of us to counter them, and if we try, we'll merely be taking ourselves to our deaths. 'The ships?' I ask, when the ealdorman doesn't have a ready response.

Ælfstan's eyes flick feverishly from the raid to the ships, a slow smile spreading along his face. There's no mirth to it, though, only the promise of death.

'Wulfheard, take most of the men and harass the rear of their fighting force. Stay alive,' Ealdorman Ælfstan cautions him. 'You're not to engage to the death, and be wary, if they realise what Icel, Oswy, Goðeman and I are about, they'll turn tail and try to save their ships.'

Wulfheard's eyes narrow at the command, but he nods sharply, calling the others together.

'And ensure two men hold the bridge,' the ealdorman further commands. That'll leave Wulfheard with less than half the number of our enemy. 'We need access to the horses,' Ælfstan continues. 'If we must flee from here, then we need those horses.'

'Aye, my lord,' Wulfheard confirms.

I'm unsurprised when he orders Wulfgar and Uor to hold the

bridge. Between them, the two can block the bridge if they stand side on. Their bellies will touch and no one will be able to drive a wedge between them. The image in my mind brings a tight smile to my lips. Before, their size was a hindrance, and yet now, it works to our advantage.

'Come on, we're going to damage those ships,' the ealdorman seems infused with determination.

I relinquish my position on the bridge uneasily, eyes raking between the raid in front, and the ships. The noise of our enemy is loud, even though the drum no longer bangs. And yet, they clatter against the wooden gates, their cries deafening.

The Viking raiders seems so convinced of their triumph that they've not even left a guard to protect either craft. For a moment, I consider whether they mean to ever leave here, and then dismiss it. Of course they do. They've not come without their wives and children to hold a monastic site in the middle of Mercia. They want the wealth that they believe is held inside the church and the outbuildings. They want, as they did at the holy island of Lindisfarne, to take the monks as slaves and steal their wealth at the same time. They think to be rich after this.

Or, they come for King Wiglaf, on the orders of King Ecgberht of Wessex, or Ealdorman Herefrith of the East Angles. Either way, they'll be rich, and that drives them on. The promise of treasures has made them confident of success.

In contrast, I hope they'll be dead by the time this is over.

With nimble feet, we dash towards the ships. Up close, they're even more massive than I'd at first feared. The craft might well be able to float in little water, but the sides of the ship overtop me, and I'm not a short person.

'How do we do this?' I query, huffing with the effort of running over the muddy foreshore. We have no fire to burn the ships with, the preferred method in Londinium. Here, we must do something else entirely.

'Do you think we can tip them over? They're already half on their sides anyway.'

I eye the boats, aghast at the ealdorman's huffed suggestion. 'No,' trips from my tongue, with no respect at all. The idea is ludicrous. My eyes have been taken by the ship head on the first of the ships, and I can see it more clearly than before. It's a menacing beast, but expertly carved, showing a long, sloping tongue beneath fierce eyes that glower with the red paint daubed onto them. The rest of the creature is black, apart from its whitened teeth, and it promises death to all who face it. I reach up, half expecting to have my hand bitten, but, of course, it's merely a creature wrought from wood, made lifelike by skilful hands, and the application of paint. It has no power over me or Mercia. The words of the scop song, which so tormented me, have been laid bare before me. This is but wood and paint. The men are merely men, and can be killed.

'We need to ensure they can't escape from here,' the ealdorman determines, coming to an abrupt stop, turning to check on the progress of our opponents, who are still out with the defences of Peterborough. Wulfheard and the rest of the warriors have taken up position between us and them. For now, our fellow Mercians don't engage with the enemy, but I don't believe they'll hold off for long.

I run my hands along the wooden strakes of the ship. I'm amazed by the thinness of the wood. The shipmen trust their lives to such strips of wood. I don't believe I'd be able to face the giant waves of the sea with only such slivers of wood between me and the promise of a cold death, dragged to the depths.

'We need to remove the oars, and the sail,' I huff, coming to the side of the first ship and peering inside it. There's a mass of oars abandoned along the middle of the ship, which is lined with chests in a neat and orderly pattern. I can also see where the mast has been laid beside the oars.

'What?'

'Without oars, they won't be able to manoeuvre out of here, and without a sail, they won't be able to use the wind either.' As I'm speaking, I jump into the ship, which leans to the side with a sickening feeling, as I brace myself against the unexpected movement. I'm not even on the water and I already feel seasick. I scamper over to where the oars are stowed and bend to scoop them into my arms. 'Bloody hell.' The oars are longer and more unwieldy than I'd thought. The enemy makes using them look effortless, but, evidently, that's not the case. 'Help me,' I command Oswy and Goðeman. They leap into the ship as well, and it lurches even further to the side. The three of us collect as many oars as we can. I can take no more than five at one time.

'Where shall we put them?' Oswy grunts.

Of course, I've not thought of that. Where can we put them where the Viking raiders won't be able to find them? I look to where the horses are, but that's just too far and would involve us running over the bridge. And the oars are too heavy to carry so far, unless we do it one at a time, and I can't see that our actions will remain undetected for that long.

'Throw them overboard,' the ealdorman confirms. He's joined us in the ship.

'Aye,' I confirm, quickly running to where the ship lists in the shallow depths, to fling the oars I have in my arms overboard. They fall with a discordant clunk of wood into the shallow depths of the river. I don't take the time to see where they go but return to remove more and more oars. The ealdorman looks for something close to the mast, and I know he seeks out the sail.

I run past him, glancing at the fighting taking place on land as

I do so. I have to move my eyes quickly, checking where I step so that I don't trip. The Viking raiders have made little progress, apart from in one place, where they've encountered fierce resistance from the king's warriors who stand outside the gates, protecting them. Wulfheard and my fellow warriors have begun to harass the back of the fighting force.

'Here it is,' the ealdorman confirms. He points down, and I see a tightly rolled mass of bleached cloth.

'That looks heavy,' I wheeze, rushing past with yet more of the oars. I can't see that we're going to be able to remove all of the oars and the sails of both ships without being seen. I'm tense, ready to reach for my seax and battle for control of the enemy ship, just so I can ensure it's little use to them, other than for allowing the current to take them at will.

With the second armload of unwieldy oars thrust into the water, I watch them being dragged along with the flow of the current towards the far distant sea.

'Help me,' the ealdorman urges. He's bent double and tries to collect the furled sail, but it's just too heavy for one man. Quickly, I grab the other end, and between us, we manage to lift the woollen sail which stinks of salt and damp and grease, but it's an effort. 'How do they do this at sea?' the ealdorman queries, and I'm thinking the same thing as we both labour beneath the vast weight of the folded sail. How big, I consider, is the damn thing? Huge, I'm sure of it. The ship might be made of lightweight wood, but it's still a heavy craft to drag through the water.

'In the river?' I ask, but Ælfstan shakes his head.

'No, we take this off the ship, and away from the river.'

I feared he'd say that, but I stagger towards the side all the same, and the pair of us manage to upend it onto the muddy bank. I'm pleased that, here, the side of the craft is lower than at the front. Bending low, and refusing to look at the fighting, the ealdorman urges me onwards with the heavy sail. I can feel sweat breaking out on my forehead and dripping down my back, but still, he encourages me. Until, eventually, we do reach the bridge. Only there does he allow me to drop the heavy load, much to the confusion of Wulfgar and Uor, who stand, ready and prepared, with shields facing the enemy. They drop them to allow us to deposit the sail on the planks of the bridge.

'We need to finish with the oars,' I huff, as we dart back the way we've come. My arms tremble from all the carrying, and after this, I'll have to take my shield and seax and attack our enemy as well. I cast an eye towards my shield, but it waits for me, on the Viking raider ship. I just need the opportunity to collect it.

'The same on the other ship?' Oswy calls. He can carry more oars than me, and I realise that, between them, Goðeman and Oswy have removed all of the oars from the first ship.

'Yes.' But the ealdorman has his eye on something else.

'What?' I query, when he makes no effort to move. Goðeman and Oswy scoop up their shields and dash to the other canted ship.

'The steering board.'

'What?' I ask again. I'm not sure what he means.

'We can't burn the ship, but we've taken the oars and the sail, and now we can disable the steering board.' His eyes are feverish as he points to what he means.

'How will we do that?'

There's a length of wood, attached to something at the rear of the ship. It's been in the way while we've been throwing the oars into the river. I can almost determine its use.

'I don't know,' he admits, suddenly defeated. From the other ship, I hear the sound of footsteps running over the wooden struts.

'We need to help the others,' I urge Ælfstan, bending to retrieve my shield and gathering up Ælfstan's at the same time.

'And then we'll think about the steering board,' Ælfstan confirms.

I jump from the ship and dash to the other one. The sounds of the battle are intensifying, but I also detect something else and look around, shocked. Not that I can see where this new sound comes from, but I welcome it, all the same.

Focused on the task at hand, I rush along the muddy water's edge, where the water laps against the sides of the land, leaving in its wake detritus from the river. I curse on seeing one of the oars slapping against the other ship and crash through the water to thigh height to collect the oar and take it with me to the rear of the other ship. We can't leave anything lying around for the Viking raiders.

With my legs slick, and my boots sodden, it's an effort to clamber onto the craft, but I manage it by gritting my teeth and using all of my strength. The ealdorman has beaten me there, but then, he's not been wading in the river.

I lay my collected oar atop the others and then struggle to grip five of them, to begin my haphazard journey along the ship. The ship bucks beneath my feet, lurching to fall further onto its side so that I trip over my feet and have to jump over a moving cask that blocks the path. The ealdorman hunts for the sail, while Goðeman, Oswy and I jettison the oars once more. I can see the majority of the burnished oars making their way along the river, caught in the current. One or two, I notice, have already tangled in the undergrowth, but to the far side of the river. I eye the bridge once more. Wulfgar and Uor aren't tasked with any of our enemy yet.

And still, the distant sound, I'm sure I recognise, is getting closer. How they've not noticed what's happening surprises me, but then, these Viking raiders are arrogant. They don't seem to expect any resistance to their attack.

I throw the oars overboard and return for more of them, but there's a ring of iron on iron, and it's far too close. I see Ealdorman Ælfstan, his shield hastily palmed, as one of our enemy leaps to fiercely attack him from where he's run away from the forward attack.

''Ware,' I bellow to the others. They stop in their haphazard advance and glance over shoulders. I scurry past them, gathering up my shield to aid the ealdorman as the dull thud of iron on wood thunders through the air.

Wulfheard clambers onto the ship, from the far side, following our enemy. A glance assures me that none of the other foemen has realised what's happening. There's just one man and he's made it beyond Wulfheard's guard. That'll bloody annoy him.

Not that Ealdorman Ælfstan seems to need anyone's help. He expertly lashes out against the enemy. His seax leaves a trail of blood pouring from the foeman's shield arm as the man mistimes his attack. Following up, Ælfstan smacks the man's face with the rim of his shield. His opponent drops his shield in surprise. It rolls towards me, the tilt of the ship and the circular shape of the shield making it seem impossible that it'll stop until it launches itself off the far end of the ship and into the water.

I jump clear from the thundering obstacle, calling a warning to the others. The shield gathers speed. Should it hit them unawares, it'll knock them into the stinking bilge water, or jettison them into the water as well. The pair continue to stagger onwards with their task. The ship lists, and I find myself falling perilously close to the deeper water. My heart thuds loudly, as I grip the side of the ship, my fingers scrabbling for the tholes. It was one thing to wade into the water, but falling in, armed as I

am, will see me sucked beneath the surface with no chance of
rescue.

Wulfheard growls from behind his opponent, and when I've
regained my balance and look once more, Ealdorman Ælfstan
has staggered backwards, one hand holding on to the side of the
craft while the foeman is very, very dead, thudding into the bilge
with a dull splash.

'Sorry, my lord,' Wulfheard huffs, and without further words,
he turns and jumps clear.

When I get a good look at Ælfstan, I gasp to see him sheeted
in another man's blood. 'Bloody hell,' I exclaim before returning
to my task.

Wulfheard has rejoined the rest of the warriors, while
Wulfgar and Uor continue to hold the bridge, ready, but with no
enemy to face.

'Did you find the sail?' I query, bending to balance yet more
oars in my arms. I don't think we need to go all the way to the end
of the ship any more, the water to the east side is far out of reach
with the ship entirely canted over, as it is. But it's an effort to
scramble upwards, against its curve. Instead, I wobble my way to
the back of the craft, passing Oswy and Goðeman as I go,
accepting that not all of my ideas are good.

'Not yet, no,' the ealdorman calls in frustration. 'It's not where
the other one was.'

'Well, it's that bloody big, it must be here somewhere. Unless,
of course, they don't have one.' I launch the oars overboard.
Looking along the river, the oars have formed what could be
taken to be a perilous and unstable bridge along the centre of its
course, suitable for ducks and otters. I wouldn't fancy trying my
luck on them, but desperate men might well do so.

'It's here,' Ælfstan eventually calls. He's at the front of the
craft, just below where the ship head rests, and I hasten to join

him. All of the oars are nearly gone. I still have no idea how to disable the steering board, but the ealdorman has found the sail. It's much better protected than the one on the first ship. A chest, as wide as the ship, has been built along its width, and the bleached sail has been carefully folded into it. But it looks unwieldy. I don't know if two of us will be enough to pull it forth. How strong these men must be to manipulate the vast quantity of woollen cloth into position.

I take one end, and Ælfstan the other, but it's just about impossible. The sail is so folded that it takes up my entire arm length just to reach the bottom of the chest.

'Oswy, help us,' I huff to the other man.

He staggers over, being careful where he places his feet on the slanted craft, and only with his aid do we manage to pull the sail forth. Then, of course, we have the conundrum of where to put it. I hear the grate of metal on wood, and glance up to discover Goðeman has found a huge axe from the ship and endeavours to slash through the wooden strakes. As he works, splinters flee through the air, and I hastily look down to avoid a flying piece of wood.

'Over here,' Oswy urges us. I can't see that it's going to be possible to do more than remove the sail from the ship, but hopefully, our enemy won't have the time to retrieve it when they're routed from Peterborough.

From far away, I hear the shouts of warriors. I don't think they come from inside Peterborough, but rather from closer by.

'Help me,' Oswy urges. He's half on the ship, and half off, the sail snagging on the tholes so that no matter how hard we try to force it clear, it simply won't go.

'Wait,' I command and creep beneath the suffocating weight of the material. It stinks of whatever's been used to treat it and keep it from sagging with the wet of the sea. I gag on the too rich aromas but finally manage to thrust my hand under the section that keeps snagging. I surge upwards, and then, as the two warriors move it away, I run my hands down the segment, ensuring no other part of the sail snags. It falls to the wet banks with a clatter, and I stand, eager to breathe in clear air.

From the bridge, I hear a cry of dismay, and turn to see Uor and Wulfgar, angling towards the south and not the north. In the distance, I spy racing horsemen, even as I realise that smoke is rising briskly into the sky from inside the settlement. I don't know if the smoke from the hearth fires was there before, and it confuses me. The Viking raiders have set no fires as far as I can see.

'What's happening?' Ealdorman Ælfstan calls, his voice filled with worry.

'Something on the bridge, horsemen approaching,' I call. We can't get to the bridge in time to help our men if the horsemen are our enemy, and I don't think we need to, anyway, if my suspicions are correct. But then the argument becomes irrelevant because at long last, no doubt alerted by the sound of thundering hooves racing towards Peterborough, the Viking raiders have all realised their ships are under attack.

23

Maneca shouts the warning that we're about to be attacked, his voice warbling with the sound of it, as the Viking raiders' cries of outrage threaten to drown him out.

'They're coming,' I shout to Goðeman, where he's still hacking at the wooden strakes of the ship, keen to scuttle them in just another attempt to make escape impossible.

'Keep them away from me,' he cries. 'I'm almost through.' I can see where he's broken through the tightly slatted strakes and glimpse the river through it, floating oars on its surface in a jagged line being dragged away by the current.

Oswy and Ealdorman Ælfstan continue to hold the sail between them, although it's unravelling from its tight folds. And the enemy is coming.

I rush back along the tilted ship and grab the abandoned shields awkwardly, one under my armpit, and one each in my hands. They're bastard heavy. I drop the one beneath my elbow when I can make no headway and ensure the ealdorman and Oswy can defend themselves. But they're still pulling at the sail.

'Leave it,' I urge them, fear making my voice jump. 'They're almost upon you.' I lay the shields down at the water's edge when neither of them takes the offered protection and rush to grab mine instead.

Jumping over the sail, much to the disgust of Oswy and the ealdorman, I surge upwards as two men come to an abrupt stop before me, war hammers and seaxes to hand.

'Bastards,' I exclaim, thrusting my shield upwards while parrying the seax blow with my weapon. My arms, weak from carrying oars and sails, both fail at the combined attack. My shield slips low so that I have to redouble my grip, whereas my seax threatens to fall to the ground.

I grip both more tightly and thrust the shield upwards. Neither foeman has a shield, and I'm unsure why. Behind them, I glimpse more of my fellow warriors coming to aid us, and also more of the enemy. I can't see what's happening at my back, but the ealdorman and Oswy haven't joined me and so must still try to move the sail, while Goðeman can be heard eagerly hacking away at the craft. The repetitive striking of his axe is a strange counterpart to the shrieks and cries of the wounded.

I shake my head, grit my teeth, and thrust with shield and seax once more. A war hammer hacks at my shield. The fierceness of it pushes my shield tighter and tighter to my chest, so that the blows rumble like horses' hooves against me, whereas the seax is able to evade my guard. I feel a slice on my chin, and growl at the sharp stab of pain, even as I force the blade aside.

'Help me,' I urge Oswy, but he and the ealdorman are busy, with whatever it is they're doing. Behind the men who face me, I can see Maneca and Wulfheard trying to get to me, but there are five foemen between us.

'Goðeman,' I call over my shoulder.

'Won't be much longer,' the git calls, his words unhurried.

'Wonderful,' I growl low, using my seax to again stop another blow from raining down on my face, as my other opponent grips his hand on my shield and tries to force it low. When, I consider, did I stop being told to wait at the back of the shield wall, and become the bloody shield wall?

I lash out with my seax, taking one of the fingers from the man who grips my shield. His grip releases with a shriek of blood, but the other man gets even closer. With my shield free, I jab it into his face and hear a satisfying crunch of bone. Both men are wounded. I lower my shield, and stab the man with the missing finger upwards and into his belly. The blade grates over his byrnie and draws no blood, but it hurts. He gasps as the air is knocked from his body, and I face the other foeman. Blood pours from his nose, streaming into his fair beard and down, down over his byrnie. It merges with the sucking water at my feet and I grin, thinking the battle more than half won, only to feel my legs taken from beneath me. I land, heavily, releasing my shield and seax as I go, for fear I'll stab myself, and there's water up to my elbows. I have nothing but my sodden feet to protect me.

From behind, I hear cries of a struggle, but I don't turn to look. Instead, my two opponents are leering down at me, no doubt deciding who'll make the killing blow, and that's the only reason I live. Their hesitation allows Wulfheard to skewer the one through the back, while Maneca runs into the broken-nosed man so that he too falls into the water, face first. Only then does Maneca thrust his seax through the man's exposed neck. The body bucks and judders, as I struggle to my feet.

Wulfheard offers me his hand, only to grimace at the pool of water that drips from me.

'Bloody bollocks,' he exclaims, while Maneca wades into the water, the dead man forgotten about. Only when I'm standing do I realise what's happened. One of the bloody oars has tangled with my feet because the ealdorman and Oswy have thrust the sail clear, and now more and more objects tangle with the river water.

The Viking raiders haven't kept their advance to the shore either. Some of them have run along the other craft, the one we've already removed the oars and sail from, and they drop into the water, fully armed, from behind the ealdorman and Oswy, and they show none of the fear I felt earlier of being in the water wearing a byrnie and laden down with iron weapons.

'Goðeman,' I call. The other man still hasn't joined us, and now none of us are in the ship, and he's entirely alone. 'Goðeman,' I holler again when there's no reply. I look to Wulfheard. He peers along the ship, and then shakes his head.

'He's on his way.' But our attention is on the attack that surrounds us. It must be that the Viking raiders have entirely abandoned their assault on Peterborough, and now need to make their escape. But we're in the way, and their ships are missing vital equipment, while Goðeman has purposefully slashed through the wooden strakes of the ship beside us. I can see little between the sides of the two ships, and it's acting as a funnel to drive the enemy towards us now that they're being attacked by the Mercian warriors who've ridden to Peterborough from the south. I can hear the distinct cry of Ealdorman Beornoth as he directs his men. It's that sound I've been hearing while we disabled the ships.

'We should have stayed out of the way,' I huff, but there's nothing for it. We either kill the men, or die here.

I gather my wet seax and shield to me, flicking my blade to release as much of the water from it as possible, only for Wulfheard to growl at me.

'I don't want to be as bloody wet as you,' he menaces.

Maneca and Wulfheard stand to either side of me, the former to the left, and coming towards us are a host of angry, frightened and evil-looking Viking raiders, of all shapes and sizes. Some carry bleeding wounds, some have shields, and a few wear helms, but most merely have a byrnie and a blade. Some have already discovered the truth of what we've been doing, their cries of outrage reaching my ears, even as they scurry from one ship to another, jumping over the water as though it's not as deadly as a sharpened blade, seemingly in hope that they'll find what's missing from the one on the other.

They won't.

'Right, let's kill the bastards.' Wulfheard speaks casually, his voice showing no fear, only resolve.

I find a grin on my face, something I've never experienced before when faced with a battle to the death, and the first of the next wave of enemy warriors rears up before me.

He's an ugly-looking brute, his nose bent and twisted in more than one place. Mind, with the size of it, I'm unsurprised it's been smacked around so many times. He has a thick moustache, almost white it's so fair, and blood drops into it, staining it pink. He's small and wiry, and before I can so much as lift my seax, he's darted beyond my guard and opened a slice along my damp arm. I hardly feel it with the cold of the water on my skin, but the blood wells, and I feel my anger build, as he retreats just as quickly.

I power myself forward, striding through the water, which now reaches over my boots. Each step is a torment of slick feet and sucking mud, but my enemy can't run from me, because more of his allies block the path. I lash out with my seax, a great sweeping arc that rains water onto my foeman that's quickly replaced with blood as my blade bites deep and true along his arm. We carry the same wounds now, and I don't rear back but continue to advance, with Maneca and Wulfheard doing the same.

I hear men shrieking and crying, and some sobbing, as we deal death. The broken-nosed man falls beneath my shield, allowing me to hack through his suddenly exposed belly as his byrnie rides high. My movements are smooth, precise, and others might curse my training as a healer, but I know where the most damage can be caused. I leave him gurgling around his wounds and advance on the next man.

He's a youth really, not a man, and he stands with the arrogance of someone who's probably never feared death before, so sure of his accomplishments. He wears a blackened helm over his head, so I can see little but eyes and lips through the chin guards that are tied tight. His weapon of choice is a war hammer, while on the other hand, a shield with some emblem on it catches the sunlight, and almost blinds me.

His shield hits me first, but I veer away from a broken nose, using my elbow as a stopper between the shield and my face. Using the same elbow, I knock into his face, his helm moving under my thrust so that he can only see fully out of one eye.

'You should have got it fitted properly,' I caution him, as my seax attempts to slash open his byrnie. But, while he might not be able to see everything, he's alert. My foeman skips aside, only to tangle his legs in another piece of jetsam and flotsam. He goes down on one knee, but I can't take advantage of his distraction, because Wulfheard's enemy has knocked him sideways, and we collide when I'm mid-stride. Somehow, we keep our feet, but my opponent rushes back to his, and I need to begin the process all over again. Not that he has time to do more than knock his helm straight, and even then, it'll be easy enough to dislodge, now I know how to do so.

His war hammer rounds on me, his swing well-aimed, and I just get my shield before the blade, but it hurts. I aim my seax towards his eyes, and when he jolts aside, I redirect it and stab through his neck, a great bout of blood erupting to blind me.

I force my seax out, but he's not dead yet, although his breath is wet in his throat. His war hammer meets my unprotected arm once more, and this time, I more than feel the impact as blood wells from just below my elbow.

'Bugger,' I cry, stepping back to be out of his reach. But the life has left him. He scored me with his final breath and now falls to the ground, tangling with the legs of one of his allies. The man explodes with rage as his legs go from beneath him, my blade embedded in his throat for good measure. 'Who's next?' I roar, the thrum of battle loud in my ears. I'm still at the water's edge, and the Viking raiders continue to try to escape. It's not as though I'm going to be short of a few enemies.

An incomprehensible sound ululates from the open mouth of my next enemy. The man has silver arm rings at the top of both of his arms. A man of some wealth and skill, I appreciate. His byrnie is fitted with fine-ringed iron and the hilt of his sword, where I glimpse it beneath his hand, is decorated with swirling emblems, not unlike those I saw on the shield that blinded me.

He's about as old as Ealdorman Ælfstan, and his movements, despite his fury and perhaps fear that he'll never leave this place, are precise and placed well.

He watches me, unlike many other of my kills, no doubt trying to see my weaknesses and strengths. I'd honour him by showing him, but I've no idea what I'm good or bad at. I just need to kill him.

I lash out with my seax, making him think I mean to engage in that way. He lifts his shield to deflect the strike, but I've already redirected attention to my shield. It has such a huge surface with which to injure my enemy, but at the last possible moment, he ducks aside, so that I don't get to break another nose.

I growl low in my throat, forced to veer away from his sharp blade, that comes for my neck. We tangle like this, seax for seax, shield for shield, and I begin to feel the strain of the ongoing battle in my weakened arms. The water and mud sucking at my feet are no help either. I can't move away from the attack. I'm as immobile as though I were merely stone.

But the man is struggling, for all his riches and battle skill. His fellow Viking raiders buffet him from side to side, and they die with increasing frequency on the blades of Wulfheard and Maneca. I can hear Goðeman now. He's finally decided to fight for his life.

And still we trade blows. Seax, shield, seax, shield. I look at nothing but my foeman. He meant to determine my strengths and weaknesses, and perhaps I should have done the same to him, but all warriors are the same. At some point, they make a mistake.

Only, it's not him who makes the mistake, not this time.

I lift my shield to counter a blow, only to feel my balance wavering. I try to lift my right foot clear of the sucking ooze, but my foot doesn't lift when I want it to. To keep my balance, I'm forced to hold my shield wide, my seax as well. The fact I should probably drop one of them isn't lost on me, but I keep a firm hold. If I'm going into the water once more, I want my shield and weapon to hand.

The warrior pounces on me, jabbing out with his seax, forgetting to protect himself with his shield, and that's when I strike. All but crouched, my arse in the water, I stab upwards with my seax, the blade burying itself deeply inside the man's exposed upper thigh. For the moment, he doesn't feel the cut, continuing to harass me. He lands a slicing blow across my neck, but it's not deep, more a score than anything else. Just as he's reversing his hold, to take the killing strike, his eyes open wide, the pain finally registering. I withdraw my seax, blood pooling into the churned water, and he drops like a stone, sending a wave of fouled water into my mouth.

I spit it aside and finally regain my balance. I'm looking for my next enemy, but there's no one there. I turn, seeking out my fellow Mercians, but they're not close by either. What, I consider, has happened now?

And then I hear the clapping. I look in shock to meet the eyes of King Wiglaf. He's as begrimed as I am, his byrnie stained, his face showing an assortment of cuts and reddened marks that'll no doubt bruise, while his seax is held pointing downwards, blood streaming from it to mingle with all the other fluids covering the mud-slick ground.

I blink, startled, with my feet still stuck in the mud, and he smirks at me.

'Well, young Icel. It seems you're determined to make a name for yourself.' I'm aware of noise all around us, but it's no longer a fervent battle. 'That, I'm led to believe, was Jarl Olaf, lord of Norway and leader of this expedition.'

I look down, note the back of the man's head, from where he's tumbled forwards and landed in the water. The place is filled with oars, the unravelling sail and many, many dead bodies.

'My lord king,' I say, finding it difficult to focus on what's happening and what the king means. I'm heaving breath into my body, aware of all the aches and pain of a long battle, and trying to shake away the battle rage that would enable me to fight on, should I need to.

'Come.' The king beckons to me and, when he realises my problem, strides towards me, offering me his hand to pull me from the water. 'You really are your uncle's nephew,' the king murmurs to me.

I take his hand, and together we work to release me from the mud's lock on my boots. They come away with a loud squelch and it's all I can do to keep my feet, as I fear I'll collide with the king.

'Not that you bloody look like it,' is his final word on the matter.

24

I'm shivering uncontrollably. I've had to strip all my clothes from my body and throw buckets of water over my head to remove the ingrained filth and muck. The action has set my chin throbbing, and my arm wounds as well, whereas my slim neck wound merely pulses uncomfortably.

My boots are ruined.

I walked away from the mess at the water's edge, where scores of Viking raiders lay dead and dying, their cries piteous, their whitened flesh shimmering under the sunlit sky, and straight into Peterborough Monastery, through the twin gates, the one knocked aside, the other hanging firmly on to its black hinges. I didn't so much as grimace at the splashes of maroon staining the polished oak. There, monks, men and women scattered aside from me as though I were one of the enemy, while Oswy rumbled with laughter behind me, following on in my steps.

'Here comes the jarl-killer,' Oswy called for all to hear, his voice rising above the shrill nickers of horses and the wounded. Some cheering and clapping greeted his words, but most just looked horrified. I noticed Edith, the woman whose facial wound

I sealed, and in her eyes I saw the dread reflected of what I've become, even as she held her son tightly to her side as though I might infect him with my battle fever.

I'm a killer, a warrior, a man who defeats Mercia's enemies, and that thrills me just as much as it terrifies me.

'Bring water,' I called to a youth, standing, mouth agape, as I dripped past him, leaving a trail of blood and mud combined in my path. He leapt to fulfil my request, and I startled at that as well. When did I become someone others hasten to obey?

Now, I feel exposed, and so, so tired. The other warriors shout to one another, discussing elements of the attack, some sobbing softly at those who are dead, while Ealdorman Beornoth's men are hardly bloodied at all. If anything, they look disgruntled to have arrived so late, when the battle was almost won. All the same, without them, I'm not sure it would have been such a surety. I consider how they knew to come? Was it just chance?

'Here.' Wulfgar thrusts my saddlebag towards me. 'Find some clothes and get yourself covered.'

'Is Brute well?' I call to him, struggling to open my sack of possessions with trembling hands, wanting to hear something from him, perhaps praise, or commiserations, or even just words that show we share the same thoughts. I could do with something to soothe my body. Something hot, or cold, or just tasty, to fill my hollow belly. My healer's mind is trying to help me.

'Aye, the mounts are all fine. None of the buggers tried to take a horse. They preferred to die trying to reach their sea steeds.' Wulfgar's words astound me, but I can't call him back, because he's moved through the mass of men standing in the courtyard, trying to swill the muck of the battle from their flesh. There are no dead bodies in here. The Viking raiders didn't make it beyond the gates. King Wiglaf and his household warriors ensured that

Peterborough was protected, even when the enemy was successful in pulling down one of the gates.

Maneca sits on his arse, a space opening up around him, as beast and man alike now stay away from the crazed look in his eyes. He runs his hand along his seax to clear the blood from it using a strip of torn tunic. I don't think it's come from his own clothes. Wulfheard is off with the ealdorman, in conversation with the king, while Uor, with his view of all that happened, has begun the story of the battle, taking over from where Oswy named me the jarl-killer.

'They stood no chance,' he bellows, as I struggle into a cleanish tunic, smelling faintly of Brute, so that it grounds me in the here and now. There's also the smell of herbs that have been crushed in my saddlebags, and they remind me of Wynflæd and my previous life. I seek out my healing pouches, determined to treat my cuts and bruises before they become even more painful than they already are. 'The gates held. The bastards stood no chance. They should have attacked at night.'

It's not only the warriors who are listening to the tale, as horses mill around the tight space, servants dashing hither and thither, while the monks wisely stay just in the doorway of their church, crowding it so that they can all hear. They wouldn't have known what was happening beyond the gates, but their chants had perhaps emboldened the king to protect his holy men.

'But they fought fiercely, all the same,' Uor continues, 'until they realised what was happening with their sea steeds.' Here he chuckles. The sound is dark and filled with delight at a deadly enemy vanquished.

I shiver again, searching for my cloak. Overhead, the sky is bright, but I'm cold, oh so cold. It might have looked easy to Uor, from his vantage on the bridge, and I might have found an inner warrior I never knew I had, but now, I'm beginning to realise just how close I came to dying on the edge of a Viking raider blade. I might not be here, now, if not for some luck.

'Four men, that was all it took, to destroy any chance of escape the bastards might have had. They offered Viking raider corpses to the wolf by the sea.'

I shake my head at Uor's words, a smile playing on my lips, as he twists the words of the scop song that so filled me with fear. I've been passed a beaker of cool water to slake my thirst, and I can also see that bowls of pottage are being handed out to the warriors, by servants who move with some trepidation through the heaving mass of men and horseflesh. There's no rhyme or reason to anything. It's certainly not the ordered place it was when we last visited.

'Four men, Ealdorman Ælfstan, Oswy, Goðeman and young Icel. They carried the shield of war and so dealt death mightily, giving swollen flesh to the raven and marking men with the print of the sword's edge.' Again, the words of the scop song slip from Uor's lips.

I smirk to hear my name mentioned with those mighty warriors.

'Goðeman fought the bastards alone, hacking great bit pieces of wood from their ship. The thing will never be seaworthy again,' Uor chortles and I realise that he's now standing on a stool, so that all can see him. He has the attention of everyone. Even the horses are quiet. 'Ealdorman Ælfstan single-handedly threw the sails of the sea steeds into the river,' Uor announces. 'Ensuring they couldn't sail from this place.'

I shake my head, smirking. It was hardly single-handed but I'll allow Uor his praise of the ealdorman. Ælfstan played his part. He laboured with his oath-sworn warriors.

'Oswy tossed every single one of their oars into the river.' A cheer greets those words. It seems that Oswy is well liked. This surprises me once more, even though we are now allies. 'All two hundred of them.'

Again, Oswy didn't do this alone, but it seems churlish to complain. And Oswy is strutting through the sea of people, to Uor's side. They clasp forearms and embrace, the cheers only getting louder until someone's shout breaks through the acclaim.

'A pity the river didn't bloody want them,' a coarse voice rejoins. It was indeed a pity, and that's why so many of us tripped over oars and why the river now has a thin line of those oars stretching far into the distance as they make their way towards the sea, as though in mockery of the Viking raiders attempt to escape. The oars are the only things that will survive this attack. Everything else is dead, or dying, or scuttled. Neither ship will be seaworthy any time soon.

'And young Icel.'

I stiffen at the words.

'Young Icel killed the bloody bastard jarl, the steerer of the sea-horses. He offered Viking corpses to the wolf by the sea,' Uor roars as he reiterates the scop's words once more.

The cheering is louder now, and even the two ealdormen have joined in, the king just behind them, emerging from the hall. King Wiglaf and Ealdorman Ælfstan are drenched in sweat and filth and muck from the battle, while Ealdorman Beornoth is still pink of cheek, the swiftness of his passage evident. I wonder if the king recognises these words, spoken at the wedding feast by the scop.

From beside me, Maneca startles as though to wakefulness, then stands to lift my left arm high above my head. He means to celebrate my triumph as more cheers ring out. I catch sight of the look on King Wiglaf's face, and worry fills me, for he appears stern and deadly in his battle garb. Have I stolen his triumph? I hope not. Maneca must think the same as he drops my arm and moves aside. Only then, a broad grin touches the king's cheeks, and he walks towards me, a path clearing for him through the mass of men, women, children and horses. In his hand, the king carries the jarl's two arm rings, worn, no doubt, by the dead man to show his battle prowess. How they mock him in death. The king's eyes glint with a knowing look.

'And the king's warriors must be rewarded as such,' King Wiglaf calls, his voice barrelling over everyone else's, as the good humour is held in check, all deferential to Mercia's king, who has won yet another victory against her enemies. 'Oswy, to you I gift a byrnie made by the most skilled of my weapons masters.'

A servant brings the item forwards, staggering under the weight of the linked chains. I consider who it once belonged to, but dismiss the thought. It doesn't matter. It's Oswy's now. Oswy bows as he takes it easily in his hands. It's of no great weight for him. His face blooms in a smirk of triumph. It's a fine gift. A very fine gift.

'Goðeman, to you I gift the jarl's sword, taken from his lifeless hand. Perhaps you will learn to row with it?' the king jokes, as another servant hands over the blade.

Goðeman stands to take the gift, his mouth opening in shock. 'My lord king.' He bows as well, and cheers once more erupt. Every man there would like to receive such a prize

'And for my ealdorman, a man of unquestionable loyalty.' I nod at those words. Whatever happened between the king and Ælfstan before we were once more sent to seek the East Anglian ealdorman, all is forgiven in light of such a triumph. 'I give him the weapons from forty of the dead warriors, to dispense with as he pleases.' This is a fine gift as well. In being so generous, the king leaves himself only half of the spoils.

Ealdorman Ælfstan nods, the light of triumph in his eyes, as he bows before his king. And then I feel the king's eyes on me.

'Now, our young Icel already has a horse, and his byrnie and seax are equally fine, once belonging to his fierce warrior uncle, what then shall I gift him?'

I didn't think to be rewarded. I am the king's sworn man. I did what I must to ensure his survival, and that of Mercia. I did my duty.

Men and women call their replies, everything from a field of sheep to a ship of my own. Although, what use a ship would be to me, I don't know. I listen with growing surprise as the rewards get bigger and bigger.

The king seems to listen, but there's a smirk on his lips, and he bids me rise. I do so, standing before him.

'Icel, Lord of Budworth, and jarl-slayer, I reward you with a symbol of what you have become, a warrior of Mercia.' And the king slips the dead jarl's two silver arm rings over my left hand, forcing them along my arms, which shudder from exhaustion.

Understanding touches the king's features, and he moves more quickly, and then, taking my left hand in his, lifts my arm high, the brightness of the sun catching the silver arm rings, evidently hastily cleaned from the muck and filth that must have coated them, and now the cheers are ever louder.

'Icel,' rips through the air, and I can't deny it feels empowering to be acknowledged as one of Mercia's warriors. A grin slips on to my face. Wulfheard, close to me, chuckles with mirth, although his nose continues to bleed, and he looks as though he might have taken a nasty bang to the side of his head, an egg-shaped lump now forming.

Ealdorman Ælfstan stands close to me as well – I think perhaps there is a slight interplay between the ealdorman and the king as to who is owed my allegiance – and then Oswy lifts me onto his broad shoulders, and I can see everyone shouting and screaming my name.

For the first time in the last two years, I consider why I ever shied away from this acclaim, why my uncle thought such was a duty and not a joy. Only then my eyes alight on Frithwine, who raced to find Ealdorman Beornoth to the south as soon as he'd informed the king of the coming attack. In that way, Frithwine was responsible for the reinforcements that ensured Mercia's victory. Tears stream from Frithwine's face. I look for Garwulf, and his brother isn't standing beside him, as he should be. I appreciate then why the king must reward men as he does. To take the risk, the chance, the opportunity to defend Mercia, can only ever be done when your life is imperilled.

Frithwine lifts his eyes to mine, a wobbly smile on his face, and I know his sorrow, for it wasn't long ago that I lost my uncle, my only family. Frithwine's grief will be long and hard. I pity him it but know there's no other way for him to come to terms with what's happened.

Oswy abruptly drops me to the ground, reawakening all of my hurts and pains, an *ouff* of pain rushing from my lips. The king has gone, the ealdormen as well, hurrying back into the hall. No doubt, there is still much to discuss.

This has been one victory, against one of Mercia's enemies, and now, we must learn the truth of the attack, and ensure Mercia is always so well protected in the future.

25

LATE SUMMER AD831

As Brute walks through the gate to Tamworth, he whinnies, and an answering call comes straight away. I grin, jumping from his side, to lead him towards the water trough. It seems that Wine is pleased at my return.

I catch sight of young Cuthred, dashing haphazardly through the horses. He's grown during the summer months and now almost reaches to Brute's shoulder as he stops before me, a wide grin on his sun-roughened face.

'Cor,' he mutters. 'Did you eat a whole cow to yourself?'

I grin, and reach out to run my hands through his hair. I've been forced to beg new tunics from the servants at Peterborough. My arms' girth has far outgrown the linen's best attempts to keep me contained.

'Did you?' I retort, eyeing his great height now.

He stands back, hands on his hips, and giggles, reminding me of the boy he is. 'Wynflæd said I needed feeding up to help her, and so I've been getting double portions.' There's wonder in his voice, that has me laughing.

'And how is Wynflæd?'

'As grumpy as ever, and as eager with the slaps,' he replies cheekily, and clasps his hand over his mouth, as I laugh to shrug away any concern he's been too outspoken.

'And Theodore and Gaya?'

Cuthred shrugs now. 'I don't know. They left, some months ago, to travel to Kingsholm. Lady Cynehild is with child, and Wynflæd has determined she must have every assistance. She's fearful that the lady is too old to live through the birth.' Cuthred at least has the wherewithal to lean close to me and whisper these words.

I nod, worry stabbing at my heart at the news. I knew it was inevitable, and in all fairness, Lady Cynehild isn't as old as some women still birthing their children, but Wynflæd's worry will be that this is her first child.

'Then, I'll pray to hear of a safe delivery soon,' I confirm, keeping my voice light so that Cuthred won't detect my fear. We're walking away from the water trough now, towards the stables, where I can see Wine's distinctive grey coat even from the gloomy interior. 'And is there more news?' I query.

Cuthred sticks his tongue between his lips, and his forehead furrows in thought. 'The queen has been busy making marriage alliances for those ealdormen who are unwed. Her son has been training with the men – oh, and he's to be married too, after the harvest.'

I nod. 'I heard,' I murmur, watching as Brute and Wine make their welcomes to one another. I once thought the two would detest one another, but that's not the case. I remove Brute's saddle, while Cuthred collects hay from the net and uses it to clear the filth of the road from my horse. I move to check on Wine. She sniffs my hand and then runs her rough tongue over my eagle scar. It's still prominent on my hand. No matter the salves I've been using on it, it hasn't faded yet. I imagine it never will. I appreciate that I've been marked as one of Mercia's warriors since that day in the woodlands, defeating the Viking raiders, even if earning the recognition took longer.

'King Ecgberht of Wessex sent an emissary to negotiate with King Wiglaf.'

'Did he now?' This I didn't know.

'Yes, but King Wiglaf wasn't here then, and the queen refused to allow the emissary entrance to Tamworth. There was a bit of a fuss about it, to be honest. Ealdorman Sigered was determined that the queen should hear what King Ecgberht had to offer, but she refused. And the king of the East Angles has also renewed his request for a permanent treaty. It's been slightly more warmly received.'

'You seem remarkably well informed,' I quiz him.

'Ah, well, double portions. I'm in the king's hall more than I'm out of it, and Wynflæd isn't as quick on her feet as she used to be. She sends me to listen to anything deemed important.'

'Come, let's visit her,' I determine.

Cuthred has my saddlebags over his shoulder, and Brute's saddle and harness have been removed and hung on the waiting pegs. Wine is comfortable, her head hanging over the stall so that she can look at Brute, who contentedly eats his hay, slurping the pieces up with his black and white nose. I consider what stories they might share with one another.

Outside, the chaos of the return of the king's warriors is clearing quickly. Men and women reuniting in joy, while the bereaved have taken themselves either to the church or to their homes to be alone with the reality of their grief.

'Where have you been?' The shriek is just that, as I bend ever lower to enter Wynflæd's workshop. She's sitting at her board, three candles lighting the delicate work she's undertaking with the herbs spread out on the chopping board before her.

'Tending to my horse, as all good warriors should do,' I retort, pleased to know her sharp tongue hasn't lessened in my absence, even if she actually meant those words for Cuthred, not me.

'Is that what you are now?' she queries, a thin eyebrow arched, recovering quickly from any shock I might have given her.

'Aye, that's what I am, but still one with a skill for healing,' I confirm. I should like to bend and embrace her, but I can't see that will get me anything but a smack to the side of my face.

'Is that why you wear those arm rings?'

I've forgotten them, and now I pull them loose with some effort. They've been resting only just above my elbows, and not closer to my shoulder, where I've been told they should be worn.

'Here, I've been keeping them safe for you,' I confirm, handing them into her open palms.

She looks from me to the arm rings, a curl of her lips at the gift. 'And why would I need such as these?' She's not going to take my gift easily, I realise.

'I believe you could buy a fortune in those exotic herbs I've heard you and Ealdorman Tidwulf discussing. I should like you to see them, and to know their potency.'

'Ah, well, I might do that,' she confirms, slipping both silver arm rings into the pouch that nestles around her waist. She stands abruptly, startling me, and forcing me to take her chair, with her hands on my forearms. Even then, I'm still just taller than she is, but she pushes my head back, peering into my eyes. All I can see is the greyness of her eyes, and the faint white hairs on her chin. Then she scoops my scarred hand into hers, and peers at it, taking it closer to the light so that she can get a good view of it. Her fingers are like ants on my hand, so light. 'I've heard of your exploits,' she informs me, as she touches the raised edges of the eagle scar. 'You've changed while you've been away.

You've healed, I know you have, and you've killed and taken delight in it, and not just through fear.'

I nod, unsure how else to respond.

'The king has richly rewarded you,' she murmurs more softly and just close to my ear.

'Aye, he has,' I confirm.

'And that has aroused some jealousy,' she continues. 'From the queen and from the king's son as well.'

I swallow, uneasy with what she's telling me.

'Tread carefully, young Icel.' She smiles then, the years driven back from her face. For a moment in the flickering flame, I see the young woman she once was, before her years and grief made her diminutive, settling on her as though a ship collecting oarsmen as she's journeyed through life. 'You're truly a warrior of Mercia, and there's no greater threat to those who lack the skills to claim the title.'

I shudder at her words, and then she surprises me, thrusting her stick-thin arms around me, and holding me close enough that I can hear the thin echo of her heart beneath her tunic.

'You've been the grandson I never had, and I love you for that, and fear for you in equal measure, my warrior of Mercia.'

* * *

The ground disappears beneath Wine's hooves too easily. I knew I had to come, and yet all the same, I'd sooner not.

When last I came to Budworth, I could hardly see for the tears that marred my face, and now, it's as though I see it all with new eyes.

Beneath the gentle shading of a late summer's day, all too soon, the settlement comes into sight, with its neatly roofed houses and storehouses, animal barns and grain stores. I would smile to see it, but it merely reminds me of all that I've lost, and all that I never knew. My uncle's home, but never mine.

'Come on, girl.' I direct Wine towards the small church, its square tower lying centrally over the length of the building. Its wooden structure is far from the stone-built churches I've seen on my travels throughout Mercia, and yet it has a certain majesty to it. I thought it only right to bring Wine and not Brute. Wine has yet to offer her own solace for the loss of her master.

The road running close to the church is absent of others. I'm far from surprised. In the distance, the sun is beginning to set, and there's a chill wind in the air. Most, I assume, will have scuttled home, to warm themselves around hearths, enjoying the fact they don't yet have to wear all of their layers of clothes to keep warm against the bitter winter cold, but aware that time is running short.

'Wait here, girl.' I dismount smoothly, swallowing against the bitterness of my pain and trying not to let the tears I want to shed fall down my cheeks, mostly obscured beneath a thick black beard and moustache. I know, without having to think about it, that I'm no longer the child who lost his uncle. No. I'm a man grown and come here to mourn a man who was my uncle, and who I miss every day, even if, on occasion, it takes me a while to remember to do so.

Wine bows her grey head, knowing where we are, and I allow my hand to linger on her shoulder as I steel myself to approach my uncle's grave. Wulfheard didn't ask me of my intentions when I asked for leave from Tamworth when I'd only just returned. No doubt, he had his suspicions. I didn't stop to think he might have wished to accompany me. I didn't stop to think I might have appreciated someone supporting me. Now I wish I wasn't alone. I would welcome someone to ensure I offer my uncle the respect and sorrow he's due.

It's not the anniversary of his death. When that occurred, I was somewhere along Ermine Street, carrying out the orders of my king. But I'm here now, and I have time to sorrow.

Swinging open the gate into the small, enclosed churchyard, I stand and stare upwards, looking once more at the wooden tower, with its square sides, until Wine's soft nicker has me remembering my purpose. With feet grown leaden, I follow the gravel-strewn path to the church door, and only then move aside, following the shape of the rectangular church building towards the western extent of the churchyard.

There's little to demarcate one grave from another, other than traces of where the ground has been disturbed, but in the far corner there's a collection of structures, some of them little more than slabs of stone, some with bright colours, and others with faint impressions of holy signs carved into them. It's towards them that I travel.

When I brought my uncle to be buried here, I was grief-stricken and hardly noticed the grave that marked where my mother lay, but I've often thought about it in the intervening time. She's been here, all these years, and yet I'd never thought to ask about it, and my uncle had never brought me to visit her. I wish he had before his death.

I eye it now, marvelling at the elaborate stone structure that marks her burial. I would have asked my uncle about it, had I known of its existence, but I didn't, and now I have no one to question about it. My uncle and their parents' burials are denoted merely by small, coloured stones, carved with the symbol of their god. There's not so much as an emblem to mark them as all related, and yet my mother's grave is almost entirely shrouded by a stone, carved with intricate interlocking patterns of leaping animals and intertwining vines, holy symbolism evident in the carved cross and bowed head of an unknown saint.

I shake my head to see it. What does it represent? Why is it even here? My uncle, with his reserved ways, wouldn't have placed such a thing here. Was it – and my heart skips a beat to think of this – a memorial commissioned by my father? I take an eager step towards it, suddenly desperate to examine the twirling patterns, only for my eagerness to falter.

Do I really wish to know, after all this time, who he was? It's evident that he abandoned me and my mother. If even Godwulf didn't know of my father's identity, and he was an ally of my uncle, then how could anyone else?

Is this stone merely a sign of my unknown father's guilt for what happened to my mother? Was it an effort to win forgiveness from our Lord God, if such even exists? I pause and then stop, looking instead towards my uncle's understated grave. His stone shows little more than an emblem depicting Mercia's battle stan-dard of the eagle, wings outstretched, mouth open in a shriek of defiance.

I angle my steps, trying to turn my thoughts towards Cenfrith, and how I wish to remember him, as opposed to how I do remember him: dying from his surfeit of wounds, bleeding his last into the dry and dusty land, his face contorted in agony.

Why I can't remember him as his usual taciturn self is beyond me. I wish I could remember the rare smiles, the minor complaints even, but, no, I remember his pain and suffering and how he gave everything that he had to Mercia. At the end, that even included me.

'Icel.' I startle to hear my name being called and turn, mouth falling open in shock, to see Lady Ælflæd, a thick cloak around her shoulders, hurrying towards me, my perplexed reeve escorting her. How often, I consider, does the man have to play host to his lord, and a visitor, all on the same day.

'My lady,' I stutter, those two words almost beyond me, so intense is my shock at seeing her.

Her face is bright with the chill and rush of the wind.

'I didn't expect to see you here,' she says at the very same time I utter the same words.

She laughs, the sound light and soft, filled with respect, as she remembers where she is.

'My sister by marriage bid me come here,' she exclaims, as I look from her to the reeve, noticing his furrowed forehead, before he remembers himself, bows his head and moves aside to allow us some privacy. He can still see us, though, from his place outside the graveyard.

I turn and notice that Wine is no longer alone. A collection of six other horses surrounds my uncle's horse. Their riders stay mounted, and I could swear that one of them was Edwin, although his head is averted from me.

Lady Ælflæd continues to speak, 'She wanted me to offer her respects.' I turn to her, thoughts of Edwin dismissed. I've almost forgotten that he punched me in Tamworth. I'm not the same person I was on that day. I don't even think I need to know why he did it. I have my suspicions.

'Lady Cynehild is well?' I query instead, reminded that she must be huge with child.

'She's very well, but unable to make this journey, and she wished someone to visit your uncle's grave site for what would have been the celebration of his birth.'

This flummoxes me, and I try to keep a track of the dates in my head. I recall the monks at Peterborough just celebrated the saint's day for the holy Paulinus, but it's too soon for the harvest festivities. Perhaps, after all, it might well be Cenfrith's birthday, had he lived.

I notice then that she carries a collection of late-flowering orange roses, their heads nodding in the sharp wind.

'You'd forgotten?' she asks me, her head tilted to one side.

'I...' I begin, and then nod unhappily. 'It seems I must have done. I missed the anniversary of his death, and came as soon as I could.'

'You've been busy, on the king's orders,' she commiserates. 'I'm sure your uncle will merely be pleased to have been remembered.' As she speaks, she settles on her heels, head bowed, placing the flowers over the small stone above my uncle's grave.

I imagine Cenfrith wouldn't have much cared if I remembered or not, but I'm uncomfortably reminded of the task my uncle left me, to give the small sigil to Lady Cynehild. I consider once more what truly happened between them. Lady Cynehild has clearly remembered, despite a new husband and a child on the way. I shake my head. I wish I understood more of events when I was so much younger.

I listen to Lady Ælflæd's words as she prays, head bowed, noting how her soft voice carries well and wishing that I could listen to her all day long. When we last spoke, at Tamworth, our conversation was observed by many, and was over too briefly. Now, we're alone. Almost. I want to ask her about Lord Wigmund. Will she truly marry him? And what does she think of him? But, instead, her prayers stop, and she turns to face me, her hand outstretched.

'Help me,' she demands. I take her light hand in mine and she rises to her feet. She smiles at me, but her cheeks now seem pinched from the cold, and the hood of her cloak has fallen over her shoulders. She should cover her face. 'I'm never truly comfortable in a churchyard,' she murmurs, shuddering as she gazes once more at my uncle's grave. And then I see her head rise, as she notices something, and turns to me. 'Who's buried there?' she asks softly, a thread of resolve in her voice.

'My mother,' I offer, without thinking, and now she rounds on me.

'Your mother is buried there?' she questions, pointing with a finger, and I nod, unhappily.

'It's quite elaborate,' I admit, shrugging my shoulders.

She nods, but her eyes are troubled, as I catch sight of them. Quickly, she moves aside. 'Excuse me, Icel. I'll leave you with your prayers and remembrances. The reeve has prepared a warm meal and a hearth for me, and I confess, I'm suddenly very cold.'

I open my mouth to stay her, but she's skipped away, her light footsteps crunching over the gravel, and now I do catch sight of Edwin, and also Oswald. I snap my mouth shut on more questions. I doubt anyone would answer them.

I listen to the horses being led away, my back towards the road, as I fixate on the flowers, and their bright shades against the dying grass of the graveyard, and only then do I make my way towards my mother's grave.

I wish I knew what had upset Lady Ælflæd so much that she left quickly, but as curious as I am about the emblems and images covering the shimmering jet-black stone, I'm at a loss as to what any of it means. I resolve to seek out Lady Ælflæd in the reeve's hall, but then another voice hails me. And it's my turn to gasp in shock.

'I thought to find you here when Wulfheard informed me you'd left Tamworth.'

'Godwulf?' I exclaim, my voice too high. 'What are you doing here?' I've seen nothing of him since we fought beside the River Nene. In all honesty, I wasn't aware that he yet lived. The alliance with the king of the East Angles only survived for as long as the attack on Peterborough. The summer months have been ones of being uncomfortably aware of our counterparts to the eastern edge of Mercia's border with their kingdom. If King Athelstan is talking of peace with Wiglaf, it has yet to have any impact on the warrior bands protecting the borderlands.

'It seems I tire of being an East Anglian, not a Mercian.' His words are filled with forced cheer. I notice then that his face is scarred, a long thin slice that has healed but with his right cheek slightly lopsided. I take the wound to be one given by a Viking raider. 'And, your uncle wouldn't forgive me if I left things as they were,' he continues, no doubt aware that I'm examining his face. 'There's much that I can teach you, and not just about being a warrior. Icel, I've come to educate you about your birthright.'

'Then you do know who my father was?' I gasp the words. It's been such a secret, I've long feared that I'm truly a bastard and not a true-born son at all.

'Alas, no, I don't. But I do know who your uncle was, and while many seem to have forgotten, I have not. Your uncle, Icel, was more than the friend of a king, he was King Beornwulf's foster brother, and the commander of the king's troops. And one day, you will be as well.'

I laugh then, for if Wigmund is to become king, then I can never be the commander of the king's troops, but Godwulf misinterprets my laughter.

His lips curled in what he must think is laughter, but which looks far more sinister, he intones, 'Yes, Icel, you've always been destined to be more than just a warrior of Mercia.'

HISTORICAL NOTES

The *Anglo-Saxon Chronicle* entries for these years have little to say, other than noting the change of kingship in Mercia from Wiglaf to Ecgberht and back to Wiglaf, alongside the deaths of a number of prominent holy men.

The marriage of Lady Cynehild to Lord Coenwulf is entirely fictional. I don't even know the names of these people, but, obviously, someone must have been the mother and father of Coelwulf II, later king of Mercia, and equally, King Coelwulf I must have had children for Coelwulf II to later claim descent from him.

The union of Wigmund to Lady Ælflæd is based on sparse historical knowledge, and I don't want to give anything away just yet.

Lady Cynethryth is named as queen in the few charters that have survived from the reign of King Wiglaf. If you're not a Saxon nerd, this might not seem too out of place, but the neighbouring kingdom of Wessex only very reluctantly adopted the title of queen for the king's wife and not until the 960s. Not even King Alfred's wife was designated as queen of Wessex. Mercia had a very different attitude towards her royal woman. Wigmund is also

named as the king's son in some of these charters. (S188, S189 and
S190 for those who might like to look at these using the Electronic Sawyer database.)

For those with a desire to learn more about this period, I
can't recommend *Ælfred's Britain* by Max Adams enough. It is
not, as the title suggests, an accounting of Alfred's Britain but
comprehensively (or as much as possible) covers the years
before his reign, and also after. It is incredibly engaging and
accessible even for readers who are new to the subject. Other
historians I would recommend for those becoming addicted to
the period would be Nicholas Higham, and, of course, I never
tire of recommending *The Earliest English Kings* by D. P. Kirby
for all I first read it a scarily long time ago, but always refer
back to it. Other histories that cover the whole of Saxon
England will likely not mention this period in more than a few
sentences, and all of them will likely be concerned with
Wessex.

Events in any of the kingdoms other than Wessex are poorly
served in any of the available sources for this time period. Indeed,
in one book I consulted, it merely said 'and nothing else is said
about East Anglia (in the written sources).' That's about all the
opportunity a writer of historical fiction needs.

The Viking raiders (you may know them as Vikings, but to go
Viking was a job description) had first attacked what we know as
England in AD793 at Lindisfarne, or Holy Island, off the coast of
Northumberland. What happened in the intervening years,
before the later 860s when the 'Great Heathen Army' arrived, is
difficult to reconstruct, most noticeably because of a lack of available sources. There is a general consensus that due to events
taking place elsewhere in the world, attacks on England began to
increase from the 830s onwards. Peterborough, or Medesham-
stede as it was known at the time, is said to have been destroyed

in the 860s, although there is some argument about this. I have made it the centre of a much earlier attack.

The Viking raiders in this narrative are not the men and women who came to England with the intention of settling, perhaps driven by a lack of available land to farm in their native country. Those characters belong to later in the ninth century, from about 865 onwards. While the narratives surrounding the earlier period of the first Viking incursions are somewhat poorly documented between the attack on Holy Island and the attacks on Wessex, the Viking raiders, or perhaps even pirates, were a problem not just for England, but for the whole of the United Kingdom, Ireland and the Frankish kingdoms, as well as much further afield. The number of attackers is impossible to determine.

The exact relationship between King Wiglaf of Mercia and King Athelstan of the East Angles is unknown. It's interesting to ponder whether they might not have considered an alliance – after all, if not for Athelstan and his propensity for killing Mercia's king, Wiglaf would never have become king of Mercia.

When determining the names of characters, I often rely on the extant Saxon charters, which can be viewed, sometimes in translation, on the Electronic Sawyer website. For Lord Wigmund's allies, I'm using the names of those men who attested later charters. I know little more of them other than their names, and family relationships are entirely fictional. But men with these names were alive in Mercia at this time. It feels good to allow them some space on the page, rather than using entirely fictional names.

Saxon churches do survive, although not many of them. They can be characterised by square towers, not at one of their extremities, but rather centrally located. In recent months, I have attended a number of online lectures and been surprised by just how much can be reconstructed from surviving churches which have been substantially redesigned in the intervening years. Those that survive are often rebuilt in stone. I have taken myself off to view one of only a few surviving Norse churches in the UK, that of St Magnus' kirk on the small Orkney island of Egilsay. It has a wonderful rounded tower!

The tale as told by the scop is an amalgamation of a translation I found in *The Scandinavians from the Vendel Period to the Tenth Century*, edited by Judith Jesch, and also two poems translated in *English Historical Documents 1* by Dorothy Whitelock, which were written about King Cnut and Erik Bloodaxe, much later than when the events of this story take place. I'm not very good at skaldic poetry, or any poetry for that matter. 🙂

As regards to Icel's oath given to the king in *Son of Mercia*. This is known as a commendatory oath. (The matter of Saxon lordship is a huge topic of ongoing discussion amongst academic historians.) This would have been a personal oath, as opposed to one where land would have been involved. It has been argued that men and women could be beholden to others through a variety of oaths, either personal or with the involvement of land. This could have made life very complicated.

Ships of this period – Viking ships, if you will – were not all the same. The most famous and easiest to conjure up are the longships called *langskip*, which might well have had up to thirty rowing benches, and would have been powered by oars with a sail, in case the wind was favourable. A *knarr* would have been smaller and powered by a sail alone, while a *karve* would have been smaller yet, with no more than sixteen benches but able to navigate in very shallow water.

I'm not a fan of narratives that present the Saxons or the Viking raiders as stupid in order for the other side to triumph. All battles will have been pitched and difficult. It's not as though one side had more or less experience than the other, and certainly not at a time when Mercia was so constantly at war. That doesn't mean that all Viking raiders and all Saxons were excellent warriors or strategists. It also means that no result can ever be assured, and again, this is excellent for a writer of historical fiction.

Icel will return. Soon.

Thank you for reading.

ACKNOWLEDGMENTS

As ever, I must thank my cheerleaders EP, ST, CS, AM, JC and MC. I would also like to thank CS for spending time with me at Jarrow Hall learning more about elements of Saxon culture from the re-enactment group there. I should clearly have done this a long time ago. And for attending Saxon conventions with me!

Huge thanks to Shaun at Flintlock Covers for managing to produce fabulous maps from my idle meanderings.

Thank you to Caroline Ridding, my editor, and to my copy editor, Jade Craddock, and proofreader, Ross Dickinson. One day I'll learn that slaughterhouse is one word, and sworn man is two – I have to, I've written it here.

Huge thanks to the whole team at Boldwood Books for their hard work and sheer brilliance.

And to my readers, thank you, as ever, for journeying into the past with me.

MORE FROM MJ PORTER

We hope you enjoyed reading *Warrior of Mercia*. If you did, please leave a review.

If you'd like to gift a copy, this book is also available as an ebook, digital audio download and audiobook CD.

Sign up to MJ Porter's mailing list for news, competitions and updates on future books.

https://bit.ly/MJPorterNews

Son of Mercia, the first book in The Eagle of Mercia Chronicles, is available now.

ABOUT THE AUTHOR

MJ Porter is the author of many historical novels set predominantly in Seventh to Eleventh-Century England, and in Viking Age Denmark. Raised in the shadow of a building that was believed to house the bones of long-dead Kings of Mercia, meant that the author's writing destiny was set.

Visit MJ's website: www.mjporterauthor.com

Follow MJ on social media:

twitter.com/coloursofunison

instagram.com/m_j_porter

bookbub.com/authors/mj-porter

Boldwood

Boldwood Books is an award-winning fiction publishing company seeking out the best stories from around the world.

Find out more at www.boldwoodbooks.com

Join our reader community for brilliant books, competitions and offers!

Follow us
@BoldwoodBooks
@BookandTonic

Sign up to our weekly deals newsletter

https://bit.ly/BoldwoodBNewsletter